2

D0371622

THE
RUINS

THE
RUINS

PHOEBE WYNNE

ST. MARTIN'S PRESS
NEW YORK

This is a work of fiction. All of the characters, organizations, and events portrayed in this novel are either products of the author's imagination or are used fictitiously.

First published in the United States by St. Martin's Press, an imprint of St. Martin's Publishing Group

THE RUINS. Copyright © 2022 by Phoebe Wynne. All rights reserved. Printed in the United States of America. For information, address St. Martin's Publishing Group, 120 Broadway, New York, NY 10271.

www.stmartins.com

Designed by Kelly S. Too

Library of Congress Cataloging-in-Publication Data

Names: Wynne, Phoebe, author.
Title: The ruins / Phoebe Wynne.
Description: First Edition. | New York : St. Martin's Press, 2022.
Identifiers: LCCN 2022003289 | ISBN 9781250272065 (hardcover) | ISBN 9781250272072 (ebook)
Subjects: LCGFT: Novels.
Classification: LCC PR6123.Y63 R85 2022 | DDC 823/.92—dc23
LC record available at https://lccn.loc.gov/2022003289

Our books may be purchased in bulk for promotional, educational, or business use. Please contact your local bookseller or the Macmillan Corporate and Premium Sales Department at 1-800-221-7945, extension 5442, or by email at MacmillanSpecialMarkets@macmillan.com.

First Edition: 2022

10 9 8 7 6 5 4 3 2 1

For all the women and girls who were made
to sit on men's laps without wanting to—
and still remember it

NOTE FROM THE AUTHOR

The Ruins contains some references to the emotional and sexual abuse of young girls. This book is a work of fiction but speaks to experiences I recognize, so that little has been invented. I write in the hope that what is true for me could be true for at least one reader, too, and might provide some consolation for the darkest moments of the female experience.

THE
RUINS

Prologue

The Château des Sètes took up the loveliest spot in the area; everybody said so. It was extraordinary in its setting, flanked by the rushing blue of the Mediterranean and the cut of the white rock. The house was tall, wide, and glowing like a cream jewel, with rows of red blinking shutters; it caught every eye that passed it from afar, whether skirting behind the grounds in a car or from the front, gliding past on a boat.

This evening the house was lit up for the Ashbys' party. As the sea grew dark, the stone sweep of the terrace was dotted with lanterns and merry guests chatting over the jazz from the record player. It was a goodbye party, to celebrate the concert and the end of the orchestral week—the children of St. Aubyn's school had performed very well, including the Ashbys' only daughter, Ruby. Many of their parents had recently arrived in the area to enjoy the concert, delight in the party, stay the night at the local hotel, and take their child home in the morning. Many of them were also there to appraise the château, envious of their own children, who'd spent their nights sleeping in tents on the land and their days rehearsing with the full backdrop of the sea.

But the high-pitched wail of a siren pierced the party's buzz. It accompanied a flash of blue light, then a swirl of red, which swung across the faces of those gathered there.

For a long moment nobody knew what to do at the sight of a police car perched on the edge of the terrace, like an uninvited guest. Adult eyes turned away politely, but the children were all agog.

A uniformed man slammed the car door, and his voice rang out. *"Je voudrais parler à Monsieur Ashby. J'ai Monsieur et Madame Fuller dans mon véhicule et c'est une histoire très délicate."*

The jazz tootled on, but a strange hush came over the crowd. In the backseat of the police car was the shadow of two dark heads. A second, younger policeman emerged from the other side of the car, just as a small voice spoke up from among the group of children.

"'Fuller'? Did he say 'Fuller'?"

A confident voice answered, a girl with red hair and frowning eyes. She moved to the front. "No, he said 'Ashby.' My father's here."

A smartly dressed man approached the first policeman, shaking his hand to draw him aside. The back door of the car opened to produce another man with short curly hair and a furious face, his eyes blotchy and his nose bloody. Behind him, a woman was hauled out. The policeman leaned his arm on the door to get a better grip on her, and she screamed, a sound that matched the earlier wail of the siren. Her white face wore no blood, but her eyes stretched wide as she gaped at the three men around her as she was lifted out of the car. The tips of her fingers were soaked red, bright against her pale hair and paler skin.

The girl standing in front of the children jolted at the scream, alarmed to hear such a sound come from a woman—from someone's mother.

1

1985

Ruby had both looked forward to the party and dreaded it. She'd been the last to leave the church after the concert, packing up her flute carefully, straggling behind the group of young musicians as they wandered back down and along the rocky path to the house. The way was lit with dim lights and the swinging flashlight of one of the music teachers, and Ruby breathed in that smell so familiar to her, a deep, damp green pine. The unseen sea was gently roiling, rumbling out a soothing encore after the heroic might of the concert.

Ruby felt a twinge of anguish. She'd so enjoyed hosting the orchestra trip this year. The performance was already over, the party would be soon, and she didn't know when she'd see Bertie again. This was his last school trip, the end to his final year at St. Aubyn's, and now he'd be going off to his next school—strict, grown-up, and boys-only. Ruby, two years younger, would be left behind. She couldn't imagine what it would be like next term: to scan the dining room empty of him every lunchtime, to never spot him playing board games in the old library or football on the lawns, to arrive at orchestra rehearsals twice a week without his smile to greet her.

Ruby clutched at her flute case, holding on to the joy of the concert: the thudding warmth of the orchestra in their altar alcove, the beat of the music under the heat of the electric lights. She'd counted every bar with the nod of her head, watching the conductor as he brought her in with a sweep of his arm, nudging the hopeless second flute beside her when she missed her entry. Even with those moments, the concert had gone brilliantly.

But on her way back to the house, her joy evaporated. Ruby felt annoyed that the whole of August lay ahead of her—empty without the daily cheer and discipline of orchestra rehearsals. Of course, she had always loved her summers in France, but she'd enjoyed having her classmates there during the last week. She'd seen her family house anew, proud of the way it looked with all of them in it. But by this time tomorrow the house would be empty except for Ruby and her parents, and their friends, the Blys. Then again, August always seemed to bring the small dread of more guests than Ruby had bargained for.

THE PARTY AT THE HOUSE was in full swing when Ruby got there. The elated concertgoers spilled out along the long sweep of the terrace: parents, staff, and helpers, all babbling in stiff English. The mothers were draped in pastel silks and linens, glittering with smiles and diamonds or precious gemstones. The fathers were elegantly casual in cotton shirts and chino trousers, tanned faces and wild hair. Congregating away from them was a throng of messy, delighted children grasping at bowls of crisps and glugging out of plastic cups.

Tables were set, heavy with lavish plates of food interrupted by swathes of green foliage or bunches of wildflowers drooping from jugs. Someone's little sister poked her finger into a bowl of chocolate mousse, then sucked on it delightedly. She turned to see Ruby scowling at her, pulling her finger out of her mouth with a laugh, before realizing who Ruby was; her face straightened and she scuttled away to cower behind her mother.

Ruby's own mother, Rhoda, petite and auburn-haired, was standing with her friend Polly, who rested a graceful arm on her pregnant belly, laughing as she recounted a story.

"Well done, darling girl!"

Ruby smiled brilliantly as the parents of one of the cellos swanned over to her. "Good evening, Mrs. Moreton, Mr. Moreton. Did you enjoy the concert?"

"Yes, dear," the woman nodded over-vigorously. "Well done—splendid!"

Ruby smiled at the confirmation. "Thank you. Have you seen my father?"

"Yes, he's been rushing around, setting up for the party."

Ruby looked up at the couple. "Didn't he come to the concert?"

"No, darling," Mrs. Moreton said lightly, "your parents have been terribly busy hosting all of this, of course. Do be good to your mother—she's been a wonderful hostess."

Mr. Moreton was surveying Ruby with a tilt of his head, his hand gripping a tumbler of whiskey against his chest. He bent to address her. "I say, you're rather good at that fluting, aren't you? How old are you, dear girl?"

"I'll be twelve in two weeks." Ruby straightened up. "I'm not normally first flute, but the girl who is couldn't come. Next year I might—"

"Jolly good." He shifted his gaze to give his wife a knowing look. "Toby Ashby's inside the house. He had a rather important phone call, I gather."

"Well, I hope it wasn't anything bad," Mrs. Moreton said with a toss of her head. "Better not ruin everyone's last evening together."

Ruby smiled thinly at the Moretons and wandered over to the swell of children, her eyes skating over the boys' heads to find Bertie. There he was, his sunny face lit with laughter as he jostled with his friends and their cups of Coca-Cola. He'd looked like that when he smiled at Ruby only a few days ago, asking if she wanted to go for a swim together. She'd barked out a "no" without thinking. He'd nodded before moving away, leaving her utterly dismayed.

Ruby bit at her lower lip, sore and overused this week from so much fluting. Even though it was evening, she felt hot, a slick of sweat under her undone hair. She was cross that her father hadn't seen the concert, cross with that phone call for distracting him now, cross with Bertie for not seeking her out that evening when she might never see him again. Cross that in the morning the other children would pack up their tents lined along the back patch of land, pile into the school coach or their parents' cars, and leave.

Imogen Bly waved Ruby over and offered her a cup of Coca-Cola. "I'm so sad it's all over."

Ruby nodded and took the cup, but didn't take a sip. The plastic felt sticky and it looked like someone had already taken a swig out of it.

"At least we've got the next few weeks together," Imogen continued buoyantly. "I can't imagine the house without everyone. But it'll be fun, won't it? I do like the bedroom your mother's given me, far better than that awful tent I've been in all week."

Ruby gave a halfhearted smile. Imogen Bly annoyed her; at home in England, she and her mother, Polly, were always coming by, or they were going there. Polly had grown up alongside Rhoda, like two plants shooting up and flowering together—or so their stories went.

Ruby and Imogen did not share their mothers' hot relishing of each other. Imogen probably wouldn't have minded being friends, but Ruby was firm in her dislike. Imogen was in the year above, and her beauty and warmth were too irritating and confusing for Ruby to navigate, so she preferred to avoid her at school.

Orchestra brought them together, although Imogen played brass— the French horn—and was always gassing at the back and blasting her instrument out at odd moments during rehearsals, just to be funny. But Imogen was well liked and had won the Maths prize three years in a row, and so Ruby generally tolerated her and her abundant black hair and too-large mouth.

"Yes," Ruby said, plastering on a smile. "It'll be fun. There's always something to do here."

She took a sip of the Coca-Cola just as a siren jolted everyone out of their revelry.

RUBY STARED AT THE WOMAN plastered against the police car, and made the connection quickly. *"Monsieur et Madame Fuller,"* the policeman had said. Ruby's head seemed to fill with the woman's scream, her twisted figure, her cold face—which Ruby now realized she'd seen earlier that evening.

It had been at the end of Holst's *Jupiter*. The audience had clapped obligingly, but one woman—Mrs. Fuller—had stood up and cheered heroically, her great voice whooping around the church, her face swollen with emotion. The conductor hesitated, his mouth slightly agape. The rest of the orchestra smiled at each other uneasily, now woken from the bubble that had been their music. Ruby had appreciated it until the church began to echo with the woman's repeated claps, her unceasing hoots.

The second flute, Annie, had stiffened beside Ruby and let out a small moan. The cheering woman was her mother.

Mr. Fuller had tugged his wife down violently. She'd let out a short cry as she fell back to her seat with a flump, her shoulders jagged and her head hanging forward.

The conductor had waited a moment before raising his baton, and the concert had carried on.

But now Mrs. Fuller was grappling with her husband as he battled to trap her arms and settle her shaking head, his own bloodied and angry face just as horrifying as her blank one. Ruby's father was speaking quick and agitated French at the first policeman.

Ruby felt sure that something terrible must have happened after the concert.

"My goodness, that woman is terribly upset." Imogen stepped up beside Ruby. "The policeman mentioned 'Monsieur Ashby.' Are they going to arrest your father?"

"No," Ruby shot back, "of course not. That's Monsieur DuPont. He's the police chief; he's been here for dinner many times. I didn't fully understand what he said."

Ruby's chest quivered with unease. She glanced at the second, younger policeman, at his tight, resentful face and folded arms. Ruby had never seen him before. He caught her eye with his severe, surveying stare, and she looked away.

A few other men had hurried forward to support Ruby's father in his conversation with the police chief. Mrs. Fuller seemed to be gathering herself to stand, her tortured features twisted, her legs almost giving way. But as her husband grabbed her arm, she screamed again, louder than before. It was as if she were being burned by a white-hot poker, and Ruby felt another bolt of alarm at the noise. In the corner of her eye she saw a small dark shape dash into the bushes—the local stray black cat that always lurked around the house. Mrs. Fuller's screaming had apparently scared even him.

"Darling! Can't you do something with her?" Ruby heard her mother's voice call frantically. "Quickly, Toby darling? We've got company!"

"Yes, Rhoda," Ruby's father turned his head to answer, "I'm well aware. Let's put her upstairs in one of the rooms."

The guests were moving across the terrace now; the adults seemed to have given up their polite indifference, their eyes fixed on the fascinating debacle.

Mr. Fuller somehow managed to fold his wife into the group of gathered fathers, Ruby recognized Imogen's among them. The mass of men seemed to warp her screaming into long, painful groans.

"Oh! How awful, Ruby!" Imogen was ogling the scene delightedly. Ruby heard a rush of whispers behind her as the other curious children joined them, crowding nearer as Mrs. Fuller was taken into the house, those heavy groans thinning out as she passed over the threshold.

"What happened?"

"Who is that woman?"

"Is she drunk?"

Ruby took a quick breath as she watched her father finish his intense conversation with the police chief. Toby Ashby stood tall and narrow, touching his glasses with attention, his neat mustache as stiff as his brown hair. Perhaps that's what it was; Mrs. Fuller *did* seem very drunk. Ruby had an aunt who spent every Christmas with them, and who usually cradled a glass of something from noon till night. She sometimes grew hysterical and shouty, just like Mrs. Fuller now, although never this bad, and never involving the police. Ruby's mother said her sister drank because she was unhappy, and because she was a housemistress in a school somewhere, without a proper life. Perhaps Annie Fuller's mother was unhappy, too.

Ruby heard her father switch to English as he challenged Mr. Fuller with a question. Yes, Ruby thought, she could see the resemblance between him and Annie, something in their pink cheeks and narrow squint.

"She crashed the car; she was drunk," Mr. Fuller answered Ruby's father loudly. "I couldn't get to the wheel in time. She was trying to get to the airport." Imogen's mouth slid open with interest, and she turned to relay the information to the others behind her.

"But couldn't you have stopped her? The trouble is, they're saying there was an accident—a hit-and-run—on the same road, and they're implying that your car was involved."

"God, no." Mr. Fuller shook his head forcefully. "We hit a wall. We didn't hurt anyone."

"Are you sure?"

Mr. Fuller hesitated, then answered, "Yes."

"Well, there will be an investigation. I'm afraid neither of you can leave the country."

A glimmer of fury crossed Mr. Fuller's face. "Can't you help us at all?"

"That is what I'm doing." Ruby's father gestured at the police car. "It's a mercy they're allowing you to stay here in the meantime."

The police chief had heard enough, and with a short bow he announced, *"À demain, Monsieur Ashby. Nous vous contacterons dans la matinée. Bonne soirée."*

Ruby's father gave a grim nod and replied, *"Et à vous, Bernard."* He turned to catch the younger policeman's eye with a *"Bonne soirée, monsieur,"* but it was ignored, and the man slammed the door on his side of the car.

The gathered crowd of onlookers ruptured and pulled back, giving the police car a wide berth long after it had rolled away into the night, without any swirl of its colorful lights.

"Bloody disaster, Toby," Mr. Fuller exclaimed.

Ruby's father leaned back to consider Mr. Fuller. "Yes, quite." His eyes hovered over the inquisitive partygoers. "We need to discuss this inside, Max."

"Yes, I'll pour a drink first. Can I get you a whiskey, too?"

A few of the parents cast dark looks between them as Ruby's father strode into the house, with Mr. Fuller hurrying behind. Ruby wondered where they'd put Mrs. Fuller, where Annie was, and whether she'd witnessed her banshee of a mother, or her bungling confusion of a father.

"Ruby, Immy." It was Imogen's father, his bulky figure heavy and his face drawn with concern. "Come along, you didn't need to see any of that. Do you want to go upstairs to bed? Or enjoy the rest of the party?"

"What's *happened*, Dada?"

"Not for you to know, darlings."

"Is it a secret?" Imogen asked excitedly.

"Well, yes, why not."

"A secret?" Ruby repeated, skeptically.

"So which is it?" Imogen's father demanded. "Upstairs or enjoy the rest of the party?"

"Oh." Imogen hesitated. "May we enjoy the rest of the party, please?"

"The party," Ruby added, quietly but decisively, thinking of Bertie. Her eyes fell on the space where the police car had been, now swallowed by the evening's darkness. "Is it really a . . . secret?"

"Ruby, you little thing," Imogen's father continued, "your flute solo was wonderful. Fancy getting all those pretty notes out of such a sliver of silver."

"A sliver of silver?" Ruby repeated uncertainly, her eyes lifting to search the man's worn face. Mr. Bly—or Lord Beresford, as people were supposed to call him—had always intimidated her. She didn't know whether it was his height, his wide stooping shoulders, or his dark, sunken eyes that seemed to flash at her as he talked.

"Yes, girl. A sliver of silver." He laughed expansively. "You're a damn sight more feminine and beautiful than Immy, with her bloody trumpet."

"Dada, do you really mean that?" Imogen turned and looked beseechingly at her father. "Don't you know it's a French horn?"

He patted the top of Imogen's head reassuringly. Ruby couldn't help smiling at the compliment.

BUT SHE WASN'T SMILING HALF an hour later when the children's part of the party was called to a halt and she was sent to bed. To her surprise, Ruby's mother accompanied her to her bedroom.

"You're going to have to share your room, Ruby."

Ruby's mouth puckered. "What?"

"Little Annie, that woman's daughter. The Fullers. They're going to stay here until your father can sort out what happened in the accident."

Ruby looked at her mother, wanting to ask her the questions whose answers she now feared. Through the double windows, a bright bloom of chatter rose up from the terrace below. Farther beyond she could hear the lively shouts of the others bedding down for the final night in their tents.

Ruby's mother was waiting for a response, but received none, so she continued. "Their daughter Annie will sleep in here, and you'll be jolly nice to her."

"Can't Imogen share *her* room?"

Her mother straightened Ruby's coverlet and thumped up the pillows. "No, darling, we're the hosts. This is our house."

"We've just hosted the whole orchestra for over a week!"

"Yes"—Rhoda's face swung to Ruby's, and their irritation sparked together—"and you did very well out of it, young lady. First flute, ahead of your time."

Ruby was almost growling; she sat on her bed to calm herself. "For heaven's sake! Having Imogen here is bad enough."

Rhoda stood up straight. "Ruby, it's been quite a trying evening. There are far more important things to be getting on with. Don't make a fuss."

Ruby spat out, "Annie can have the metal bed, not mine."

Rhoda glanced over at the antique metal bed set near the long windows as a sort of sofa. "Yes, fine. Move your teddies. And find her some sheets, can't you?"

"What?" Ruby's mouth curved with disbelief. "Can't Lisette do that?"

A voice called out from below. "Rhoda!"

Ruby's mother stepped over to the window's balcony and peered out, a strategic smile placed on her face. "Coming!" She turned back to her daughter. "Lisette is busy tidying up, which you know perfectly well. Stop being such a boor, Ruby, and get this done."

She sashayed to the door, ignoring Ruby's incredulous face, and clicked it shut.

Ruby wanted to slam the door instead. Annie in her room! That little urchin constantly by her side, like she had been in orchestra, the second flute to Ruby's first. Thin and pale and insipid, with her wide eyes and cringing mouth. And now her mother, some strange creature, so unlike the other mothers, involved with the police and staying in the house.

Ruby scowled as she lifted her teddies off the metal bed, settling them carefully in her wardrobe, arranging them to face each other in mutual embraces. She was an only child, and had been her whole life—why should she suddenly have to share everything? It was certainly true that the Vaughan Williams *Greensleeves* duet with Annie had gone very well, both in rehearsals and during the concert—Ruby had done all the heavy lifting, of course. But she did have to admit being impressed by Annie's efforts. Perhaps Annie knew how to rise to a challenge, then. Well, Ruby would give her plenty.

Ruby stared resentfully at the metal bed, wondering where to find any spare pillows or where the sheets were actually kept. She'd never made up a bed in her life. Maybe she'd take some pillows from her parents' bed—her mother's side, just to spite her.

2

The fan in Ruby's bedroom whirred back and forth as she stared at the ceiling. Annie was still asleep, her eyelids swollen and pink as if she'd cried through her dreams. Ruby sighed wearily. She'd left the shutters open last night by mistake and now the room was roasting with the morning heat. She knew the coach had already left, and that if she ventured downstairs there would be nobody but Lisette, elbow-deep in last night's dishes. Ruby could picture her wizened French face now, pointed with resentment as the dishwater overflowed and the soapsuds slipped to the floor.

She couldn't work out how she felt—cross, sad, or bothered by Annie and her mother. The house would take on a strange foreignness with Annie and her parents, Imogen flouncing about too, and heavens knew who else hadn't been scraped away after the party. They would probably talk loudly during siesta time, watch television during the day, hang their wet towels and swimsuits over the balconies, and make everything look ugly. Her mother would no doubt be all the more sour, too—she threatened to return to England earlier and earlier each summer, always moaning about the boredom, the heat, and the damage to her perfectly fair complexion.

Ruby didn't like any of it. She turned to glare at the sleeping Annie accusingly.

Last night she'd made a small noise while Ruby was undressing. "What's that?"

"What?" Ruby lifted her face; Annie was clutching at the spare nightdress Ruby had given her, and gazing at a crumpled pair of knickers kicked aside on the floor. It was a small change from the sad expression she'd worn since entering Ruby's bedroom, apologetically dragging her bag.

"Oh, it's nothing." Ruby felt her resentment give way to shame as she turned away.

"Are you ill?" Annie said fearfully.

"No," Ruby huffed, standing up straight in her nightdress. "It's my period."

"Oh, wow." Annie seemed to look at Ruby with new eyes. "I suppose you've got boobs like the older girls. But you must be one of the first in the year to get your period. Do you wear a bra?"

"Only sometimes."

"Oh! It must be wonderful to wear a bra."

"I haven't got many—" Ruby heard her voice crack. "My mother hasn't taken me . . . You make it sound glamorous. It isn't."

Annie turned away, her face awash with sadness again. "I'd love to have boobs and my period."

Ruby hadn't answered. At the beginning of the orchestra week there'd been a sudden brown sludge in her knickers, and she'd held on to it like an ugly secret. But then the brown sludge gave way to darker blood. She'd waited a full day before reluctantly telling her mother, who was alarmed, insisting that Ruby should have been taught all about this at school—that's why they paid all that money to send her there, for goodness' sake. And for now, she definitely wouldn't be able to swim.

Then came Bertie's invitation to the pool, Ruby's favorite place, and she'd had to say no. She'd still stepped outside to watch him splash about, hoping her presence might be bright enough to sway his attention. But after her sharp rejection he'd dipped and dived among the other girls instead.

"I'll never get boobs because my mother doesn't have any," Annie had volunteered, tying her hair into a ponytail.

Ruby tucked herself into her bedclothes. "What's wrong with your mother, anyhow? Why did she want to go to the airport straight after the concert?"

"I don't know," Annie said heavily. "Probably because of my father."

"Oh."

Annie spoke up again. "Tomorrow morning everyone will be gone. Is it okay if I'm still here?"

Ruby turned her face to the wall and said, "Yes, it's fine."

Annie sniffed. "Thank you."

"Why are you crying?"

"It's nothing. Thank you for the nightie. My clothes are all really dirty now, after the week in the tent. I hope I can get them washed." Annie sniffed again. "Thanks for letting me stay. I don't know what I'd do otherwise."

Ruby scrunched up her face. "What do you mean, what would you do? It's not as if you'd have to walk back to England on your own."

"No, but . . . I don't know."

Ruby hadn't said anything else, and soon fell into a heavy doze. But now she lay awake staring at the ceiling, bright with the hot morning. She supposed it would be nice to sleep in in the mornings now, if her mother would let her, and not worry about the strict orchestra rehearsal schedule, letting go of any thoughts of lessons or dormitories or homework—even if Annie and Imogen were lingering around.

She wondered how long the Fullers would stay, these uninvited and intruding guests. The orchestra trip meant that her parents had already taken on more than they usually did during summers at the château. Ruby loved it there, just like her grandmother had, and they'd spent many long hours there together. But her grandmother had been gone for three summers now—and Ruby had come to love the château even alone, amusing herself while hearing her parents' voices just far enough away. Visitors would traipse in and out, one couple after another, the odd child in tow but none her own age. She'd sweeten herself for them, play her flute, or the piano downstairs, laugh at their jokes, smile, and then go away to swim or read or play to her heart's content. She skirted under the eyes of all of them. At least that's how it had been every other summer. But not this one, it would seem.

Ruby scratched her arm. She'd left her mosquito net open—it would serve her right if she'd been bitten all over. She punched at her pillow. She hadn't even said goodbye to Bertie, and she didn't know how to write to him at his next school, or even if she should.

The fan winnowed away from her and onto Annie's head, brushing at the hair across her forehead. Ruby closed her eyes again, but her thoughts were too busy. She let out a frustrated sigh and kicked herself up and out of the bed.

BREAKFAST WAS READY ON THE terrace, which stretched out in front of the château like a flat amphitheater in wide appreciation of the sea, the view interrupted only by several pine trees that shot up high and straight, dark green and forever dropping needles. Now that the party and the orchestral week were over, the dining table had been restored to its proper place, as had the shallow games table and its armchairs a little beyond, and farther away the sun loungers sat, returned to their sun spot and posing under a huge, drooping parasol.

Ruby took her usual seat at the table, facing away from the house and toward the sea, her face sheltered by the dappled shade from the trees above. Annie sat beside her as Ruby thumbed open a piece of baguette, took a knife, and pulled out a glop of Nutella from the pot. She drizzled it thickly over the bread as Imogen's father and her own chatted over breakfast.

"I like your house so much, Ruby," Annie said, her eyes still tight and misty.

Ruby opened her mouth to respond, but Annie's father, Max, answered first.

"It's not really a house, Annie. It's a *château.*" He sat down heavily beside Ruby, who stiffened at the vinegary whiff of alcohol coming from him. "Choose your words wisely, dearie."

Annie shot a look of quiet loathing at her father, and the silence caught the attention of Ruby's father.

"It is a château, you are right, Max," Toby Ashby shrugged genially, "but it's on the smaller side, not like those in the Loire Valley. It belonged to my parents."

"Don't be so humble, Tobes." Imogen's father, Angus, leaned forward and clapped Toby's shoulder hard enough to shake the newspaper in his hands. "It's practically a country estate."

Ruby's father grinned. "You should know, Angus. You're the one with the *proper* estate, *Lord Beresford.*"

"Really?" Annie's father leaned forward with interest as he lifted a croissant from a pile set out in a neat basket.

Angus ignored him and spoke only to Toby. "Nonsense. I won't have any of this second-son self-pity. You've been morose about it since our university days."

Max's round eyes were drinking up the pair of friends. Flakes from his croissant fell around his mouth as he spoke. "Ah. So, you're the second son, are you, Toby?"

Ruby didn't know why no one had yet mentioned Mrs. Fuller. In her mind she could hear the woman's painful screams, her long groans, even now. She was probably still asleep, but Ruby thought Mr. Fuller could at least show some consideration for his wife.

"Yes, Max. Second son." Toby gestured toward the house vaguely. "This place is the bulk of my inheritance, with a few other bits. My brother got the UK residence. This is why I work, and Angus here doesn't have to."

"And what is it that you do?" Max asked Toby with his dogged energy. Angus tilted his head back and surveyed Max through narrowed eyes.

"I'm a barrister."

"The greatest," Angus said heavily, using his napkin to take a croissant from the basket. "One of the youngest Queen's Counsels in his day, even though that's old news now. His fiftieth birthday looms this Christmas! By then he'll be on track for a judgeship."

"We *hope*." Toby smiled genuinely. "I've got a big case on, and I've taken August to prepare for it. If I do well, yes—the judgeship could be on the horizon."

"It will." Angus nodded back, slicing open the croissant with his knife before looking around for the jam.

"And how long have you known each other?" Max asked.

"We were boys together," Angus said warmly.

Ruby finally finished slathering her piece of baguette with Nutella, stabbed the knife into the pot, and passed it over to Annie.

Max looked from Toby to Angus. "So, when does the boozing start, chaps?"

"I say"—Angus leaned forward, his height and broad chest looming over his part of the table—"shouldn't you see to your wife?"

"She's asleep," Max answered with a firm nod. "Far better like that if you ask me. I've given her a pill."

Toby readjusted his glasses but said nothing. Ruby saw that his eyes were wrinkled and weary, even though it was morning. He turned to Angus. "Where are the ladies?"

"Recovering, I think," Angus replied with a smile.

Imogen appeared in the doorway, looking sleepy, her black bob messy across her forehead. She put her fingers through it, trying to flatten it down.

"Good morning, young lady," Max said as he turned to appraise her. "Who are you? I ought to get to know all your names if I'm staying."

"Are you staying?" Ruby turned her head slightly toward Max.

"Ruby, don't be rude," Toby interjected quickly. Ruby bowed her head, but not before she saw Annie's cheeks flush.

"Sorry."

"Don't say 'sorry,' say 'pardon,'" Imogen sang out as she stepped toward the table, "or so Mother's always saying." She smiled at everyone jovially, touching her father's shoulder tentatively as she passed him. She nodded obligingly at Max. "I'm Imogen Bly. Angus and Polly are *my* parents." She waved toward Ruby. "And that's Ruby Ashby. She's the daughter of Toby and Rhoda, who have *this* place. Then there's Annie Fuller"—Imogen squeezed out a laugh—"but of course you know her, she's your daughter."

Ruby never understood Imogen's ease in the way she spoke to others. Ruby could perform if she knew the people well, or if she took direction from her mother, but she didn't have this easy warmth that extended to anyone Imogen met—from the children, to the parents, to even Lisette. Ruby didn't understand it, and she didn't like it.

"Pleased to meet you, Imogen. Pleased to meet you all." Max turned to Ruby, who frowned through a mouthful of Nutella. "Please call me Max."

"Oh, we won't call you that," Imogen called out as she chose a seat near her father. "It's not the done thing. You're 'Mr. Fuller.'"

Max smiled thinly, uncertain of Imogen's humor. From a first-floor balcony, fresh squeals of delight rang out, and every head turned to look. An auburn head appeared in the gap between the shutters, smiling and blinking down at them.

"Darling," Ruby's mother called out, "do we know when the others are arriving?"

"Oh, in a few days or so. Harley will let us know when he and Liv leave." Toby folded his newspaper. "Come down for breakfast, Rhoda, please."

"No, darling . . . you know I never eat breakfast. Neither does Polly. Anyhow, we're not made up."

"We've got guests."

"Not important ones, darling."

"Oh, you are a tease, Rhoda," Angus called up loudly, and she flashed a bright look back at him.

Ruby reached for a jug, considering her father's words. She hadn't realized Harley Montgomery was coming this summer. She poured some orange juice over her cup, and it splashed to the side.

"Ruby!"

"What?" Ruby answered her father waspishly. "Lisette can clean it up."

Toby looked affronted. "At least offer it to the others."

Ruby raised the jug jerkily. "Annie? Imogen?"

"Yes please," Annie answered eagerly, wiping her hands on her napkin and extending her cup forward. Ruby stood and leaned over, her arm straining with the effort.

"Well." Toby tugged at his newspaper again. "Keep your eye on the time, Max. We've got an appointment at the mayor's office at midday."

"Not the *gendarmerie*?" Angus asked in his low voice.

"No, thank God. Much easier if we stick to your original story about the separate accident. And beyond that"—he shrugged genially at Max as he raised the pages of his newspaper onto the dining table—"I suppose we can consider some boozing."

"Well, I don't see why we can't start now." Max stood up brightly. "Got any champagne we can mix this with, for mimosas?"

He leaned over to grab the jug of juice from Ruby. She looked at him, at her suddenly empty hand, then at Annie's empty cup. Annie was staring blankly into the space in front of her, her face vacant. Ruby hesitated, and sat down.

Angus frowned at Toby, who gave Max a weary smile and answered, "Yes, perhaps . . . I'll have Lisette hunt some down."

RUBY WENT UP TO HER room, but Annie followed through the door before she could close it.

"You fancy Bertie Simmonds, don't you?"

Ruby froze, but felt strangely glad to have his name mentioned. "No."

"I noticed, sometimes, sitting next to you in orchestra . . . you looking at him."

Ruby turned her face away, reddening.

"I don't think he knows, though," Annie carried on. "He's too busy messing around with his friends. But if he had, he probably would have liked you back. Boys are stupid."

"Not all of them," Imogen interrupted, pushing through the bedroom door. "Who are you talking about? What are we doing today?"

Annie and Ruby looked at each other.

"Could we go for a swim? I'm ever so hot."

"Oh." Annie smiled for the first time that morning, and clasped her hands together. "Let's."

But Imogen was staring around the room. "What an awful mess it is in here. And it smells a bit."

Ruby followed Imogen's gaze, seeing her rumpled bedclothes, the piles of books on the tiled floor by her bed, her hairbrush, uncapped suncream, and jewelry strewn across the dressing table. The wardrobe door was hanging open, and the curtain by the long windows tugged with the limp breeze. Annie's things were scattered beside the metal bed, too—an inhaler, a diary, a battered yellow Walkman—while her dirty clothes were piled underneath.

Ruby felt frustration rise up in her chest and suddenly wanted both girls out of her bedroom. Was this how it would be—this slow invasion of her space, the two of them prodding her first in one direction and then the next? "All right, the pool," she finally said. "You go ahead, I'll just grab my things."

Annie disentangled her swimsuit from her pile of dirty clothes, then followed Imogen out. Ruby stayed where she was for a long moment before shoving some things into her linen basket, taking up her book, and moving over to her balcony. She could hear the fathers' chatter rising from the terrace, Max's cackling laughter coming through the stiff and rickety railing. Ruby pulled her shutters closed with an almighty crack, and went downstairs.

On her way to the pool Ruby heard her mother mention her name from the living room. She hovered near the doorway to listen, and saw Rhoda settled close to Polly as they chattered together. Imogen was every bit her mother's daughter, from her animated face to the thick black hair tumbling past her shoulders. The only difference, Ruby thought, was Polly's slight American twang, which had softened after more than two decades in England.

"Do you know how many nannies Ruby's had in London? Toby's mother was the only babysitter Ruby would tolerate for long. Thank goodness she's been boarding the last year."

"She's hardly a little terror, Rho."

"Oh! Well," answered Rhoda, "she is compared to the delightful Imogen. But then, we've not had much time for her—Toby's forever at work and I'm on so many guilds and committees. Oh how I miss them when I'm here!"

"I just take Imogen with me to those," Polly said lightly.

"Which is why you're involved in so few, darling." Rhoda smiled. "Children are supposed to be seen and not heard."

Ruby cleared her throat and said, "Mother, will you ask Lisette to bring us our lunch to the pool? Just some sandwiches should be fine."

"Ruby! Don't creep up like that," Rhoda answered sharply, turning in her seat to see her daughter. "And no, I'll not do your little errands for you."

"It's for *our guests,* not me," Ruby retorted, quickly retreating into the hallway and through the front door, still wondering where Mrs. Fuller was.

The sunlight of the terrace revealed the three fathers reclining in the lounge chairs and admiring the sea. Max had pushed his chair close to the balustrade, and set his feet along the railing. Ruby cast her eye along the long edge of the terrace; there was a gap in the balustrade where it broke into steps down to the sea, before its run along the green lower lawn. Ruby avoided the stone stairs that staggered down into the water, and the flat expanse of scalding rock that stretched out beside, bleached and grooved by many summers of use, with a wooden deck that extended over the waves.

Max was already speaking in a slur, a cigarette tipping out of his mouth. Ruby's nose curled with the unfamiliar smell; she noticed that all three men were nursing spindled glasses of some yellow drink, so she gripped her book tighter and made her way to the pool.

"Ruby, darling," Ruby's father called out from his lounger. "Come here."

Imogen's father was sitting up and surveying her too. "What's that you're reading, young lady?"

Ruby hurried over to them, and blinked with surprise when she saw the cigarette in her father's hand. Angus was waiting for her response. "Oh." She glanced at the cover cautiously. "It's Agatha Christie."

"Ruby reads them religiously. We've got quite a few here; they were my mother's." Toby blew out his smoke, waving it away from his daughter. "Ruby's fascination with them seems a waste. Didn't the woman once say she was a sausage machine, churning out the same shape but different contents?"

Angus wasn't having any of it. "Nonsense, Tobes. They're brilliant. Is that *Murder on the Orient Express*? One of the best." He flashed a dark smile at Ruby. "Let me know what you think when you've finished it."

Ruby hesitated, seeing the brightness of his eyes. She answered carefully, "I do like it so far, Mr. Bly. But *The Body in the Library* is my favorite."

"*The Body in the Library*?" Angus thought about it. "That's Marple."

"Yes . . . I suppose Poirot is a more exciting detective."

He nodded jovially. "He is. I'll borrow one from the shelves here, then. We'll chat about them when you've finished."

"All right," Ruby said, nodding back, considering how that might impress her English teacher at school.

Angus studied her briefly under his thick eyebrows. "I shall keep you to that, little thing."

"Really, Angus." Toby turned his head to light another cigarette, now propped up by his mouth. "Ruby, why aren't you keeping up with your side of the hosting? Go and join those girls. I've spoken to you about this before."

"I'm just joining them now, Father." Ruby turned away quickly, only to hear long peals of double laughter coming from the direction of the pool. She glanced up at her closed bedroom shutters, her jutting balcony burning in the direct heat. Other rooms' shutters were, whether open or closed, ever fighting the persistent crawling plants pulling at the wall's crumbling patches of stone. Ruby hurried on her way.

Far behind the house, the land was enclosed by a long thick wall and a pair of tall gates, from which the ribboned driveway swung through staggered plots of land. There was a narrow olive grove whose sun was blocked by the house, a wild and unattended vegetable garden with two knotted fig trees, a tennis court with spurts of grass growing up around the rotten net, and the now-empty stretch of flattened, dry grass where the tents of the young musicians had been set up. At the edge nearest the road, a rectangular patch was cordoned off and never touched, save for wild animals that sniffed at the many wooden crosses pushed into the ground.

Tucked beside the house and away from the edge of the bay was Ruby's favorite spot—and her destination—the swimming pool. Once an old *bassin,* it was thick with stone and the occasional clump of moss that had collected around the taps at the far end. Shrouded by low trees, it was protected against the sea wind. Ruby didn't like to admit it, but she was frightened of the unpredictable Mediterranean, and preferred the soft, flat pool water in its own leveled nook.

The source of the double laughter was some kind of swimming competition between Annie and Imogen, who now paddled beside each other to share a hushed conversation. Ruby forced a smile as she approached them. Annie saw her first and quickly fell quiet. Imogen lifted her head cheerfully, but even so, Ruby knew they'd been talking about her.

"What are you playing?" Ruby bit her lip as she dropped her book and suncream on one of the chairs. "Can I . . . umpire perhaps?"

"I don't think so." Imogen narrowed her eyes. "We're playing Marco Polo. You have to close your eyes and grab the other person, then if you—"

"Yes, I know Marco Polo," Ruby said. "I'll just watch."

"I was just saying," Imogen said loudly, "I can't believe I've never been here before. Normally I spend August with Gramps in America, or at camp by the lake."

Ruby put in bluntly, "Your mother's been here many times, though. Your father, too."

Imogen looked taken aback, and Ruby felt a dim beat of gladness. Imogen answered, "Well, I see *your* mother all the time in England, at our house."

"Yes, well."

"Well," Imogen said, glancing sideways at Ruby, "I'm happy to be here now—it's lovely. Mama says I'm a young lady now and should learn to be one, instead of spending my days up trees and down pits."

"Oh, up trees and down pits in America? Sounds fun!" Annie laughed, and Imogen laughed too. Ruby sat down on a lounger and turned her face away from the sun.

RUBY SAT UP WITH SHOCK—SHE'D dozed off and hadn't put on her sun-cream. Her nose felt a little sore, and her cheeks were burning—her mother would be furious.

She blinked anew in the sunlight, gray shadows hovering about her vision. It was a long, tall woman, floating toward the pool like a spec-ter. Ruby wondered if she was still dreaming.

"Oh." Annie was sitting on a deck chair in the shade, hidden by the hanging ivy. Her swimsuit was dry, and she was smiling. "Hello, Mum."

Mrs. Fuller muttered a small greeting, but Ruby didn't hear it. The woman's eyes were slightly swollen and her blond hair was misshapen. She had deep marks across her face as if she'd slept badly.

Annie left her chair and came forward. "Mummy, this is Ruby; it's her house. She's the first flute."

Her mother nodded as Ruby forced out a blotchy smile, staring at the woman in a trance.

"And this is Imogen, Mum," Annie said loudly, pointing at the doz-ing Imogen. "She played in the orchestra too, in the brass section. She's asleep, I think."

In the next moment, Mrs. Fuller swept off her silk kaftan and dove into the pool. She drifted easily through the water, her long slim arms moving just beneath the surface. There was an unsteady silence as Annie watched her mother, her face full of anticipation. Ruby watched her too, this tall, unspeaking woman—so different from the joyful audience member at the concert, or the hysterical banshee in the police car. Ruby couldn't help feeling uneasy, so she distracted herself by dragging her chair into the shade, away from Annie and the pool, and opening up her book.

Annie's mother resurfaced and paddled a little above the water, breathing loudly. As Ruby frantically found her place in her book, she tried not to reconcile those vigorous exhales with the groans she'd heard the night before. Imogen did not stir from her sleep, her face soft and relaxed.

Annie sat down near her mother, dropping her legs in the water. Ruby couldn't help but watch the woman's swimming progress, steady and controlled. When she reached the middle of the pool, she suddenly plummeted.

After a long moment, she reappeared above the water.

"Mummy." Annie's voice was fearful. "What are you doing?"

She went under again. Swirls rose above her head, her hair lifting with it. Ruby counted, just like she was used to doing in orchestra. A few bubbles blew to the top of the water.

The moment stretched, long, then longer. Annie splashed into the pool. "Mum!"

She tugged on her mother's arm as she rose out of the water, coughing.

Annie was searching her mother's face, as was Ruby, who wondered why Mrs. Fuller said nothing. Imogen sat up, awoken by the splashing water. "What's happening?"

"Mum, please," Annie said. "Don't do this again."

But Annie's mother had already darted out of the water quickly, sharply, and was moving toward the steps. She turned to Ruby as she held her kaftan to her body. It shrank against her wet skin.

Ruby lifted her book defensively, avoiding the woman's eyes.

Mrs. Fuller twisted her hair to squeeze the water out of it. She tilted her head away from Ruby and smiled bracingly at her daughter.

As Mrs. Fuller moved away, Imogen resumed her slow doze, and Annie splashed into the water again, her face taut. But Ruby's heart glimmered with anxiety. Something was still very wrong with Annie's mother. She found her page and forced her eyes to read.

AT DINNER RUBY FELT RELIEVED that Lisette had laid a section for the girls at the end of the table, to separate them from the adults.

The food was already out, long dishes of roasted vegetables, a bowl of buttery squashed potatoes, and slices of roast lamb so rich that the juices seeped out of it. Ruby drew the serving spoons together and helped herself. As she scooped up a helping of aubergine and courgette, she nudged a set of wine bottles nestled together on the table, and their heavy clinking drew Max's attention.

"What a lovely sound. Like a bell, summoning me to drink." Max clinked his empty glass against one of the bottles. "Shall I open the first, Toby?"

"Ruby, manners." Rhoda cast a long scowl toward her daughter. "Serve others first, for heaven's sake."

Ruby sat, ignoring her mother. She had washed before dinner, but the sun and salt air still clung to her skin. Everybody else looked thoroughly clean, with their neat shirts and oiled faces. Imogen's face had turned a soft olive color, her eyes brightly surveying everyone gathered there.

"It's Market Day tomorrow," Polly announced with a turn of her pretty head. "Rhoda and I went last week—it was just lovely. Will you come, girls?"

Annie looked at Polly desperately, wondering if she was being included.

"Yes, I'd like to," Imogen said, nodding easily.

"You'll have to get up early"—Polly glanced at her daughter affectionately, reaching out her arm—"lazy bum."

Imogen went to her mother and touched her hand with her own. Smiling, she turned to the other girls. "Annie? Ruby?"

"I'd like to, if I'm allowed," Annie answered quietly.

"Of course you're allowed," Ruby said irritably. "Yes, let's." It would take up part of the day at least, she thought.

"Let's all go," said Max with a nod from the other end of the table. Ruby looked at Mrs. Fuller, sitting drowsily beside her husband. Her bowed head drooped over her empty plate—a far cry from Polly and Rhoda, perfect pictures in their soft linen dresses and immaculately tousled hair. In fact, very few of the mothers at Ruby's school looked like Polly and Rhoda, and many of the older girls commented on how attractive and youthful they were, which annoyed Ruby.

She frowned and looked around the table. Nobody else seemed to be concerned by Mrs. Fuller's appearance.

Before dinner she'd passed her parents' bedroom. To Ruby's surprise, her father's voice had sounded ill-tempered; she'd seen him struggling to attempt to tie a cuff link as she peered around the door. "We can't just kick them out. This is very serious, Rhoda. I couldn't persuade the mayor to drop it. The police will need to record their versions about the accident and about the other car—if it was indeed them. The Fullers are associated with us now—it's all flowing through me."

"But how could you let it get this far, Toby?" Ruby's mother hovered at the double windows, checking for any curious ears outside. "And why are you behaving like that around him—as if he's one of our set? The smoking, too?"

"He's all right—it's not his fault his wife's a joke. Should make you proud."

"Proud?" Rhoda laughed darkly. "What, that I can keep myself together?"

"Yes, and that you make me proud, too."

"Well, I'm clearly not enough for you, Toby, if that Leonard woman is on her way here."

"Oh, Rhoda, we don't know that she is," Toby said crossly. "She mentioned it in passing, and I said it would be a pleasure. I very much doubt she'll take me up on it."

"Of course she'll take you up on it—she's always rushing after you. And Harley encourages it. I hate that you ever met her, never mind everything else!"

Ruby's father buried his silence in fussing with his sleeve, and her mother carried on. "I wish you weren't so beholden to that man. Must he know everything about our financial problems?"

"Oh, Rhoda, hush!" Toby burst out.

"And if I see any gambling on those tables"—her mouth twisted with resentment—"I'll be out of here like—"

Ruby cleared her throat to announce her having wandered in. "What is it that Mrs. Fuller has done, and why are the police involved?"

"Ruby, don't just barge in here, please." Toby shook out his arm with frustration. "We're having an important conversation. Off you go."

Ruby's chest heaved. "Well, actually, I agree with Mother, and I wish the Fullers would buzz off."

"Well, do my ears bleed? I never thought that godforsaken daughter of ours would ever agree with me!" Rhoda crossed her arms and glared out of the windows.

"It doesn't matter two hoots what you or Ruby think—that family cannot leave this place."

"I suppose Annie's all right," Ruby declared. "I only meant her parents. She's a bit of a weed, but I do feel rather sorry for her."

"That's enough, from both of you," Toby said firmly, giving up on his cuff link and drawing his hand through his hair.

Rhoda made an irritated noise and turned away, though not before she muttered, "Ruby, do change for dinner."

"Yes, leave us," Toby reiterated. "Now."

At dinner, as Imogen scraped her fork around her plate, she asked, "What's it like then, Ruby—the market?"

Ruby looked at her simmering food, which seemed too hot for the weather, and answered, "Vegetables mostly, and some soaps and things. Bits of jewelry."

"Oh, lovely!" Annie exclaimed.

Imogen hesitated before asking Ruby, "And the boys in the village? I thought I saw some hanging around that fountain in the square when we all went in for ice cream."

"I . . . don't know."

"Ruby wasn't looking at *them,*" Annie said lightly.

Ruby threw Annie a hot look across the table, and the girl's face twisted with regret. But a strangely loud whimper from Annie's mother turned every face toward her. Her chin had fallen flat against her chest in a painful-looking pose.

Angus muttered to Max, "Put her upstairs, old boy."

"Do you think so?"

"Yes," Toby said firmly.

Rhoda and Polly tittered with laughter as Annie's mother seemed to fall forward with another whimper. Max's face lightened when he saw their response, and he took his cue from them. "I'll leave her be. My mother used to fall asleep in the middle of the table all the time."

"Max," Angus stated in his low voice, "we insist. Take her upstairs."

"Easy, my man." Max gave a teasing smile. "Not your house."

"Max." Angus placed his fist on the table, his voice almost a growl. "Not in front of the children, surely."

Toby glanced at his friend. "Yes, Angus is right, Max. Take her upstairs, old boy. Think of your daughter."

Mrs. Fuller's head hung limply to the side and her mouth began to drool. Polly laughed uncertainly, while Annie's face dissolved with horror.

"Well." Max took up his glass of wine and drew a long sip. "Isn't it the girls' bedtime anyway?"

Through the strange and brief silence, Imogen spoke up. "We're not children. I'm twelve—I'll be thirteen in three months."

Angus closed his eyes with irritation as Toby frowned.

"Yes, quite, Imogen. You're growing up." Max focused his smiling gaze on her. "And you must be tired from all of last week's orchestrating."

"Orchestrating?" Ruby exclaimed. Angus stood, and seemed to use the advantage of his height even more than usual as he glared down at Max. Ruby could see the canopies of the pines above his great head, and wondered what he would do next. But then Max was standing too, his arm nudging his wife to join him. He tugged at her, saying, "Come on, darling. Let's take you upstairs."

"I'll give you a hand." Toby bent forward, throwing his napkin on the table.

Angus glanced over at Ruby and Imogen, and lastly at Annie. "It's all right, Annie. Your mother will be fine. Too much sun." His eyebrows drew together in dark pity. "She's had a difficult time of it, I'm sure."

Annie only nodded.

Ruby released her breath, not realizing she'd been holding it. Imogen's face was curious, and thoroughly confused. The incongruous trio of Annie's parents and Ruby's father staggered back toward the house, which stood tall and ready to receive them.

3

The next morning, the blue sea greeted Ruby in consolation, wide and broad from the height of her second-floor bedroom. She felt Annie stir behind her as she checked for her mother and Polly outside, wondering whether they'd been chattering away all night and would somehow still be there now, as bright and annoying as ever. The table gave them away with its untouched croissants and two used coffee cups. Of course, Ruby thought—the two women had already gone ahead. She could picture them freshly pressed, stalking elegantly through the luscious colors and noises of the market.

But there was a police car parked at the side of the house again, set impertinently on the edge of the terrace. There was no one there, and no conversation coming from any open window below. Beyond the scratch of the crickets and the whirl of the sea, the silence seemed to pound in Ruby's ears.

She rushed downstairs. As she reached the bottom banister, Ruby heard the dark squabble of voices coming from her father's study. The large hall mirror caught her white nightdress as she passed. She stopped short at the doorway.

Angus was staring down the young policeman, who raised his head in defiance as Angus said, "He's already told you, man, he won't speak to you. Bloody upstart. Get your chief!"

"Angus, let me handle this," Toby said in a strained voice.

"*Messieurs.*" The policeman cleared his throat, and Ruby could just see the back of his neck, the clean line of his hair above his neat white collar. "*Je ne peux rien faire pour vous ou pour vos associés. Le jeune homme est mort.*"

"*Oui, je comprends,*" Toby said with firm irritation in his voice, "*mais je me suis entendu avec votre chef, Monsieur DuPont.*"

The policeman bowed his head. "*Il faut respecter la loi, Monsieur Ashby.*"

"*Oui, bien sûr.*"

"*Cette personne, votre victime, est morte hier soir.*"

"*Morte.*" Ruby moved beyond the doorway, she knew that word.

"*Il n'est pas le notre, monsieur!*" Toby cried out.

"Dead?" Ruby asked suddenly. "Who is dead?"

Both Angus and Toby turned to face her, momentarily stunned, before Toby yelled, "Ruby, get out of here!"

Ruby didn't move. Toby stepped toward the policeman with a rub of his mustache. "*Alors, merci, monsieur.* We understand you perfectly."

The policeman nodded and ducked through the door. Ruby's feet felt glued to the floor. She realized both fathers were still wearing their pajamas and looked absurdly childish, given the formality of the policeman.

Angus tilted his head carefully toward his friend. "Have a care, Tobes. This is a difficult thing."

"Not you, too! Do you have any idea—"

"Yes." Angus put his heavy hand on his friend's shoulder, his features sterner than ever.

"Yes," Toby said, nodding slowly, "yes, you do. But I mean—coming here without his chief, dropping that bombshell on us . . . Does he have any idea how much my family has given over the years to the village, how much they owe us? How dare he? My father—"

Toby pushed his glasses against his nose and swooped on his daughter.

"Ruby, darling . . . I wish you wouldn't hang around at doors."

"I . . ." Ruby's throat seemed to crack. "I wondered if you would take us to the market. I think Mother has already left."

"Oh." Toby's eyebrows drew together in strange relief. "Yes, all right. Let's . . . gather the troops. I'll need to go to the village with Max, thanks to all this." He raised his arms wearily.

Angus squeezed Toby's shoulder again and looked at Ruby. "We'll just need to dress, little thing. You too. Give us a minute."

Ruby went to Imogen's room first, and was surprised to find the shutters and windows open, with Imogen propped up on her made bed, fully dressed with a magazine split open in front of her.

"Oh, sorry." Ruby hovered at the door.

"It's all right," Imogen answered easily. She closed her magazine and put the lid on the pen she was holding. "Are we going out? Mother said—"

"Our mothers have already gone. My father said he'll take us."

Imogen's face crumpled. "Mama's gone? But at bedtime she told me—"

"She's gone," Ruby repeated. "Didn't you know?"

"No, I'm not allowed in my parents' room." Imogen pushed herself off her bed. "Here or at home—it's the rules. I'll see you downstairs . . . You're not even dressed, you know."

In her own bedroom, Ruby found Annie holding up one of her necklaces against her chest. Annie dropped it quickly, red-faced at being caught.

"I'm so sorry, it looked like lily petals, I haven't seen one like that before, I . . ." Annie fussed as she picked it up, until Ruby said, "It's all right. Will you wake up your parents? We're going to go to the market."

"Oh, of course." Annie laid the necklace carefully on Ruby's dressing table. "I must dress, though, and I . . ."

Ruby had already wandered over to her wardrobe to scan her dresses. White, blue, violet. She picked out a white with broderie anglaise detail, remembering that she liked how the little cap sleeves looked over her shoulders. Tugging it out, she glanced at her teddy bears stacked together, glad that she'd put them away. She pressed the dress against herself, and turned to see Annie looking over enviously.

"Sorry." Annie glanced down at her pile of dirty clothes, in spite of herself.

Ruby tried to smile. "Would you like to borrow something?"

"Oh!" Annie's face lifted. "Really?"

"Yes." Ruby glanced back regretfully at the open door of her wardrobe, across the row of treasured fabrics. She couldn't bear to see the eagerness in Annie's face, especially now that her mother was in trouble and somebody was perhaps dead. It was all very confusing.

"I don't know which one, though . . . My dresses might drown you, you're so small."

Annie's shoulders sagged.

"Perhaps a skirt and a top would be better." Ruby went to her chest of drawers and tugged out the first items she saw: a white cotton set with blue flowers. Annie took them gladly, lifting off her nightdress to pull them on, delighted even with the boxy top, the dragging skirt. She widened her eyes to seek Ruby's approval, and Ruby responded, "It'll do, don't you think? Let's see about washing your clothes. I'll ask Lisette."

"I haven't had a bath for a few days, either."

"Neither have I, but your hair looks fine, if that's what you're worried about."

"No, I—"

"I'll go first in the bathroom, if you don't mind." Ruby took her dress and rushed through the door. She washed her face, dressed quickly, and left the bedroom without Annie—very glad that asking Lisette about the laundry would give her something to do.

The kitchen was a terrible mess: champagne glasses and smaller tumblers soaking in their own dirty fluid; small plates stained with chocolaty-looking goo. Lisette appeared from the pantry with a weary look on her face, so Ruby ducked away. She'd ask about the laundry when they returned.

Thirty minutes later, Toby declared that they were ready to go, although Ruby noted the absence of Annie's mother. Angus had to drive, seeing that only the Blys' car was available. Of course the Fullers' hired car wasn't there.

They were slightly too many for the Volvo, so Toby had Imogen
sit in the front beside her father, while Annie shared the backseat with
him and Max. Ruby would sit on her father's lap. Angus scratched his
thick dark hair and insisted after Max's teasing that no, he wasn't too
hungover to drive the short distance to the village.

Ruby was annoyed that she would be the only one without a proper
seat. She threw her strappy basket in the trunk and shuffled awkwardly
onto her father's lap. As the car bumped along the drive, her knees
jolted against Imogen's seat in front. She stared past the long spray of
lavender lining the tunnel of trees, the swing of the land along the bay
and toward the village, feeling every stir and turn of the car, thinking
about that young policeman and his harsh words.

Her father didn't seem to be interested in making her more comfortable; he reeked of wine like the other fathers, and the closeness of
those in the back made it very hot. He'd pushed the hair roughly off
his face and it stayed where it was, sticking up as he adjusted his glasses
with a round cough.

"You'll have to come with me to the *mairie* again, Max," Toby said.
"We'll need to speak to some people after this . . . unfortunate devel-
opment."

As they drove into the heart of the village, the market grew busier, and Imogen and Annie gasped at its colorful bustle. Toby directed
Angus to the car park, and Ruby jumped out of the car as soon as she
could, tugging at her rumpled dress to smooth it. There was a small
splotch of something near the hem, and she picked at it.

"Ruby, are you coming?" Annie asked. Ruby let go of her skirt and
followed the others.

The Tuesday market stretched from the harbor toward the main
square and through narrowly threaded streets. The long rows of stalls
seemed to be linked together, running along the outline of the square,
taking a breath only at the large water fountain in the center. Thick
plane trees sheltered the space, hanging tall as waiters shifted parasols
to better cover the circular tables littered with wineglasses and coffee
cups. But even the brightness of the market couldn't temper the ripples
of anxiety in Ruby's chest.

"Can we go and have a look on our own, please?" Ruby touched her father's arm as the group neared the busy café on the square.

Angus answered, "Good idea. Off you go, girls, and we'll get a table over at the café there."

"Aha," Max said. "Yes, I'd love a coffee . . . or better? Hair of the dog, they say."

"No, Max." Angus turned to face him. "You're off to the *gendarmerie*."

Max looked at Ruby's father. "Now, Toby? Are you sure?"

"The *mairie*, yes," Toby said, and Ruby saw that her father's face was more wrinkled than ever, his mustache twisted with the unhappy shape of his mouth.

The girls broke away and sauntered around the busy square, stopping first at the dress stand, then a fruit stall, where the merchant had sliced up some pinkish melon. All three girls took up a piece and had a taste. Imogen made a happy noise and took another, smiling sweetly at the merchant. Annie next stopped at the woodwork stall, and fiddled with a little toy delightedly. It was at that point that they realized they had no money between them.

"Have we even had breakfast?" Imogen asked as they made their way through the crowds to follow the narrow streets up and beyond.

"No," Ruby said.

"Let's go back, then."

The girls returned to the café, where their fathers sat swimming in a cloud of smoke that drifted above a basket of croissants. As they approached they saw that Annie's mother had joined the three men, sitting bolt upright with a frightened look in her eyes.

Ruby felt a fresh ripple of alarm run through her as she turned to Annie. "Where did your mother come from?"

"She came in with yours earlier," Annie offered weakly. "My father said."

"Oh."

Imogen lifted her voice as they reached the table. "Dada, where's Mama?"

Angus leaned forward to tap his cigarette above the ashtray, his shoulders stooping.

Imogen tried again, louder. "Father, where's Mother?"

"No need to shout at me, Immy." Angus turned his head irritably. "She came past with Rhoda. They went to smell soaps or some nonsense."

Imogen made a small noise and stepped forward to pull at one of the croissants. She took a great bite, frowning as she chewed. Annie moved toward her mother magnetically and muttered something in her ear. There were no spare chairs for them, and Ruby checked for any to pull up, but all the nearby tables were full.

Ruby's father was talking to Max.

"So, that was encouraging, I think. We'll need to make a police statement. You'll both have to swear to individual affidavits—after we make sure they say the same thing—and then we'll go from there. I've had to pull quite a few strings, but let's hope it's enough," Toby finished with a tight nod of his head.

Ruby's words flew out of her mouth before she could stop herself. "But someone died, Father."

Toby looked at her with quick shock, before Max turned to answer coolly, "No one that we have to worry about, Ruby. After all, people die every day."

Ruby's eyes fell to the ground, but her heart seemed to beat through her head.

"Indeed, well," Toby said slowly. "I've managed to pacify the other side—for now, but I rather think you should get out of here as soon as you can."

"Of course. We'll put the statements together, collect our passports, then see where we stand." Max turned to his wife. "What do you think, dear?"

Annie's mother shook her head at her husband, the circles under her eyes dark and deep. Ruby took a short breath—she couldn't understand how fragile and changeable this woman was. Mrs. Fuller bent to whisper something in Annie's ear.

"Oh." Annie's cheeks colored with discomfort. "I can't buy cigarettes, Mummy."

Mrs. Fuller muttered something stronger as she pressed a coin into her daughter's palm. Annie stared at her hand.

"Cigarettes? Any particular brand?" Toby said. "Ruby knows where the *tabac* is—she gets her sweets there every week."

Ruby was stung, and spoke up. "Not anymore, and anyway—"

"Are you mad, Tobes?" Angus joined in. "They'll never sell cigarettes to twelve-year-olds."

"I'm eleven," Annie said pathetically.

"Well, Rubes can try," Toby insisted. "They've known her since she was tiny. They're only peasants."

Ruby scowled at her father. She rather liked the man with the wide smile at the sweet shop. She didn't think of him as a peasant—and she certainly didn't want to be involved in any buying of cigarettes.

Mrs. Fuller made a strange noise as she beseeched her daughter again, but her husband turned to accost her, his voice low and electric. "For fuck's sake, you've already made a disaster of yourself. Stop making such a fuss!"

Toby and Angus regarded Max curiously, while Annie went to grasp her mother's hand; but her mother only waved her away. Imogen was looking at Mrs. Fuller with wild fascination, the girl's half-eaten croissant hovering at her mouth.

"Now, boys," Max said, his voice changed as he heaved a bag onto his lap. "Have you seen this hunk of cheese? We can have it for lunch, Toby, as my gift to you for letting us stay. Guess how much it cost!"

Angus leaned back in his chair and considered Max carefully before saying, "Is that all you're going to contribute to your little . . . holiday here?"

Max's smile didn't fade. "Point me in the direction of the best local winery and I'll buy the Ashbys a case."

Toby laughed politely, and Max's smile brightened even more. The girls remained standing. Ruby looked through the crowds to see if she could spot her mother and Imogen's, but they were nowhere to be seen.

The drive home presented another problem, as they had added to their number. Ruby's father squeezed into the back next to Max, whose wife sat beside him, with Annie folded on her lap. Imogen sat cheerfully next to her father in front, chewing on something she'd persuaded him to buy her. Ruby got in with difficulty, Max drawing back as her head swung toward his. Her long hair touched his chest, his chin, and the tip of his nose as she moved, and Max closed his eyes for a moment.

"Sorry," Ruby said as she settled on her father's uncomfortably bony legs.

"No, not at all," Max answered, as Toby guided Angus out of the village toward the main road. Ruby winced at her discomfort, annoyed that her mother had gone ahead with Polly, left Annie's mother with them, and allowed the Fullers to continue to trample all over their hospitality.

Under her father's instructions to Angus, Max spoke so quietly that Ruby's ears strained to hear. "Lovely dress, Rubes . . . fits you perfectly. Been admiring you from afar, lovely girl."

He touched his finger across Ruby's thigh, and it seemed to burn her skin. Prickling with horror, she didn't look at him, but shuffled over to move closer to her father. She pulled her hair along her shoulder and across her chest like an extra barrier between them. Annie was gazing out of the window on her side, oblivious and sitting uncomfortably across her mother's lap.

A distracted Toby sat back as the car joined the main road and the bay opened out in front of them.

"I say, Max," Angus called from the driver's seat. "Tell us more about your cheese. Will that make up for manslaughter, I wonder?"

Max looked straight ahead, smiling with his eyes narrowed.

"Oh, no need to talk like that. I'm feeling rather cheerier about it after that meeting." Toby gave a sigh so great that it shifted Ruby's position. "The mayor won't let the other party press charges. Looks bad, you know, for them . . . The British abroad bring a great deal to their economy. They need us. They *certainly* need me."

"Always handy in a crisis, aren't you, Tobes. I adore you for it," Angus boomed out. "You're a lucky man, Max—you both are—to have this guy on your side."

Toby sighed again, and Ruby gripped at Imogen's seat in front of her as her father spoke. "Well, we're just lucky it was local. I'm not sure how far my influence extends beyond this small part of France."

"Oh, nonsense, old chap, your parents were conquering English aristocrats," Max said smoothly. "I can already tell that they worship you here."

Ruby heard Angus scoff. She felt the burn again on her thigh, and focused her gaze out the window until they reached the gates of the château.

4

Ruby went to her bedroom first, rubbing roughly at her leg. She pulled off her dress and winced as the waistband snapped. She didn't want to wear it anymore—Mr. Fuller had touched it. He'd touched her skin, too, but she couldn't very well pull that off. Her hair tumbled across her face and she pushed it behind her ears, feeling very hot and upset. She caught sight of Annie's pile of clothes lying under the metal bed, still dirty, and flung them into her linen basket.

In her parents' bathroom on the first floor, she let the hot tap run and squirted big white globs of bath cream into the rushing water. She dabbed in a few drops of lavender essence, too. Once the bubbly foam rose over the top of the bath, Ruby stepped in, forcing herself into the scalding water and pressing harshly at her thigh. The zing of the wet heat seemed to blister her skin. Taking her mother's shampoo, the expensive-smelling one, she rubbed her hair harder than she ever had before. She took the body brush and thrust the bristles along her arms and legs—anything to scrape away that sensation of Max's fingers on her deadening skin.

Dead, Ruby repeated to herself. *Who* was dead? And why was everyone so calm about it?

Half an hour later, she wrapped herself in her mother's luxurious dressing gown, feeling smaller than ever. The steam seemed to follow her and her damp footprints as she left the bathroom, the floor tiles cold beneath her feet. In the wide corridor the tall shutters snapped and clacked with the sea wind, the curtains billowing. But there was a figure tripping down the stairs from the second floor, hesitating, smiling at Ruby curiously. It was Max, and he gave her an appreciative nod as he crossed the landing and carried on down the stairs.

Ruby closed her eyes to still the hammering of her chest. She tugged her dressing gown closed and dashed up to her bedroom, pulling the door hard behind her. Her heart beat so fiercely that she felt it in her fingers, her mouth, her head.

An hour later she forced herself downstairs, in a clean dress and bearing her dirty linen basket to leave with Lisette.

The voices of the other two girls pulled Ruby outside and toward the sea rocks. The stray black cat was lying along the balustrade, his head set neatly over his paws. Ruby wanted to pet him as she passed, but decided not to disturb his peace.

Annie's mother was lying in one of the hammocks set across the lower lawn, near the sea wall. Her figure was bundled up like a corpse, but her arm draped down to the ground. A wineglass had tipped on its side, its red fluid spilled across the trimmed grass. Ruby hurried past, imagining Mrs. Fuller being nudged hard, swinging high, and toppling onto the watery rocks beyond. *Morte.* She or her husband were responsible for someone's death the night they'd been brought home in the police car. And now Ruby knew for certain that Mr. Fuller was a bad man.

The flat spread of the rock seemed wider than ever as Annie ran across it to greet Ruby. It was a brittle white in the sun, marked with ridges and nooks, drawn out by its wooden diving pontoon and a rusted metal ladder bolted into the side. The sea slapped against the rock relentlessly, its blue-black waters churning and tossing. Ruby looked at the sea cautiously. It was darker than usual, even as it glistened in the afternoon sun.

"You missed lunch—your mother was calling you," Annie said kindly as Ruby approached. "And you've washed your hair—how lovely it looks! You know, Ruby, you're like the Iris Fairy, with her red hair and yellow flowers. I expect you look lovely in yellow."

Ruby avoided Annie's enthusiastic gaze as she carried on. "Although you look a bit like the Yarrow Fairy, too—does pink suit you? Or even the Queen of the Meadow—that could be your mother. I can't pick." Annie smiled in quick embarrassment. "I have a book at home; I wish I could show you both."

Imogen called out from the deck chairs, "I remember the Flower Fairies. Which one do I look like?"

"I've already decided," Annie tittered, turning toward her. "You, Imogen, are the Fuchsia Fairy, so beautiful and unexpected. I love fuchsias in the garden and always want to pop them, but then that damages the flower, so I don't. But your mother looks just like the Poppy Fairy, so beautiful. She ought to wear red more, Imogen."

Imogen smiled carefully at Annie, saying, "The Fuchsia Fairy—I'll certainly take that. Which are you?"

"Ah, thank you for asking, but I'm not sure." Annie hesitated. "I think I'd be the Lily of the Valley Fairy. Rather plain, but fine enough."

"And what about your mother," Ruby said breathlessly as she followed Annie to the deck chairs, "is she—"

"Don't be mean, Ruby," Imogen shot out, giving Ruby a pointed look.

"I wasn't." Ruby hesitated, taken aback by Imogen's tone. She meant no impertinence, but she couldn't cast away the image of Mrs. Fuller slumped over their dining table, then stiff and fearful at the market, and now swollen in the hammock.

Imogen beckoned Annie along the wooden pontoon for a dive into the water. Ruby looked around anxiously. It was the wrong time of day for her—there wasn't any shade, and she hadn't brought her suncream. She wondered whether she should dangle her feet in the water and bow her face away from the sun. Her hair was still damp from the bath, offering some small mercy from the beating heat. Ruby bit her lip and pressed again at her thigh.

WHEN IT CAME TO DINNER, Ruby decided that she didn't want to stay too long. She wondered how she'd manage it—even with the adults paying so little attention to her, she couldn't exactly dismiss herself. At the table she took up a seat as far away from Max as she could, and said very little. She didn't dare stand up to remove her plate before anyone else, so she nibbled at the vegetable lasagne and damp salad leaves until the parents moved to the farther edge of the terrace.

The sinking sun seemed to follow her into the living room, where it reflected off the small square television screen. Ruby slid down into one of the plush armchairs and kicked her legs over the armrest; from here, she thought, anyone passing the door wouldn't see her. She focused on the screen, hoping the blur of colors might distract her from that burn in her thigh, from the strange curl of anxiety that had been lodged in her chest ever since the concert party.

A series of music videos soon slipped into a French soap opera. The evening's darkness took over, and Ruby was able to better see the figures on the screen.

"Oh, here you are," Imogen said.

Annie added excitedly, "Can we watch, too?"

"Oh." Imogen hesitated for a moment. "I'm not allowed to watch television—my mother says it rots the brain. We prefer reading together, or lately she sings to the baby bump."

"My mother says the same about the brain," Ruby added dully. "But I don't care."

She could hear a shout from outside, and Imogen said, "They're playing poker."

Ruby turned her head slightly. "Who?"

"The dads. My father isn't any good, I think he's just watching." Imogen moved forward, mesmerized by the luridly dressed characters moving across the screen. "What is this?" She flopped down on the floor in front of the television. Annie moved to an armchair and imitated Ruby's pose, placing her thin legs over the armrest.

"My father is very good," Annie added quietly.

Ruby turned up the volume as two angry women barked at each other in French. One slapped the other. Ruby didn't blink, but Annie let out a small exclamation.

"Oh, goodness. What is this?" Imogen asked again.

Ruby took up the remote and switched over to a noisy advert. It was loud, and Imogen laughed as the animation rolled along the screen. Ruby picked at a hole in the armchair, where two round scorch marks had allowed the stuffing to be pulled out and fiddled with.

An angry voice came through the door.

"Turn it down! How dare you! Ruby!"

Ruby turned to see her mother's pretty face contorted with fury.

"Sorry, Mrs. Ashby," Annie volunteered, glancing at Ruby desperately. Ruby adjusted the sound and sank lower into her chair. She thought of her bedroom, and how many steps it would take to get there, two floors away, without being seen or challenged by anyone.

By the time Annie came to bed, Ruby was feigning sleep, facedown, her hand pressed carefully between her thigh and the mattress. Annie entered the room in a towel and smelling of lilacs. Ruby recognized the scent of her mother's expensive shampoo and looked up.

A pile of clean clothes, folded and ironed, was waiting on Annie's newly made bed. She was pressing them into her chest, into her face, her damp hair falling forward as she checked each article of clothing, gratefully breathing in its freshness. Her breathing soon slipped into small sobs that shook her frail shoulders.

Ruby hadn't expected that. In the dim darkness, she remained still, before turning her face into her pillow to smear away her damp eyes.

5

The next day carried on with a numb hush. Ruby's father and Max went out for hours, and Ruby felt a strange relief at having them gone. She followed Imogen as she approached her mother after lunch, during the quiet afternoon siesta.

"Stop wriggling about against my chair, Immy." Polly put her hand over her belly. "What is it that you want from me?"

Ruby would have turned away, but Imogen stayed where she was.

"I would like," she attempted in a calm voice, "to go to the village for ice cream with Ruby and Annie—when she's finished with her mother. We could walk."

"You can't *walk* to the village, Immy," Rhoda cackled. "Someone might accost you on the path."

"Can't you just"—Polly flung her arm out—"run around here and have fun? For heaven's sake, don't be a burden, Immy. You know I'm suffering today with my swollen feet."

Imogen reeled back as if struck. "And you, Mama, don't be unkind."

Rhoda sat up. "Don't tell your mother how to behave, thank you, Imogen. Now buzz off, you two."

Ruby fiddled with the tips of her hair, her eyes wide and embarrassed at her own mother rebuking Imogen, but thankfully Polly's voice softened when she saw her daughter's abashed face. "Well . . . I might need to go to the pharmacy later for my pills. I'll take you in then."

"Oh, how tiresome." Rhoda adjusted her sunglasses. "Yes, I suppose I'll need to go to the bank for Toby—thanks to Max cleaning him out with those card games. How I wish he'd bloody leave!"

"Hush, Rhoda, not in front of the children."

Imogen turned to Ruby, her eyes sad. "Shall we go and have a swim in the sea, then?"

"Oh," Ruby said, distracted by her mother's words. "I'd rather the pool?"

"The sea is tons nicer."

"No," Ruby answered dully. "The salt hurts my skin, and there's no shade."

"Don't forget your suncream, Ruby—your freckles are worse each day," Rhoda interrupted.

Imogen's shoulders sank. "Oh, all right. The pool it is, then. Mama, will you tell Annie to join us if you see her?"

"Oh no." It was Polly's turn to adjust her sunglasses. "Not if I have to speak to her mother."

"Dreadful woman!" Rhoda added waspishly. "Mind you . . . I envy her medicine cabinet."

The two women dissolved into laughter.

Imogen moved away, and Ruby followed her. The pine trees above rustled with a turn of the wind while the needles scattered across the terrace floor.

The pool was deserted. Ruby applied a thick layer of suncream to her nose, then began wading around the shallow end, tilting her head away from the sun.

"Let's dive together," Imogen said. Her thick dark hair was slicked around her face, but Ruby could make out the wide grin connecting the bright apples of her cheeks. She was surprised at the swift lift in Imogen's mood.

"I'm terrible at diving." Ruby shook her head. "The water goes up inside my nose."

"I'll teach you how to do it. It's easy."

Ruby looked at her feet, magnified through the water, looking white and ugly. "I don't find it easy."

"I'll *teach* you, I said." Imogen smiled again. "Go on."

Ruby moved toward the pool steps. "No."

"Honestly," Imogen huffed as she splashed about in the deep end, "no one is any fun today. This holiday is simply—"

"What about me?" a new voice interrupted. "I can be a lot of fun, if you'll have me."

Ruby turned and immediately screwed up her face against the sun, but not before she caught the silhouetted shape of Max.

Imogen looked at him doubtfully. "I'm sorry, Mr. Fuller?"

"Where's Annie?" Ruby asked urgently, submerging her body fully in the water, leaving only her head above the water. Her long hair swirled around her, like a webbed protective collar.

"She's in her mother's room," Max answered simply.

Ruby slipped underwater and swam to the far edge of the pool, away from Max, who threw his towel over a lounger and undid his shirt in quick, tight movements. Ruby pushed herself out of the water, and said, "Perhaps I'll go and see if she needs anything."

"Ruby, are you going?" Imogen frowned, spreading her arms to swim toward the shallow end. "Don't go."

Max moved to Ruby's side as she collected her towel. She wrapped it around herself tightly, and inched past, careful not to touch him.

"Ruby?" Imogen said again.

"She's off." Max nodded, smiling down at Imogen keenly. "Did I hear mention of a diving competition?"

"Oh . . . yes." Imogen squinted at Max. "Are you any good, Mr. Fuller? I won the cup last term."

He dove into the deep end just as Ruby passed the last corner of the pool. She felt the water splash her feet.

Before she reached the edge of the house, she glanced back, terribly aware that she ought not leave Imogen alone with Max. She saw him climb out of the water, then put his hands under Imogen's splashing arms and pull her out in one movement. "Well then," he exclaimed. "Let's have a look at what that cup's worth!"

Imogen laughed awkwardly as she staggered backward. "All right then. But I warn you, Mr. Fuller, I'm terribly good."

Ruby turned to face the house, ignoring the beat of alarm in her chest. She hurried inside, past the hall mirror where her face reflected dark and distorted. On the second landing she heard Annie's voice coming from the Fullers' room, so she left them to it, suddenly cold in her towel.

Passing the mirror in her bedroom, she turned this time to observe her shadowy figure. Her fingers, her arms, her legs seemed long and spindly to her; her bumpy breasts were unwelcome and incongruous with the rest of her. Imogen was thicker around the limbs, yet somehow more lithe in her movements. Annie looked still very much like a child, especially when she was laughing with Imogen, exposing her tiny pearly teeth. Ruby didn't like it when Annie and Imogen stopped chattering to turn to check her expression. She didn't know if it was because they were talking about her, or because they thought they needed her permission, or because they feared she would spoil their fun. Regardless, Ruby resented it, and was ready for Annie and her parents to leave.

She squeezed out her wet hair over the sink in her bathroom, and lay back flat on her bed, dampening the linen sheet. Her breathing seemed to level out as she watched slants of light slide across the wall through the crack in the shutter.

RUBY'S EYES FLEW OPEN AT the call for dinner.

"Ruby! *À table!*"

She looked around her. Annie had obviously been in and out without waking her; her things were arranged differently on the metal bed. Ruby rubbed her eyes and scrabbled to remove her still-damp swimsuit, her hair dry but slightly matted. She pulled on a nearby discarded dress and forced herself downstairs, into the hazy evening light. Everyone was already seated, so she drifted toward the children's end.

"Ruby, you haven't dressed."

It took Ruby a moment to respond. "I have."

"That's not dinner wear," Rhoda scolded. "And you might have brushed your hair."

Imogen glanced at Ruby before piping up with, "Mama, I have a bone to pick with you . . . we never went to the village. You promised."

"Tomorrow, darling," Polly answered vaguely. "Don't pester me now."

Ruby checked Imogen, who looked quite tired but well enough— and then Annie. Mrs. Fuller wasn't there, but Max was tucking delightedly into his food, a veal escalope with a mushroom sauce and a scoop of fluffy rice. Two vases of fresh wildflowers were set at each end, with some kind of herby green stems, and Ruby was grateful for their small, aromatic barrier.

Her father was deep in conversation at the other end of the table. "So it'll just be a rather large fine to pay now that the affidavits are accepted. They'll return your passports, and then"— Toby spread his hands with a nod to Max—"you ought to get going."

"Jolly good." Max smiled with a joyful raise of his wineglass. Angus, too, was sitting back and smiling, but not in the same way. Max carried on, "And when are your friends the Montgomerys arriving?"

"In three days. Saturday."

"Well," Max said, nodding, "we'll go then. How does that sound? Easy handover. I'll give the wife the warning and I'll book the flights over the phone tomorrow. No problem."

Toby nodded with a touch of a frown, missing the sharp look his wife gave him. Ruby looked back to the other girls.

"Where is your mum, Annie?"

"She's eating in her room," Annie answered, her eyes fixed on her plate.

Imogen chirruped a little too loudly, "Oh, lucky! Don't you think, Ruby?"

"Yes, of course." Ruby held her breath and let out a tentative smile. "Well, Annie, if you've only got three days left, we should perform a flute duet before you go. Wouldn't that be fun?"

Annie nodded, her eyes still gazing at her untouched food.

The prospect of the Fullers' departure filled Ruby with relief. She had little energy to join in the general dinner conversation, but tried instead to consider how quickly three days could pass.

LATER, RUBY SUGGESTED A GAME of cards, and went to fetch a pack from her room, her grandmother's set from Las Vegas, the preferred pack from all the casinos she'd ever visited. The cards had been used in play, which had left them thick, grainy, inky on the sides, with the top right edges cut. Ruby liked how severe they still looked, how large the numbers were. "Caesars Palace," the back said, which to Ruby sounded like tall marble pillars and spinning roulette wheels, with women wearing black furs and satin gloves sitting beside balding men with monocles. Somewhere hot and in America, somewhere far away where her grandmother had had a wonderful time.

Ruby had adored spending time with her grandmother, in France on holiday and in England on long weekends, lounging in darkened rooms playing cards or sewing together with their minute fingers, her grandmother's coarse black hair and hers strawberry-blond, dangling over their work. Ruby would read aloud to her, short stories mostly, by a writer with a French-sounding name. Her grandmother said the words had ruined her eyesight, but Ruby thought that the embroidery must have too, and the piano pieces that she would sight-read while Ruby sat humming along to the long and somber notes.

Her eyes were the darkest Ruby had ever seen, lined into a thick almond shape with black pencil. Someone had once said that Nancy Ashby was "rather Latin," which Ruby didn't completely understand; nor could she make sense of people's dripping remarks about her heavy perfume or her loud, thick laugh. She certainly couldn't square the glamour of her grandmother with her boring Latin lessons.

Ruby clutched her pack of cards and went over to Imogen and Annie. They were leaning on the balustrade looking out at the sea; it was pearly blue and strange with the end of the sunset.

"These geranium pots are lovely all along here," Annie was saying to Imogen, "so pretty with the sea moving behind. I should like to paint a picture of them. Or press the flowers, perhaps?"

Ruby narrowed her eyes at the plants that peeped over that part of the balustrade. She'd barely noticed them.

"You're so knowledgeable about flowers, Annie," Imogen said kindly.

"I've got the cards," Ruby announced.

Imogen turned around quickly. "No, I'd rather not. I don't feel like it."

A disappointed Ruby wandered over to the far end of the terrace, to a seat by the low coffee table and its accompanying wicker arm-chairs. She shuffled her cards and smiled at the numbers and suits, red and black. Swiveling around her chair, Ruby kicked off her shoes and hooked up her legs on the balustrade wall, her dress tight against her thighs. She shuffled again.

Ruby heard her mother shout over to her. "Put your feet down, Ruby! Close your legs—it's not decent."

"Oh darling, stop shouting," Toby interjected, "it's fine. She's a child."

Rhoda scoffed at her husband, but Ruby put her legs down anyway, since the adults were approaching. She couldn't ignore the hot spread of shame across her cheeks, feeling the glare of her mother—or worse, Max's stare.

"Rubes, why don't you play a bit of flute for us," her father suggested.

Ruby bent over to collect the cards that had fallen from her lap. "Oh no, please, Father, not now."

"Yes, do," Rhoda said. "That nice teacher man loved your playing, Ruby, he kept saying so, even if it was pure flattery to us as the hosts . . . Didn't he give you some project for next term? Although," she added, turning significantly to Polly, "we're not sure she'll—"

Ruby's heart jumped into her throat. "He's not a 'nice teacher man,' he's the head of Music, Mother." She sat up, bunching the playing cards together in her haste. "And yes. He gave me a concerto to learn for next term."

"Can't think why. Holidays are holidays, after all," Ruby's father said vaguely. "Sounds awfully complicated."

"Well, now, you two," Angus contributed. "Sounds like quite an honor for Ruby, and not flattery to you at all, Rhoda. He wouldn't have—"

"Don't tell Rhoda what it was, Angus," Polly interjected. "What on earth do you know about it?" Her husband simply shrugged.

Ruby continued to straighten her cards, very aware of her fingers. She tried to remember a magician she'd seen last Christmas, shuffling a pack of cards by fanning them out. She wondered if her grandmother had ever been able to shuffle like that; Ruby liked to imagine it. She sighed a small breath of relief as her father led the group of adults back to the dining table with promises of after-dinner drinks.

Imogen stood over Ruby's shoulder. "I loathe card games." She raised her chin haughtily. "We're over them in our year."

Annie hovered behind Imogen, and to Ruby's surprise, so did Angus. His bulky figure bent forward so suddenly that both Ruby and Annie jolted with surprise as he spoke.

"Ah, so Imogen is very grumpy and won't play." Angus pulled up a chair and settled opposite Ruby. "Annie, will you?"

Annie hesitated, but after a prod from Imogen she straightened up and answered, "No, thank you."

"Fine. Hurry along then, you two," Angus said, and Ruby felt a twinge of anxiety at having the heat of his attention like this, separate from the others. He reached forward and took the cards from her small hands. "Lovely cards—well worn, and not by you, I think. What'll we play?"

"Well"—Ruby looked up at him, at his thick fingers as he moved the cards between his hands—"do you know Three Blind Mice?"

"You'll have to show me, I'm afraid."

Ruby nodded slowly, then said, "All right. Twos, sevens, and tens are special."

Imogen scoffed, moving farther away, but still watching.

Ruby explained carefully as Angus leaned forward, his thick eyebrows knitted together. After a quick practice round, Angus laughed. "Yes, I understand. Time to play properly now."

Ruby nodded, a little awkwardly. Annie had already wandered to the balustrade to watch the sky darken, and Imogen had joined her, casting Ruby quick and hot glances.

"Tell me about your concerto, little thing," Angus said.

"Well, it's Mozart, with a harp," Ruby replied quickly. "There's three bits to it. I can do the first easily. But the second movement is very hard."

Angus chuckled. "And there's a harpist waiting in the wings, is there?"

"Well, yes, Sally Deed plays, and she's in Imogen's year. She's rather splendid, actually—" Ruby stopped, worried that she'd spoken too much, embarrassed about her excitement.

"Sounds ideal. I don't know anything about music. I enjoy as much of Imogen's blasting as I can handle, but there's something rather beautiful about the flute."

"I think so," Ruby answered, a little shyly.

"Well, you make a jolly good sound," Angus said measuredly. "You and Annie had a lovely duet during that concert. You ought to play it again before she goes."

Ruby looked up at Angus—the curls of his thick steely hair, his sunken expression, his round, intimidating gaze. He really looked nothing like her own father, and she couldn't see Imogen's resemblance to him at all.

"I did mention it. Do you think I should try again, Mr. Bly?"

"Yes, why not." Angus nodded seriously. "It might cheer her up, poor thing. I imagine she needs our support, with parents like that." He gestured over to the clustered group of adults a little away from them, Toby pouring out some newly produced whiskey across several tumblers.

The late evening was settling in now, and the lights from the house shone over them. Imogen started to dance to the jazz records whose sounds now drifted across the terrace, and she pulled Annie toward her. Ruby watched them for a moment, flicking the cards between her fingers. The jazz reminded her of the concert party, and the police car. Her father was somehow sorting it all out, but Ruby was no closer to understanding what had happened.

"Angus, come here!" Rhoda called over. "You can't be serious, playing cards with the children."

He shook his head jovially and called back, "Perfectly serious, Rhoda."

Polly looked over, too, with a peculiar expression on her face that washed away as soon as Rhoda made some sort of joke. A few minutes later, to Ruby's surprise, she'd won the game. She laughed, for the first time that day.

Angus chucked his hand into the mess of cards. "I say, you're a lot better than your father at cards, aren't you?"

Ruby looked up, confused. "My father?"

"Sorry, little thing, not what I meant at all."

"Mr. Bly." She looked at Angus's exposed hand. "Did you let me win?"

"It's Lord Bly, Ruby."

"Oh, yes. I . . . forgot," Ruby said quickly, gathering the cards together, her cheeks hot.

"I'm teasing you, little thing," Angus said, waving her apology away with a laugh. "It's actually Lord Beresford. But nothing gets past you, does it? Let's have another round."

Ruby squinted at the cards as she amassed them. She didn't know whether she should feel relieved or mortified.

"Best of three." Angus leaned forward and collected the cards efficiently, ushering her hands away. "Let me. And I promise not to let you win this time."

Angus shuffled and dealt the cards as a burst of laughter came from her father. Ruby sat forward, determined.

6

Three days later the Fullers left in a wave of exaggerated regret. The adults grasped each other and exchanged their pleasantries, and Annie gave Imogen a small squeeze before she got into the car, chattering nervously about what awaited her back at home—Girl Guides and visiting her aunt's cottage by the sea. When the car rolled down the drive, Ruby felt a rush of relief as she returned to her room, now hers alone. She was glad to break away from the hot stupor she'd fallen into the last few days, swinging from her bedroom to the pool to meals on the terrace and then back again, hovering above the small friendship Annie and Imogen had established.

The crickets were incredibly loud that morning, and Ruby wondered if they had always been scratching away like that and she had simply got used to them. Was it possible that they could fill each day with such a jarring screech and no one else noticed?

A few hours after the Fullers' departure, another car arrived, spilling out four people when only the two Montgomerys were expected. The unexpected pair stepped out of the back of the large Range Rover: a mother and daughter, brown and soft, and in stark contrast to the older couple that stepped out of the front. Ruby and Imogen couldn't help staring at the unexpected and uninvited girl. She was wearing a loud and colorful T-shirt so big that it left gaping holes at the arms and hung long over her loose and rumpled shorts. She had pale brown frazzled curls cut short all around her head, and thick glasses that sat on a firm nose and made her eyes look small. Ruby guessed at her being around sixteen, just ahead of them in age.

But this new creature wasn't looking at them at all. She was appraising the expansive terrace, the bustling sea, the tall line of the château that stretched all the way up to the canopy of pine trees.

"Wow!" She pulled an exaggerated face. "What the hell! Mum, you didn't really describe—"

"Ned, darling, come and get your things." The girl's mother tugged open the trunk. She had very short hair combed slick over her head, and wore a brown linen dress cut perfectly for her neat and muscular figure.

Toby went to help the woman with her bags as Rhoda muttered furiously to Polly. In a mirrored movement, Imogen turned to Ruby.

"Who are those two?"

"I don't know," Ruby said quietly, anxious over her mother's reaction. "I've never met them before. I thought we were only expecting the Montgomerys."

The Montgomerys were a smart, cream-colored husband and wife, their countenance as severe as their perfume. Harley was a very tall and portly gentleman with a dry blue stare and a rapidly balding head, whom Ruby found quite a bore in a pestering sort of way. His linen suit flashed in the sun and shone against his silk pocket square, which was as blue and eye-catching as the sea behind him. His wife, Liv, matched him in dress, but her marbled and downcast eyes gave her a timid demeanor, and she'd barely said a word to Ruby in all the years she'd known her.

Imogen's father moved forward to greet Harley stiffly, but with familiarity. Harley's face filled with warmth as he drew Angus into a slapping hug.

"Oh." Imogen inhaled sharply. "Does my father know him?"

Ruby frowned again. "Yes. Didn't they all go to university together?"

"I've never heard of this man." Imogen attempted a laugh. "I've never seen him before."

The two men were equally tall, and seemed to make one great monster. When they pulled out of the hug, Ruby looked at their arms, as strong as gorillas'. But in the next moment, Harley turned his attention on her.

"Hello, little Ruby Booby Rubes." His voice was a low bass. "You're growing up. Jolly good to see you—and who's this?"

"I'm Imogen," Imogen answered quickly, still a little bewildered. "Imogen Bly."

"Imogen, of course. We've never met." Harley nodded at her, pleased. *"Bonsoir, mademoiselle, je suis Harley."*

Imogen declared, "It's *'je m'appelle,'* actually."

"'Course it is, you little minx." Harley chuckled. "Call me Major General Montgomery. And that's Liv . . . my present wife."

"*Present* wife?" Imogen's mouth puckered.

"Yes dear, number two, and let me know if you'd be willing to do the job next time around. Can't believe we've never met. I see your beast of a father regularly in London, with Tobes. But I very rarely get invited to your country estate."

Imogen's face was creased in confusion.

"That's enough, Harley. Hello, I'm Ned Leonard." The teenage girl moved forward, nudging Harley out of the way. "My mum dragged me along with her, as stowaways in Harley and Liv's car. Apparently she and your dads are all old chums. I'm not babysitting either of you, so get that out of your head right now."

Imogen's mouth untwisted. "We don't need babysitting—we walk to the village on our own."

Ruby glanced at Imogen, surprised at the lie.

"Oh, well." Ned considered her, flashing that wide smile again. "Glad to hear it."

Imogen scoffed. "What kind of a name is 'Ned,' anyway?"

Ned's smile faltered, and she answered, "It's mine, that's what it is." And she moved away, replaced by her mother.

"Hello, you two, I'm Georgina Leonard. Ruby and . . . Imogen? Good to meet you." She smiled broadly, and Ruby saw the daughter's smile in the mother's. "Don't mind Ned. She's probably got a bit of heatstroke—too long in the hot car." Her eyes lingered over Ruby's face for an uncomfortable moment. "It's wonderful to meet you. It really is." Her face snapped to Imogen, her smile unwavering. "Both of you. I've known your fathers for a very long time, you know. We all studied together—among other activities—at university. Ned and I were just passing through France on the train, heard Harley was on his way, and thought we'd pop by."

Harley boomed out at Toby, "This is the tenth year you've been here, isn't it?" His eyes lit up as he surveyed the colorful landscape.

"Well"—Toby's head tilted as he regarded his friend fondly—"the tenth year since I inherited it, yes."

"How momentous." Harley nodded his head. "We shall celebrate. Can't stay too long, though. Nanny's looking after the dogs, but you know how they are with her. It's jolly good to be here at last, at Number Seven."

"Number Seven?" Imogen couldn't help but ask.

"Yes, dear Imogen, Château des Sètes—it means 'Castle of the Thirsty,' but it sounds like *numéro sept*. So that's how I address it. Number Seven, the Mediterranean." Harley gave a small bow of laughter as Imogen frowned, nonplussed.

Ruby had learned to ignore Harley and his remarks whenever he was around, usually during the holidays or at Christmastime. But she couldn't help but feel a fresh interest in the curious new pair, Ned and Georgina Leonard, so energetic and colorful and exotic, even if they did have the bad manners to turn up out of the blue.

As they walked toward the house, Imogen regarded Harley with a careful eye, and whispered, "I'll miss Annie . . . but I'm glad her father's gone."

"Oh, why do you say that?" Ruby asked warily.

Imogen hesitated on the steps. "Well . . ."

"Well"—Ruby nodded as Imogen's face changed—"I'm glad too."

Imogen gave a brief smile but turned away and moved down the

steps. Ruby watched her stride across the terrace and toward the balustrade. Ruby wanted to join her, but couldn't seem to move her feet.
Anyway, she knew her mother would want her to welcome their guests,
offer them a drink, and then bark the orders at Lisette. Show them to
their rooms, though she had no idea where the Leonard pair would
sleep. These were her father's friends, and she had to be on her best
behavior. She also wanted to look at that Ned person more, and she
ought to tidy her bedroom now that Annie had gone, in case the new
arrivals were given a tour of the château.

AT DINNER RUBY WATCHED IMOGEN, who looked queasy from the
start. She'd asked her father something, leaning close to his ear, but he'd
brushed her off, which surprised Ruby. Imogen was wearing a short
gray dress but moved awkwardly in it, while Ruby felt confident and
cheery enough to wear her broderie anglaise dress again, clean and safe
from the now-departed Mr. Fuller. In an attempt to cheer Imogen up,
Ruby politely offered her the serving plate first. Imogen looked cautiously at the pile of penne pesto, then nodded, and picked up the bowl
of parmesan afterward.

"Thank you."

Harley was speaking in his long, tired drawl. "Are the girlies really
sitting at the end . . . Shouldn't we be teaching them all manner of
things, such as conversation at dinner? They're hardly children anymore."

"Oh"—Rhoda sprung to her feet—"of course, Harley. Ruby, move
up here—you too, Immy . . . Polly, stay where you are. Liv, just here.
Georgina there, Edwina at the end. There you go, gents," she coaxed.
"You move around us however you like."

"Well, I refuse to sit near my wife," Harley growled good-naturedly.
"So I'll find the best spot I can."

Ruby and Imogen were promptly moved into the middle of the
table. Ned smirked and took up Imogen's chair. Imogen looked thoroughly dismayed at being placed in such a position, but Ruby didn't
mind the attention at all. She fluffed out her hair and smiled as she

looked at the faces around her, lit by the outdoor lanterns and supported by the luscious scenery around them. Angus sat beside Ruby,
rounding on her with a tight wink, while Imogen stared over at him
sullenly. Polly and Rhoda made sure they were sitting close together, to
continue discussing whatever grasped their attention: the new arrivals,
perhaps, or some new irritation Rhoda had found in Ruby.

Harley sat beside Imogen and woke up the table with his great deep
voice. "We saw the Cressels before we came down. They had a small
dinner."

"No! Did you!" Rhoda swung the bowl of pasta in a sudden gesture. Ruby could see that her mother was envious, and that same envy
crossed Polly's face, too.

"She's rather fond of Liv, so we were included," Harley said with
delight, fully aware of the effect of his words.

"Is she?" Rhoda set down the bowl.

"And how do you find her, Liv?" Polly asked.

"Rather stilted, I thought," Harley answered before his wife could
reply. "The pair of them are rather dull."

"Dull, indeed! They are only one of the greatest families in the king-
dom," said Rhoda.

Harley shrugged delightedly. "Well, I just like to see his horses,
and his dogs. He has a devil of a pointer, and his horses are brilliantly
trained. God, I already miss my hounds. And the cricket—I need to
check the scores, actually."

Liv raised her graceful head. "She's so generous. We both grew up in
Northumbria, a place she very much cherishes."

Rhoda bristled at this unsatisfactory answer, while Polly pressed
Harley, "Who else was there?"

"The Ridleys and John Olding. Are they on your Christmas card lists?"

"Yes, of course. How lovely to have seen them," Polly said.

"We don't much care for that sort of company, Harley," Angus said.
"At least not as much as our wives do."

"No, I know," Harley said with a thrilled humor, "and I'd probably
have to agree—it was a ghastly evening. The pheasants were full of
shot, and they couldn't get any hot water for the bath."

"For the bath?" Rhoda repeated, stunned. "Did you stay over-night?"

"Hasn't he shot grouse with the Prince of Wales?" Polly asked at the same time, and Harley nodded, even more delighted than before.

Rhoda pushed her food around her plate. Ruby knew what her mother was thinking, how much she longed to be in England, plan-ning her next dinner party, some scheme within her social circle, her next trip to London or to the dress shop. Ruby looked up at the trees, across at the sea, breathing in how much she loved this house—her grandmother's favorite place, more than any other at home. But the view, the sounds, the smell of the château had changed somehow over the last few days.

Half an hour later, just as the plates were being cleared and Rhoda was sliding open a white box of *patisserie* cakes, the phone rang in long peals, startling the group.

"Ruby, answer it," Rhoda said irritably, lifting each cake out of the box and onto a platter.

"Me?" Ruby squeaked.

"Yes, you," Rhoda insisted. "Don't try me, girl."

Ruby prickled with indignation that her mother was taking out her social anxieties on her, but knew better than to argue. She pushed her chair out and dashed across the terrace.

It was Max, his voice as unwelcome as the discomfort Ruby felt in hearing it.

"Ruby, for heaven's sake, why have they sent you? Get your father. It's urgent."

By the time she got back to the table the chatter was easy again, the stack of plates at the end waiting for someone to carry them away. Imogen was watching Ruby, wide-eyed and waiting for some horrible confirmation. Ruby spoke a few words into her father's ear, her voice quivering.

"What's that?" Toby turned his head so hastily that Ruby flinched. "Speak clearly, Ruby."

"It's Mr. Fuller," Ruby repeated loudly, her cheeks flushing.

Ruby returned to her seat with her head lowered, her face hot from the sharp rebuke and the terrible uncertainty of what Max might demand from her father over the phone.

Toby eyed his wife warily when he returned to stand by the table. Harley's curiosity was evidently too much to bear. "What's happened, Cashby, old friend?"

"It's nothing." Toby touched his glasses dismissively, but couldn't conceal the note of worry in his voice.

"It's not 'nothing' at all, is it, Toby?" Rhoda said, reading her husband's face. "Tell me it's not a returning guest."

"You're not serious! Not that woman!" Polly's eyes blew wide.

"No, not her." Toby drew his eyebrows together. "Just him."

"What's happened?" Harley demanded.

"He missed the flight or—didn't get on it? I couldn't understand. The thing is"—Toby seemed to address the table—"he could get a hotel . . . but you know what those are like around the airport. It's already past nine o'clock." He turned to his wife. "Has Lisette changed the room yet?" She turned her face away. "No. There you are, you see? It's easier this way."

"Easier for *him*," Rhoda added firmly, with a strained smile. "We won't discuss it further. He can stay one night. He'll go to a hotel, or back to England, tomorrow."

"Is Annie okay?" Imogen burst out suddenly, her face very agitated.

"I say, old boy," Harley interjected, looking from Imogen to Toby, "this is all rather exciting. What's the story?"

Toby threw himself into his seat. "It would seem that Max—whom you've not yet met—and his wife had a row, and she got on the plane with her daughter, and he didn't. Or rather . . . she booted him off. Made quite a scene, he said."

"Sounds brilliant." Ned laughed. "I'll be sad not to meet *her.*"

"Sounds like a very unpleasant business," Angus said gravely. "And a bore for you both."

"But Annie is all right?" Imogen tried again.

"It would appear so." Toby took off his glasses and pinched the bridge of his nose. He closed his eyes for a brief moment.

Ruby sat back. So Mrs. Fuller had gone, hopefully with Annie, and

Max was returning for one night. She wasn't sure where to put her anxiety. She wasn't sure she could really picture Mrs. Fuller on a plane, shaking next to poor Annie the whole journey. Nor Mr. Fuller, back here at the house, alone. Ruby forced a smile for the rest of the table, and didn't look at Imogen.

WHEN THE TAXI ROLLED IN, Max was full of frantic but unapologetic words. "I couldn't stay on that plane with her." He addressed Toby so loudly that those on the terrace could hear. "She's going to see her sister, and I'll go back home in a few days. I'll be able to get some sense out of her after that."

"I thought she wouldn't let you on?" Toby said as he helped Max with his bag. Ruby fiddled with her playing cards by the coffee table and pretended to not be listening.

"Well, how could I go with her? After all the dreadful things we've suffered here, thanks to her?"

Toby glanced at Angus, and said, "Should we phone her to make sure she's home all right?"

Imogen had already gone upstairs to bed, but Ruby had promised her she'd wait to hear anything about Annie. The women had remained outdoors, Liv going alone to paddle her feet in the pool even though it was dark. The men had retreated to the living room, smoking and playing records, their conversation low and constant as they waited for the beep of the taxi, and the arrival of another man.

"No. I'd rather not," Max answered. "But a stiff drink will do me fine." He gripped Toby's shoulder tightly as he moved toward the table. "Thank you. It's been a trying day."

"No need to air your dirty laundry, man," Harley called out to Max as he approached. "Stiff upper lip, pronto. We'll have one of the ladies fix you a drink. Rhoda!"

Max glanced up, relieved, as Harley pulled him in for a handshake.

"I'm Harley. One of Cashby's best people. Welcome to our crowd."

7

2010

Mrs. Cosgrove woke up agitated; she had dreamed about the château again. That grand house perched by the water, tinged with sunlight and heat. The memory of it was permanently lodged in her mind, like an azure blue aneurysm, sharp and painful with every blink.

Mrs. Cosgrove's eyes adjusted to the light of the hotel room. She looked at her small suitcase. Just how long did she expect to stay? The room was small and densely furnished—too much velvet and mahogany for the hot weather—but it had a long window with its own red jacquard seat and a fine view of the village square.

It was Market Day. She lit a cigarette and watched the people move beneath her, streaming past the flat, colorful tops of market stalls. The sun came through the thick plane trees, settling atop a pile of tressed garlic bulbs and leafy green basil plants, across a slate of silver necklaces, on the bare shoulders of a teenage girl. Mrs. Cosgrove took a drag of her cigarette and nodded to herself. The village was undoubtedly busier since her last visit over two decades ago. The area was wealthier now, and she could hear the happy hubbub of many different languages. She was glad of this—her own clipped accent might slip in between and she could pass by, unseen.

Mrs. Cosgrove glanced around for the ashtray, but there wasn't one. She frowned with annoyance and moved into the bathroom, where she dropped the stub of her cigarette into the toilet bowl. She heard the hot tip sizzle and die before standing back and flushing it away.

Mrs. Cosgrove went back to her suitcase and started to undo her folded clothes, frowning at the creases in her linen suit. She knew she ought to have unpacked last night, to let the soft fabric drop. But she moved efficiently now, hanging each outfit in order along the rail. She had planned on four days, but she would stay until it was finished.

At the bottom of her suitcase sat a sunglasses case, a spare plug adapter, a small pouch for underwear, and two stray lipsticks that had fallen out of her washbag and were probably softening with the heat. And a copy of *The Iliad*. Mrs. Cosgrove winced seeing it, but couldn't stop herself from running her fingers over its pale cover. Her nails were painted a rich dark red, Chanel's *Rouge Noir*, James's favorite. She'd had them done before she'd left. But there was no need to perform anymore, Mrs. Cosgrove thought, not here anyway, and especially not now that James was gone. Even so, she'd probably keep it up—all of it, even the smile that had etched itself into the small wrinkles beside her eyes. She didn't know any other way.

This trip, this "visit," had stood at the forefront of her mind since the death of her husband, now that she was finally free to move around as she liked. She'd brought the thick leaflet from James's memorial, with his smiling face on the cover—a photo somebody else had chosen because she hadn't had the heart. Still, the event had been a fitting tribute, thanks to the loving swarm of people, the mournful swell of music, and the many important figures who spoke so warmly. Mrs. Cosgrove had stayed silent as the program went on, everyone around her interpreting her stillness as a sign of deep mourning.

His death had shocked her into the very bewilderment that drove her here to France. Yes, she'd been content in the early days of her marriage—happy, if that was indeed an option for her—but any budding love for James soon hardened as she felt the leash of their marriage tighten, and she'd beat her wings against the heavy cage of their union like some unhappy bird. She'd soon turned away from him completely. Not with anger or disappointment, but with coldness. And that coldness seemed to have permeated his very soul, lodged itself in his heart, and sped up his aging process. It might have even given root to his heart attack. Mrs. Cosgrove wasn't sure how she felt about his death. She only knew that she hadn't felt a great many things since she was a child.

The memorial leaflet had slid into the pages of *The Iliad,* and Mrs. Cosgrove quickly pulled it out. She didn't want them touching each other—they were two entirely separate things.

Her heart beat steadily at the thought of finally being here. But it struck with something like fear: fear of those people in the village below; fear that the woman at the hotel's reception downstairs might recognize her; fear of last night's cabdriver, who seemed to note how she held her breath as they drove near the château, on that side of the bay.

Tomorrow was Mrs. Cosgrove's meeting with the estate agent. He'd sent over the details of the house via email, and the glossy pictures had tripped her backward, memories slapping her across the face. Tomorrow afternoon he would thrust a brochure full of those images into her hands, and take her to see the place again with her own eyes—and then everything would be a reality. Mrs. Cosgrove wondered if that confrontation would make her feel something, anything, again.

She wondered if the brochure, or the agent, would detail the true history of the château. How the Ashbys had cut off the house from the rest of the village many generations before; how they rebuilt the deep walls around the property, cleared the mess off the land, pruned the gardens to perfection, scrubbed away as much of the château's history as they could, and filled the elegant rooms with treasures from wealthiest Europe, Eastern Asia, and anything else that had caught the elder Mrs. Ashby's eye in the British auction rooms. They had created their own piece of heaven on the edge of the bay.

It was well known that the Ashby family had escaped the Fall of Singapore during the Second World War, and returned to England. But Mrs. Nancy Ashby, the matriarch, missed the warmer climate she'd grown accustomed to, and several years later persuaded her husband to search for a second home abroad, in France—close enough to drive from their country pile in England, and far enough away from her father, the Fifth Viscount Deering, and his domineering disapproval. They soon found the Château des Sètes, and Mrs. Ashby made it her home for several months of the year. The château became both new and terribly old—a place where the Ashbys were luxuriant, beautiful, and safe. They could parade through the village, spending their money generously in the restaurants and local shops, sharing their expensive jollity with gaggles of visiting friends, before retiring to the splendid decadence of the house and its expansive grounds.

Mrs. Cosgrove wondered, too, whether the brochure would indicate how a few decades later, under Mrs. Ashby's second son, the love and care for the château began to fade. The edge of the bay was unforgiving—the sea wind was tight on hot summer days, the front of the house didn't quite face the right angle for renewing daylight, and the ancient walls split against the burn of the sun.

She knew that the brochure certainly wouldn't mention how very few of the French locals chose to go near the house after the war; or that they believed it would be forever governed by the great number that had died there—the refugees and rebels who'd been kept in the attics, tortured, and then killed at the hands of the occupying enemy. The château was cursed, they said, its aura black and its first English mistress an inevitable victim of its tortured history.

Would she, Mrs. Cosgrove, now open up those troubled gates again, and become its next English mistress?

The phone rang, jolting her out of her reverie. It rang in one long tone, and then stopped. She turned from the bright window, past the red curtain to the red wallpaper and the red bedcover.

The phone rang again, and she stood to answer it. The other person spoke before she did.

"Cossie? Have they put me through, or not? Monsieur?"

"Hello?" Mrs. Cosgrove's voice was thick. "Good morning?"

"Oh, God," said the voice at the other end of the line. "Cossie, what are you *doing* there?"

"Alexandra . . . is that you?" Mrs. Cosgrove cleared her throat quickly. "How on earth did you find me?"

"You told your mother where you were going."

She bristled as her friend continued, "*Why* have you gone away so soon after James? I can't believe it. Aren't you worried about what people will say?"

Mrs. Cosgrove's voice was louder than she expected. "No, and I feel insulted by the question, Alexandra."

"Don't be ridiculous. You belong at home. James's family were—"

"I had to come here," Mrs. Cosgrove insisted, looking around wildly, almost expecting Alexandra to burst through the door. "And Alexandra, I don't remember telling my mother. We've barely spoken in the last year."

"Don't be ridiculous, of course you've spoken. You've just lost your husband, for heaven's sake." Alexandra's words came tumbling out. "I just don't understand why you've gone to France—to that *place,* after that terrible summer! Why on earth would you want to return?"

"It wasn't what you think it was."

"Of course, Cossie, what happened . . . is well known," Alexandra said cautiously. "Even though you never speak of it."

"Well, I need to be here now. I need to see it through." Mrs. Cosgrove reached across the desk for a cigarette. "I can't explain it, and I don't have to answer to you."

"You're not going to hurt yourself, are you?" Alexandra suddenly asked.

Mrs. Cosgrove let the silence hang between them. "No."

"Well, I'm glad to hear it. Miranda was asking where you were, you know; you've let us down with the church bazaar."

Mrs. Cosgrove thought of the lofty church hall, bubbling over with busy and happy people, just as it should be, after she'd put so much into it. The lists of prizes she'd overseen, the persuasive letters she'd written for the donations, the book stall she'd meticulously alphabetized, the invitations she'd sent to every wealthy name in her address book. Alexandra was right—it was a lot to give up. But somehow it had entirely slipped her mind.

"You say 'us.' Does that include you?"

"Well, yes," Alexandra answered sheepishly. "They've asked me to step in. You know, in your place."

Mrs. Cosgrove felt a sting in her tongue as she said, "I'm so glad."

"No, no . . ." Alexandra stuttered defensively. "Cossie."

"I'm happy for you. You've been angling for a way to get in with Miranda and that gang. I should congratulate you."

"Now, hang on." Alexandra hesitated. "I've been doing nothing of the sort—and what about Robert, does he know where you are—"

Mrs. Cosgrove had a terrible urge to slam the phone down, but instead she answered in a measured voice, "No, Alexandra, and do not tell him, please."

"I'm worried about you. Everybody is."

Again, Mrs. Cosgrove let the silence stretch between them. She sat up straight, tapping her cigarette on the desk, ready to light when the conversation was finished. "I must go, actually, Alexandra."

"Just come back," her friend said urgently. "And when you do, we'll talk through things."

"No thank you, Alexandra. Not with you."

Mrs. Cosgrove dropped the phone and fetched her lighter from the bedside table. She stared at the flame for a long while, letting the skin of her thumb rest on the roller. Beyond the door of her room she heard two male voices in some kind of loud but muffled argument. The flame caught her finger, and with the sharp pang, she dropped the lighter. As she bent down to collect it, the unlit cigarette drooped in her mouth.

Was Alexandra right? Mrs. Cosgrove looked over at the taxi card the driver had given her, which she'd placed strategically next to the phone. She could call, right now, have him collect her things and take her back to the airport, back to the cool air and the reprieve of England. Back to Alexandra, and Miranda, and the church bazaar, and all the other events that would line themselves up, waiting to be ticked off before the next revealed itself. A never-ending chain of social calls and smiles and thanks and flowers and tea. To be endured alone, without James to complain to, without the great bulk of his position and personality to hide behind.

Her stomach arched and gurgled—she'd probably missed breakfast. She could call room service . . . but the taxi card seemed to call to her. Mrs. Cosgrove felt a sudden rush of emotion; the beat of her heart quickened as she remembered that other trip back from the airport, all those years ago. She pictured three girls bound tightly together in the backseat of the car, holding each other. Their hot breath, clammy palms, and her overshadowing fear of the man in the front, the man driving. It had been a scorching day, and someone had suggested ice cream. The windows were open and the breeze smacked their faces and tore at their hair.

She'd done all she could to ease the heat in the car, to maintain the light tone in her voice, to appease that man in the front. The other two had seemed to do the same. Still the sweat had prickled at her neck and between her fingers.

Mrs. Cosgrove sat down on the bed to shake away that memory, to return to herself. But she couldn't. Her demeanor that day, the way she had composed herself in that car, to that man—she knew that she still behaved like that now.

When was it, she asked herself, that her youthful joy turned sour, when this strange exterior rose up and crystalized around her? She knew exactly. It was that summer.

8

1985

Ruby struggled to sleep that night. She thought she heard the phone ringing, summoning her downstairs. Closing her eyes, she saw herself outside at dinner, then running across the terrace to answer. She told herself that it couldn't be ringing, not again. In fact, it usually never rang at all—Lisette answered it promptly during the day, and no one ever called at night.

But in the morning, Ruby heard it again, as clear as a bell over the fresh shriek of the seabirds. It rang long, and stopped. Through the crack of her shutters, agitated voices bubbled up from below, and Ruby's worry forced her out of bed and downstairs. On the terrace, a frantic Max was rushing through his breakfast, sitting opposite her father, who looked equally disheveled. Ruby saw him share an alarmed glance with Angus.

"Of course, I'll take a taxi," Max said between mouthfuls. "You've got guests."

"Just take the car, as I say," Toby urged, "and bring her back. You'll only panic in a cab."

Max pulled a grateful face as he scraped a nub of butter onto his last fragment of toast. Ruby narrowed her eyes at him, and asked, "What's happening?"

"Bring *who* back?" Imogen added, emerging behind Ruby, who jolted at seeing her. Imogen's soft face was even more alarmed than her own.

Toby didn't answer, so Angus took up the reins. "It's Annie, girls. Her mother left her behind. She's at the airport."

"What?" Imogen's voice grew cold. "Overnight? Where did she sleep? She's only eleven!"

"Imogen." Angus's face hardened. "Don't make it worse."

"Yes," Toby added. "Don't worry, Imogen darling, these airports know how to look after wayward children."

Imogen's voice was shrill. "She's not a 'wayward child'!"

Ruby stayed stiff and silent.

"Max is just about to go and collect her." Toby stood with a weary frown. "Don't panic, either of you."

"But poor Annie!" Imogen cried. "She's been all alone!"

Max's expression shifted with an idea. He smiled. "Imogen darling, why don't you come with me in the car."

Imogen hesitated. "Oh, I . . ."

Max waited for her response. Toby was hurriedly collecting the breakfast things, and Angus stood to help. Ruby wondered whether they were trying to hurry Max along; she could feel the steady beat of the silence.

Imogen's voice sounded smaller when she answered. "Isn't it very far?"

"Not too far—an hour perhaps," Max replied fluidly, maintaining his gaze.

"I'd rather not, Mr. Fuller."

"Oh, don't be disagreeable, Immy." Angus leaned forward to gather up the used napkins.

"I'd really rather not—"

"Don't fuss, Imogen," Toby interrupted. "Do what Mr. Fuller says. There isn't time, and it might cheer Annie up to see a friendly face after the night she's probably had."

Imogen looked desperately at her father, then at Toby. Lastly she glanced at Ruby, who was already saying loudly: "I'll come too, then."

Max regarded Ruby carefully. "All right. It'll be jolly. We'll stop for ice cream."

"Buy some baguettes, will you?" Toby said distractedly. "Lisette's not here till later."

"Only on the way back," Ruby said firmly. "We need to fetch Annie first. She must be terribly frightened."

"Yes," Imogen agreed. "Where did she sleep?"

Max looked back at the breakfast remnants. "I'll get my things. Then we must go." He added with a quick laugh, "No time to check the financial index!"

Just at that moment a shutter flew open, which drew all the faces upward. Ned stuck her head out of the window and exclaimed delightedly, "Lovely! Not a cloud in the sky!"

RUBY AND IMOGEN SETTLED INTO the backseat of Toby's car. Max started the engine quickly, but spent a good deal of time adjusting the seat and moving his hands about the gearstick and steering wheel. He addressed the girls cheerfully, joking about having them read the map to direct him, trying to catch their eyes in the mirror. Ruby responded with equal cheer, careful to say the right thing, and even more careful to fill the silence that the muted Imogen left beside her.

When they arrived at the airport, Max pulled into the short-term car park and insisted on going in himself, and alone. Ruby was glad—she was hot and exhausted, though it was still only mid-morning. As she leaned her head on the car window, she felt a small pressure on her arm. Imogen released her fingers, but met Ruby's gaze with misty eyes.

"Thank you for coming, too."

Ruby nodded and turned back to the window. She pushed open the car door, and stepped out into an even heavier heat. She winced at the choking stink of the cars, the shouts of porters tugging at a luggage trolley, the flash of the sun across the metal car hoods. Her feet seemed to stick to the hot tarmac beneath her sandals.

What would it be like with Annie back, Ruby wondered, now that there were more people than they'd ever had at the house, and more than her parents seemed to be able to manage? Ruby sighed out her dismay at this strange summer, and pushed her fingers through her fringe as she muddled through her thoughts.

From the other side of the car, Imogen exclaimed, "There she is!"

Annie's dress was dirty and very rumpled, and she trailed a small suitcase behind her. She stopped to say something to her father, but he gave no acknowledgment as he took the suitcase from her and hurried toward the car.

Imogen bound Annie into a hug; when she let her go, Annie shook a little before standing up straight.

"There, there. All better." Max slammed the trunk and moved around to pat Imogen's shoulder.

Imogen ignored him, her face bursting with questions for Annie. "I'm so glad you're all right. What happened?"

Annie's voice cracked a little, and her shoulders shuddered. "Well, the air hostesses took me to a cabin room with a sofa to sleep on. I was never alone, but I didn't really sleep."

"That sounds terrible."

"It was all right," Annie insisted, with a glance at Ruby.

"What happened to your mother?"

Annie didn't answer, but raised her eyes to glower at her jaunty father as he slammed the door and settled into the driver's seat.

"Perhaps Annie doesn't want to talk about it," Ruby said dully. "Let's just get home."

Ruby made sure that Annie was sandwiched between her and Imogen in the backseat to stop her gentle shaking. Max switched on the radio in the front. Ruby scowled as he searched for stations; the scratch of pop music was abhorrent to her ears.

The small party didn't stop for ice cream, or baguettes. Nobody mentioned it, and when they got back to the house, no one was there to greet them. Ruby wordlessly guided Annie up to her bedroom, Imogen a strong support behind them. Max left his daughter's suitcase at the bottom of the stairs, and went to find the others.

The two girls decided to leave Annie to sleep on the metal bed, although Ruby wondered whether she should offer the girl her own after the night she'd had. Imogen sat beside Annie as she tucked her feet under the covers, and Annie suddenly said in a rush:

"I didn't want to say in the car, but it was horrible; they argued like never before. Daddy says that Mummy has been more . . . excitable since we've been here, and he's right, but he's so horrible to her. He was so horrible that they escorted him off the plane! And I ran after him, but I shouldn't have. I thought Mummy would follow too, but she didn't! Oh, I don't want to think about it!"

"You don't have to think about it, Annie," Ruby told her. "You're here now. You're safe."

"Yes! We'll cheer you up," Imogen added. Annie laid her head on the pillow, and Imogen started lightly stroking her hair away from her temples. Ruby watched them.

"This is what my mother does for me when I'm upset," Imogen said as Annie gave a weak smile.

Ruby pulled the shutters closed and turned toward the other two in the new darkness. "Shall we go for a swim, Imogen? And come back later to check on Annie?"

Imogen moved her hand away from Annie's head as she thought about it. "Oh, in the sea?"

"Yes," Ruby said staunchly, "all right."

They went down to the rocks and the pontoon, passing no one on the terrace. On the steps, Imogen paused and separated from Ruby, going to her mother on the lower lawn. Polly was balancing on one of the twin hammocks, Ruby's mother on the other. Imogen leaned toward Polly, saying something and touching her mother's arm tenderly but tentatively.

"Haven't you?" Ruby heard Polly say from under her broad sunhat. Imogen's mother raised her voice and shifted forward, jerking the hammock. "Rhoda, they've had no lunch."

"Oh, how boring," Rhoda answered lazily, lifting her hat. "Immy darling, do ask Lisette. Ruby knows what to do. Ruby!"

Ruby took a step back so that her mother wouldn't see her.

"Or . . . save your appetite," Polly suggested, settling back in her hammock. "We're going to Saint-Tropez for dinner."

"Where? *Sant* what?"

Polly raised her voice automatically. "Don't fuss, please, Imogen."

"If Mr. Fuller is staying, Mama, shouldn't we go home? I'll speak to Dada—"

Ruby looked out at the sea. It was very blue today, and not rough at all. She wondered if she should go on ahead; she didn't want to listen in like this. She pulled at her bundle of swimming things anxiously.

"No, darling, our holiday is just starting," said Polly.

"Oh God." Rhoda laughed. "I suppose they *will* be staying here, won't they, if it's just the two of them? Bloody Fullers. How frustrating not to be able to control who comes into one's own house." With another laugh, Rhoda leaned over her hammock and drew a tall clinking glass to her lips. Polly laughed too, but Imogen didn't move, and raised her voice persistently.

"But . . . it's not fun here anymore. We can take Annie with us— she'll fit in the car— back to her mother, or her aunt . . ."

Ruby turned away, her cheeks growing as hot as the weather, just as Rhoda shrieked, "How rude, Immy! What an ungrateful little thing you are!"

"Quite, Imogen. Mind your manners around your hostess," Polly said steadily, her American accent coming through suddenly. "You're being a brat."

Imogen's face dropped with astonishment. Before she could apologize or protest, her mother added in a stern voice, "I've told you we've got reservations in Saint-Tropez for dinner. We'll be getting ready in a few hours. So, you just have your swim and wash that mess of hair afterwards, and mind you wear your best dress. All right?"

Ruby politely avoided Imogen's shamed look as she returned. The steps to the water were slippery as the two girls tripped down, and Ruby wondered dimly what would happen if she fell and slid and smashed down into the sea. She hopped over to the flat rock instead, behind Imogen.

Three people were already there, lying prostrate in the deck chairs, draped haphazardly with colored towels strewn across the rock. Ruby hesitated before dashing past them. She dropped her things on the far edge of the pontoon, pulled off her dress, and leaped into the water.

The cold salt of the water curled into her eyes, her scalp, her nose, and she bobbed up like a cork, coughing. She could already feel the sting of the salt water against her legs, the current beating her back toward the rocks. She spotted Imogen in the water, swimming farther out.

Hopping up the ladder, Ruby turned away from the others, suddenly self-conscious at the three new pairs of eyes. Ned was there, with her mother, and Harley. Harley was asleep, his mouth slightly open and his tummy round and high as it swelled and relaxed with his breathing. Georgina may have been asleep beneath her sunglasses too, since she lay so still under the enormous red straw hat settled over her face. Only Ned eyed Ruby, through the semi-opaque blue circles of her sunglasses. She had a pile of books beside her, a pen in one hand and a rolled cigarette in the other. She wore a bright blue swimsuit, a darker shade than her sunglasses, baggy and revealing the flatness of her chest.

"Hello," Ned said with a wide grin. "What drama for our first day! Where's the abandoned little girl?"

"She's asleep." Ruby pulled at her towel, adding, "And she's not abandoned."

Ned tutted at her rolled cigarette. "This damned thing keeps blowing itself out." She dropped her pen and pulled out a lighter. Ruby watched her shield the flame behind her hand, sucking in the cigarette as she did so. Her nails had been painted blue, but they were square and stubby and badly chipped. Georgina's fingers and toes were painted a shining red, the same red as her large sunhat.

"You've timed it well—these two only just dropped off, after talking endlessly about their university days . . . club dinners and disputes in the pub and that sort of nonsense. And Harley's time army training before that—even more club dinners! Never heard anything so boring in my life." Ned tilted her face to survey Ruby. "Cat got your tongue?"

"No." Ruby turned to check the sea behind her, spotting Imogen's black head. The sun was strong—she needed to apply her suncream. "Are *you* at university?"

"No, I'm seventeen; I have my A Levels next year. This is my last summer with my mama, then I'm free. She wanted me to spend it with some of her university friends, hoping they'd rub off on me. But I'm already far ahead of her." She gestured at her books.

Ruby couldn't see the titles. She caught a whiff of the cigarette smoke, and wanted to cough again. Ned continued to smile and said, "I don't think your mother expected us. She certainly seemed cheesed off at lunchtime, though she tried not to show it."

"She's always cheesed off," Ruby said, before feeling a flush of disloyalty. But Ned was already sitting back and pulling the bookmark out of one of her books to resume her reading.

Georgina's head moved, and she took in a stilted, uneven breath. Her red hat slipped to the side. Ruby took her cue and went back in the water.

"THANK YOU FOR LENDING ME a dress," Annie said darkly as they got ready for dinner. "I've got hardly any clothes at all now that my proper suitcase went off with the plane. Whatever will I do?"

"I'll lend you things, Annie—it's only a day or so," Ruby said encouragingly. "There were some things from last year that my mother was going to give to Lisette's granddaughters; I'll have a look for them." She hesitated, and lifted an item off the fresh pile of laundry behind her bed. "For now, just wear this—it's one of my smaller dresses. It's important you look nice tonight, since we're going out."

Imogen emerged wearing a beautiful sleeveless dress that buttoned up at the front, then fell freely all the way down to her feet. Ruby admired her as she came down the stairs, but didn't say so.

"Goodness, don't you three look like angels of the night?" Harley said as he came out of the living room, clutching a tumbler of whiskey above his belly, which he swung toward them. He frowned at Imogen, and said, "You're quite beautiful enough for a harem, you know." She returned a tight smile, without looking at him. He tried again, "Yes, you'd better watch out tonight—you might get stolen away in one of those delicious yachts." He nodded heavily, and his drink sloshed in his glass. Ruby hoped it would splash and stain his crisp white linen shirt. She imagined him having to go upstairs to change and then be too late to join them. But the whiskey stayed inside the glass, and Harley was still talking. ". . . you must all look after your virtue."

Ruby lifted her chin. "Thank you, Mr. Montgomery."

"The correct answer is, my dear—'*I would not be so stupid.*'"

"Oh, you are a tease, Harley," Rhoda interjected from the living room door.

"A tease? My wife doesn't think so. Hasn't laughed for years. Mind you, she's lucky she's with me—no one else wanted her. Too religious, too stuck up." Harley lifted his head to call into the living room. "What do you think of these angels, Liv?"

Liv didn't appear in the doorway, nor did she respond. Ruby often wondered why she never joined in—whether she was drunk, like Annie's mother, or unhappy, like Ruby's aunt at that school. Liv's face never seemed to change—her jaw seemed permanently set, her eyes deliberately turned away from the conversation at hand.

"I wouldn't know anything about angels, would I, Harley?" Liv finally answered from the living room.

Ruby insisted the three girls stay together, in the family car, with her father driving. Her mother sat beside him, very cross about something. Annie dawdled at some boughs of lavender and pulled at one stalk, crushing the seeds in her palm before drawing her hand to her nose to smell it. Imogen stood at the car door, ogling Ned's attire. The older girl was wearing the same overlarge shorts as yesterday, but had thrown on a red military-style jacket with brass buttons.

"She looks terribly odd, doesn't she?" Ruby said as the three girls settled into the car, Annie still smelling the lavender seeds.

"I just think she might be hot in that jacket," Imogen said with a shallow laugh, and Ruby felt a strange wave of relief.

In the car she kept her face against the window and admired the darkening view of the sea, the cliffs, the dusk-lit towns they passed through. It was a bit of a drive, but she liked Saint-Tropez. To Ruby, it spoke of two worlds—an old-fashioned French village mixed with the glamour of a classic French movie. As they drove along the curve of the bay, she peeked over the walls to see the seafront houses, some long, flat, and white, others traditional but slighter versions of their château. She liked to wonder what was happening inside those houses, and beyond them—did they have pontoons, flat rocks, their own boats, perhaps?

They parked the car before the harbor and walked into the heart of the town, past the buzzing restaurants that lined the water and the boats hunched up together alongside. An artist was sketching out a rough landscape, with his other paintings displayed around him; a little farther up a saxophonist was playing an old tune and smiling. Ruby watched him and his expert fingering. She didn't know much about the saxophone, but the keys didn't look too different from her flute. She took out her purse, wanting to drop a coin of her pocket money into his glossy open case, but she was overtaken by the laughing Ned, who threw in some change and gestured at the saxophonist, wiggling her hips in tune with his music, before turning back to smile at her mother.

"There's so much going on here. Is it a special night?" Imogen asked Ruby, her eyes so full that she bumped into Annie beside her.

"I don't think so." Ruby smiled with a shrug. "It's been like this every time I've come."

"I wonder what day of the week it is. The days sort of merge into one here, and everyone is sort of . . . relaxed," Imogen said, looking over at her mother, in thick conversation with Rhoda. "It's not really what I expected. We're quite on our own, aren't we? My mother barely notices me here. She's nicer to me in England."

Ruby glanced at Imogen, but didn't need to answer her. She thought Imogen's mother was rather kind, but perhaps too clingy. Rhoda always regarded Ruby from the corner of her eye, while Polly often touched Imogen's hair, pulled her into an embrace, placed her hands on both sides of her face, and stared into her eyes, their smiling faces a mirror of each other's. Ruby thought it more likely that Polly's pregnancy had changed things for Imogen, rather than it being this holiday's fault.

Imogen cast a wary look in Max's direction, and then Harley's. Ruby saw it, and frowned.

They wandered past an ice cream parlor whose double doors were spread wide open and displaying rows of colorful flavors, sauces, and toppings. Seeing Annie's and Imogen's eager faces, Ruby asked her father if they could have one.

"Later, after dinner, Rubes," he batted her away. "Although the restaurant will have as wonderful a dessert menu as you can imagine, darling."

Harley turned to acknowledge Ruby and the other two girls, his white-gray hair moving as he spoke. "Order anything you like, girlies. I'm paying for dinner."

"Harley." Toby's voice was warning but warm.

"What? I'm easily the richest of any of us; you know that well after all the money I've lent you. Ha! In fact isn't this summer trip a bit of payback for everything I've done for you?"

"Of course, Harley, you're always welcome here. Remind me how long you intend to stay?"

Harley let out a roar of a laugh. "As long as our friend Angus is staying . . . Listen, why don't we nip to the casino after dinner, and I can win even more from you, dear Cashby?" Harley suggested teasingly. "Perhaps your château, if you'd dare to stake it."

"Quite the jester, Harley, aren't you?" Angus interjected.

"Oh, come on boys, let's hit the tables. You can trust me, I'm a major general."

"Do you ever stop going on about that?" Ned sighed. "'Major general'—what does it even mean?"

Angus smirked and gave Harley a short slap on the shoulder. "It means his balls are so shriveled that he needs a name to hide behind."

"None of that, please," Georgina called out. "Ned, leave them to it."

"Quite, George. Leave Haz to his shriveled balls," Angus responded.

Ned guffawed, as did Harley. "Glad you're all now picturing my balls. But I do fancy a good old roll of the dice after din-dins."

A regretful look crossed Toby's face. Ruby noted his silence, and the fact that her mother's fury hadn't abated during the drive. Rhoda had now glued herself to Polly's side, complaining loudly that if they didn't stop walking soon she'd lose her appetite.

At dinner their long table was so full of laughter that other diners in the restaurant turned to look. They were well positioned at the front of the restaurant's terrace so that they could enjoy a good view of the painted sailing boats bumping along this section of the harbor, and unfortunate passersby had a good view of the loud, extravagant Brits enjoying their meal.

Harley sat at the head of the table and roared every time he laughed, even as he ate. Ruby had chosen a spaghetti Bolognese, but worried about staining her dress with every mouthful, and regretted her choice even more when she saw Imogen's steak haché frites. Ruby considered asking for a chip, but Max, seated beside Imogen, took a few from her plate with his chunky hand, so Ruby concentrated on her spaghetti, and Imogen ate no more after that.

The conversation seemed to bounce around the university days of the four, their banter moving so quickly that Ruby couldn't keep up. She tried chatting with Annie and Imogen instead, to no avail.

"You two were always sucking up to old Nestor, weren't you," Harley accused Toby with a slam of his hand on the table.

"Well, whenever we tried to find you, you were growling in the nave."

"I can't understand anything you lot actually say," Ned said, rolling her eyes. "What's a nave?"

"Harley sang bass in the choir, in our college chapel. The nave is where the choir performed, Ned," Toby replied, and Rhoda's face grew even more sour.

"He growled all right," Angus declared. "Both in the nave and in the pub."

Harley grinned proudly as Toby continued. "The other singers used to knock for us to come and drag him out of the pub in time for Evensong. Even George had to help . . . she was the only one that could convince him." Georgina smiled as Harley let out a laugh that shook the whole table. He managed to add, "It was the tenors that used to complain about me. Us basses knew what was what."

Georgina's smile turned wistful. "You were beautiful princes, all three of you. It was the best time of my life. It's wonderful to be here and catch up with you all."

Harley added quickly, "And get what you're owed. Yes, there are many of us here for that." Ruby looked at him, but Angus took over the conversation, and she focused on Annie, seated opposite her.

By the time pudding came, Harley's drunken chatter had him confusing his university professors with his teachers at school. "Yes . . . old Pelforth, that was the man. History master. Used to give me a good rogering, I was only a little tyke, so you're right, Tobes . . . that wasn't at Cambridge at all."

"Harley!" Liv said loudly.

Ned almost spit out her wine. "Is this Pelforth now in prison?"

"Don't listen to any of the rubbish that comes out of Harley's mouth, Ned," Georgina jeered.

"Not rubbish at all, dear girl. We were *all* given a bit of a rogering, it was the done thing. Doesn't make you a bumboy. Jolly good practice if you ask me, good to get the juices going . . . if you don't mind the pun. Did it to the young'uns when they arrived too." He gestured to Angus and Toby, who sat opposite each other. "Would have done it to you two if you'd been around then."

"Disgusting man!" Georgina called out with glee. Rhoda and Polly reached for their wineglasses. Under his laughter, Toby threw a horrified glance at Ruby, who was busying herself with the girls and their pudding choices at the end of the table. Angus's face was impenetrable.

Max leaned forward, a thrilled look on his face. "So, Toby . . . you and Angus went to school *and* university together?"

"Yes, they rescued each other. Still do." Georgina's eyes seemed to sparkle, and her daughter took the opportunity to pour herself another glass of rosé.

"We rescue *and* punish *and* destroy each other," Angus said grimly, taking a glug of his drink.

"Steady on, Gus, always so serious." Harley drew his eyebrows together.

"I shouldn't be where I am—*wouldn't* be where I am—without Angus," Toby answered Max. "At Cambridge, Angus paid my fees when my scholarship was in jeopardy."

"How noble of him," Max said, without sarcasm.

"Talking about fees now, are we?" Harley leaned forward.

"Couldn't be without you, old friend." Angus sat back, surveying Toby under his eyebrows. "You're the one that got me into that mess in the first place."

"What do you mean?" Ned asked eagerly.

Angus gave a rare, grateful smile. "Toby tricked me into applying to Cambridge. He filled out my form at school and handed it in to the headmaster."

"Really?" Max winced as he took a sip of wine.

"Terribly sappy, aren't you, you two?" Harley said, somewhat bitterly.

"I love it," Georgina said, smiling.

"So do I." Ned smiled too, tipping her pinkish glass to her mouth again.

"Talking of school," Toby said, attempting a shift in the conversation. "What's your favorite subject, Ned?"

She licked the rim of her wineglass. "Latin."

"Latin?" Toby's face opened with surprise, while Angus tilted his head.

"Yes," Ned replied confidently.

"I'm jolly good at Latin," Imogen piped up, her voice suddenly very young. "I'm good at the sentences and things."

"I like the stories, too," Annie volunteered.

Ruby didn't have anything to add—she didn't enjoy Latin. Her teacher always marked her pages with big red circles and arrows pointing the words in different directions.

A waitress handed the puddings around, and Ruby thanked her quietly.

"It was Toby's subject, you know, and mine: 'Greats'—the Classics," Angus's warm voice came in. "Toby was as gifted and graceful as old Apollo and his lyre. Top of the whole year. I wasn't."

"And were you both speaking endless Greek to each other?" Ned urged.

"No one speaks ancient Greek fluently—that would be impossible," Toby answered seriously. "The fact is we don't know much about spoken ancient Greek. You'd have to work out the endings as you spoke them . . . Latin is slightly different, because you have Roman comedy and their sort of street-chat . . . Well, anyway." Toby hesitated, momentarily embarrassed by his earnest train of thought. "To answer your question, Ned . . . Angus and I struck a perfect balance between talking up the Classics fellows and talking up the ladies."

"No balance at all, Toby—there were hardly any ladies." Angus was shaking his head now. "That's why we recruited George from the Languages Department."

"Yes, only she—and one other—kept the two of you occupied all those years," Harley muttered into his wine. "Your first loves."

"We did work very hard," Toby said, ignoring Harley's comment, concentrating on Ned. "I was a Latinist, Angus was the wild Greek."

"And Harley was . . . ?" Max pressed.

"A historian—you know, the *recent* past," Harley answered proudly. "The army saw me through my university days in the History Department."

Georgina called the waiter over to order another bottle of wine. "More rosé, chaps? Or red?" Max raised an empty rosé bottle and tapped the label. Georgina smiled at him.

"Toby should have been a professor," Angus said, and his friend winced regretfully, answering, "No, I go where I'm told."

Ruby frowned at her father, trying to work out his meaning. Harley added, "Yes, you do as you're told, and you only argue when you're told to, Tobes. That's what you're good for." Harley grinned. "And now both of your erudite degrees are wasted—Toby on grim professional pursuits and Angus on his lordly family firm." He tilted his head to gesture at Georgina down the table. "Your degree too, George, now that you've gone into hats. Don't need languages with hats. Or do you sew Italian poetry into the seams?"

Max laughed.

"There are no seams in hats, dear boy," Georgina retorted happily. The waiter reappeared with another bottle, and Harley turned to Max. "What did you study, man, and where?"

Max raised his empty glass of wine and grinned. "I studied Maths—well, Economics. At Bristol."

"So, you're ahead of us." Harley leaned over to nudge his glass for the waiter to fill it up too, almost elbowing his tarte tatin. He nodded at Max importantly. "These are the subjects of the future. We're all humanitarians over here, learning about what's been, not what's coming." Harley cleared his throat heroically. "I've made my son Hugo apply for PPE for that very reason—Philosophy, Politics, and Economics. Though he's such a cringing weed I don't know if he'll stand it."

"You have a son, Mr. Montgomery?" Imogen asked. Ruby looked at her anxiously. She didn't think the children should be contributing; the conversation seemed not meant for their ears.

"Yes, dear Imogen, and it's a hopeless case. He's thoroughly disappointing, just like his mother was, as a wife. Top marks at school, of course, but he can't hold up a debate, can't catch a cricket ball, can't speak to a girl to save his life." He took a swig of his wine, before gesturing toward Angus. "Should have got you to shoot *him,* Gus, like you did that boy. Then again, I do need an heir. Was hoping Liv would provide me with a spare, but she's hopeless."

Ruby looked at the sallow Liv briefly, before turning her hot face to the tablecloth, her hands pulling at her napkin. Shoot what boy?

"I say, Harley—watch your words. We're only having dinner," Toby said with false cheer.

"The worst thing is," Harley laughed easily, "Hugo is no fun. The whole point of having kids is to get pissed and have a bloody good laugh with them. My boy doesn't know what he's got in life, or even what he's got between his legs. He's hopeless, and children are supposed to be the future. Speaking of which . . . Gus, Tobes, Max, what are you doing about properly educating these lovely girls?"

Toby smiled wistfully as he concentrated on his crème brulée. "Ruby's got two years left at St. Aubyn's, though she's old for her year . . ." Toby nodded at Angus. "And Imogen has one."

"What, neither of them going to their mother's school?" Harley snorted, looking between Rhoda and Polly as he continued, "You have such happy stories about that place . . . That woman you introduced me to at Christmas! Hilly, I liked her, though her husband was a tosspot. Slip of a thing, lovely profile—one of your horsey friends, Rhoda?"

"Hilly's mostly dressage," Rhoda answered flatly.

"Oh, Hilly Wheeler?" Polly sat forward awkwardly. "Such a hoot! She was always getting into scrapes. Mother used to say she was just like our dachshund, quite untrainable. We don't see her enough. She lives in Russia now, with her husband. He has an accent that could raise blisters on your skin!"

"Yes, I remember him. Diplomat?" Harley hesitated. "And you refuse to send your girls to this wonderful school?"

"We're discussing it," Rhoda said with finality, Polly giving her a supportive glance.

Max was puzzled. "So you four went to university together, and these two went to the same school? Blimey, that's a small world."

Harley turned to Max bracingly. "Yes, our society tends to keep itself small, and very well endowed."

Ruby turned away to observe the view, the people passing by, lit by the string of lights glimmering along the harbor. The evening was sinking into darkness, and she thought longingly of the ice cream parlor— anywhere that wasn't this table.

"Yes, you'd think they'd have had enough of each other, Max," Rhoda said pointedly, nodding over to her husband and his friends. "You old men and your constant haranguing of each other. It's true what they say about children of the war, so morbid and morose. Polly and I are all sweetness and light."

Harley turned to the two wives, his voice bright again. "Not as sweet and springy as your daughters. Oh, the burden of daughters, and you can't even deflower them yourselves! Don't you think fathers should be the ones to do the honors—wasn't that the way in ancient Greece?"

"No, Harley, old chap," Toby answered in a strained voice. "Not at all."

"You're no fun; neither is Angus here with his moods. I'm glad I've got dear Max, and his great youth." Harley gave Max an appraising look. "New money, aren't you? Promising for England."

Ruby looked at Max. It hadn't occurred to her that he was younger than the other fathers, but his face was tighter, more supple, his jawline lined with grayless stubble, his eyes keen and alert. Now that she was thinking about it, he made Harley look positively ancient with his white hair and tall forehead, but the age of Toby and Angus seemed to fall in between the two, thanks to their worn and lined faces, their gray-marred hair. Liv was ageless in her cold and unspeaking way, but certainly older than Ruby's mother and younger than Georgina. Georgina must have been the same age as her university friends, but was clean, tanned, handsome—more alive and much younger in spirit than any of them.

"Honestly, Harley," Ned attempted, "you're just full of corkers, aren't you—'deflower their daughters.' Are you a bit of a creep?"

Harley turned to Ned, his eyes now bulging with alcohol. "You should mind your own business, Edwina. You're underage too, darling, and rather letting the side down. Two of these girls have bigger tits than you. I bet you're gasping for it."

Ned's mouth opened with horror.

"Ned, darling," Georgina moaned. "Don't. It's only a bit of fun. Best not to react."

"That's enough wine, I think," Liv interrupted stiffly. "Shall we get the bill?"

"Yes, let's," Toby said with an anxious laugh.

"I'll get this." Angus sat back to bury his hand in his pocket, his eyebrows knotted together. "I'd rather not have Harley lord it over the rest of us, make us pay in other ways. Your husband, Liv, needs a hard reset; we just need to find the batteries."

Harley gave Angus a small look of loathing, just as Georgina laughed merrily and said, "Oh, Angus, you always knew how to topple an argument. You should have been the barrister."

Angus kept his gaze on Harley, but didn't respond. Ruby watched the tension pass through them, feeling her anxiety push at her cheeks, her eyes.

"Well." Toby raised his glass. "Shall we say three cheers to the holiday?"

"Three cheers to Harley, chief entertainer?" Max suggested.

"Ah." Harley patted the table, and the tension seemed to ease. "Quite right, young man. I like your style."

Max nodded seriously. "Thank you for your compliments, Harley, I *am* a modern man, a man of the future."

Georgina cackled and Ned widened her eyes as she refilled her glass of wine.

Max sat back in his chair, smiling around the table and tapping his hands on the tablecloth. He rested his eyes on Imogen. As his arm slipped beneath the table, Imogen's waist and hips seem to swivel and stiffen. She looked up at him anxiously, before glancing across at Ruby, and then down to her lap. Ruby watched as Imogen bowed her head with some private, reddening shame. Max's maniacal smile lifted as he stared into the space in front of him, his arm remaining under the table.

Ruby realized what she was seeing, and suddenly felt very hot. A white light seemed to blow out in front of her, and she dropped to the side.

"Ruby!"

SHE WAS REVIVED LATER BY a cold flannel and the comfort of a soft reclining chair. Somebody was talking to her as she opened her eyes.

"Are you all right, little thing?" Angus was stooping over Ruby, but she saw only the bright lights of the restaurant ceiling as the noise of the place came back to her. "You fainted. Overheated, your mother said. Your father's just gone to fetch you a glass of water. We're going for a little walk, or would you rather go straight home?"

"No, no." Ruby sat up. "I'm all right to walk."

She didn't look at his face, and took the glass wordlessly from her father when he appeared a moment later. She gulped at the water, straining to hear the reassurance of Imogen's voice.

9

After dinner the group wandered to the far edge of the harbor, under a wide archway where the stone pavement fell away and the sea spread out toward another bay, or—as Ruby liked to pretend—toward Italy or Africa. But the vista was a thorough black now, and Ruby could hear only the smash of waves against the breakwater rocks. Her nose wrinkled with the whiff of briny sea air as she followed Imogen with her eyes.

The adults were arguing.

"I absolutely insist we go to the casino—even Polly and Rhoda want to," Harley was bellowing at Toby. Ruby's father gave his wife a beseeching look, but she was having none of it. It was soon suggested that Liv drive the girls home.

Ruby wanted to pull her father's arm, insist that he take them; but her voice would be drowned out by the crash of water against the rocks.

"If Liv won't do it tell her I'll push her into the sea." Harley shrugged his great shoulders. "She's only good for taking orders."

Georgina muttered, "Liv doesn't want to be around the children, Harley, you know that very well."

Harley shot back, "Ever since her personal tragedy, of course."

Angus grimaced. "Come on, man. Wasn't it your tragedy, too?"

"Hardly," Harley snorted. "You can't attach yourself to the thing if it's only a year old, can you?"

Ruby looked at her father, confused.

"I'll take the girls," Angus spoke up in an electric voice. "I've had quite enough."

"Angus!" Toby said. "Come on."

"Polly," Georgina began, "insist that your husband stay!"

"My husband listens to nothing I say, Georgina," Polly called back from the archway, her arm in Rhoda's.

"Oh, Angus . . . do stay, *please*," Harley said sarcastically.

The girls were taken home in a silent car. Angus busied himself with the road, hunching forward, his frown deepening. Ruby tried to remain polite and chatty, but her voice faded in and out between the rumble of the car. She still didn't dare speak to Imogen.

Ned sat in the front passenger seat with her legs spread, one knee pressing against the glass of the window, her curly head tilted in the same direction.

Annie stretched her arms behind her, and Ruby caught a whiff of the lavender seeds she'd crushed earlier. Ruby suddenly asked, "Is there a Lavender Fairy, Annie?"

"Yes," Annie said quietly, "but she doesn't look like any of us."

"Why not?"

"She's always smiling."

Ruby looked askance at Annie. "What do you mean?"

"Mummy said that once—that the parents at school smile without smiling," Annie answered, her eyes drooping. "She's with my aunt now; I must phone to see if she arrived safely."

"Oh. Do you have the number?"

"Yes. Mummy always had me learn it, in case of emergencies."

Ruby frowned. "What kind of emergencies?"

Annie shrugged as she shifted her head. "Mummy has always been frightened. She was right to be, really."

Ruby stared out at the orange streetlamps flitting along the dark road. "What about Mrs. Montgomery? Which fairy would she be?"

"One of the Winter Fairies, I think," Annie whispered. "I daresay she could be the Snowdrop Fairy. Not her hair, but her expression . . . or perhaps the Horned Poppy Fairy—pale, and always looking the other way. Yes, that's her."

Imogen made a small sleepy noise.

"Are you talking about fairies, you girls?" Angus asked.

"Yes," Ruby answered, "Flower Fairies, Mr. Bly."

Angus chuckled delightedly, "Oh to be young, and careless, to think on such things."

Ned muttered something in response, and Angus laughed. Ruby watched the lights from the road shine and swing across the side of Angus's face, past the thick grip of his hands on the steering wheel. She closed her eyes.

The three girls were asleep by the time they reached the house.

THE FOLLOWING DAY BROUGHT A *brocante* to the village: a summer flea market. Ruby had a bright idea and suggested that the three girls stay behind to enjoy some freedom at the house without the adults. It was only between the long hours of congregating together that Ruby could actually breathe, and she wanted to extend that as much as possible, as well as cheer both girls along.

They were enjoying a bungled game of Marco Polo in the pool—Annie was too easy to catch, and Ruby couldn't help peeping to cheat—when Ned appeared. She had a rolled cigarette in her hand and tapped the falling ash on the paved stones. Ruby stopped paddling, noticing that Ned was still wearing the same pair of dirty shorts.

"I thought I'd take us all to the village, to see the *brocante*," Ned said. "It's almost lunchtime."

"Oh yes, let's!" Imogen yelped, shooting up from the water. "This game is boring now, and my fingers are all pruny."

Ruby wasn't sure. "Really?"

Annie looked around, her eyes still closed but her face glittering with water. "Have we stopped playing?"

"Yes, really," Ned answered Ruby. "Where's your sense of adventure?"

"There's no car."

"So? We can improvise. They're probably all staying there for lunch, so we can eat a bite here and make our way to join them for ice cream. Don't want to miss out, do we? There might be some fun antiquey things to buy," Ned added, then took another drag of her cigarette.

"That sounds like a nice plan," said Annie, nodding. Imogen looked at her, and said, "Well, if Annie thinks so, then we're definitely going."

"A bit of fresh air for us ladies." Ned sat down disjointedly on a lounger, and struck a pose. Imogen and Annie laughed, and Ned smiled at the attention.

Ruby was glad, but hesitant. "All right then. But don't they say that only mad dogs and Englishmen go out in the midday sun?"

"They do," Ned said solidly. "So everybody has to wear one of my mother's hats."

In the hallway there was a new stack of hats under the stairs that Ned passed off as gifts from her mother. Imogen took out the ugliest one—black, with netting—and made a funny face as she moved over to the hall mirror. She stood on tiptoe to see her face better. Annie took a neat straw hat and Ruby took the one at the bottom, with a scalloped brim and a blue ribbon that almost matched her dress. Ned had her own hat; it was broad but floppy, and Ruby could just about make out her sarcastic smile underneath its folds.

Imogen went to swap her black hat for a better, plainer one. As she glided past the grandfather clock, she ducked her head.

"What's wrong?" Ruby asked.

"It's just"—Imogen's smile froze for a moment—"why doesn't that clock have a face? And why is there a skinned cat on the wall over there? And those strange helmet hats?" She jerked her head. "It's very strange, I think. No offense." She turned her back on Ruby to rifle through the hats.

"No, not at all," Ruby answered emptily, feeling a flush across her cheeks as Ned watched her reaction. "They've always been on the wall, and the clock's always been empty. I've never really wondered about it."

Imogen shuddered in response as she regarded her chosen hat. "This one is lovely, don't you think, Ned?"

Annie was checking her reflection in the mirror, but caught sight of the jug of wild poppies displayed to the side of it. Ruby associated poppies with Remembrance Sunday, so they felt wrong in the house, basking in the block of sunlight coming from the door, drooping hopefully toward the sea.

"I keep noticing these lovely arrangements," Annie enthused. "Almost every day there are new flowers. There was gaura the other day, and some cypress spurge, I think."

"Lisette always makes an effort. She likes it to look nice," Ruby said.

Ten minutes later Lisette armed each of them with a half-baguette sandwich and they wandered down the coastal path. It was bordered by the sea wall on one side and little houses on the other. Ruby breathed in the woody, sea salt smells, and watched the water lap against the stones. She could feel the sun burning the back of her creamy shoulders while her sandals slapped on the stones. It had been a long time since she'd walked this path.

As soon as the bay swung around tighter, they came to the village. With the sea behind them, they wandered past the harbor, up along the main street toward the long, tree-lined square. Annie and Imogen let out squeals of delight, for every corner and flat space of the square and its main street had been set up with long tables and low awnings, filled with antique bits: shining crockery, rows of cracked china, or a dish full of tangled jewelry. Not just the tables, but the pavements in front of each stand spilled over with old garden pots or rusted metal garden chairs, covered over with an old rug supporting trinkets or bits of wooden furniture.

There was plenty to look at, but Ruby liked to study the vendors, many of whom were locals that had raided their cellars for treasures. All were French, from their tanned, wrinkled faces to their washed-out striped shirts and braces. Ruby had always enjoyed the *brocantes* when they happened; many of her childhood toys had been bought from them and played with, after Lisette gave them a good scrub. Ruby smiled as she surveyed the village through Imogen's and Annie's brightening eyes.

Ned chose the café on the square, near the fountain. As they approached, Ruby heard Harley's voice from across the square, and they saw that his back was turned to them. Ned straightened up and pulled a warning face at the girls, with a finger to her lips.

"Let's go home and have a drink. This is all a bit peasant, isn't it?" Harley was saying, casting his critical eyes over a stack of postcards and old books. "Not exactly Sotheby's."

Angus countered, "What did you expect, Harley?"

"Well, you can say what you like," Toby said, moving slightly ahead of them, "but the Jeffers found a postcard from the *Titanic* last year, and it was worth a bloody fortune!"

Max lifted a book on a nearby stand uncertainly. He replaced it quickly before wiping his hand on his trousers. Annie made a small noise, and Ned swept her arms across the three girls, drawing them back and away from the square.

"Worth a fortune, was it!" Ruby heard Harley shout at her father. "Bad luck, old boy . . . just what *you* needed!"

A little farther on, they spotted Georgina chortling as she unfolded a heavy-looking bedsheet. "I can't get past the idea that somebody probably died in these," she said to Liv, tossing the unfolded bedsheet back on the stand and ignoring the beseeching look of the vendor. Liv hastened forward holding an armful of old nightdresses and helped the woman refold the sheet, speaking to her in fluent French.

Ned took the girls on a small detour, and by the time they returned to the square, the adults were gone, and they attempted the café again. It was a sleepy afternoon, and even the waitress seemed to speak drowsily.

"Goodness me." Ned raised her eyebrows as the waitress went away. "I didn't realize my O Level French was so decent. How come you don't speak French, Ruby? You spend enough time here."

Ruby heard Ned's accusatory tone, and answered. "I understand a few words, but Mother always said I shouldn't bother."

"Shame." Ned leaned forward on her elbows. Annie did the same, smiling, her soft blond hair falling about her face.

"This is lovely, being here. Thank you, Ned." Annie hesitated. "'Ned' . . . I've been wondering . . . is that a nickname?"

"Annie!" Imogen interjected, half-warning, half-joking.

"It's all right." Ned leaned toward a suddenly anxious Annie. "Yes, it's short for 'Edwina.' Can you imagine? After my grandmother—but I'm only called Edwina when I'm in trouble."

". . . And what are you reading? You've always got so many books," Imogen chirruped. Ruby hadn't noticed that Ned had stuffed a book into the wide pocket of her dirty shorts, but she wondered whether Ned was expecting to go off and read, whether she meant to abandon them there in the village, leaving them to their own devices. Ruby felt a flutter of panic at the thought.

"It's for Latin; we've been given a story to translate over the summer." Ned pulled out the slim volume and thumbed it open. "Ovid's *Heroides,* number five. Oenone and Paris, do you know it?"

Ruby hadn't seen many books like that. The newspaper shop in the village sold only French books, or *Asterixes*—no Agatha Christies, and no other English books, unfortunately. It was one of the few things she missed about England.

"Paris was the Trojan prince," Ned continued. "He was a shepherd at the beginning of his life, you see, and didn't realize he was a prince, because his parents were told he'd bring about the destruction of Troy, so they tried to get rid of him as a baby, but he survived. Anyway, he grew up in the mountains and fell in love with Oenone, a mountain nymph, and she taught him all sorts of skills and things, and they lived very happily together, and even had a son."

"How lovely," Annie said.

"Hang on . . ." Ned snorted and tossed her book aside. "There's more to it than that. Paris—as a supposedly harmless mortal—was then chosen by Zeus to pick the fairest goddess between Hera, Aphrodite, and Athena, and give her the prize of the golden apple." She lifted her small sachet of tobacco, making to roll a cigarette. Ruby watched Ned disapprovingly as she continued, nudging her glasses up her nose.

"Paris chose Aphrodite, because she promised him the most beautiful woman in the world, Helen of Sparta."

"Oh!" Imogen said excitedly. "Yes! I do know this story! Helen of Troy? Paris and Helen."

"Indeed!" Ned raised her eyebrows at Imogen, evidently pleased by her enthusiasm. "And once she's promised to him by the goddess, he goes to get her. Trouble is, she's married! So he steals Helen from her husband Menelaus of Sparta. He's recognized as the prince of Troy by that point. He takes her back to Troy, Menelaus follows with his allies, and that's the beginning of the Trojan War."

"But what about Oenone?" Annie called out.

"Well, Paris abandoned her, didn't he?"

"So what does she do about it?" Annie touched the table anxiously.

"Not much in the *Heroides,* apart from complaining." Ned sneered at the slim volume of Latin. "But in another version of the myth, she sends her son to lead the Greeks to Troy, against Paris." Ned paused, holding her hand over her cigarette to protect it as she flicked her lighter on.

"For revenge?" Ruby urged, leaning forward in spite of herself.

Ned sucked in and blew out her cigarette. "Yes. But Paris doesn't recognize his son, and kills him."

Annie shrieked while Imogen grimaced and said, "That's terrible!"

"Poor Oenone, losing a husband and a son!" Annie clutched at her mouth.

"Wait." Ned touched each of their hands in turn. "That's not the end. Paris is later wounded during a battle, and he returns to Oenone to seek her help since she's so good with healing herbs and things."

"And does she?" Annie spoke through her fingers.

"No." Ned grinned widely. "She rejects him, and he dies on the very mountain slopes where he grew up."

Imogen's face twisted. "That's not a very happy ending."

"What did she do next?" Ruby urged.

"Well, disappointingly, Oenone feels so guilty about not helping that she throws herself onto his burning funeral pyre. I mean, she could at least go out with a bang," Ned tittered. "But the part I'm translating is just a letter, from Oenone to Paris, telling him off for abandoning her. There seems to be a strange bit where Apollo ravages her, but I may have got that wrong . . . I'll need to check with my teacher when I get back."

"I don't think I'll ever have a husband, or children. It all seems quite hard!" Annie burst out. "I'd rather just have friends."

"Oh, really?" Ned laughed.

"Yes, like sisters. None of us have sisters; it's such a shame. I've always wanted one."

"No, indeed." Ned tipped her cigarette ash into the ashtray, and looked up at Ruby. "What do *you* think of the story?"

Ruby looked at Ned. "I don't know, it all seems . . . rather complicated."

Ruby sat back in her seat, feeling a strange niggle of confusion—at the wistful look on Annie's face, the indifference on Imogen's, the strangeness of the story. The waitress finally arrived with four banana splits and four small glasses of water, and Ruby gave her a relieved smile.

The girls started eating. Halfway through her chocolate ice cream scoop, Ruby felt full; she looked guiltily at the dish and wondered whether she should have taken a sweep of the vanilla and strawberry too, all three flavors in one go, since she wasn't allowed more than two scoops of ice cream a day. With a shrug, she dropped her spoon and took a gulp of water.

Ned was chewing on a piece of banana. Mid-mouthful, she said, "Harley's a bit of a twat, don't you think? Shame his wife can't rein him in."

The three girls shared a surprised glance, but Imogen was the first to answer, saying carefully, "What's wrong with Mrs. Montgomery?"

"Ruby . . ." Ned's small eyes widened at Ruby through her glasses. "Haven't you told them?"

"Told them what?"

"You mean you don't know?" Ned's mouth opened with surprise. "I would have thought you did, seeing as he and your father are such good friends."

"I don't know anything. I only know she's a bit of a pain," Ruby said defensively. "Or at least, my mother says so."

"She's *in* pain, more like it. Married to *him,* can you imagine?"

Ruby opened her mouth importantly, "I know that he was married before; he has a son, but his first wife died—"

"Yes, he was hoping for a larger brood. He has an heir, but wanted a spare. You heard him last night. Anyhow, he and Liv did have a little baby boy, but he fell out of a window."

A grim silence spread across the table before Ruby found her voice. "What?"

"He was a toddler. He was playing, and climbed up onto the windowsill in his bedroom, and fell out." Ned kicked one leg over the other and sucked on her cigarette. "They found his little broken body only minutes later."

"How terrible!" Annie cried, while Ruby absorbed this new information.

"They got rid of the nanny," Ned continued. "But I gather it was Liv's fault somehow. And neither of them have forgiven her for it."

"But," Annie spluttered, "I hardly think it could be anyone's fault! That's the saddest thing I've ever heard. They shouldn't blame anyone; they should just let themselves be sad about it!"

Ned snorted again. "Don't count on that level of emotional honesty, Annie. These are toffs you're talking about. They specialize in suppressing every feeling they've ever had."

"It is sad, though, Ned," Imogen insisted.

"When did that happen?" Ruby asked.

"For the Montgomerys it's more of a family dishonor." Ned's eyes lit up wickedly. "Then again, I suppose you know all about that, don't you, Imogen? Covering things up?"

"Me?"

"Your father, Angus."

"When did that happen to the Montgomerys?" Ruby repeated, considering how long she'd known Liv—how many summers, Christmases, anniversary parties had passed without her ever having heard that story.

"Five years ago, Mum said. They were married only a few years earlier. He married her for her money—so now there's definitely no love between them." Ned cleared her throat. "You're too young to have met Harley's first wife before she died, I suppose. I think your father was in love with her, too, Imogen? She rather interests me."

"What?" Imogen frowned and glanced at a confused Ruby.

Ned pushed her glasses up her nose and said quickly, "I'm just curious about people, that's all. Anyway, do you reckon Liv might have wanted her son to die, perhaps like Oenone did, just to punish Harley, because she realized he was such a pig?"

Annie tittered politely, but stopped when she saw that Imogen and Ruby didn't join in. Ned scowled at the three of them and stubbed her cigarette into the ashtray.

"You girls have no imagination. Well, one of you needs to pay for these ice creams, I've got nothing on me."

Annie and Imogen looked around helplessly for a moment, before turning to Ruby, who said automatically, "Oh. It's all right, my mother gives me an allowance." She touched at her bag as her cheeks reddened. "I don't know how much this all adds up to."

Annie opened her small wallet obligingly, moving the coins between her fingers. Imogen said, "Ruby should do it, Annie, she's our hostess."

Ruby tugged the plastic dish toward her, determining how much to pay. With the coins in her purse and the single note, she had just about enough.

They left the café and meandered toward the harbor. Along a narrow street, Ruby caught sight of Liv walking ahead, swinging her bag behind her as she strolled through the open doors of the village church. Ruby halted and watched, as the others, hot and tired, drifted after Ned.

Liv sat in a pew and bowed her head. Above the altar, a circular hole in the ceiling cast the stone alcove in a warm shaft of light. The orchestra had held their practice concert in there several days ago, performing to smiling locals. Ruby had been so proud of their glorious acoustics, had been mesmerized by the glowing light that shone down and touched the top of Bertie's head. How different things were, then. How things were changing still.

"Ruby?" Annie called, and Ruby followed.

As they wandered down toward the harbor, a villager leaned over her balcony to shake a thick rug. Ned reached out a warning hand to guide the girls around the falling dirt, and as she did so, an old woman coming the other way stepped out of their path and into the street. Ruby gave the old woman a grateful glance, but hesitated at her stiff, bitten face, her dark eyes stamped with misery. The old woman's features became stiffer still as she took in Ruby's face, her reddish-blond hair. It seemed to spark some understanding in her, and she cried out:

"C'est Mademoiselle Ashby?"

The old woman's mouth twisted with horror as she uttered the name, and Ruby stepped away from her, alarmed.

"Ruby!" Ned called out. "Come on!"

Several yards ahead, Annie and Imogen surveyed Ruby and the old woman curiously. Ruby hurried over to join them.

"Don't dawdle," Ned huffed. "I expect your fathers are already home and furious with us."

"Why?" Ruby asked hotly.

"Well, you've run off, haven't you?"

"No." Ruby felt her heartbeat hot in her mouth. "We haven't run off. Lisette knew."

Ned merely shrugged.

Along the coastal path, the sun had lowered and shone directly into their eyes, the heat somehow stronger than before. Ruby winced and tugged her hat lower, trying not to recall that old woman's face, the way she had said her name. Ruby pushed past Ned to lead the little group, distracting herself by considering what she could do when they got back. Perhaps she could make everyone a drink from the kitchen, some squeezed oranges, like Lisette sometimes did.

But when they got there, the château stood quiet. The cars had returned, but the adults were nowhere to be seen.

10

2010

Mrs. Cosgrove swept her gaze over the hotel room. She'd remade her bed and tidied her clothes. Yes, it looked all right; there was nothing to alarm whoever might come and clear her lunch things away, nothing to reveal that urgent scream of her heart.

She needed to get out. The clink of ice and the pop of sparkling water were still loud in her head, and the remnants of the club sandwich had gone sour with that eggy smell.

Outside the hotel room window, the market was winding down now, a few shouts signaling the merchants folding away their tables and the slam of van doors announcing the pack-up of their wares, as a few stragglers milled about for last-minute bargains or a forgotten bag of nectarines. In a moment she'd go down and have a coffee, and perhaps some kind of ice cream—whatever she liked, now that she could. Hopefully one of the village cafés would have a proper espresso machine—they couldn't be that uncivilized.

She also had to go to the *tabac* for more cigarettes. What would Alexandra say, if she knew that she'd resumed such a terrible habit?

Mrs. Cosgrove left her room and let the door fall back softly, and

as she did so, the clean air of the corridor burst through like a wave
of clarity. She wondered if her room smelled bad—infected not just
by the whiff of her lunch, but by her black thoughts, her coldness,
the memories of her cruelty toward her husband. She had never been
more desperate to escape her own head. She had to go out; this was
intolerable.

Mrs. Cosgrove could smell the sea as soon as she stepped through
the hotel doors, brushing past a pair of men who came through. Salty
air paired with the sickly scent of dead fish brought in for the market.
Perhaps later she'd wander down to the harbor, sidle to the short stretch
of beach along the bay, and keep her face away from the glimmering
spot of the house on the other side. It would be a pleasant walk, one
that the locals probably took all the time.

She wondered fleetingly whether James would have liked this place.
Such a thought surprised her; she hadn't expected any memories of
him to pursue her here. James didn't belong in this place, nor had she
allowed him to belong anywhere near her inner thoughts, though he
was the kindest of men, who never let her say a harsh or judgmental word
about their peers, whose great generosity astounded her, but never softened her.

Their marriage had been just like her parents' marriage—shining on
the outside, but cold everywhere else. It had been a decent connection—
she'd been the top of her set, and well suited to him. Later it became
a contented union, inasmuch as contented meant satisfied. Satisfied
to sit across from each other at dinner parties, smiling at each other
while speaking to everyone else, then sitting across from each other in
matching armchairs in the living room at home. Filling those married
hours with social engagements and trips to the opera or the theater, and
personal hobbies for the empty moments in between.

Still, James had been one of the few who hadn't questioned her
about that summer—in fact, he'd shielded her from the challenges of
others. His acceptance of that, and of their lack of children, meant that
James provided a safe haven within which she could both unravel and
hold herself together. For that, she now realized, she was grateful.

Mrs. Cosgrove chose a café, the most modern and the busiest, although the early afternoon heat had driven away many patrons. She heard French voices coming from a nearby table and took a seat close by.

Perhaps Alexandra was right. Mrs. Cosgrove couldn't remember many things about her decision to come here—it had simply run through her like a bolt of energy, forcing her to arrange the car, book a flight, and go. She couldn't recall telling her mother. When she thought back to those days after losing James it was as if she had been drugged—passing through rooms, conversations rolling on without her, a glass of wine nudged into her hand whenever it was decent. On the morning of the funeral she'd been surprised that the sun had risen, and the reception afterward had arrived with alarming alacrity. Was it then, that someone mentioned the château—or later, at the memorial, had she overheard something?

Alexandra had been the one filling up her glass, embracing her with one arm, standing before her as people attempted to speak to her. She'd gathered the flowers, collected the cards and letters, putting them aside for Mrs. Cosgrove to read later. Was that kindness, or something else?

Directly across the square, on the edge of the circular spread of tables, was the very spot where Ned had begun to tell them about the Trojan War, and of Paris, Helen, and Oenone. At the time Mrs. Cosgrove had rather liked the story, but now it seemed morbid and ghastly. All the stories from that summer haunted her—and all those women, tossed about by the desire and ambition of their male counterparts. Those stories had seemed to repeat themselves through her life, like some hideous, cruel joke.

Her ice cream arrived, three scoops. Mrs. Cosgrove's eyes almost bulged with the indulgence. They gave her a long spoon, and a tall glass of water; her coffee sat neatly beside. She had a sudden urge to pour her coffee over the ice cream, to see what would happen. Or to order a Grand Marnier and pour her coffee into that, bury it and herself in drink so that she didn't have to hear her thoughts.

Grief was wreaking havoc in her mind. She'd not deserved to be at the funeral. She'd not deserved to have James. And now, without him, what was the point of her? What was her place in society now? Yes, she'd grown into him—the familiarity, the companionship, the ease of following behind him. According to the others, their marriage had been a great success, childless or not. Mrs. Cosgrove had always wondered whether her own rancor had dried up her organs of increase, just as King Lear had cursed his daughter. Perhaps her father had managed to curse her too, from afar, as punishment for that summer. She had willed her childlessness—but James hadn't, and she was paying for it now with this bitter guilt.

She brought her fingers to her mouth distractedly. Her teeth pulled at the hook of a broken nail and she spat it onto the ground. She glanced at the mess of her fingers and saw that her nail polish was chewed, torn, and ugly. Not only that, the tips were stained with her lipstick—which must be blurred and ruined by now. Mrs. Cosgrove couldn't help being entirely disgusted with herself.

She lit another cigarette and held it to her mouth. The ice cream lay untouched.

That afternoon with Ned had been brief but happy. For a moment, everything had felt full and colorful and safe in her young mind.

"Excuse me, madame?"

The harsh voice couldn't possibly be addressing her.

"Excuse me, if I might be so bold."

Mrs. Cosgrove wanted to laugh at the man's formal English drenched in a heavy accent, but his expression warranted no laughter. She turned and took in his round chin, his decisive nose. "Yes?"

"You are alone?"

She hesitated, leaning away from him. "Yes?"

The man put his hand on the chair and leaned forward. "I recognize you. You have been here before."

"No."

"You are English?"

"Yes." Mrs. Cosgrove drew her cigarette to her mouth again, and narrowed her eyes at the man.

"Yes." he nodded heavily. "You have been here before. Sniffy English. I have seen your face, your hair, your pale skin before. During the summer, here. Buying your *bonbons* in the *tabac.*"

"My hair?"

"Beautiful hair." The man leaned farther forward, his eyes boring into Mrs. Cosgrove's face.

"Excuse me." She turned her head away with distaste. "I'd rather be left alone."

"You know the Ashbys?"

Mrs. Cosgrove whirled around with a spray of cigarette ash. "Cosgrove is my name, not Ashby."

"Ah." The man's eyes lit with fresh purpose. "But you know of them. The château is for sale. The château we all discuss, often. And once it is sold, the Ashbys will be gone forever." He stood up straight, almost defensively. "Why do you come here? You . . . you must be the age now of those daughters."

"No," Mrs. Cosgrove said loudly.

"Yes, the accident of that summer. They say it was the daughters' fault."

"No!"

The waitress appeared at the table, touching the man on the shoulder. *"Mais laisse-la tranquille, Bruno. Ce n'est qu'une touriste."*

The man ignored the waitress, his face tense. "You hide from the police, you use the mayor. But us, the villagers, we knew. We *know*."

Mrs. Cosgrove stood so abruptly that the waitress gasped. With a small *"Desolée"* she took up her bag and left the table. The waitress called after her, her cheeks flushed with her own embarrassment. Mrs. Cosgrove hesitated before rifling through her purse for a note to hand over with another *"Desolée."*

The man was leaning his weight on the table, his sleeve hanging over the untouched ice cream as he declared, "These questions, madame, they are not from me. They are from other English. The Englishmen here today, yesterday." He raised his finger. "You, *petite fille,* must be careful to return here."

Mrs. Cosgrove shook her head furiously as she spluttered, "What Englishmen?"

"Englishmen," was all the old man answered, "at the hotel."

She gave no response as she fussed with her handbag. In the next moment she rushed across the square, down the main street, and toward the harbor. Away from the man, the hotel, and any phantom Englishmen asking questions. Mrs. Cosgrove strode forward, every step matching her thundering heartbeat.

11

1985

Ruby came down for dinner. She hadn't changed her dress, since she hadn't seen her mother at all that day, even at the market. She'd smoothed it over her tummy and pulled her long hair out of the collar, before brushing it and Annie's, who hadn't changed either.

The terrace was splendidly lit with lanterns again, and the table laid heavy with food. But as she approached, she saw that her mother's face was thunderous. When Rhoda caught sight of Ruby, her eyes flashed anew.

"Ruby, how dare you! Go up and dress immediately."

Ruby reeled back but somehow answered, "I am dressed."

"You are *not*." Rhoda's voice was hot. "You look a state!"

"I—"

Ruby hadn't prepared herself for this confrontation, and was aware that everybody was listening.

"I'm sorry, Mother." Ruby hurried along the table to appease her, but Rhoda grabbed her arm and whirled her around.

"And fancy running off like that this afternoon! What on earth has got into you?"

"I told Lisette; she made us baguettes for lunch," Ruby protested pathetically, her arm stiffening under her mother's grip.

"Who do you think you are, gallivanting around the place, making a mess in the kitchen, shouting and behaving disgracefully, the other girls taking their cue from you? You're the hostess, for heaven's sake, and you behave like some spoiled brat!"

"Shouting?"

Rhoda wound her daughter in tighter. Ruby said nothing more, full of fear. Her mother's face was close now, her features pointed with anger.

"And those oranges, the mess you left in the kitchen, that's the last straw! You will behave, young lady. You will be held accountable to your father, and to me! No more running about doing whatever you like! I'll set you a routine and see how you like that!"

"I say, go easy on the little thing," Angus spoke up into the strained silence. Polly cast her husband a hot glare, before turning in support of Rhoda. Ruby didn't dare look anywhere other than her mother's face.

"Yes," Ned added tentatively. "Mrs. Ashby, it was me that took them to the village . . . I thought it would be all right. I apologize if I was wrong."

Rhoda did not turn her head. If anything, her fury intensified.

Georgina made a further attempt. "Rhoda, darling, I do apologize for Ned's actions. But there's no need to *yell* like this and ruin our dinner. It sours the mood."

"Quite," Harley had a go in his resounding voice, with a lift of his wineglass. "Take this sort of thing inside, darling."

Rhoda let go of Ruby's arm and almost spat at her daughter. "Sit down, then, and shut up."

Ruby kept her flaming face down for the duration of dinner. Annie and Imogen didn't glance her way once, as if her disgrace would be contagious.

Ruby gave up following the conversation, which soon grew hearty again. She wanted to bury her face in her meal—to tear at the chicken breast with her knife, to spear her broccoli with her fork. Max was apparently pestering Toby, just out of Angus's earshot, with his desire to stay longer.

"Give me a week."

Toby hesitated, then repeated, "A week?"

"I'd like to see if there's something I can do for that woman, or her family."

Toby's face darkened. "I don't think that's a good idea at all, Max . . ."

"Well, let's see. I'd also like to repay you, Toby, for your kindness."

Harley's voice came in. "Doesn't Toby owe *you*, Maximus, after the cards?"

"Ah"—Max's face seemed to flicker delightedly—"well. Give me a week, Toby, and let me see what I can do."

Ruby didn't look up, but she could tell by the swelling assertions of Harley and Max that her father was going to concede. By the time pudding was served, Harley was grinning from ear to ear as he declared Max a kindred spirit, causing Ned to laugh with dismay. Toby seemed to have receded into himself, while Rhoda's face remained clouded with fury. It was at least an hour before she injected herself into the conversation again, turning to Polly for entertainment.

Angus peered at Ruby over the great glass bowl of tiramisu, layered and creamy like silk. He spoke in his low, musical voice. "I say, little thing, fancy a game of cards? I've remembered a jolly game I could teach you."

Ruby lifted her eyes to his, but couldn't control her wobbly lip.

"Better not," he answered carefully. "Tomorrow, then. I'll make sure."

Ruby felt Imogen glare at her, but she was too miserable to consider why.

RUBY LAY AWAKE IN BED while the evening carried on without her. Her mother had dismissed her thoroughly after having her collect the dishes and carry them inside. Ruby couldn't hear the other girls' voices beyond her balcony, even though she'd thrown the shutters open wide. She felt miles away from their hot escape of an afternoon.

When Annie finally came in, she passed Ruby wordlessly and sat on her own bed, ruffling the bedclothes.

Ruby sat up mechanically to avoid Annie's prying eyes. She passed her small bathroom, crossed the dark landing, and moved down the staircase, then across the first-floor landing into her parents' bathroom. Ruby closed the door behind her, sat, and waited with the lights off, hoping that Annie would soon fall asleep and the day would be over. She stared at the empty spot where her mother's lilac shampoo had been, and turned on the tap to cancel out the rush of worrying thoughts in her head.

When Ruby finally came out of the bathroom, she could hear a dull shouting coming through her parents' bedroom door.

"*How* can you expect me to compose myself, Toby, when that girl is here?"

Ruby inched closer to listen—her mother's voice was somehow angrier than it had been at dinner, and seemed louder over the hush of the sleeping house.

"I can't exactly send her away, can I?" Toby answered frantically.

"You can. I can't believe you allowed both of them here! In front of me, in front of Ruby and everyone else, to see!"

"Yes, it was ballsy of her to come, I did try to warn you . . . But Ned will be an adult soon, she'll be off to university next summer, and Georgina wanted—"

Rhoda's voice was a screech now. "She wanted all of your friends to meet her, finally, properly—your illegitimate daughter! Your *first* child!"

Ruby's heart beat thickly, in her mouth, in her chest.

"It's a disgrace!" Rhoda continued. "And for her to take Ruby off for the afternoon—"

"Ned has no idea I'm her father—Georgina insisted—"

"Shame on you! Shame on them both! I'll not stand for it! A man in your position—how could you have—"

"That's enough!" Toby's voice grew stronger. "Quiet, Rhoda; you will be heard! This is *not* something I shall discuss. They are staying, and you are keeping out of it. And if you don't like it, you can leave and take Ruby back to England with you."

There was a dim slam, but Ruby couldn't tell where it came from.

She slid down the wall and sat in the corridor. She looked out the tall windows, at the glimmers of light from across the bay, pinpricks that Ruby watched dance about. Boats, perhaps, enjoying the water. The house was entirely silent now, the only sound the push of the sea against the rocks, and the awful words that still echoed in her ears. Could she crawl to the balcony and climb over? Fall splat on the steps below, and be found in the morning? It wasn't high enough—she might not die. Ruby sat there for a long time, wondering.

12

Ruby's mother set her a routine, just as threatened.

She was allowed a quiet breakfast and a swim in the morning, before flute practice, lunch, and a siesta in her room, during which she'd stare listlessly at the ceiling, trying not to see Ned's face imprinted on her father's. Later in the afternoon she could swim again, or join the others for an activity. Then Ruby would return to the house, wash, and choose her clothes for the evening with her mother. She'd then play her flute again until dinner, to entertain their guests. At dinner she would help, and eat properly while avoiding anyone's eye, before being excused for an early bedtime.

The other girls did what they liked for the next few days. Ned had taken to watching loud films in the living room, and Annie and Imogen often joined her, settling beside each other on the sofa. Ruby had caught a few minutes one afternoon, drawn there by the noise and her distraught curiosity about Ned. The girl's features seemed magnified in Ruby's mind: the glint in her eye, the turn of her voice, the tilt of her head—even the way Ned moved her hand as she drew her cigarette to her mouth. It seemed so obvious now, and Ruby wanted to both scream it from her broken balcony and bury it in the foundations of the château. Ruby hated her, even as she told herself it couldn't possibly be true, Ned couldn't possibly be her father's daughter.

Ruby had stood behind an armchair, the one farthest away from Ned, keeping her hand on the headrest and ready to dash at any moment. It was a gory but adventurous film—one scene had particularly compelled her, where a foreign man pulls out someone's heart by muttering a spell in a dark cave. Just at the most critical moment, an adult voice came in behind her.

"Ned!" Georgina demanded. "Why are you watching this nonsense? You didn't bring these videos with you, did you?"

"Yes, Mother," Ned answered simply, without turning away from the screen.

"Can't you watch something lovely like *A Room with a View*? That was such a treat—Florence was utterly sublime, and those wonderful dresses . . . Lucy Honeychurch had hair rather like yours, Imogen."

"Who?" Imogen asked, confused.

Ned twisted back to sneer at Georgina. "Yes, I suppose you only really notice the costumes and the hair, don't you, Mother?"

"Oh tush," Georgina scoffed. "What nonsense you talk."

"Less nonsense than *you* talk."

Georgina grinned and shrugged at the younger girls as she left the room. Once she'd closed the door, Imogen turned to Ned. "The way you talk to your mother is not the way we talk to our mothers."

Ned smirked, still watching the television. "You'll learn."

Imogen raised her eyebrows and glanced at Annie; they were both impressed. Suddenly Imogen caught sight of Ruby.

"Ruby! Did you know that Ned is sleeping in the attics?"

Ned burst out laughing. "Not all of them, just one little cell."

Ruby didn't answer—she didn't go near the attics. "Cells" is exactly what they were. She refused to listen to the stories about them, but far worse, she'd been locked in there for a whole afternoon one summer when she was very little, by a particularly mean older boy. He'd been a friend of Harley's son, Hugo, who was tolerable and even played snap with Ruby whenever he saw her—but his friend that summer had been awful, and bullied Hugo, creating such a fuss that Harley never brought Hugo to the château again. That afternoon in the attics had dented itself in her memory: how she'd roamed from cell to cell, howling through the shadowed hours, banging at the locked door until Lisette came to open it. It gave Ruby the shivers to think of Ned sleeping up there.

Upstairs, Rhoda had removed Ruby's pile of books by her bed and those on her shelf, replacing them with old annuals titled *Happy Book for Girls* and *Girls' Summer Best.* Ruby glared at them contemptuously, glad that she'd saved *Murder on the Orient Express* by hiding it under her pillow. Annie, however, had opened one of the annuals and thoroughly enjoyed it. Ruby wanted to roll her eyes—they were all filled with nonsense, tall tales interspersed with guides to sewing or flower pressing—but still, something nudged at her heart seeing Annie's innocence in liking them.

During the siesta that same day, Annie returned to the bedroom with Imogen to resume her reading, while Imogen closed her eyes and set her head on Annie's pillow. The two girls were tangled together, just like they had been on the sofa.

"There's a funny story here about two girls who have their bikes stolen," Annie said excitedly, nudging the annual into her lap, "and they discover it was two boys at the local school, so they decide to play a trick on them!"

"Hmmm?" Imogen said dozily.

"And there's another one about a turret room ghost." Annie smiled giddily. "You know, the girls in these stories are very clever, like you two."

Imogen turned her face toward Annie, and muttered, "We aren't clever."

Ruby's head snapped up from her Agatha Christie. "Yes we are."

Later, Annie and Imogen had already left for a swim when Rhoda appeared to check on her daughter and remind her that she was to keep away from the colorful Ned, who was too rough and unfeminine an influence. Ruby nodded but avoided her mother's pointed gaze, feeling the truth pass between them.

Ruby didn't quibble over the rules. She felt entirely disengaged, floating above the others and looking at them all anew. Her father, her mother. And Ned—her sister? *How* could that be? She remained silent, obedient, not wanting to be agitated, not wanting to be touched.

But touched she was. Several mornings into her new routine, Ruby was wearing a stiff white dress from last summer that was now too tight around her chest. Her mother had insisted that she wear it, even though Ruby was uncomfortable. She compromised by wearing her soft swimsuit underneath, instead of a bra, but it made little difference.

Harley saw her approach the breakfast table, and greeted her with a wide smile as the sea sparkled behind him. "Come here, darling Ruby. Are you still all upset?" he said, patting his leg. Annie and Imogen raised their eyes. "You look lovely today. Come and sit on my lap."

Ruby glanced at her father as he turned the page of his newspaper, shook it out, and resumed his reading. Harley patted his lap again, smiling all the way to his dry blue wrinkled eyes. There were no other adults to refer to—so Ruby felt she had no choice but to go and sit.

Harley pulled at her waist and jiggled her bottom over his knees as she settled there. "Lovely. Now, isn't that nice?"

Ruby could smell the hot vinegary stink of alcohol coming from him, and was glad to have her back to his face. She shifted her weight a little, trying to sit more comfortably.

"What's the game, Rubes?" Harley jostled his knees up and down and Ruby jolted about with him. "Horsey, horsey?"

"Oh, I don't know," Ruby answered weakly, feigning a small laugh as she pushed her hair around her neck and toward her chest. Her father peered over the top of his newspaper with a clearing of his throat; seeing her laugh, he returned to his page.

Ruby tried to smother her mortification as Harley jostled her about on his lap. It wasn't the first time he had done this, but she'd hoped he would stop once she got older. Now, it seemed less playful, and more something else. The morning's heat was already bearing down on her, but Harley's warm breath on her neck was much worse. She focused her attention on the table in front of her and wondered how long she'd have to stay in this position. As she did so, she caught Imogen's stare, her eyes soft with horror as she watched. Annie was busy spreading chocolate over her bread.

"Aren't you enjoying yourself . . . ? Oh, all right." Harley squeezed his hands around Ruby's waist; she sat up straight in resistance. "Off you go then, for now. We'll try again another time." He patted the side of her buttock and she took her cue, moving away. She felt strangely light-headed as she wandered to her seat, her thoughts reaching for anything other than the burn of his hands against her skin, the nauseating rhythm of his legs. Ruby pulled the Nutella toward her. Her hands shook as she pushed the knife into the pot, but her shoulders shook even more when she heard her mother's voice call out from behind her.

"No, Ruby, no more Nutella!" Rhoda insisted. "Just butter and bread, or try a *biscotte* instead of the bread. Your figure is changing."

Ruby nodded without turning around. She let the knife go and pushed the Nutella back toward the middle of the table. Harley was tearing at a croissant with vigorous enthusiasm.

"Ah, Rhoda." Toby dropped his newspaper at the approach of his wife and her friend. "Good morning, darling. And you, Polly. Where's Angus?"

"Imogen, you too. No more Nutella." Polly nodded at Imogen, ignoring Toby's question. "Rhoda's right—you girls are growing up. Time to watch yourselves."

Imogen turned to her mother, stricken, while Annie set aside her freshly spread bit of bread, bowing her head in small shame.

LATER THAT MORNING, RUBY WAS pleased when Annie and Imogen asked to join her during her swim. Her disappointment was heavy when they found the pool already occupied, the four men laughing and talking in a swirl of smoke that even the sea air couldn't dispel. They'd pulled together several sun loungers, and a spray of playing cards was scattered between them. A bottle of something empty languished on the stones at their feet, alongside two drained glasses. Georgina sat a little away from them, her skin turning browner in the sun, with

Ned beside her, poring over a book. Imogen led the girls away, moving around the other side of the pool to the shade under the trees.

"Good morning, Annie." Max smiled over at them. "Ruby, Imogen?"

"Hi, Dad," Annie replied dully.

Rather than responding, Ruby looked at the cat lying flat along the side of the pool and said, "Hello, *minou*."

"Is that his name? Little bastard." Harley rolled out a laugh.

Ruby wanted to scowl at Harley, but instead she said, "He's a stray, but '*minou*' is what you call a French cat, Lisette said."

"He's skin and bone—he's a ratbag," Harley retorted.

"No he isn't." Ruby stepped forward. "We feed him biscuits every day."

"Ruby." Toby interrupted his conversation with Angus and turned to his daughter with a cough. "Don't be ridiculous. Of course he's a little ratbag. Let Harley have his fun."

Ruby gazed at the yellow eyes of the cat as he studied her, apparently in some kind of mutual understanding. She busied her hands with burrowing into her bag, and pulled out her book, just to have something to hold.

"Shall I take you girls over to the sea?" Angus asked with a nod of his head.

"Yes, Dada, please," Imogen said quickly.

Ruby nodded back, one hand gripping at her bag, the other her book.

"Oh, Annnngus," Harley bellowed, "bowing out early, again!"

Angus's face stiffened with irritation. "No, no."

"Don't break up the party—we need four for the game," Max said crossly.

"Oho, Angus will always do the dutiful thing, Max," Harley sneered. "He's a pillar of society, after all. A life peer all the way back to his medieval ancestors."

Angus's voice was lower than usual as he answered, "Yes, Harley, and I imagine you'd like to *buy* your way into a peerage, wouldn't you."

The three girls stood and waited, not knowing whether Angus would keep to his word. Annie looked at Imogen hopefully.

"Oh no, I *do* accept tradition, and I revere it, more than you." Harley nodded heavily, just as Max piped up, "Are you in the House of Lords, Angus?"

Angus pushed his hand through his thick dark hair, and turned to the girls. But Harley hadn't finished.

"He should be, but he isn't. Because he's the doomed Earl of Beresford. Lord Beresford, Angus Bly. His wife and child, the Honorables."

Ruby turned to Imogen and asked, "Are you an Honorable?"

"Yes, she is now that her father is the lord," Harley answered. "Rather fun that he married an American, but she was an heiress in search of a title, wasn't she!"

"Well, I liked the look of her; I thought she'd do," Angus added, giving the group of men a wan smile.

"I bet you did."

"Harley, honestly," Toby muttered, "your envy is showing."

"Oh, hush, old friend. You're almost as nothing as I am. What are you . . . the second son of the daughter of a viscount? A nobility so distant, it hardly counts." He gestured over to the other side of the pool. "Even Georgina has more of a right to a peerage than you—at least her father was knighted for services to industry."

"Hardly," Georgina laughed, tipping her hat off her face. "My father was a tradesman. You're obsessed with these titles, Haz . . . It's terribly ugly."

"Oh, I'm *sorry*," Harley replied sarcastically, "didn't you have to buy your way into London Fashion Week, George?"

"Ha!" Ned squealed, nudging Georgina with her foot. "He got you, Mother dearest!"

Harley took a measured sip from his glass, his eyes darting at Angus. "I do like to tease his ladyship, here. But it's his best mate, Tobes, that really needs to watch himself. He's the one with no money left!" Harley narrowed his eyes, his mirth slipping as he said seriously, "I don't know why you won't just sell this place. I've already helped you with your many properties in England. I could buy Number Seven off you easily."

The silence spread cleanly across the pool area as Toby's expression filled with astonishment. Ruby felt her face flush, and she gripped her book tighter.

Harley continued confidently, "God knows the place needs some care and attention, which I'd be able to give. Mind you, its history is pretty sullen, needs a good cleanup, too. That cemetery, for one thing!"

"Cemetery?" Ned asked.

"During the war, young Edwina, the Germans took over the house. Anyone they caught trying to escape by boat—Jews, vagabonds, whatnot—they brought them here. Even members of the French Resistance."

"Nazis?" Ned screwed up her face with curiosity.

"Oh, do be quiet, Harley," Angus said disgustedly. "And stop bloody drinking."

"Yes, they were all put in the attic, weren't they, and shot. Then buried en masse, over there. Those poor souls need to be put to rest," Harley continued deliciously. "The whole place needs tightening up—everyone can see it. Shame on you, old boy, for letting it come to this."

Angus said, "Harley, come on, I don't think—"

"To be honest," Harley chortled, and Ruby glared at him, alarmed that he was still speaking, "it looks like old Max might win the house off you soon anyway, the way you're going with the cards. Clever young Max will outstrip us all."

"Here we go again." Ned sat up and addressed the group of men. "You're like cocks fighting, the way you talk to each other."

"Cocks?" Harley shot back, evidently thrilled.

"Yes, always have been." Georgina grinned, tossing aside her hat this time. "You too, Max, you're a ripe new cock." She lay flat again, pleased with her interjection.

"You remind me of the heroes in *The Iliad*." Ned lifted her book away from her lap. "Appallingly behaved."

Toby blinked with surprise, and Angus glanced at him.

"Tell us, then." Harley was pleased, and gestured at Ned from across the pool. "Didn't Alexander the Great carry a copy of *The Iliad* everywhere?"

Ruby blinked her eyes with frustration, and looked longingly beyond the pool, toward the house.

"Well, you're an Agamemnon if ever I saw one," Ned said sharply, sitting forward properly now. "Bossy, rude. Arrogant."

"Do go on," Harley said expansively. "Find a hero for all of us."

Ned pulled a face at Harley, before considering each of the men in turn. She pushed her glasses up her nose, taking a breath to gather momentum. "All right, here we go . . . Toby is your Odysseus—obedient, kind, appeasing. Angus is your Achilles—moody, unruly, the silent brooding one."

"I hardly think—" Toby started.

"And Max?" Georgina interrupted.

"Max . . . I don't know." Ned shrugged. "Some young Greek upstart?"

"How dare you!" Max laughed uncertainly. "I'll have you over my knee."

"Oh no, you won't," Ned answered coolly.

Harley raised his glass with gusto, and a swirl of wine sprayed into the pool. Ruby watched the red liquid spread into the blue-clear of the water, like blood.

"Didn't Agamemnon and Achilles fight over a girl?" Harley tittered. "How fitting!"

Ned smiled. "Yes, Briseis."

"Your mother must have told you all about it," Harley went on, "how I swiped Angus's first lady love from under his nose. Old Nestor's daughter . . ."

"What was her name?"

"Little Clara. She was a lovely, sweet thing when we were at university, totally unaware of herself, and unlike any other girl we'd known before."

"I didn't like her at all," Georgina put in, nodding at her daughter. "Far too sweet for my taste—and very feeble. As young as you but not nearly as savvy. No wonder Angus treated her like a porcelain doll and Harley treated her like a plaything."

"Yes, I rather enjoyed how gentle she was." Harley smiled and threw up his hand dismissively. "But as a wife she grew bitter and shriveled up—"

"What was it that Old Nestor used to say, about being remembered?" Toby interrupted, noticing Angus's stricken face, and attempting to shift Harley's attention elsewhere. He continued in a deeper voice, imitating their professor, "'Boys, you must be remembered. Remembered as heroes, remembered as *worth something.*'"

"Heroes . . ." Harley repeated. "The roles that Ned has given us!"

"That's not what I meant," Ned said dully.

"Well, Angus has public recognition. He'll be remembered," Max spoke up with a fresh look of respect on his face. Angus scowled and turned back to the girls.

"But has he got the heroic spirit?" Harley shook his head. "What do you say to that, Ned? He knows he's bound to die—death stands in wait for him. For all of us! He needs something permanent and lasting, to win glory, in order to be remembered."

"Well done, Harley, excellent recall for a non-Classicist!" Toby clapped a hand against his chest. "Didn't realize you were paying so much attention during those long lectures in our rooms."

"I think it might be a little late for any glory on my part. I have accepted my fate," Angus said in his querulous voice, not nearly as merry as the others.

Harley met his tone. "Yes, and you've not paid the blood price yet, have you? So you're doomed."

"Indeed, no," Angus conceded, "I haven't."

Max asked, anxious to keep up with the conversation, "What blood price?"

"Payment for death, for his sins," Harley declared. "First: murder, and then—hushing it up! Making everything so much worse for his lordly self. I had to step in, and thanks only to my connections, we managed to sort him out. But all it takes is one word from me, and his carefully constructed world comes tumbling down."

"Harley, please," Toby urged him.

Ruby frowned, confused. Ned glanced at her mother with a similar expression.

Harley sat back easily, looking around the pool area with a laugh. "But it's not just Angus who has the blood price hanging over him, is it? There's already been a murder here this summer . . . hasn't there, Max?"

"That's enough, Harley!" Angus muttered torturedly, his eyes like hot beads of light. "You've had too much to drink. We've all heard *enough*."

"I haven't." Ned sat forward. "What's this about—"

"Leave it, Ned." Georgina sat up as her daughter spun around to face her.

"What are you, Mother, the pacifier?"

"Yes." Harley laughed hoarsely, meeting Ned's curious gaze. "She doesn't like it when we don't *get on*."

"Our Cambridge days shall stay in Cambridge, and everything else between then and now," Toby said decisively, with a quick glance at his companions spread across the loungers.

"Does your dalliance with Georgina *after* Cambridge count then?" Harley gushed at Toby. "And the various anniversary reunions there-after?"

"Oh, Harley, you are a tease," Georgina tittered.

"His what?" Max looked up, and Ruby turned her burning face away before she could hear anything else. That comment, she'd under-stood.

Angus stood up heavily. "I'm taking the girls to the sea. They shouldn't be listening to any of this rubbish. You're all . . . we're all a disgrace."

"Oh, a true Achilles, spoiling our fun. Swift-footed Angus! Off you go then." Harley waggled his fingers rudely, and Ruby winced. "Take the little girls away, before I wrap them up and keep them for myself."

"Come, girls," Angus said wearily, but Harley followed Ruby with his narrowed eyes, squinting to see the book in her hands.

"What's that *you're* reading, Ruby Boobs, a bit of Greek, too? A real pair of brainy girls you've got here, Toby!"

Ruby looked up in dismay. Nobody had reacted to Harley's group-ing of her and Ned, but a terrible apprehension rose in her chest as she answered.

"It's *Murder on the Orient Express,* Mr. Montgomery. I've almost finished it—"

"I know it!" Harley interrupted. "That's the one where all the passengers have a go, one stab after another, isn't it? Everyone except Poirot, of course." He laughed out a massive belch. "Pardon me."

Ruby's face crumpled as her mind flitted through the book's characters. Every one of the passengers, "one stab after another"?

"I say, Harley," Angus almost shouted, "what a brute you are, spoiling it for her."

"Oh, come on, Gus. Everybody knows the ending to that one."

Ruby looked up at Angus. His eyes were darker than ever as he glared back at Harley. "Ruby didn't."

Harley shrugged. "She shouldn't be reading it anyway—her mother's forbidden those, I heard."

"Has she?" Ned said hotly from the other side of the pool. "How peculiar!"

Harley turned away from Angus and the girls. "You'd better run along to the seafront, old boy, if you've lost your sense of humor. We don't want any of your grumpy nonsense here."

As they walked, Angus's face seemed to slacken and relax as Imogen and Ruby darted ahead gratefully. But Ruby saw his eyes flash anew when he addressed her.

"I'm so sorry about Harley, Ruby. He should never have spoiled the ending for you. You must be furious." He paused. "Perhaps I'll have a read of your book while you're in the water, little thing. I'll remind myself of the story; we could discuss it afterwards. I wish Imogen read more, like you."

They passed the lower lawn and heard the voices of Polly and Rhoda floating up from the hammocks, completely concealed by two huge parasols covering the shifting glare of the sun. Ruby squinted at them painfully, while Angus concentrated his gaze on Ruby's careful steps. In the next moment she hurried to the long expanse of rock, where Annie and Imogen were already climbing down the ladder and into the sea.

———

RUBY WAS GLAD TO BE in the water, regardless of the bitter salt or the unpredictability of the waves. She hoped that the rush of the sea would block out the voices and images in her head. But even then, under the water, she could hear her father's voice saying in his bedroom, *"She's my daughter,"* tenderly, insistently—about Ned. Differently from how he spoke about Ruby. She could hear Harley's voice even louder, spoiling the Agatha Christie ending, swirling his glass of red wine into the clear pool water. And Max, too, his piggy eyes keen and laughing as he shuffled the playing cards.

Ruby pushed her way back up to the surface, choking the salt water out of her throat. The other two girls were farther off and gliding past each other gracefully, falling into squirts of laughter. Ruby looked back to the pontoon; Angus was standing at the ladder, apparently alarmed by her coughing and raising one arm to better see. He clasped her book in his other hand. Ruby felt relief flood through her as she swam back to him.

13

2010

Mrs. Cosgrove woke abruptly, as if somebody had shaken her. The daylight came thickly past the curtain to inform her of the lateness of the morning. As she raised her head, her hair hung in strings up from the pillow, still damp. Her head seemed to thump as she pushed herself up to sit, and she saw through blurred eyes the two buckets of melted ice on the desk. The single ashtray was piled high and stinking. Squinting, she could see several glasses marked with her lipstick; her white pillow was similarly streaked with pink-red stains and black smudges. She put a hand to her mouth—her lips were swollen, too. Her hair against her face smelled of that familiar soapy lilac scent. She had bathed, then, but hadn't washed her face—or perhaps reapplied her makeup? She couldn't remember doing that.

Her dreams had been haunted by the inky black sea and the scrape of the stones. Had some curious nighttime part of herself gone to the harbor beach—to the château itself? She had no recollection beyond her return to the hotel and her one, two, three gin and tonics.

She'd dreamed of Englishmen with unknown faces and the same tight accent as her own. The voices were looking for her, talking about her, somewhere here in France. And how well Mrs. Cosgrove knew the habits of Englishmen, and Englishwomen—forever thrusting themselves forward with their dripping comments, their prying eyes, coming and going into their friends' houses, their friends' lives. The brightly false compliments they threw out at each other, the insults directly and indirectly combative, the resentment and loathing played out in passive games. All of it masking their greed, ambition, and desire to live the high life, know the right people, be seen in the right places. Had she learned to play the same games, to join in with the charade? Was it some covenant that they had all signed, and accepted?

The typical Englishmen had certainly found their place at the château that summer, and perhaps here again, now.

The man's questions at the café yesterday had muddled her—challenging her in that rough French accent, his mouth hanging open delightedly at her shock. She didn't like the way he had looked at her, how his eyes had scoured her face, her figure. *Your beautiful hair,* he had said. *They say it was the daughters. Yes, you hide from the police, but we know.* Between her damp head and her dirty bedsheets Mrs. Cosgrove shuddered.

She remembered returning to the hotel after a long walk the previous afternoon. She hadn't gone up to her room, but wandered past reception toward the shallow and shaded courtyard, where a few bodies languished among the dropping ivy and someone's child dipped in and out of the pool. The concierge had followed her, though, and presented her with a phone message from Robert Payne.

The wrong Englishman, she'd thought, and not at all welcome. She couldn't believe the boldness of the man, the impertinence! The message seemed to burn in her hand the longer she held it, so she took it up to her room.

Now this morning the message from Robert Payne sat on the desk, torn out of the envelope. Mrs. Cosgrove couldn't ignore it as she pushed herself out of bed. Phrases seemed to ring out in his voice now, *Come back to me, my little vixen, how dare you leave me at a time like this,* and his ultimate demand, *I need you back here, I need you to warm my bed again. I shall call again soon, perhaps in person.*

In the bathroom doorway, she stopped short. There was another glass on the floor, marked red at the rim, like the others—but smashed. She wasn't safe here, but she was safer than in Robert's urging, thrilling, horrible clutches back in England. She cringed at the lack of courage that had led her to go along with the affair. From this distance, her behavior was a disgrace, but at least she'd exiled herself with this visit.

Her makeup bag was open, its contents in disarray, and the shower curtain had been twisted back to reach the sink. The floor was wet, but her copy of *The Iliad* sat in the far corner, safe and dry. She caught her marred reflection in the bathroom mirror, the deep dark circles under her eyes—that hungry, frightened look she used to hide so well.

Mrs. Cosgrove bent to wash her face quickly, scrubbing away the stains of the night before. But the broken glass had pricked at her foot and let out a rivulet of blood, which now spread across the floor of the bathroom in short whirls.

She collected the broken glass in the paddle of her hand, and dashed it into the bin, before scrubbing her hands thoroughly once again. She winced as the small shards of glass scraped at the skin of her hands, her feet. Her foul breath was a mix of soured alcohol and cigarette smoke, and her toothbrush seemed to have gone missing.

Returning to the bedroom, she turned over her stained pillow and lay down flat, her face pressed against the mattress.

Sometime later, a knock sounded on the door. "Housekeeping?"

"Non, merci!"

"Pardon?"

Mrs. Cosgrove raised her voice. *"Non, merci! Plus tard."*

Another part of her dream flew into her mind. She'd seen her father, his face drawing toward her as he folded her in his arms. She could remember being pressed against him, that earthy smell of his chest. She had felt so warm and safe there, but the smell was decidedly unearthly, since it belonged only to her dream, which now cleared in her mind's eye. Her father's face had been turned away from her, his eyes searching for another. He was not there, and hadn't been for many years.

And now James was gone, too.

She considered how the staff of James's firm had admired him, and her too, though only for her appearance. During their last Christmas do in the city, and under many watchful eyes, Robert Payne had approached her with his slippery, seductive voice. Was that where someone had named the château, spoken of its sale? No, that was more than six months ago. The mention of the château was more recent.

Mrs. Cosgrove pushed herself upright and went to the wardrobe. She took out her swimming things, wrapped herself in a thick dressing gown, grabbed a towel, threw on the hotel slippers, and made her way downstairs; perhaps the rush of water could drown out her thoughts.

She felt a sudden flush of shame as she moved through the lobby. Bare legs, bare face. With a shock, she realized it was the first time in years that she'd been in public without her veneer.

The dining area of the courtyard was deserted except for a few guests finishing their breakfast and a waiter clearing away tables. At the poolside an older couple lay reading their books.

She dove into the pool before any of them could notice her, first dropping her dressing gown and room key by the wet poolside. She held herself underwater and saw again her father's face, fierce now, any of the warmth in her dream suddenly withdrawn, as it had been when she was a child. Was it that same grief that had brought her back here to France? Losing James, and losing her father? The same unresolved, uncomfortable anguish?

She pictured her mother's face instead, very much alive but even more unknowable, nodding sorrowfully at James's memorial, then cheerfully joining the other well-dressed women at the dining tables.

Mrs. Cosgrove pushed herself deeper into the water, holding her breath, her knees against her chest. At secondary school she'd been one of the best swimmers. They'd all praised her elegance, her posture while diving. They'd had diving competitions that summer, hadn't they?

She pulled herself out of the water, her breathing coming in great gasps. The older couple didn't waver from their joint concentration. Climbing out of the pool, Mrs. Cosgrove pulled at her swimsuit, feeling the suck of the water against her skin. She remembered her resistance to her husband whenever he'd drawn close to her, with his soft, trying tenderness. How she had loathed those hands being anywhere near her. She'd known so little about him, and their intimacy had been so sudden. His hands were different from the touch of the man who first touched her, a touch that felt like daggers all over her skin as a child.

That attention must have been her fault. She must have encouraged them all, smiled and tolerated it. Mrs. Cosgrove wondered whether she'd played games with every man she'd ever met. She'd gone further, by taking a lover in Robert Payne—or he'd taken her, and she'd allowed it. He'd spoiled her with gifts and furtive messages and frantic professions of desire—it was everything that she'd been told to hope for from a typical love story—and she'd played her role perfectly, disgustingly, behind her husband's obliging back. She'd performed so well that Robert now demanded she reprise her role. Well, she couldn't think of anyone she'd less like to go back to. His hands, too, had been strong, invasive, and insistent.

Perhaps now was the time for Mrs. Cosgrove to stop playing along. Her gasping stiffened, and she took an almighty cough.

In the dining area, two remaining guests turned at the noise. They were a pair of men in soft linen suits: a shorter, older man with white flyaway hair and a narrow face, and a middle-aged man with a heavy build and an agitated expression. In one moment Mrs. Cosgrove took a decent look at them, before ducking to lie down on her sunbed.

In the next moment they were quarreling with the waiter as Mrs. Cosgrove tried to listen, breathing in slow motion with her eyes closed. She guessed that the harsh and furious voice belonged to the middle-aged man, but she couldn't be sure. He spoke exaggeratedly in bad French, and the waiter seemed to give up his part of the argument.

Mrs. Cosgrove realized that she recognized the middle-aged man. She'd seen that grim face compose itself to appraise her. An evening at the Banqueting House, perhaps? Or a friend of Robert's that she'd met at a soiree? She'd definitely seen those eyes pass over her, as so many eyes did—friends' husbands, her own husband's friends. Appraising eyes and softly daggered words. These male faces who had shaped how she carried herself—her father, his friend Harley Montgomery, and then Max Fuller—all gone now, yet still larger than life.

Mrs. Cosgrove didn't dare turn for a second glimpse. She focused on her damaged nail polish instead, tempted to tug off some of the smooth edges with her teeth, or to take her razor to them and tear off the dark color. The razor her mother had never taught her how to use. How could her mother mean nothing, and all those men mean everything?

Her body dripped with the pool water as she sat shivering in the shade, soaking through the towel and the cushion beneath, her things at the other end of the pool. Waiting for the men to finish their breakfast and their conversation; desperate to hear, to determine why they were there, and whether they were The Englishmen.

But of course, Mrs. Cosgrove already knew the answer to that.

14

1985

After a slow breakfast the next morning, everyone climbed into their various cars to go to a nearby beach hotel. Ruby was looking forward to a day away from her stifling routine, and to being around people beyond their party.

It was a modern hotel: a rectangular block of white, with ribbed balconies and wide windows. Steps ran down toward the beach and split the long deck into a restaurant and bar on one side and an oval-shaped pool area on the other. Heavy pine trees offered ample shade, their thick tops so dense that they refused to sway with the sea breeze. Beyond the hotel's broad deck, the beach's yellow sand was lined with rows of luscious cream-colored beds, fluttering parasols, and short, square tables pushed into the sand. Ruby admired the exotic stretch of blue Mediterranean in front of her, altogether more inviting here thanks to the slow slant of the water's approach, the softness of the sand underfoot, and the shallow early water so easy for paddling.

Ned's shorts seemed to have been washed for today, but she wore an old stringy T-shirt emblazoned with the word "Heart." She looked strange next to the neat prettiness of Imogen's matching blouse and skirt and Annie's blue dress, an old one of Ruby's and very fetching on Annie's small figure. One of the beach attendants smiled at Imogen and asked her how many towels they needed. Ned answered in her stilted French.

"Ruby!" Rhoda called out. "You mustn't go in. Ruby!"

Ruby waited while Rhoda ordered a large gin and tonic with a slice of cucumber and a *Perrier rondelle* for Polly. Rhoda returned to her daughter when the drinks were ready, her auburn hair glinting with the sun.

"Don't go in the sea until after lunch."

Ruby protested, "But that's more than an hour away—"

"You mustn't have a wet dress during lunch," she said irritably. "And your hair must stay dry."

The men were moving toward the bar too. Ruby lowered her face, and her voice.

"But is Imogen—?"

"Polly's determined to disagree with me." Rhoda added thickly, "But you're not *her* daughter, you're mine."

"Honestly, Rhoda," Polly said, sipping her bubbling Perrier.

Rhoda lifted her gin and tonic. "I'll show that blasted woman how to raise a daughter properly. Just look at Ned! What a horrible example she sets."

The other two girls eyed Ruby confusedly when she skittered back to them and insisted that she preferred to stay in the shade by the pool before lunch.

"Shall we save you a bed then, for afterwards?" Annie asked.

"Yes, please," Ruby answered, before turning away, tugging on her basket laden with suncream and her mother's old annuals.

The girls sprinted across the beach and into the sea, wading and kicking up splashes at each other. Ruby dropped her hot feet into the pool instead and glared at one of her books; *School Friend,* the cover read. She had thought she'd try to smuggle another Agatha Christie into the binding of the annual, but she'd finished the *Murder on the Orient Express* that very morning, and found that Harley was right. Her dismay at the ending being spoiled filled her eyes with tears that had blurred the words. Before closing the book, she'd spotted an early page with its corner folded, where Angus had read up to. Ruby wondered whether she should hand it over to him or keep it in her bedroom.

Her father and Angus were at the bar, laughing with Harley; Georgina and Max were chatting on one of the sofas, separate from her mother and Polly, who'd invited Liv to join them with her own gin and tonic. The smartly dressed barmen were throwing their shakers around with quick laughs among piles of lemons and limes and rows of thickly colored bottles.

Ruby remembered once going for tea at Claridge's in London with her grandmother on one of their long weekends together; they'd stayed so long into the early evening that she'd taken Ruby into the bar. Ruby had sat high up on the stool and ordered a Virgin Mary for herself and a Bloody Mary for her grandmother. The barman had grinned at her as he'd created the bright, strange concoctions. Ruby still remembered the smell of that tomato drink, and the shimmering lights of the glorious bathroom, the mirrored walls, and her grandmother's cackle as she tried all the creams.

They'd done the same thing in Le Meurice in Paris, where the high-ceilinged bathroom was even grander and the bar was full of men smoking thick cigars next to a tinkling pianist and tootling saxophone player. Ruby had loved it, even though they'd played jazz, and her grandmother had so many cocktails that they'd been the last people to leave, by which point Ruby had fallen asleep with her soft head on her grandmother's arm.

Ruby stared across at the group of her parents' friends near the bar. How different things were, she thought. Now, here. She thought that somehow her grandmother might have admonished Ruby's father, put Ned in her place, rebuked Harley for his comments, shooed them all away, and ushered Ruby over to sit next to her.

AT LUNCH, ANNIE'S THIN HAIR was thick with water, while Imogen's black tendrils were soaking the chest part of her dress, which she didn't seem to notice as she sucked on some melon. Max was gazing at Imogen as he took small sips of wine, his eyes round and keen, barely hearing Ruby's father talking at him continuously.

The decadent lunch was making her feel queasy: delicate plates of baked aubergines blistering with tomato sauce and cheese sat beside a deep dish of ratatouille; paddles of steaks simmering with garlic butter lay next to stacks of mussels sitting in sauce with their shells partly open. Harley was mopping up a final glob of garlic butter with a piece of baguette, drawing it to his slopping mouth before reaching back for more. Ruby closed her eyes briefly, listening to the longing pull of the sea as sweat trickled down the back of her dress.

". . . You see, they've now found fingerprints on the body, old boy— your wife's," Toby was muttering to Max. "She didn't get out of the car to have a look at the—"

"I'd rather not talk about this on such a glorious day at the beach."

The heat seemed to beat against Ruby's brow as her father carried on, "My dear Max, you can't avoid this conversation. And you really ought to get going back to England. If they can prove that it was in fact your car involved, then your affidavits are false, and then if they catch the lie about your wife being the driver . . ."

Angus was talking over them, and his musical voice tugged at Ruby. She turned her head.

"A little bird tells me it's Ruby's birthday in two days." Angus's face softened with kindness. "What are we doing to celebrate? Toby?"

Toby turned away from Max and said with some irritation, "Rhoda?"

Ruby looked between her father and mother. She'd never wanted a birthday celebration less.

"Oh, yes, of course," Rhoda said irritably, fluffing up her hair with her fingers. "It's so tiresome to have to bother with a birthday during the holidays, rather than the school dealing with it. Imogen has hers in term time, doesn't she, Pol?"

"Quite right," Polly tittered with a nod at Rhoda, "Imogen has a cake delivered and a present from her father and me . . . a bit of a singsong with the boarding mistress and the other girls, and that's quite enough."

Imogen set down her melon rind and looked at her mother, appalled.

"Ruby's a summer baby, is she? Hotheaded, they say." Harley nodded over to Ruby with a wide grin as she turned her face away.

"Ruby's lovely," Angus said.

"Ye-es, she *seems* lovely, doesn't she," Harley continued, "but I see
the way she looks at me, at all of us, buried in her thoughts. Mark my
words, she'll turn out hotheaded, very like her grandmother Ashby.
And even more so when she discovers that there's nothing for her to
inherit—what a rotten birthday present, Tobes!"

Toby bowed his head into the silence.

"What can you mean, man?" Angus cried out. Rhoda looked up
nervously, just as Ruby turned her face to the floor.

"Oh, you all know that etiquette is not my middle name." Harley
smirked. "I'm talking about the château, Gus. I'm putting an offer together; I've got Max on board too, with his new-money riches—"

"Harley, do not speak in this manner. Remember what we discussed," Liv said sharply, and the table turned, surprised to hear her
voice. Harley gave her a brief look, full of loathing.

"Oh, yes," Angus's voice rolled forward as he eyed Max brutally.
"Old Haz brags about being the one with the money, but it's his wife's
after all."

"Not at all. And I have even more influence than money, my friend,
as you well know."

"Yes, your society chums and your army chums and heavens know
who else you meet as you climb the ranks—all of them so easy to co-
erce! But Tobes and I see you for what you are, even if you have got us
over a bloody barrel. 'Major general' indeed . . . you've only ever been
one of those chaps stuck behind a desk." Angus slapped his hand on
the table and Ruby jolted.

Harley drew his eyebrows together haughtily. "I was in Nigeria fif-
teen years ago, thank you. And in Ireland."

"Oh, but you can't *talk* about it." Angus winced, tearing at his food.
"How convenient. Too grand to actually *do* any of the work—even
though you're *not* grand at all."

"Angus," Toby said wearily, "don't."

"Bit rich coming from you, Gus—you've never done a day's work in your life!" Harley spluttered furiously. "And my 'chums,' as you call them, were the reason you avoided prison all those years ago. They came when *I* called them, in *your* hour of need, even though you'd barely spoken to me in decades. They were certainly handier than Toby, the law man, who drew a blank in your case. Those same chums have helped Toby out, in his turn—with the tax man, most recently, I seem to remember."

"Prison?" Ned queried.

"Yes, yes, we're forever in your debt," Angus almost shouted, "and you won't let us forget it. Don't forget you've done very well out of us, too."

Ruby stared into her food, taking apart Harley's confusing comments in her mind—these small bullets of unknowable ammunition that he seemed to hold, ready to use against her father, and Imogen's.

"I haven't at all." Harley's face hardened. "I've always been there for you boys, and I've had little gratitude for it. Worse, I've had little acknowledgment. I made it all the way to the Ministry of Defense before I retired, with no help from you fellows."

"Ministry of Defense!" Max repeated, impressed. He raised his glass to Harley and took a cheery sip of his wine.

"Yes"—Angus's heavy features seemed to tighten—"awarding and promoting an incompetent swine, just to get rid of you. But whatever happened to *cause* your early retirement, Harley? Was it . . . fiddling with the boys?"

Harley snarled at Angus, "This is all because of old Nestor's daughter, isn't it? Clara. Your first love, my first *wife*. Very petty of you to've let it dent our friendship so hugely."

"Oh, here we go." Angus drew his hand through his thick hair, which flashed steel gray in the sunlight. "You know, Harley, you and the army makes sense. It accounts for your emotional violence."

Harley shook his head furiously. "Well . . . at least I've learned to control my temper. Unlike you, dear Angus!"

Ruby blinked at the two men—two bulls ready to charge, the heat of the day beating between them, red flags in each other's eyes. Imogen was watching her father, terrified.

Ned suddenly chimed in, "Are you sure you two are even friends?"

Georgina laughed a big laugh, breaking the tension. Toby let out a sigh, and Angus glanced at him. Ruby didn't turn her head, but she could feel the other two girls as stiff and exhausted as she.

Twenty minutes later Ruby ordered a pudding with a quick check that her mother was looking elsewhere, but when the waitress placed the *tarte du jour* in front of her, Rhoda spoke such a rebuke at Ruby that she felt the full torrent of her words.

"Oh, let her have it, Rhoda, now she's ordered it," Toby said wearily. "I'll have a spoonful if you insist."

"Appalling!" Rhoda said.

"Appalling indeed." Harley let out one of his rolling laughs. "Don't let her ruin that beautiful figure. This is a precious age, unspoiled girls caught in their nebulous beauty, before they get too old."

"That's it." Ned stood up, her face twisted with disgust. "Harley, you're a disgusting perv. I don't want to sit here listening to you. What are your military medals for . . . being a creep?"

"Pipe down, Edwina dear," Harley said, glaring at her. "I've already told you—you're just jealous; you can't bear the lack of attention."

"Ned, darling, leave it," Georgina said, placing her arm on her daughter's arched back.

Ned bit her lip, then shook her mother's arm away. "Girls, come to the beach."

Imogen and Annie stood to follow Ned. Ruby toyed with her pudding.

"Oh, she's not even going to eat it now!" Rhoda barked out. "Bloody argument for nothing!"

Ruby looked up, her eyes almost swimming with tears. "I will, I will, I promise!"

"Do you know how much a place like this costs for a day?"

"Hush, Rhoda," Toby said, checking the other tables of guests sitting around them.

"Well," Harley chortled, "it would cost much less if you had a head for personal finance, dear boy."

Ruby pushed a large chunk of apple tart into her mouth miserably, and felt Ned standing behind her. She scowled down at Ruby, "Finish the stupid cake or don't, Ruby, and let's go for a swim."

Ruby stood up clumsily, not wanting to go anywhere near Ned, but wanting to stay at that table even less. She was still chewing, her eyes wet, as she turned away from the table and toward the beckoning sea.

RUBY LAY ON HER SUNBED beside Annie, quietly turning over the horrible things she'd heard and seen at lunch. Rhoda and Polly were in the shade of the pine trees by the pool, keeping Polly's pregnant belly out of the heat. Liv sat with the girls, but made no acknowledgment of them while she read her international newspaper. The men were playing in the sea, the tension at lunch now transformed into aggressive splashing games. Harley's thick stomach hung low, protruding over his swimming shorts. Max's chest was tight and muscular, and he swam in small, biting strokes. Angus and Toby seemed to move as one, although Angus was taller, broader, and more looming. Ruby had watched them tentatively while she paddled in the shallow water, pushing the squelch of the wet sand between her toes. She'd swum alone and only for a short time, before rushing back to her bed to wrap herself in a hotel towel.

Harley eventually left the men in the sea and strode over to the row of sunbeds. He shook the water out of the little hair he had left.

"Look at your Greek heroes, Ned," Harley called out, pulling at a towel and gesturing toward them with his roaring laugh, "playing with each other on the Trojan beaches. We just need you lot to play the slave girls."

"You're more like lumbering Trojans. Especially you, Harley." Ned kept her eyes on her book. "I wish I'd never mentioned it."

"What happened to those heroes, Ned, remind me?" Liv eyed her husband evenly, as if she knew the answer.

"Well, they were victorious," Ned said begrudgingly.

"There you are, you see?" Harley was jubilant.

"But when they got home . . ." Liv said in a soft voice. "What happened then?"

"Well." Ned sat up, taking the bait. "Achilles never made it home. But he knew that it was his destiny to die there, at Troy, with glory. Odysseus took ten years to return to Ithaca, after the ten years of the war—so once he got home, he had to convince his wife Penelope it was really him. And then he had to defeat the load of men—enemies, rivals—waiting for him there." Ned's face lifted with a grin. "And then the great leader, Agamemnon. Wasn't that you, Harley? He was stabbed in the bath, by his wife."

"What?" Annie spat out. "Stabbed by his wife?"

"Yes," Ned cackled.

"Why?"

"The king of the Greeks," Liv repeated darkly. "Stabbed by his wife in the bath. What an indignity."

Harley's face hardened at his wife's words, but cheered up as Max appeared behind him, chanting, "King of the Greeks, yes. King of the Greeks!"

Ned ignored him as Imogen stood up to return to the sea. She turned to Annie and Ruby. "Shall we—"

"Want to go for a swim in the pool, Imogen, clean ourselves off?" Max interrupted, smiling. "How about another diving competition?"

"Oh, er . . ." Imogen looked around anxiously for her mother. Her father was still out swimming with Toby. Her face seemed to crumple.

"Come on," Max coaxed, "and when we're back we'll order everyone ice cream."

"Er . . ."

Ruby saw the girl's burning face, and turned away quickly. She planted her feet in the sand in front of her.

"Annie? Ruby?" Imogen suggested weakly.

Annie shook her head with a simple shrug. "Oh no. I'm no good. I'll stay here—I want to hear more of Ned's stories."

Ruby shook her head without moving.

Imogen followed Max toward the pool, her shoulders sagging and her damp hair spreading down her back. Ruby lay flat, her heart beating as she felt every second of Imogen's absence. When Imogen returned twenty minutes later, she was shivering.

"Are you all right?" Ruby asked, sitting up.

"Mr. Fuller ordered us some ice creams, but he wasn't sure about the tab, so he put it on your father's," Imogen said quietly.

"Are you all right, Imogen?" Ruby repeated.

"The pool water is cold," Imogen answered.

Ruby studied her face, before saying, "It's cleaner, though . . . the pool water, and you won't get a rash."

Imogen shoved her hands between her thighs as her face tensed, her eyes narrowed with quivering emotion.

"What flavor ice creams did you order?" Annie asked.

"Oh, one of each," Imogen answered, her voice a stuttering whisper. "I thought we could share." She hesitated, and added, "Do you really get a rash from the seawater, Ruby?"

"Yes, usually. It's my pale skin, and the heat."

"But the seawater is beautiful here, sparkling." Imogen's voice wobbled as she spoke, and Ruby studied her face again. Her eyes were filled with tears, and there was a queer turn of her soft mouth.

"It's part of a nature reserve, I think, and that's why there are so many trees," Ruby answered carefully. "Not like the open bay, where our house is."

Imogen nodded, almost imperceptibly.

Ruby felt completely miserable. She watched Max rejoin the men with a triumphant shout.

Ned set her book down heavily. "Who wants more story time?"

"Yes!" Annie cried.

"Not today," Ruby said at the same time.

"Yes, today!" Annie leaned toward Ned beseechingly. "The wife who stabbed her husband in the bath, please."

"She can wait. We'll do another wife. Odysseus's wife, Penelope." She glanced at Ruby with her eyebrows raised. "What do you think, Ruby . . . I've compared Odysseus to your dad. Perhaps his wife is similar to your mother, too. Shall we hear about them?"

"Please!" Annie said.

"Well, Odysseus didn't originally want to go to the war," Ned began.

"He didn't?" Annie asked brightly. "I thought he was a hero."

Ruby refused to listen—she was more concerned that Imogen was still shivering. As she tried to throw her towel over Imogen's shoulders, their eyes met.

"Heroes can be reluctant, and powerless, and humble, and many more things, Annie," Ned continued. "Anyway, all the Greek leaders were summoned to fight at Troy to get Helen back. But Odysseus had a new baby and didn't want to go. So when Agamemnon—the big-boss Greek king—turned up to recruit him, Odysseus pretended to be crazy and plowed up the beach."

"Why is that crazy?" Annie asked.

"Well, you don't 'plow' a beach, Annie—it's made of sand." Ned rolled her eyes. "But Agamemnon knew Odysseus wasn't mad, so he put the baby in front of the plow. Of course, Odysseus stopped plowing—he wasn't going to kill his own son. So off he went to war. For ten years! Actually, twenty, because it took him ages to get back to Ithaca. During that period, his wife Penelope patiently waited for him, but he took his time, and he had affairs on the way."

Ruby stiffened.

"He had affairs?" Annie repeated.

"Penelope was having a miserable time keeping away local princes, and they all moved in, drinking the wine and eating all the food. And since Odysseus didn't immediately return, they presumed him dead. They each wanted to marry Penelope, you see, and take the kingship for themselves. Her son was growing up, too, but he'd gone off to look for Odysseus, and hadn't returned."

"So what did Penelope do—how did she keep them away?" Annie gasped.

"She told them she was sewing a waistcoat for her husband—"

"Sewing a *waistcoat*?" Ruby blurted out, in spite of herself.

"Yes . . . it sounds weird, but that's how things were. The women did a lot of sewing."

"My mother doesn't sew," Ruby said bluntly.

"I'm *sure* she doesn't," Ned said with a touch of sarcasm. "But we're not directly comparing Penelope to your mother—or are we?"

Ruby looked at Ned. Her long spindly legs. Her father's blood, her father's brain. Ruby felt sick with her hatred. Even if Ned had defended them from Harley's disgusting talk, even if the other girls liked her. Ruby turned away, but her ears betrayed her by continuing to listen.

". . . every day Penelope waited for her husband to return. She told the local princes that she wouldn't marry anybody until that waistcoat was sewn. Every day she sewed, and every night she undid the work she'd done that day. Finally, Odysseus came home."

"Oh, I'm glad," said Annie.

"Yes, but he was outnumbered, and wary of confronting these men that had taken residence inside his palace. So he disguised himself as an old homeless man, so that no one would recognize him. There's a really sad bit where the dog realizes it's him, after so many years . . . it gets all excited, jumps about, but then collapses and dies." Ned shook her head regretfully. "Anyway, Odysseus gets invited for dinner—sorry, I forgot to say his son Telemachus is there, too. He's returned home and he knows who Odysseus is, but he plays along, saying that he's bringing this homeless man into the palace for dinner. The only other person who has worked out who he is is an old chambermaid."

"Not Penelope?" Annie asked.

"No, not Penelope."

"It's sad about the dog," Imogen burst in unhappily.

"Anyway, at dinner it's someone's idea to challenge the suitors and say that the only person who can win Penelope's hand is the one who can do this big challenge: string Odysseus's old bow and arrow and shoot along a row of axe-heads. It's a big old heavy thing and very difficult to use. So they all have a go but, of course, they're helpless with it."

A low voice came in behind them. "What's this—axe-heads?" Angus was leaning over from behind, his tall figure casting a shadow. "I hear ice creams are on the way. Everything all right, girls?"

"Go away, Angus." Ned smiled up at him, tilting her head right back. "We're discussing new ideas about ancient things. Something you'd know nothing about."

"Ancient things and Greek tragedies are my speciality. Something I know everything about." He nodded at Ned, before smiling diffidently at the three girls, striding over to settle on a spare sunbed beside Ruby. Imogen's eyes were wide as she followed her father's movements.

"Did Penelope watch the men have a go with the axe-heads?" Annie asked hurriedly.

"No, she'd been dismissed back to her room, by her son. Can you believe it? Anyway." Ned sat back. "Odysseus wants to have a go with the bow and arrow, and of course, the suitors laugh at him—an old man, thinking he can do what the young princes can't. But then he does it! He strings the bow, and shoots the arrow through the axe-heads."

Angus turned to Ruby, speaking under Ned's voice. "Have you got yourself another murder mystery to be getting on with, little thing? From the bookshop in the village, perhaps?"

The dark beads of Angus's eyes seemed to gleam at her, and she stuttered to answer. "Oh, not yet. They only sell French books, Mr. Bly." Ruby shook her head gently, saddened to remember her ruined Agatha Christie ending. "I used to get *Asterixes* there . . . but I never understood the French."

"The language hasn't rubbed off on you, little thing," Angus said fondly, just as Ned stopped talking. Ruby turned her head and caught a strange glower from Imogen.

"Imogen's really good at French," Ruby answered Angus carefully, her voice growing louder. "Imogen's much better than me at so many things, since she's older."

Angus tilted his head toward his daughter, who seemed alarmed at the sudden attention.

"You're absolutely right." Angus sat up properly, his body overlarge on the sunbed. "She surpasses me in every way—I can't think why she wants to have anything to do with me."

Imogen cast her eyes away from her father.

"Angus," Ned said sharply, leaning forward to see past Ruby, "can you go away? You're stealing my audience."

"Oh, I do apologize." He leaped up, and with a broad smile moved down the beach to join the other men.

Ned lay back on her towel, pleased. "So then . . . the best bit is,

Odysseus turns his bow and arrow on the suitors—the men at the dinner. He grabs more arrows, and kills them one by one."

"Oh!" Annie cried out.

"Yes! Crash bang wallop, all the suitors are dead! And he's reunited
with Penelope."

"Oh, good!" Annie smiled. Ruby felt a flare of relief, too.

"But not before she tests him. She doesn't trust this man, even after
the homeless disguise has been removed."

"What did they do with all the dead bodies?" Ruby asked sharply,
annoyed that she was listening again, but dimly glad that Ned's story
seemed to no longer bear any relation to her actual parents.

Ned wrinkled her nose at Ruby. "I don't know. Burned them, probably. That's not the point." She gave Ruby a withering look before continuing, "So to test Odysseus, Penelope asks him to bring their marriage
bed into the main hall of the palace, to consummate the marriage."

"That's not a test," Annie said.

"Well, it was, actually." Ned shuffled along her sunbed, tucking her
knees in under the shade of the parasol. "And Odysseus knew it. His answer was . . . 'I cannot bring the bed through, darling Penelope, because
I carved the wood myself, from the olive tree that grows in that room.'
The bed was made from a living olive tree and couldn't be moved. And
because Odysseus knew that, Penelope knew it was him! So they were
reunited." She glanced at Ruby again. "I suppose they did have to go
around appeasing all the suitors' families for murdering them, but
since the citizens were so happy that their king had returned . . ." Ned
shrugged. "It seemed okay."

"That's not what I was asking," Ruby said quietly.

"I like Penelope!" Annie exclaimed.

"The thing is, she was patient. So patient! The Greeks considered her
an amazing and worthy wife of such a hero . . . especially since Odysseus spent so much time with other women, seven of those ten years
with Calypso."

"Who is Calypso?" Annie frowned.

"Odysseus's secret girlfriend." Ned scratched her leg in one long
stroke and looked at Imogen as Ruby blanched. "But at least Penelope

got her husband back. I don't think many of the other heroes' women were quite so lucky after the whole Trojan War fiasco."

Annie nodded importantly, but Ned was cross. "What's wrong with you, Imogen? Why aren't you saying anything? You've lost all your pluck today."

Imogen turned her head stiffly. "Have I?"

"She's fine," Ruby said abruptly.

Ned regarded them both. "If you say so. Well then, tell me what you think of old Penny-lope?"

After a moment Annie volunteered, "Yes, I like her. I like these stories—they take me out of my thoughts."

"Is that all?" Ned tutted. "Should have known I couldn't discuss anything with you lot. You're only children, after all."

She stood abruptly, kicking a wad of sand over the girls' sunbeds.

Harley and Max were walking up from the shore, sinking into the hot sand and shaking off the salty water. Harley sucked at his lip, and Ruby heard a strand of their conversation.

". . . Marriage without a bit on the side is as undesirable as Stilton without a glass of port. Just look at Prince Charles!"

"Indeed." Max nodded joyfully.

"You'll have to come to my club in London, Max, when we're all back."

"Yes, I can't wait."

The waiter approached the girls with three ice creams. Annie watched the tray sail toward them with a squeal of delight. Imogen tucked up her legs and pushed herself into the shade.

15

On the way home Ruby understood from the conversation in the car that the adults were going for drinks in the village. Ned wanted to go too, and Liv would stay behind as the remaining adult.

Once the cars pulled away, Ruby retreated to her parents' bathroom. She washed herself carefully, scraping out the gritty sand underneath her toenails and scrubbing at her elbows. In the mirror she checked carefully for any rashes, worried at seeing something red and raised on her left thigh, and around her waist.

Ruby looked down at her small toes, neat and clean now. She wondered if she should paint them, and paint Imogen's and Annie's too. Her mother had rows of beautiful dark colors. Should she offer? Ruby hesitated. The truth was she didn't want Imogen—indeed, any of them—to look prettier than they already did.

Ruby folded herself up in her father's thick dressing gown, pulling the collar around her and catching the musky mint of his scent. The dressing gown cord followed behind her as she crept down the stairs and outside, dragging as she crossed the paved stones of the terrace barefoot. At the balustrade, Ruby gripped the railing and looked out at the sea. The horizon was a blur of dark blue and black; hardly any boats twinkled back at her this evening, nor did the slim crescent of the moon.

But the little black cat caught sight of her, and darted over, leaping onto the balustrade and pushing his face against her pale hand. She stroked his head, his back, feeling the gentle rhythm of his heart through his chest; she tried to breathe along with it. The cat settled a little away from her, propping up his head on his paws and closing his yellow eyes.

Ruby turned back to the house only when she heard Annie calling her name.

Very late that same night there was a soft knock at her bedroom door. A sleepy Ruby stumbled to switch on her lamp. Her mother never bothered to knock, and nobody else came up here besides Annie, who was asleep. Ruby found herself half-fearful, half-cross as she switched on her lamp.

Imogen was hovering in the doorway. "Please, can I come in?" She dragged a coverlet behind her and clutched a pillow to her chest.

"Imogen?" Ruby whispered. "What's wrong?"

Imogen's eyes were red with tears. "Please just let me in. I'm not safe in my room."

"What's happened?" Ruby asked again, alarm flaring through her chest.

"Imogen!" Annie cried out, suddenly awake. "What's happening?"

Imogen held Ruby's gaze. "Please, can I sleep here? We could share your bed? Or . . ." Her teeth pulled at her swollen lip desperately. ". . . I'll sleep on the floor?"

"Won't your mother check?" Ruby said. "I might get into trouble with mine."

"No," Imogen answered emptily, "she's stopped doing that now the baby is coming. She'll never notice." Her voice caught in her throat as she spoke again. "Please. Please, Ruby."

"You can share my bed, Imogen," Annie said, rubbing at her eyes. "If you sit here, you can smell the jasmine from the creeper outside. It reaches all the way up here from the door of the house."

Imogen let out a sob as she waited in the doorway. "Please be kind, Ruby, please."

As Ruby looked at Imogen, something within her slotted into place. "Of course. Of course." She took the pillow from Imogen, before standing aside and throwing it onto her bed. She was fully awake now.

"Thank you."

Ruby said quickly, "Don't thank me."

"Okay." Imogen hiccuped, touching at her eye with her sleeve. "Top to toe? I've done that before . . . with friends."

"Oh."

"Just please let me stay."

Annie asked, "Imogen, are you all right?"

"They're all horrible, aren't they?" Imogen's face puckered with emotion. "I thought I knew how things are. But here, this is . . . they are all so . . . even my father."

"Your father is kind, isn't he?" Ruby stood at her bed, pulling at the bedclothes. Her voice was tight as she spoke. "And a good friend to my father, I think."

"You think that because he likes you. He doesn't always like me. I always have to concentrate when I'm with him, but you get on well with him," Imogen said bitterly, her voice stronger now. "I suppose you've simply *got* everything—red hair, pink cheeks, blue eyes—haven't you? You could be a doll! Everybody says that at school."

"My eyes are brown. And you're much prettier than me." Ruby turned and caught Imogen's furious, defiant face in the dim light. She felt her own soften as she added, "You've got lovely thick dark hair and dark eyes—"

"I wish I had *no* hair and *no* eyes—then nobody could look at me, and I'd see nothing!" Imogen's voice grew hysterical. "But it's too late for that! I—"

Ruby had an urge to grasp Imogen, to hug her to stop her from speaking—but Imogen's thunderous face prevented her. Annie was standing now, and placed a gentle hand on Imogen's arm. "Tell us what's wrong?" she asked.

With a warning glare at Ruby, Imogen turned to Annie. "Nothing, don't worry. It's really nothing."

"Only if you're sure." Annie's hand slipped from Imogen's arm.

"I'm fine. Better to go to sleep."

Annie moved back to sit on her bed, tucking her feet under the covers. "I loved that beach place we went to today; it was such a treat." Her voice bubbled gladly. "And that story about Penelope? I can't stop thinking about it."

"Who?" Imogen asked blankly. She gave Ruby's newly prepared bed a queer, dead look as she lifted the bedclothes.

"Penelope."

"I'm so sorry, Annie, I am very tired. Would it be okay"—Imogen took a heroic breath—"if we went straight to sleep?"

"Do you want me to brush your hair first?"

"No, no. Thank you," Imogen managed as she fell flat, pushing her face into her pillow.

Ruby switched off the lamp and found her way to her side of the bed. She lay in the darkness, careful to stay on her half, careful not to touch Imogen.

THE NEXT MORNING IMOGEN'S JITTERY nervousness woke Ruby, who opened her eyes blearily until her confusion settled. A faint dart of light came through the shutter, so she could tell it was still early. Ruby sat up and saw that Imogen had dressed herself badly in some of Ruby's clothes, and was tugging at the bedclothes.

"Oh no, you're awake." Imogen gestured over to Annie. "Don't say anything. Don't say anything, please."

Her face was riddled with shame. Ruby saw a bloodstain on the sheet, brown tinged with red.

"Sorry, sorry," Imogen fussed as she climbed over the bed to pull the sheet up from the farthest corners. "I know it's disgusting."

"It's not, really," Ruby said thickly, moving over to help. "Poor you, Imogen."

"And in your bed too!" Imogen almost shrieked. "You were so kind to let me sleep here!"

"Hardly. And it's not disgusting, Imogen, I've got it too, now. I know what it's like."

Imogen stopped to look at Ruby as she got out of the bed. "You've got your period, too?"

"Yes."

"No"—Imogen seemed to be looking through Ruby, her face tense and bitter as she seethed—"you *don't* know what it's like. *He said* I was disgusting. So don't *you* say I'm not. Don't you say *anything*!" She pulled hard at the sheet, finally tearing it away from the bed, from Ruby's grasp, and rolling it into a bundle.

Ruby's eyes grew wide. "But Lisette—she'll have to know to wash the—"

"Besides her, then," Imogen muttered, glancing around her, "no one else. And don't wake Annie."

"Let's leave the sheet in the bathroom, for Lisette. We won't take it down ourselves, in case anyone sees. Did you sleep all right?"

"No." Imogen's face darkened. "There were strange noises in the night, coming from upstairs, from the attics. I can't believe you didn't hear it."

"No," Ruby said, her need for Imogen to be all right trumped any other emotion. "I expect I'm used to it. It's an old house."

"I think this place is horrible."

"Listen," Ruby said carefully as she leaned forward, "I could tell my mother about what's upsetting you. Or *your* mother. Imogen, really! Mr. Fuller is—"

"No." Imogen dropped the bundle to the floor and grabbed Ruby's arms to hush her, casting an urgent glance toward Annie. "No, no, it's my fault. I must have done something."

"You haven't." Ruby was astonished. "How can you think that?"

"Please be quiet!"

Annie's little voice penetrated their bubble of shared horror. "What's happening, Ruby? Imogen? Are you playing a game?" She lifted her sleepy head from her pillow and pushed her bedclothes aside. "What time is it?"

Imogen hesitated, silently pleading with Ruby before whirling around. "It's very early; sorry, Annie. We were just changing the bed around—it's not a game, no. We're sorry to have woken you."

Annie smiled at them, still sleepy and confused. Ruby added persuasively, "Yes, it's very early."

"What fun having us all in the same room," Annie said serenely, closing her eyes and stretching her arms out long. "Is it too early for a swim, do you think?"

16

Ruby took charge that day by navigating the girls around the adults.

Thankfully, all four men were ensconced in a televised sporting event that occupied them through the afternoon. The sea grew rocky as the sun dipped in the sky, and the pine trees swayed heavily above them on the terrace, so the three girls had little choice but to go to the pool.

Annie was determined to see whether she and Ruby could swim an underwater length in one breath, or at least to see how far they could reach. Imogen insisted on umpiring. Ruby agreed wholeheartedly, still anxious over Imogen's hard expression, and over the extra layers of clothes she refused to remove, even in the dense heat.

Annie swam the farthest. Surprising, Ruby thought, considering her thin frame, but she put it down to her own distracted weariness. She suggested best of three.

Ruby's head bobbed up from the water, blowing the air through her nose as the bubbles sloshed around her; she rubbed her eyes to see Annie ahead of her again. At the far end of the pool she saw Imogen's laughing face, and Ruby felt a bloom of gladness.

After a quarter of an hour Annie pulled herself out of the pool for a game that would include Imogen. She suggested making a sort of camp with the deck chairs, beyond the pool house. Ruby asked that they stay away from the patch of land farther along, hoping that Annie wouldn't ask why. They got to work, and Ruby felt grateful for Annie's suggestion and the command of the girls' imagination. Ruby collected some fallen branches and a strange, gnarled bit of broken vine. Annie was overjoyed at those, and Ruby got a queer sort of satisfaction out of cracking the sticks and crafting them to a purpose, even though they kept catching the fabric of her swimsuit. Imogen, in her sundress and cardigan, volunteered to do the dirtier bits, but they all had messy knees by the time the sun glowed low in the sky.

Annie had just found some pinkish wildflowers to decorate their camp when a new pair of voices arrived.

"Girls, what are you doing?" It was Polly and Rhoda, swinging their baskets and ready for a late afternoon sunbathe and swim. Ruby stiffened at the sight of them, as did Imogen, though for a different reason.

"We are building a camp," Annie said triumphantly; Imogen managed a small smile for her mother.

"A camp?" Rhoda pulled a dark face. "Not very ladylike. You're hardly squirrels. Polly?"

"Oh, let them"—Polly shrugged, still sleepy from her siesta—"use up some of that wonderful energy they have."

"Perhaps." Rhoda scowled as she threw her basket into a lounger. "But look at their shins."

"I only want a quick dip to cool down. Leave them to it, and pretend we haven't seen them," Polly finished, just as Imogen's face dropped.

Annie chirped up again. "Did you know there are two types of creeper along the wall here—Virginia creeper and passionflower? It looks all the same, but here over the pool house, it's mixed together. And—is that clematis?"

Rhoda squinted at Annie. "Yes, it is. Aren't you sweet?"

Ruby glanced at her mother, anxious at her meaning.

"There are so many flowers here that I've never seen before," Annie tittered on. "I wish there was a book on it."

"There might be one," Ruby offered. "There's a small library in the living room, and a large bookshelf in my father's study; you should look."

"I wouldn't dare go through your bookshelves, Ruby," Annie said softly. "But it's all right; I can make do. I've recognized some of the herbs—there's sage, and rosemary. You can smell the thyme from here—it's all around the back terraces."

Imogen chimed in, "How lovely. Where did you learn all of this, Annie?"

"My aunt showed me when I was little. She's the one who had me join the local Girl Guides chapter, and now I have more badges than the other girls." Annie's cheeks shone pink and her eyes narrowed. "But I shouldn't brag; I'm sorry."

"Good afternoon, lovely ladies!" Max called out, interrupting their chatter.

Ruby's voice lowered as she spoke to the other girls. "Let's go. Let's go back to the house."

"Really?" Annie frowned. "Let me just—"

In the next moment Max was behind them, hanging over his daughter to better see. "Hello, girls, what are we up to?"

"Nothing Mr. Fuller," Ruby said forcefully, trying to bore holes in his head with her eyes.

"No smiles for me this afternoon, girls?" He looked around cheerfully. Ruby took a tiny step toward Imogen, who seemed struck dumb with fear. Ruby saw dark but merry circles under his round eyes—and beyond him, her mother watching. She lifted her voice, "Sorry, Mr. Fuller. We're going back to the house now."

"No you're not. Come on, Annie, come and have a swim. You all look terribly hot, and dirty. Come on, girls." He tried a laugh, and Ruby could smell the huff of alcohol on his breath.

"Oh, do we?" Annie dropped what she was holding and looked at her father uncertainly. "Only if we can play a game in the pool, Daddy. I am rather hot."

"Yes, darling," Max said impatiently, "come along. Imogen?"

"I'm not supposed to be swimming . . ." Imogen said automatically, biting her lip furiously as he stood over her. "Mr. Fuller."

He tapped Annie's shoulder, urging her forward, before pushing past Ruby to take Imogen's arm. They seemed to step toward the pool as one.

"You are playful, Max," Rhoda said pointedly as she shifted her lounger away from the pool and toward the sun. "I can't think what's come over this house since you've been here," she added cattily as she shifted Polly's lounger in the same manner. "Such exuberance, you lot. I can't keep up with you."

"Ah, yes, quite right. Come on, girls," Max said, with a quick laugh. "We're going for a swim. I think we all need it. Imogen?"

"I am not supposed to be swimming," Imogen repeated faintly.

"Why ever not, darling?" Polly asked, tilting her head toward her daughter as she settled on her bed. She raised her arm to shield her eyes from the sun. "Take off that cardigan, you must be boiling, Immy."

Imogen looked at her mother, then back at Max, her face immutable but her eyes weighed with a terror that Ruby recognized. Polly lay back on her lounger with a hand on her belly. Rhoda settled beside her, their backs to the girls.

"She must swim," Max insisted.

"She won't," Ruby said.

"Yes, she will," Max muttered. He stepped forward to pull at Imogen's clothes. "Do as your mother says. Take this off. And this."

With a quick movement he removed her cardigan from her flailing arms. He raised the skirt of her dress and pulled at it, trying to tug it up over her waist. It was no easy task, and Max tutted in frustration as the fabric pulled and stretched over her face, her body tight and stiff. He left her dress uprooted, and pulled at her knickers instead. Imogen resisted sharply now, and her small hands found his as she pushed him away. Max insisted, "You can swim in these!"

Ruby darted toward the two of them. "No, she can't. She's not supposed to swim!"

Max's arms were a cage around Imogen's body as he tried to free her from her clothes. Her dress lowered for a moment, and Ruby saw Imogen's miserable eyes, her mouth bolted shut. Ruby felt a confused Annie take a step back behind her. Max held Imogen as if she were his, and their twisted tableau at the edge of the pool lit a flame of fury in Ruby's chest, in her throat.

"Mrs. Bly," Ruby shouted. "Mrs. Bly!"

Polly made to sit up and turn back, but her round tummy inhibited her. She squinted and raised her arm again. "What is it? What's the matter?" She tried to launch herself to the side and gave a dismayed laugh. She leaned over to nudge her friend, saying, "Rhoda, I can't see, the sun is *so* bright. Are the girls all right?"

Rhoda swiveled her head without raising it, and peered through her sunglasses, answering, "Yes, yes, to be sure."

"Immy, my Imogen," Max said feverishly. He gripped Imogen around the waist, lifted her up with a great shout, and jumped into the water. With a short shriek Imogen clawed at him to be free, pulling at his arms in the air. But Max did not relent, and held on to her as they fell in together. The splash was wild and loud, and Ruby watched them as if in slow motion. The conjoined pair seemed to sink and settle at the bottom as bubbles lifted gently to the surface.

Annie cried out, confused and horrified. Ruby simply stared at the dark fuzzy blot rising through the water. Imogen burst through the surface, alone and spluttering. Max rose soon after, a short distance away, with a wide and triumphant grin. Imogen spat out the water from her mouth, sobbing hysterically, her black hair slicked all around her face as her dress floated up around her like the wings of a damp moth, Max behind her, composed, a mocking look of hurt on his face.

"Immy! Is that you?" Polly cried out, an anxious tremor in her voice as she sat up.

Imogen threw her arms out in front of her in an effort to swim to the poolside, away from Max, her mother, or anyone else. She clung to the stone, gasping for breath, before trying to lift herself out, weighed down by distress and her wet dress. Ruby rushed to help, giving Imogen her arms to pull her over the edge. She looked around for a towel, for help from Annie. Ruby didn't know what Max would do next, whether he might swim over, reach out, and pull both of them in. The two girls grappled with each other until Ruby finally lifted Imogen out of the pool, her sobs filling the air.

"Immy, I'll get you a towel. Calm down. What's happened—did you fall in?" Polly moved jerkily to pick up a damp and discarded towel. Ruby ducked out of the way as Polly pushed her daughter into the towel, trying to keep her upright, her bump getting in the way of any embrace. Annie swayed uselessly behind them.

Imogen pulled the towel tight around her body, sobbing, sniffing and spluttering out dribbles of water. Polly put her hands around Imogen's face, but she shook them away. "Imogen? Settle down now."

Max waded through the water, moving toward the steps. He laughed, "Be a sport, Immy!"

Rhoda turned back from her sun lounger with a cross face. "Really, Imogen, there's no need to make such a fuss. Stop that crying—you've got your mother now."

"Imogen?" Annie attempted agonizingly, and Ruby touched her arm to hold her back.

"She didn't fall in?" Polly asked.

"It was a game," came Max's smooth reply, as Ruby shot him a dark look. "All in good fun."

Polly's face changed as she looked from her daughter to Max. Her dark eyes seemed to hollow out, and Ruby could see that she was thinking fast. Finally, she said, "I'll take Imogen back to the house."

"Really, Pol?" Rhoda said, frowning. "But you wanted a dip. Just put her on a lounger, let her dry out and settle down."

"I'll come right back, Rho." She patted Imogen's shoulder at the same time as she patted her round tummy, and they stood up together. Rhoda huffed and lay back on her lounger, pulling out a magazine from her basket.

Ruby followed Imogen and Polly as they hobbled toward the house. Annie did the same.

"Annie, stay here, please," Max demanded from the pool steps, and she drew herself back to her father. But Max was grabbing a towel and marching toward the house.

Imogen's sobbing was steady now; it was the only noise that Ruby could hear, and she felt it echoing in her chest. Near the house, Imogen slipped on the terrace and fell into her mother's side, but Polly was so slim and unsteady on her feet that she could barely support her. Ruby dashed forward to help. By the time they reached the main steps, Imogen was making such a sorry racket that Angus and Toby appeared at the door.

Angus's voice was urgent as he strode down the steps. "What's happened, Pol? What's wrong with Imogen? Why is her dress wet through?"

"I can't tell," Polly said between Imogen's sobs. Angus went to his family and gripped Imogen's shoulders with his heavy hands. This seemed to make her sob even more; she pushed out of his grasp and leaned her head into her mother's neck. Ruby stepped away from the three of them.

"What's happened?" Angus demanded again, his face rippled with anxiety. He looked at Ruby for a moment, then back to his daughter.

Ruby felt as if she'd trespassed into an adult conversation, her damp hair now dry and matted, her legs full of scratches and her knees dirty. Behind her, Max's horribly calm voice chimed in. "There, there, little Imogen. It was nothing, Angus. We were playing in the pool."

"*Who* was playing in the pool?"

"Imogen and I. And Annie," Max answered evenly.

"She's fully clothed, man!" Angus glared at Max.

Polly shook her head. "The girls *were* playing, Angus. I saw it."

"Was it playing? Imogen?" Angus demanded.

Imogen was still sobbing, so Polly said, "Can you take her? I can't—"

Angus stepped forward to receive his daughter, but she fell between Polly and him. He seemed to be rippling with rage. "Will someone explain what has happened here!"

"Angus," Toby interjected from the top of the steps, "calm down—look, it must just be a misunderstanding . . ."

"Can't you see how upset she is?" Angus almost roared at his friend, his face fierce as he tried to take Imogen in his arms. "That's not a bloody 'misunderstanding'!" In the next moment he turned to Ruby, his thick eyebrows knotted together, and asked, "Ruby. Was it playing?"

Ruby felt herself light up at the fury in his face. She looked straight at him, before answering firmly, "No. It wasn't playing."

Almost immediately Max's voice lifted fretfully, "Now hold on—you're not going to believe the word of a child over mine, are you?"

Angus closed his dark eyes for a moment as if to calm himself. He pushed his daughter back into the arms of his wife, and addressed Max. "I think it's time you made your way home, Max, don't you?"

"I don't think that's your decision, Angus," Max said carefully, not without a note of panic.

Angus jerked his head at Toby at the top of the steps. "Tobes?"

Ruby saw her father glance hesitantly from Angus to Max.

Just then, Harley appeared, his reading glasses perched on the end of his nose as he stepped up beside Toby to survey the scene. He seemed to draw the attention of everyone; his voice was falsely soft as he said, "Dearie me. What have we here?"

"I'd like Max to leave," Angus answered brutally.

"Ah, typical Angus, bossing us about." Harley smiled. "Not your house, is it, Angus? Not your say."

Angus's flaming eyes sought out his friend. "Toby?" he said again.

"Be a sport, old boy." Harley went to slap Toby heavily on the shoulder, which jolted him slightly forward. "We do love Max here. I'd let him stay, if I were you."

Ruby concentrated on her father, whose boyish face and twisted mouth seemed at great odds with each other. She wanted to block out Harley's slap and heavy comment and whatever control he thought he had. Polly was almost falling over her desolate daughter; Angus was stiff and furious, ready to pounce on Max.

"I am inclined to agree with Angus," Toby finally said. "It is time for you to go, Max. I think we've bitten off more than we can chew this summer, what with the orchestra trip, and rather too many guests. And as I've said, things might heat up with the police at any moment. It's been a jolly time, but . . ."

"When?" asked Max, his voice brittle and his face incredulous.

"Tomorrow, Monday, I think," Toby answered quietly.

Max turned away with a scoff. Harley raised his eyebrows, muttered a snort of surprise, and went back inside the house.

"I can help you make the arrangements, if necessary," Toby finished.

The gathered group broke up quickly. Toby tripped down the steps to join Angus as a two-man barrier between Max and Imogen, while Polly and the girls moved around them. Imogen was shivering despite the towel her mother had pulled around her. Ruby took one of her arms and Polly the other as they mounted the steps.

Inside, they hobbled along the hallway, hearing the buzz of the cricket scores coming through the television.

"Can we take her to my room, Mrs. Bly?" Ruby asked once they'd reached the first floor. "She slept there last night."

Polly nodded silently, struggling with the weight and awkwardness of her daughter.

Imogen didn't seem to mind either of them undoing her from her wet things, before setting her on Ruby's bed. Ruby dropped the towel on the floor and handed Imogen a fresh one from her bathroom to wrap up her wet hair, while Polly dealt with Imogen's underwear. With a hum of surprise, Polly found the sanitary towel in her knickers, now swollen with water, and lined with streaks of blood. Ruby wondered about draping Imogen's wet things on the balcony to dry, but thought better of it, and squeezed them into the bath instead, before placing them carefully over the chair of her dressing table. Polly went to fetch Imogen a clean set of underwear, asking Ruby if she had a spare sanitary towel.

Once Imogen was clothed again, Polly turned to her daughter. "What can I get you now, darling Immy? A Nutella sandwich, perhaps, or a cold glass of water?"

Imogen didn't answer. When Polly left, Ruby was relieved.

"Don't leave me alone." Imogen was whispering so quietly that Ruby bent to listen. "Please, Ruby. Don't leave me alone."

Ruby nodded, and sat on the bed, looking out at the balcony, and the strip of sea beyond. Imogen was saying something else, and Ruby turned to hear properly.

"I hate him. I hate him."

For the first time, Ruby felt truly frightened. She went to the long windows and pulled the shutters closed. In the darkness, she tiptoed to the edge of the bed, before lying down alongside Imogen, breathing carefully, trying to block out the mess of worries in her head.

JUST BEFORE DINNER, ANNIE STEPPED into the bedroom, hesitating when she saw the two girls drenched in darkness.

Imogen raised her head from the pillow. Ruby sat up too, and her brain seemed to thump with the sudden movement.

"I'm quite sad," Annie said, her eyes adjusting to locate the other two girls. She put her hands out in front of her gingerly. "I think I'm leaving tomorrow. Are you all right, Imogen?"

Imogen's eyes filled with tears. "Yes."

Annie took a breath and said carefully, "Am I leaving because of what my father did at the pool?"

Imogen let out a small gasp, and Ruby quickly answered, "Maybe you don't have to leave. Maybe you can stay, Annie, and your father can go?"

"Oh," Annie said gravely as she moved over to her bed in the darkness. "No, he would never allow that. He is in a terrible mood. I can't wait to get away from him and back to my mum."

There was a pause before a quick knock startled all three of them. Ned came in with a push of the door. "Hello, ladies. I gather my little story elf is leaving tomorrow."

"Yes," Annie said quietly. "I believe I am."

"And apparently Imogen is particularly upset about it? I seem to have missed a lot this afternoon." Ned's voice sounded too loud in the quiet darkness. "Do you want another Trojan War story before you go?"

"Yes," Annie said quickly, glad to be distracted. Ruby felt a dim sense of gratitude, despite the constant irritation she felt toward Ned.

"It's about Iphigenia, and how badly she was treated," Ned continued as she moved into the room. The door closed behind her and the darkness reigned again. She kicked something, trying to find somewhere to sit.

"Badly treated?" asked Annie. "Did she get revenge, then, like the others?"

"No," Ned answered seriously. "Sadly, the other way round. Can we open the shutters? I can't see a thing."

"Oh." Annie's face folded with confusion. "Is she a wife?"

"No, she's a daughter."

Ruby stiffened. "Whose daughter? I thought you were telling us about the wives?"

Ned shrugged as she passed her hands over the walls. "No, I'm just telling you the stories I know . . . We've been talking about the men of the Trojan War, and the women that suffered because of them. Wives *and* daughters."

Ned had found the dressing table chair, and sat down. "So, before the Trojan War, the Greek ships needed good winds and waters to get to Troy. They say there were a thousand ships sailing from Greece to Troy. To be victorious on their quest, to have good fortune, they needed to please the gods. Do you know about that sort of thing?"

"Yes," Annie said excitedly. "Sacrifices and things. Goats, or sheep, is that right? Saying prayers, holding festivals even . . . to make the gods happy, and bring good luck."

"Sacrifices, yes!" Ned almost yelped. "So, Agamemnon, the king of the Greeks, thought to sacrifice a pure animal. A virgin animal—and the best virgin animal? A virgin girl. Better than a virgin girl? A virgin *princess*. But where to find one of those?" Ned let out a hollow laugh that seemed to linger horribly in the darkness. "He chose one of his own daughters, Iphigenia."

"What?" Annie gasped. "*His* daughter?"

"Yes, he tricked her. Iphigenia thought she was getting married, so off she went to her wedding—can you imagine?" Ned laughed again, and Ruby winced. "And then, he sacrificed her."

"She died?" Annie demanded.

"Yes, on the altar—he slit her throat." Ned nodded. "Isn't that awful?"

Ruby was suddenly cross. "Why are you telling us this now?"

"It just came to me, I don't know." Ned shrugged. "Hang on, it's all right, Iphigenia's mother avenges her later—"

But Ruby interrupted, "This is a horrible story. She was killed by her father—just so that he could have a decent journey and good fortune for his army in the war?"

"Yes, he *sacrificed* her."

"But," Imogen said, her voice dry and stilted, "didn't you say that Mr. Montgomery was Agamemnon? He doesn't have a daughter."

A sharp click of the door produced a shaft of light and Rhoda's auburn head. The soft glow of the beam lit up the four young faces that turned to her.

"What are you all doing in here? And why is it so dark?" Rhoda's eyes flashed at Ned. "It'll be dinnertime soon. Ruby, you must practice your flute. And early to bed for all three of you, I think." She hesitated. "You'll be getting up early tomorrow, I imagine, since you'll be saying goodbye to Annie and Mr. Fuller."

Imogen's face stayed fixed to the ceiling, and Annie cast her eyes away regretfully. Ruby dared to ask her mother, "Must we go down for dinner?"

"Of course you must!" Rhoda was appalled.

"Imogen isn't well," Ruby persisted.

"That's not for you to say, girl." Rhoda shook her head. "Her mother can decide whether she comes down for dinner or not. Honestly, does no one respect Polly or myself!"

"Well, if Imogen has to go down," Ruby somehow carried on, "then can she and Annie and I all sit together, at the end of the table? Please?"

Rhoda tilted her head at her daughter. "Well, since it's Annie's last night, then I suppose that's all right."

Ned said cheerfully, "I'll monitor them at dinner, then, as the almost-adult, Mrs. Ashby. We'll have fun."

Rhoda's mouth twisted as Ned stood up confidently, then strode toward Rhoda and past her out of the room. Rhoda waited a moment, before giving Ruby a firm look and closing the door. The three girls were left in darkness.

17

2010

Mrs. Cosgrove woke to the blazing sunlight across her face. The breakfast terrace had been cleared, and she was the only remaining guest by the hotel pool.

She could feel the burn across her cheeks as her thoughts hurried together. Today, this afternoon, she would go to the château.

Mrs. Cosgrove collected her things. She left the pool courtyard and moved through the lobby, tightly grasping the belt of her damp dressing gown.

The same two Englishmen she'd spotted on the breakfast terrace stood near the reception, listening to a third man in an official-looking uniform. She passed them with enforced courage, keeping her face blank.

There was a flash of color as the middle-aged man moved his arm, revealing a brochure in his hand. It drew Mrs. Cosgrove's eye, and she knew what it was before her mind could make sense of it: the booklet was thick and dense and filled with colorful photographs of the château, its blue sea and white rocks. She held her breath as she glided by.

The man who held the attention of the Englishmen spoke in gentle and labored French. His voice paused, and he spoke more loudly as she reached the stairs.

"Mademoiselle?"

She whirled back obediently. Her hair was wrapped up, her figure bulky in the towel and dressing gown—only her clean and unmarked face peeped out. The official-looking man's eyes were filled with curiosity, but Mrs. Cosgrove turned and continued up the stairs. She'd thought he would accuse her with the Ashby name—just like that villager had yesterday—but he hadn't. She was glad—there was no "Mademoiselle Ashby" here.

But there had been a strange note of torture, of anguish on one Englishman's face as he'd checked hers. Fear thudded through Mrs. Cosgrove's chest as she fished out the key from her dressing gown pocket and considered the man: his height, his thick curly hair, his broad shoulders, his heavy leaning on a cane despite his middle age. He was less than a decade older than her. She did know him, and he knew her. The shape of him was so similar to the shape of one of those hideous, powerful men that summer—but the face wasn't.

She found her hotel room newly tidy and ordered—the ashtray emptied, the glass shards cleared away, the drops of blood on the bathroom floor wiped clean; even her hangover seemed to have knocked itself out. Robert's message, now folded up and put aside on the desk, also seemed not to matter anymore. What was vital was here, and now. This man downstairs, and that house.

An hour later, Mrs. Cosgrove chose the beige linen suit. She had brought it for this purpose, and felt its significance as she did up the buttons. Her sunburned face peeked through her foundation, and gave her a surprisingly renewed glow. Her hair wasn't fully dry, but she knew the outside air would finish the job, and she didn't want to risk the hotel hair dryer. She circled her eyes with dark eyeliner—anything to distract from those emerging eye wrinkles, or the tears that would inevitably come when she beheld that glorious horror of a château, that place of murder.

Lastly, she sprayed perfume on her wrists and across her neck.

The Iliad seemed to wink at her from the bathroom floor. She nudged

it away with her foot, farther under the crook of the toilet. She wondered why the cleaning lady hadn't picked it up.

Downstairs, the estate agent was waiting for her, a young, eager
man who sipped at an espresso as he leaned against one of the leather
armchairs in the lobby. He jumped up when he saw her.

"Madame Cosgrove, I think it is you?"

"Yes, Monsieur Berne," she heard herself say, "I am pleased to meet
you."

"Non, non, c'est moi."

"Merci, monsieur."

The estate agent's face rippled with merriment. "Please call me Jean-
Pierre. I am enchanted to meet you and show you the Château des
Sètes. It is the most beautiful house in the region."

"Yes, of course," she answered nervously.

In the small, hot car, she held herself upright as the man chattered
away. The town passed quickly, the houses folding into the dry yellow-
green countryside along the bay. She sat on her hands, breathing slowly
as if to soothe the tremor of her heart. The estate agent had placed the
brochure on her lap, and she gazed at it.

"I must tell you, madame, that there is another interested buyer."

"I see," she answered steadily.

"Yes"—the estate agent swung his face to hers—"he claims he has a
connection to the Ashbys. But you say you do not?"

"No, monsieur."

"The Ashbys were a celebrated family here once, but they are not so
now. It is a complicated history; you understand how these things are."
He tilted his head from side to side. "And it is not often that tourists
come to this corner of Provence."

"I do not know the Ashbys," Mrs. Cosgrove repeated.

He checked the road, but looked back again to study her face for a
moment. "Of course. Forgive me." He put both hands on the steering
wheel. "Now, I myself have always favored pretty women, and I feel
sure that you will make your offer first . . . Or at least that we shall find
your offer more favorable!"

Mrs. Cosgrove turned her agitated face away—away from his dry

French charm, from the short blue glimpses of the sea, and toward the rambling walls and dry undergrowth crossing her window.

A long moment later, the car slowed and Mrs. Cosgrove's heart stuttered along with the engine. "We are here," the estate agent said. "I must open the gates. You will excuse me a moment."

Mrs. Cosgrove finally looked up.

The gates were tall, rusted, and bolted shut. In her memory, they had always stood open, but today they were clenched together by a heavy chain, which the estate agent now unpicked with his keys.

Beyond the gates was the long vault of trees that stretched toward the château. And farther on was the roof of the house—innocent, insolent, waiting for her approval. Waiting for the final renewal of her trauma.

18

1985

The following day was Ruby's birthday, and never had she felt so reluctant to celebrate. There was a clutch of small presents scattered on the breakfast table—foreign objects dappled with sunshine that Ruby was expected to open with joy and surprise—but she wasn't sure she could summon such a performance this morning. She'd watched Annie pack her bag slowly, sadly, piling her things on the metal bed, and felt torn between anguish and fury. Ruby had given Annie more clothes than she needed, and lent her a suitcase for the journey home. She imagined her at the airport, with her father, that monster, who might again abandon this small shaking thing with another tricksy moment.

Lisette had prepared a fresh bunch of yellow flowers with greenish foliage that sprung out joyfully from the table. Ruby glared at their naïve innocence before turning to her mother. "Can't Annie stay?"

"Stay?" Rhoda repeated loudly as the others moved around them, busy with breakfast things.

Imogen glanced urgently at Ruby, who added quickly, "Not both of them, Mother—just Annie?"

"I don't think so, darling. You can't very well separate father and daughter. It's time for them to go."

"But she's happy here," Ruby pleaded.

"Don't make things unpleasant, please, especially on your birthday," Rhoda said warningly. "You understand nothing, Ruby—you're a child."

Ruby leaned closer to her mother and muttered fiercely, "He's a monster. Please, Mother, Annie isn't safe with him!"

Rhoda raised her arm to brush Ruby away. "My goodness, you're so theatrical. Will you be quiet? They *must* leave."

But Annie had overheard; her serene face was awash with hurt as she stood by her usual seat.

"Annie, dear," Polly intervened, her voice soft, "you've been utterly lovely to have, and I hope the other two have treated you well—don't let them worry you with their vivid imaginations," she said, waving her hand at Imogen and Ruby. "It's a shame to have you go, but that's the way things are."

Desperate, Ruby tried another tactic. "Don't *you* want to stay, Annie?"

Annie looked over the table, at the pile of presents, the beautiful fresh bouquet. "No. I can't stay if my father has ruined it."

Max soon appeared with a brief smile for everyone but Imogen, whom he treated as if she weren't there. The men filed around him, resuming their slapping and patting of shoulders.

Shortly after, a cool black taxi arrived and rolled right up to the terrace, just like the police car had done. Max and Annie handed their things over to the driver silently, Annie giving a peaky look to Ruby and Imogen and a wan smile to Ned as she got in the car. Max took a little longer, but after a reassuring bow from Toby and a hefty hug from Harley, he slid into the front passenger seat and the car pulled away.

At the table, Ruby sat uncertainly as everybody watched her munching through breakfast. She lifted a present off the top of the pile, and her mother screeched, "Wait, Ruby, not everyone is here. Where is Ned? She must see this."

Georgina murmured, "I think she went back to bed, Rhoda; she was in her pajamas."

"Oh?" Rhoda raised her eyebrows disapprovingly. "Well, then."

"Come on, Rhoda," Harley sneered as his tummy thrust forward, "it is terribly funny how you've assembled us all here. Rather formal for a child's birthday."

Ruby lowered her face with embarrassment.

"Open your presents, Ruby," Rhoda said forcefully, "and you, Harley, eat your toast and be quiet. You're just sulking because your plaything has gone."

"I'll only be quiet if you crack open some champagne so that we can have mimosas." Harley lifted his glass of orange juice cheerfully.

In response, Ruby hurriedly tore at the wrapping paper, regarding each present blindly and forcing a smile onto her face. Her parents had given her a red leather vanity case and a shining green gem necklace. Ruby thanked them, glad that the eyes around the table were starting to rove away from her, uninterested. Harley had no gift, but bluffed through in his usual way:

"Well, I haven't got her a present, Tobes, but I suppose paying for her last three years of school releases me from any obligation! Angus too, perhaps, for all those previous years."

Ruby looked up, thoroughly confused.

Toby countered, "Harley, not here, not now."

"No, not the done thing," Harley jeered. "Well, Ruby, I promise you a first-rate ice cream with all the trimmings in the village. How old are you now?"

Ruby hesitated, looking between Harley and her father, before answering, "I'm twelve."

"Twelve scoops then, with twelve toppings." Harley's face lifted into a hoarse grin. "How's that?"

Ruby couldn't help but check her mother's face; Rhoda shook her head in a tiny movement. Ruby didn't mind—she couldn't think of anything she wanted less than twelve scoops of ice cream, especially from Harley. Toby had acquiesced to Harley's other request and was twisting open a bottle of champagne, which seemed to delight Georgina, who held her glass forward at the pop of the cork.

Ruby opened the gift from the Blys, a red hardcover notebook with a red enamel fountain pen in a small pouch. Polly's face brightened as Ruby turned it over in her hands. "I thought you could record the summer, Ruby, like we used to, Rhoda . . . a summer scrapbook, or journal, since we're all having such a lovely time." Polly smiled invitingly at Imogen, whose miserable eyes turned to Ruby. Ruby blinked, horrified at the thought of recording anything at all from this summer.

Ned's sudden appearance at the table prompted a small cheer from Harley, who sloppily poured her a mimosa in a juice glass. Ned giggled delightedly, and Georgina looked up at her daughter, then across at Ruby.

"Sorry, Ruby, we didn't have time to get you anything," Georgina volunteered vaguely. "I'll treat you to some sweets in the village."

"My turn." Angus nudged a poorly wrapped brown paper present toward Ruby. It was a tatty offering, but his smile was sincere. "This is from me, little thing."

"What do you mean, Angus?" Polly said hotly. "The journal and the pen were from all of us."

Angus answered his wife without turning. "This one is personal."

Ruby tore it open, her fingers quick and excited.

It was a beautiful copy of Agatha Christie's *Death on the Nile*. The cover illustration showed a painted Egyptian mummy's head, with a silver pistol swimming in front of it. Ruby touched the cover with her finger; she was delighted, but confused. "But—how did you get this, Mr. Bly?"

"I ordered it"—Angus creased his eyes into a smile—"from the bookshop in the village. Arrived jolly quick; gave the man a generous tip."

Ruby smiled. "Thank you, Mr. Bly."

"It's my favorite one."

"Yes." Ruby almost laughed. "I know."

Angus threw Harley a glance. "No spoiling the ending this time, old man."

"Couldn't even if I wanted to." Harley topped up his glass with foaming champagne, and it sparkled along with the sea behind. "Don't know that one. Although rather hilarious that *you* would be so fond of books about murders."

Harley's eager eye watched Angus stiffen at the comment, and Toby scoffed unhappily. Ruby concentrated on her book.

"Here they go again." Ned jerked her head toward Harley and Angus, sipping her mimosa. She narrowed her eyes at the cover of Ruby's new book. "There's a film of *Death on the Nile*. It's brilliant, with Mia Farrow. She's in *Rosemary's Baby* too. I've brought that with me—maybe we can watch it today. My birthday present to you, Ruby, a film showing!" Ned chuckled.

"The book is always better than the film," Angus said dismissively. Ned pulled a face at him, which he received with a smirk, before turning to nod at Ruby again.

The sun seemed to burn hotter, touching the top of Ruby's head through the trees' shade. She glanced at Imogen as she finished her breakfast, unable to tell if she minded about the present from Angus. Her solemn mood was etched into her face, in her eyes and around the corners of her mouth, and Ruby felt it deeply. As the bubble of chatter at the table grew—buoyed by the mimosas, no doubt—Ruby's last wish was for Imogen to be happy.

Ruby placed the book at the top of her new pile, and looked up at Angus. He was still smiling at her.

"A mimosa for the little one? Baby's first taste?" Georgina suggested, handing a glass to Ruby, who didn't take it.

"Absolutely not," said Toby with a grin. "Not for another year or two, at least."

Georgina handed the glass instead to Liv, who took it, but let it rest on the table. She moved over to Ruby, saying quietly, "I'm sorry you've nothing substantial from Harley and me. I only recently discovered it was your birthday, so I've got you something very small." She leaned over Ruby's chair, placing a small blue paper bag in front of her. "Happy birthday, Ruby."

"Oh." Ruby was very aware of Liv's flinching presence, so she tore at the paper bag quickly. It was a beautiful leather bookmark, long, dark brown, fringed along the bottom, and embossed with the shape of a woman. Ruby looked at the etched-out figure: she was wearing armor and swirling a flag, her hands holding it upright, her face gazing upward. *"Jeanne d'Arc,"* it said at the top.

Ruby didn't want to like it, but it was interesting, and very smart. She'd been using old postcards as bookmarks, and this would do very well. She could even imagine using it at school next year—it would go nicely with her schoolbag, its leather the same rich brown.

"It's Joan of Arc. She's a saint, in France," Liv explained. "Only a little bit older than you when she heard her calling, to go and fight, to defend the French against the enemy."

Ruby politely thanked Liv, touching the embossed leather with her finger, and smiling in spite of herself.

"What is it?" Imogen asked, and Ruby handed it over for Imogen to see. Ned leaned in, too, to have a look. She said, "Oh yes, Joan of Arc. Died when she was nineteen—burned to death by the English." Ned gave an approving nod to Liv, before standing to light herself a cigarette. Liv gave a small bow and moved away, returning to the house with no breakfast. Ruby was struck anew by her stiff and unemotional manner, so different from the lurching excess of the rest of the adults.

Imogen shrugged and handed back the bookmark. "It's nice." Ruby lifted her new Agatha Christie book off her pile of presents. She pressed the bookmark into the early pages, just inside the cover. She was pleased that the present-giving was over, and pleased to have another murder mystery to read, one that her mother couldn't take away, since it was a gift from someone her father held dear. She looked up again at Angus, who was laughing at something Toby had said across the table, gleaming at him with those beads of dark light in his eyes. Ruby set her knife neatly on her plate, infinitely more cheerful than she'd felt an hour before, and hopeful that the day might continue to improve.

IT WAS AN EXCEPTIONALLY HOT day, and after lunch most of the party went to the village. To her mother's surprise, Ruby hadn't wanted to have a birthday lunch out. She couldn't bear to be the cause of the group streaming through the village, disturbing the locals with their loud voices. A small part of her also worried about seeing that old haggard woman again, with her pained *"Mademoiselle Ashby?"* Instead, Ruby stayed in her room to read, wanting some kind of silence to process Annie's departure, and to consider how to console Imogen in the coming days.

Ned also stayed behind, complaining about the intense heat, that the pool water had grown warm, that even the sea was no longer cool. Just as promised, she put on one of her horror movies and insisted that the two girls join her in the shuttered darkness of the living room to watch *Rosemary's Baby*.

Ned smoked cigarette after cigarette, and the smoke hovered in the air, past the small screen, which held the girls' gaze throughout.

Ruby thought it was an all right sort of film, and felt very sorry for the lady, but the ending was frightening, particularly with the walls caving in. Ruby didn't dare look at the walls around her—even though it was early afternoon in the living room she knew so well—and kept her eyes fixed on the screen.

But just when Rosemary was crying out "What have you done to his eyes!" Ned laughed. It was a hollow, dirty kind of laugh, as if she were thrilled by Rosemary's grief. Imogen didn't seem to move or react, but Ruby felt so bothered that she stood up and drew back toward the door, keeping one eye on the end of the film.

At the beginning of the credits Ruby was still lingering. Ned clicked the machine to rewind the tape and muttered, "I need to write some of this down," before slipping out of the room, ignoring the girls entirely. Once the door closed behind her, Imogen turned to Ruby and spoke so firmly that Ruby realized she'd been preparing her words for some time.

"Ruby, please may I move into your bedroom, into Annie's old bed? Would you mind, dreadfully?"

"Of course." Ruby tried to erase the final images of the film from her mind. "Let's do it now. I'll get some sheets from Lisette. Or she may already have done it. She sorted the other ones jolly quick yesterday."

They left the room by the light of the television, and its gray-white buzz followed them out.

Lisette had been busy cleaning one of the other rooms, now empty of Max. She was happy to hand over the sheets for Ruby to use, even though she insisted in her broken English that it was her job, and that Ruby was very kind to want to do it herself, especially on her birthday.

Ruby noticed a clutch of flattened wildflowers flutter to the floor as she tugged the dirty bedsheets away from the small metal bed. She stared at them for a short moment, before picking them up to place carefully on her dressing table. Imogen hovered around her, collecting the sheets with a heavy face. "I'm sad to see Annie go," she said.

"Me too," Ruby answered, laying out the wildflowers meticulously.

Imogen sighed a little. "I hope she makes it to her mother."

Ruby turned around. "What do you mean?"

"Well, her father . . ." Imogen's eyes widened. "He seemed so horrible toward her mother? And horrible to Annie."

"Horrible overall," Ruby added, frowning. It hadn't occurred to her that Annie might not make it back to her mother. Now, this new, fresh agony nagged at her mind. "I'm sure she'll be all right"—Ruby shook her head—"and we'll all see each other again in September."

Imogen sank onto the bed and suddenly pulled the new bedclothes toward her, clutching at the pillow anxiously. She started to sob in great gasps. Ruby watched, terribly alarmed as Imogen buried her face in the pillow and cried out in a muffled voice, "It's all my fault!"

"It's not," Ruby insisted, too mortified to offer anything else.

"It is. And I can't go back in my bedroom. I won't." Imogen lifted her face with a sob, before pushing her head into the pillow again. "He said I was disgusting. He—he tried to put his hand there."

"Where?" Ruby asked, astonished.

"But his hand was stained with it, with . . ." Her voice shrank to a shrieking whisper. "It was *disgusting*—and he was so angry! But I've never felt so . . . so glad."

"Imogen." Ruby couldn't move. Her chest thundered with shock; she didn't know what to do or say to make it well. "I'm so sorry."

"And then, he had *me* do things. With *my* hands."

"No! Imogen. I'm so—" Ruby stepped backward gingerly and sat on her bed.

Imogen raised her head again, seeing Ruby retreat. "I knew it. You don't understand. Well, I don't want to talk about it, and neither do you. You never do."

"No, it's not that, I—"

"You never do!" Imogen cried out. She turned over. Ruby turned her face away too, seeing again those darkened images from the film. Within a few minutes Imogen's breathing slowed. Ruby lay on her bed, contemplating the ceiling as the heat pounded at the shutters and the crickets scratched out their never-ending song.

RUBY AWOKE WITH A JOLT. The chatter on the terrace was loud and full of hilarity. Imogen's bed was empty, and Ruby felt a sting of betrayal at her absence. She knew she ought to go down immediately so as not to annoy her mother, even though it was still her birthday and she should be able to do as she pleased. Straightening her dress, she checked her reflection, her newly twelve-year-old face. She wondered if it had changed, if she had grown during the night. Was this what it was to grow up, to really see things for what they were, to be left to make sense of it on your own?

She brushed her hair and straightened her fringe before leaving her bedroom. The noisy bustle from outside reverberated through the open hallway and seemed to draw her forward to hold the door open for a very busy Lisette, who held a wide tray laden with drinks.

Lisette gave her a weary smile as she acknowledged her. *"Merci, ma bichette. Bonne anniversaire encore."*

"Merci," Ruby answered politely. She stepped into the syrupy yellow of the early evening, feeling a wave of nausea as the heat hit her. There was a new kind of jazz coming from the record player, fast and complicated as it crashed into Ruby's ears. She frowned; her mother was dishing out a minced curry, and its spices curled sharply in her nose.

"I don't know who put this on," Harley spoke over the music, "but

I'd kill to listen to some opera. Have you any of those sorts of records? I love that *Madame Butterfly*."

"They're in the living room," Rhoda answered distractedly. "Toby's mother's."

"Oh yes," Harley boomed out, "old Nancy Ashby would've loved that woeful soprano, those screaming notes." He turned to eye Ruby keenly. "Oh, here she is, born again. Rubes looks just like her, doesn't she, Tobes, apart from the hair? No doubt she'll grow to be just as mad."

"Mad?" Ruby asked in spite of herself.

"Mad as a hatter." Harley swiveled his head. "I'll take you, Ruby Boobs, to the Royal Opera House when we're back. Late birthday present, and you'll dress up nicely. We'll see one from Puccini's middle years . . . *La Bohème, Tosca*."

"Didn't he die after a car accident?" Ned said darkly.

"Not at all, he died of a sore throat." Harley smirked. "You know how overdramatic those Italians are, just like your grandmother, Ruby. She was unlike anybody I've ever known."

Angus interrupted fiercely, "She was wonderful—she was just eccentric."

"It was more than that and you know it! No doubt infected by some Singaporean insect; she grew progressively worse as she aged. I always felt for poor Grandfather Ashby—Nancy was his very own madwoman in the attic, just like Rochester's wife. Thank God the sons turned out all right." He tapped the side of his head and glanced at Toby.

Confused by the noise of the jazz, the allusions to her grandmother, and the thought of Harley sitting beside her in the Royal Opera House, Ruby rather lost her appetite. She winced as her head throbbed uncomfortably.

Once the dirty plates were scraped and stacked, Polly stood and asked with a bright smile, "Who would like a cocktail? Any requests?"

Harley smiled at Toby and Angus knowingly, and said, "These women do have their skills, don't they, lads?"

When Polly returned with the cocktail orders, Harley moved around the table to top up the wineglasses for dessert. Ruby concentrated on the spot on the table in front of her; people seemed to be hovering about and she wanted desperately to sit still, her headache now worse than ever.

"Darling Immy," Polly said cautiously, "Lisette asked me where to put your clean washing. Apparently you're no longer sleeping in your bedroom?"

"Imogen?" Angus swung around, glancing first at Ruby, and then at his daughter. He asked severely, "Why aren't you sleeping in your room?"

His eyes were narrowed and cross; Imogen's mouth clenched together and she didn't answer.

"Goodness me, what a mystery," said Harley lightly. "I wish she were sleeping in my room."

"It's my fault," Ruby suddenly answered, looking up at Angus. "I missed Annie's company after she left. I asked Imogen to share my room."

"How lovely, Immy!" Polly exclaimed. "A sleepover! Just like Rho and I."

"Yes," Ruby insisted, not turning her face from Angus.

Rhoda stared Ruby down, as if to decipher her real meaning. Ruby gave nothing away, focusing on Angus's glittering eyes, convincing him of her words. Toby mumbled, "You might've let us know what was happening, Ruby darling. I do like to know what's going on in my own house."

Ruby lowered her face quickly. She didn't know how to respond—of all the things going on in his house, how could her father be cross about this one small detail? She closed her eyes, barely listening to Harley relate a story about some noble family called the Ogden-Booths and their lack of money for heating, the holes in their cashmere jumpers, and the rats in their Queen Anne sofas. He called for Liv to back up his story, but she'd returned inside.

Ruby opened her eyes to see Angus shake his head as he tipped the wine bottle into his glass. "The Ogden-Booths are dreadful, Harley. Families like that have dust in their veins. I'll never understand your need to know these people."

"And I'll never understand your refusal to network within your own set, Angus," Harley answered. "Never mind your aversion to lavish parties."

"Yes, you two have become proper old curmudgeons since you got married." Georgina chuckled, with a sly look at Toby.

"This is ugly talk," Rhoda said as she slammed down her cocktail glass.

In the next moment a white box of *patisserie* cakes appeared and was passed around for everyone to take their preferred slice. Even though it was her birthday, Ruby took nothing, and couldn't even look at the white box, now smeared with cream and chocolate and raspberry coulis.

Her favorite pudding had always been at her grandmother's, where the cook served up chocolate mousse in dainty old-fashioned teacups. Ruby missed her grandmother terribly. She had always made a fuss of her birthday. She remembered the glassy sweets Nancy Ashby hid in a drawer, wrapped in foil that Ruby used to untwist delicately with her fingers. She'd liked to treat Ruby to sweet things, and often declared that she was rewarding her for being her granddaughter, and a girl—which was much harder than being a boy, she used to say.

Sometime later there was a shriek across the dining table. Rhoda's chest was drenched, her face smeared; the ends of her hair clung to her face. A laughing, drunken Harley stood opposite her.

"You said you were hot!" Harley insisted, roaring with laughter. "I thought I'd cool you down."

"With your brandy?" Rhoda spat out.

"There was ice in it!"

Ruby looked for her father, to see what he would do—but his face had collapsed with laughter. Rhoda turned to appeal to him, but Toby only said, "Come on, Rho, you were being a bit of a beast."

"Be careful, Harley," Rhoda shot back, "or you may no longer have a hostess!"

Polly was at Rhoda's elbow, saying, "Is that all you're going to say, Toby?"

Toby looked at the two women with a dazed smile, and Ruby's head thumped painfully.

Rhoda stormed back to the house, with Polly trailing after her. The rest of the table broke up soon after, and Ruby hesitated for a long moment, mortified that her parents' disagreement had been there for all to see, for Ned's and Georgina's eager eyes.

"I think I might go to bed." Imogen sighed as she stood, casting a hateful glance around the table. "Good night, Ruby."

Ruby stood aside to let Imogen pass, and wondered if anyone remembered that it was still her birthday.

19

2010

The car passed easily down the drive—too easily for Mrs. Cosgrove. The land was as overgrown as the bushy brambles that rose up to choke the distant house. They passed the dilapidated tennis court, with its hanging net and wild tufty grass; the olive grove, swallowed up by other saplings and their brush; the fig tree at the turn, wide and full, the ground below spotted with rotten fruit. Beyond that would be the swimming pool, murky and strewn with algae or vine leaves from the creeper, and beside it that innocuous graveyard for those unmarked dead. Oh yes, Mrs. Cosgrove remembered every square meter.

The château was waiting for her. The red shutters had been thrown open, the many wide-eyed windows staring, daring her to enter. She moved slightly ahead of the estate agent, drawn to the challenge. She didn't take in the blue of the sea, or the mottled light coming through the tall trees.

"Madame Cosgrove, attendez!"

She almost skipped up the steps, from some dimly remembered habit, knowing their height and depth so well. She didn't know what compelled her—the sick fright holding her chest had been overtaken by some giddy and compelling force. The front door, that second-floor balcony, that dark room nestled inside, upstairs; that was her aim—and she the arrow drawing toward it.

But once the estate agent unlocked the house, Mrs. Cosgrove hesitated at the threshold. She could scarcely comprehend the tall hallway and the arch of the stairs in front of her, in their strange and inky blackness.

"It is very dark, yes," the estate agent said, without apology. "The design is traditional and intentional—the thick walls dictate that such a building is cool in the summer and warm in winter."

Mrs. Cosgrove forced herself forward. She took in the long wall beside the staircase, set with dark and elaborate portraits of the family, seeing anew the peculiar painted details: the monkey scrounging around the floor beside one woman, or a small cowering Asian boy beside the white family. Worse was that skinned cat on the wall, set above the display of safari hats and helmets. Her throat clenched. Nothing had changed—even the hallway mirror that was cracked at the edges, dusty and stained now, and that grandfather clock beside the stairs. It stood, stalwart and tall, painted with oriental figures, but without a face and offering no sign of the twenty-five years that had passed since she'd last seen it.

The estate agent let the door slam behind him, and the cloak of that familiar darkness swallowed her once again. She stepped forward and felt something underfoot, a broken tile shifting—she remembered performing the same movement once before, her child self bending to slip it back into place.

"We shall start with this room, *madame, s'il vous plaît.*"

"*Oui,*" she answered.

The estate agent gestured to the living room, pulling open the curtains with a small huffed exasperation at the housekeeper's lack of preparation. Mrs. Cosgrove felt as though she were inhaling dust as she took in the sofa, the bamboo armchairs, the long dresser, the embroidered rugs, even the small television—all the same. The piano's top was closed, and its stool was tucked under, unplayed and unloved. She held her breath as she moved through the other rooms—the study, the dining room, the kitchen—ignoring the sales jabber of the estate agent throughout. Everywhere, that strange old glamour, everywhere the faded splendor, as if shadows had huddled throughout every room, passing the years and drying up the house with their stilted breath.

Mrs. Cosgrove followed the estate agent up the stairs, her courage faltering with each step. The first-floor corridor was laden with white plaster dirt—a piece of the ceiling had come down and cracked all over the floor. The hole was covered over now with glue and wet newspaper, but hadn't been repainted, and it drew her eye up as she wandered past.

"Ah, oui." The estate agent followed her eye, and nodded sagely. *"Il y a pas mal de renovations à faire dans la maison!"*

The bright light at the end of the corridor illuminated the grime of the house, the cracked tiled floors, and the dust falling from the beams burrowed through by ants. Every bedroom seemed to have a choking emptiness that stirred something within. But it was the other rooms, the ones on the second floor, that had once caused Mrs. Cosgrove pain, that now made her head heavy.

She was drawn there like a magnet, just as she had been to the front door. The noise in her head seemed to suck her up the second staircase and hummed louder now that the estate agent had stopped talking. A door behind them slammed with some gust of wind, but she didn't react.

Mrs. Cosgrove moved hastily along the corridor, determined to see one bedroom in particular.

The shutter was open, but the trees had grown so thick that their full and leafy branches crowded the balcony and blocked out the light. Mrs. Cosgrove gasped. She might have stepped back in time, seeing the beds in their same positions. The trio of the dressing table, the wardrobe, and the chest of drawers stood proud but weary, waiting for the next occupant. The room had been cleared but not cleaned, and a small veneer of dust covered everything. The bedroom was smaller and tighter than she remembered.

Her eyes flicked to a spot on the floor. She couldn't help it, but there it was, that long, wide stain. It was brown now. With a flash Mrs. Cosgrove remembered it, a bright, clean red, spilling out. She'd been surprised how much blood there had been, how much was needed to drain a human of their life.

"Madame Cosgrove, have you been in this room before?" the estate agent asked abruptly.

"No, I haven't. No." Mrs. Cosgrove tried to gather herself as she returned to stand beside the estate agent. "I told you, monsieur, I've never been here at all."

"Then you have heard the stories . . . ?"

"The stories?" She glanced at his face, his profile bathed in shadow from the peculiar light of the bedroom.

"It was terrible. You must have seen the headlines. I was a young boy then, but of course I remember it." The man shook his head gravely, and stepped into the room. "Terrible what these English do to each other. *Les Anglais.* Men playing, and it goes too far."

Mrs. Cosgrove didn't know how to respond. She focused on the balcony again, measuring her movements, her thoughts.

"But it was many years ago," he decided. "Hush, we will not speak of it."

"No." She ducked back into the darkness of the corridor.

The estate agent cleared his throat and followed her. "Of course, as I say, the house needs some special care and attention"—he opened the door of a nearby bedroom—"to bring it into this new millennium. I wonder if you are the one to take it on, Madame Cosgrove?"

"No, I—" Her head felt heavier than ever. "I must get some air."

"Of course, madame, but there is much more to see. Would you like to take a look at the attic rooms? There is much space on the—"

"Not those, no." She stumbled past him, hurrying to the stairs. "I must go outside."

20

1985

Ruby had slept badly again, thanks to the film Ned had put on after Imogen went to bed and the adults grew rowdy. Ruby's long siesta forced her awake late, and the horror of the film, *Carrie,* had transfixed her all the way to the end. She'd felt so sad for Carrie, bullied at school, bullied by her mother—and in some strange way Ruby thought it was quite right that all those horrible people should have died like that. The ending left her feeling confused as she brushed her teeth and plaited her hair for bed, and the unease lingered this morning.

Imogen asked Ruby if she had something she could wear.

"Oh," Ruby said, glancing at a pile of clothes Imogen had tossed under the metal bed, "aren't you giving Lisette your laundry?"

"Yes, but"—Imogen followed Ruby's look—"not those ones. I don't want to wear them again, or even touch them. They aren't . . . clean."

Ruby stopped, worried that she understood Imogen's meaning exactly. She turned to her wardrobe and pushed her hand through her dresses to find something for Imogen. Tucked in the back were her small teddy bears, facing each other in their tight embraces. The sight of them upset Ruby for a moment; she glanced over to the metal bed, where they belonged, and where they might never be again. She looked across at Annie's wildflowers on her dressing table, then back to her wardrobe again.

"I've got something that would fit you today, and we can always persuade our mothers to buy us some new things." Ruby added slowly, "How does that sound?"

Imogen nodded and kicked the small pile of clothes farther under the bed. Ruby closed the door of her wardrobe, thinking that perhaps she should collect Imogen's pile herself. Lisette wouldn't understand why Imogen needed them gone, she'd merely wash the clothes and return them clean and neatly folded on the small metal bed. At least Max Fuller had left—though the prospect of menace still lingered in the air. Ruby wasn't quite sure why.

AT BREAKFAST ANGUS AND TOBY were rustling their newspapers, not fully awake.

Ruby hurried over to her father, and asked under her breath, "Did Annie get home safely?"

Toby smiled amiably. "I don't know, darling, should I phone and ask?"

"Yes, please."

"All right." Toby nodded. "I will. Did you have a good birthday, darling?"

Angus looked up to hear Ruby's answer.

"Oh, yes, Father, thank you," Ruby said, smiling even though she was sure her eyes betrayed her. She returned to her seat just as a voice called out:

"What-ho! Good morning!"

Harley eyed the group from the top of the steps as he pulled his ratty dressing gown over his striped pajamas. It was a hot morning, and he moved through the small daggers of light that passed through the trees.

"Well, well, well, isn't it too hot for white people!" he said with a laugh as he approached the table. He tied the string of his trousers tighter, and as he did so, Ruby saw bristles of grayish white hair through the gap. She looked away with sick disgust, but Imogen had seen too, and dropped her buttered biscotte. Ned made a strained noise as she sipped at her coffee.

Harley muttered as he approached the table, "I've had wonderful dreams about little girls and birthdays and the opera."

Angus's voice came in strong. "Harley, not now."

"Oh come now." Harley's face spread into a wide, sickening grin. "I'm on holiday, we're in this heavenly place, this place of old luxury . . . a place out of time. Isn't that why artists come to this part of the world—to study the light, and make love?"

"*Must* you tell us your every thought?"

"Yes I must, my dear Gus." Harley leaned over Imogen to reach for the coffeepot, and she jolted backward as if she'd been electrified. "You could do with having a sense of humor yourself, you know. I do feel sorry for darling Polly and little Immy having to put up with you and your moods . . ." He sat down heavily and surveyed Angus. "I wonder, if I hadn't taken my first wife from your loving embrace, Angus, perhaps you'd have survived. You'd have dedicated yourself to her, instead of dedicating yourself to self-destruction, and the terrible disappointment you were to your father."

Toby dropped his newspaper with dismay, ready to mount a defense of his friend, but Angus was prepared, leaning forward keenly, saying, "Your memory is quite something, isn't it, dear Hazzer?"

"My memory is entirely intact, thank you. As is my emotional state—unlike yours. You *are* like Achilles! One moment we've got your generous spirit, then your bloody wallowing, next your exaggerated grief, and always last, your dreadful anger." Harley poured himself a large black coffee, lifting the *cafetière* theatrically high. "Perhaps this inner torment of yours is your fatal flaw."

Angus began folding his newspaper wearily, creasing the corners deliberately as if to soothe himself, his thick eyebrows bolted together. But something rippled through Toby as he sat with his friend, and he pointed his finger at Harley. "And there is *your* flaw, Harley. All you ever see in Angus is his money, his title, his role in society. You've never let him just be a man."

Harley scoffed, surprised by Toby's outburst. "But he's not just a man, he's the Earl of Beresford. And he's a disgrace."

Imogen winced uncomfortably as her father threw his paper aside and stood, his face sunken into itself as he stalked toward the house. Harley's voice followed him as he went: "And look at poor Imogen, having such a father! Imogen mustn't be made to put up with that—she's a perfect picture of loveliness, with that gorgeous sultry mouth." Harley took another slurp of his coffee with a joyful jostle of his knees. "Look at the way she's looking at me! Yes, we must ensure she grows up in a bag of feathers . . . soft and plenty to pluck."

"Harley, you'll make me vomit into my tea if you don't stop. You don't have to jizz over the whole table," Ned cut in, grimacing into her teacup.

Ruby glanced at the distraught Imogen, wishing with every fiber that Liv might appear to admonish her husband, or that her own father might intervene. Why didn't anyone make Harley stop?

"Quite right, Ned," Toby said with a snap of his paper and a rub of his mustache. "Honestly, Harley, did you wake up on the wrong side of bed this morning?"

"Oh, what's wrong with everyone these days?" Harley barked as he dragged a half-baguette toward his plate. "Our hostess was very sour last night, and now you lot. This is supposed to be my summer holiday, for heaven's sake. Days full of fun. Ah!" He paused, struck with inspiration. "Tennis! A tournament between the three of us. Agamemnon versus Odysseus and Achilles, why not? That'll sort Angus out—I'll thrash him. And Ruby and Immy can be our little ball girls. Dainty girls, running after the balls"—Harley slurped on his coffee again—"cradling the balls in their hands . . ."

"You are a disgusting, dirty old man," Ned said in a dark voice as she stood up. "I won't sit here and listen."

Ruby glanced at Imogen, who was looking toward the door, to wherever her father had gone, leaving her alone at the table. Ruby wondered how long it would take for her heart to regulate its furious beating.

———

Tennis was a bad idea, since Harley did thrash the other two, and his roaringly happy mood continued past the shouts from the court. Ned had at least managed to rescue Imogen and Ruby from ball girl duty, and they spent that part of the day by the pool, Imogen gently coaxed into the water by Ned. Ruby lay on a sun lounger and sidestepped them both, still hurt that her father had so openly supported Ned at the breakfast table, when he so rarely raised his voice for her.

Lisette bought them a tray of lunch, but Ruby didn't touch it, and tried not to watch Ned pick at the warm goat cheese with a long breadstick, or suck at her fingers where the cheese had dribbled a little. Ruby forced herself into the pool to join Imogen, but the water felt very cold, even though it was the middle of the hot afternoon. She submerged her head beneath the surface, hoping to ease the sharp prickles of discomfort all over her skin, all over her thoughts.

A sudden screech came from the terrace, and the two younger girls stood upright in unison. It turned into a long, agonized cry, like that of an injured animal. Ned raised her head behind them, her ears covered by her Walkman headphones. Imogen and Ruby glanced at each other fearfully, then dashed out of the pool, grabbing their towels and hurrying along the side of the house to see what had caused the noise.

Someone had driven right onto the terrace, a battered old French car, gray and rusted, just like the ones in the village.

There was an old woman hovering beside it, her face as worn and gray as her car. Her mouth hung open, and with a groan she cried out in French:

"*Mon fils! Vous avez tué mon fils!*"

Toby and Angus rushed out the front doors, but hesitated on the steps. Ruby saw her father's shocked face assess the situation.

"*Mon fils!*"

With a jolt, Ruby recognized the old woman—it was the one who had confronted her in the village, who had used her name so accusingly.

"You have killed my boy!" the old woman screamed again. "*Mon fils!*"

Toby was near her now, and went to put his arm around her, but she pushed him off. His voice was earnest. *"Madame, pourquoi vous venez ici?"*

Angus's face was stiff with comprehension, and he called out carefully to Toby. "It's her, old pal, it's the mother. She's found you."

Ruby felt Imogen shift beside her.

"You, *un de vous*"—the woman's French accent was heavy—"my brother tells me; he works for the mayor. One of you hit my boy in the car, hit him and run, and kill him." She started to push at Toby furiously. *"Un de vous!* Kill my boy! It was you?"

The old woman's words seemed to punch Ruby in the chest just as the woman pushed at her father, and she realized she was wrenching at her towel, pulling at it between her hands, as the woman screeched, "You lie, you make the mayor *lie*! You are *criminal*!"

Ruby's father spoke quick French while using the shape of his upper body to surround the old woman. She swatted at him again, but he was stronger. She resisted, turning her arms inward to curl away from him, her face snarling.

Liv appeared, carrying her handbag and a shopping bag slung over her shoulder, presumably returning via the coastal path from a walk in the village. Assessing the situation quickly, she lowered her voice in an attempt to soothe the woman, who had started to scream again, *"Mon fils!* MY BOY!"

Angus turned his anguished face away, and strode back into the house.

"Dada?" Imogen said quietly, just as Liv set her things down on the edge of the terrace, drawing the woman back to her car and away from the dazed eyes of Ruby and Imogen. Ruby heard Liv say to her father gently, "Toby, the children shouldn't see this."

"I hardly think you should intervene," Toby answered stiffly, attempting to lift the woman from Liv's embrace. "This all happened before you arrived."

"All the same . . . let's take her back to the village. Or into the house? It sounds like she needs an explanation. And I really do think that the girls shouldn't see this."

"I don't want her inside," Toby said forcefully.

Ruby and Imogen remained on the terrace long after Liv and Toby managed to wrestle the woman into her car, with Liv taking the wheel and steering back down the drive, the Ashby car following behind. The old woman's terrible words reverberated about Ruby's mind as the girls finally moved through the front doors and into the house. Her son, hit by someone's car, killed, and the mayor knew. And her father . . .

In the hallway, Ruby saw Angus, his great figure bent in half as he sat on the stairs. His face was white and stiff with distress. Ruby stepped ahead of Imogen and wondered if he would notice her; she imagined climbing into his lap and nestling there, to comfort him and in turn receive comfort.

The spell was broken when a voice called from the top of the stairs. "What's happened, Angus?" Polly asked. "What was that screaming?"

Angus jerked into motion. "Nothing, dear. I'll be right there."

"Is that you, too, Immy? Come on up," Polly insisted.

It was only then that Angus noticed Ruby, before tilting his head to acknowledge his daughter. His eyes were glistening as he turned quickly to climb the stairs.

21

During the main course at dinner, a very irritated Rhoda nudged at her daughter. "You are awfully sullen, Ruby. So was Lisette, earlier—what's happened to the pair of you?"

"Leave her, Rhoda, we're all out of sorts," Angus said sternly. Ruby glanced up at him gratefully, before lowering her face again.

"It does look like something—maybe a bit of heatstroke," said Polly, who herself had pink splotches across her cheeks. Ruby looked across at Imogen helplessly, desperate to dismiss the prying adults, but Imogen didn't meet her eye.

"Whatever it is, do buck up, girl." Rhoda leaned in to Ruby's ear. "I haven't forgotten your schedule; it's been woefully ignored these last few days . . ."

Imogen didn't eat much, but Ned took her in hand later on, pulling her to dance along to the jazz records. Ruby watched Imogen's face swing from cold anxiety to hot laughter as the music flowed over the group. Ned wriggled her skinny body and tussled at Imogen's hair fondly, dragging her hand down her arm. The two figures bumped at the balustrade behind them, the sea swaying with approval beyond. Imogen suddenly looked as grown-up as Ned, smiling easily with her, while Ruby felt younger than ever, some Cinderella stuck in a Grimm fairy tale as she helped her grouchy mother clear the plates.

Ruby wondered whether she could disappear to her favorite spot at the pool under the cover of evening. It would be dark, but she knew how to prise open the door to the pool house and find the right switch for the pool lights. She could put her feet over the edge, and make great blue-white swirls with her legs as she read. The trees around her, the sun loungers, even her legs would be lit up with that pale, murky blue. Moths and other insects would join her to worship the light, and the calm. She might even drop some beads of water over her forehead, as a sort of holy blessing.

But Ruby didn't want to risk further wrath from her mother. She returned to her bedroom instead, to pour herself into *Death on the Nile* as the jazz floated up past the shutters. She took care to lean her dusty feet against the bedstead and away from her clean bed linen. She didn't want to get ready for bed yet—she would wait, for she had a question for Imogen.

Besides, her book was troubling her. The first death had occurred on the Nile cruise: a woman had been shot in the head while she was sleeping. Ruby hadn't minded too much—the woman was horrible anyway, and most of the other characters didn't like her. Ruby preferred the best-friend character, who was quite upset but very spirited, and who was someone Poirot liked too, which Ruby thought boded well. She couldn't yet work out who the killer was. She pressed the pages into her chest for a long moment, before slotting her new bookmark into the back pages and carrying on.

Imogen came in sometime later, greeting Ruby as she pushed through the door.

"Ned showed me her room . . . in the attics. It's horrible up there."

"Oh." Ruby looked up from her book, uncomfortable at Imogen's remark. "It's fine—it's an old house."

"There were flies in the sink, and marks on the walls. I didn't like it at all."

"Then don't go up there again," Ruby answered defensively.

Imogen pushed the door softly but firmly closed. "Ned said that prisoners in the war were kept up there, and tortured. I thought it was another one of her stories. Have you ever been up there? I refused to stay, especially now that it's dark."

"Ned doesn't know anything. But yes, I have been up there, and I don't like it either."

"So why is your room up here if you're scared of the attics?" Imogen shuddered as she moved over to her bed, adding, "I'm sure I hear noises from up there, during the night . . ."

"I moved up to this bedroom last year because my mother didn't like me downstairs," Ruby replied evenly, "and she doesn't like it when I use her bathroom."

"This house is horrible. How can you stay here so long, and every summer?"

"I love this house," declared Ruby, sitting up and looking out at the soft pine treetops and the glittering sea. "It's what I know. We've moved house three times in England—my mother's always looking for a change, she says, but here has always been the same. Even after my grandmother died. She loved it here, and I loved her."

Ruby smiled, remembering her grandmother's pale face glimmering in the shade of the trees. She'd spent all her days outside, lounging on the lower lawn, on the terrace, or by the pool. Life in France was outside, so different from the inside life of England. But Ruby did remember her grandmother inside the château, nestled serenely on the sofa, and then the hump of her body in the bed when she was ill. They took her to the French hospital soon after, so Ruby never got to say goodbye—and for that reason, she never really thought of her as gone. Sometimes Ruby thought she heard her grandmother's voice in the corners of the château, when the floors shook as she ran up the stairs or when she turned on the groaning water pipes.

"I think this house is frightening, and I can't believe you can't see it," Imogen finished.

There was a jolly cry from outside, and a small pause, before the usual adult chatter resumed. Ruby lamented that she could rarely hear

the sea in the evenings, or the rumble of the waves, over the adults and
their constant banter.

"They are all very drunk, I think." Imogen threw Ruby a look.

"Yes," Ruby said.

"I do like Ned, though. She's kind." The moonlight slid across Imogen's face as she tucked her legs into bed. "I like her more and more
every day. She hasn't told us any stories since Annie left, though, has
she? Oh—did your father have any news on Annie getting back?"

"No, I don't think he followed it up," Ruby said unhappily.

"I'm sure she's fine. Didn't she mention her aunt by the sea? In
honor of Annie, I'll ask Ned for one of her stories tomorrow. But you
don't like them, do you?"

"It's not that I don't like them. I just—" Ruby couldn't find the
proper words. The truth about who Ned was beat in her chest, a dark
secret. She couldn't share it, because she knew it would mean something to Imogen—that she might have an opinion about this piece of
information, and it would bring their carefully composed world tumbling down. Here, in this room, Ruby needed things to be safe.

". . . I find her stories slightly morbid," Ruby finally said. "And I
prefer when things are nicely tied up at the end, and when people behave themselves."

"That sounds like a fairy tale, Ruby. I don't think that's—"

"Aren't Ned's stories just ancient fairy tales? Many of them are
nonsense," Ruby shot back, slightly cross at Imogen's rebuke. Besides,
didn't Imogen's family have their own dark secret? One that had pressed
at Ruby's heart every time she'd heard it mentioned—and now she'd
carved out a question ready for answer.

Ruby closed her book and set it under her pillow. She cleared her
throat.

"Imogen, can I ask . . . What is the disgrace that Harley sometimes
talks about, about your father?"

"The disgrace," Imogen repeated dully.

"Yes." Ruby waited.

"Everybody, it seems, is a disgrace," Imogen replied in a muffled
voice.

Ruby could hear a long peal of laughter, bouncing off her shuttered windows. "I meant the thing about the 'boy' . . ."

"Yes. It's a secret. Nobody knows about it—at least, I was told nobody did."

Ruby was silent.

"My mother says it's the worst thing that's ever happened to us," Imogen continued, looking at Ruby now. "If people find out about it, then Father will be in a lot of trouble. Granny is still so cross, she blames Grandfather's death on him . . . There was a role he was supposed to fill, you see—Grandfather's role after he died. He's a lord, an earl—you know that."

"And you're an Honorable," Ruby added unhelpfully.

Imogen hesitated before carrying on. "Yes, but Dada was supposed to be a politician as part of it—a 'peer,' they call it. But he had to give it up, because of this thing that happened. All because of that hunt one day. It's a tradition—our family hosts a hunt every year, to impress a lot of important people. But then a young man got shot—one of the beaters, who gets the birds out of the bushes. He died. It was an awful accident, and really a mistake. But my father shouldn't have been shooting at that point, they said. He was being 'impulsive' . . . Granny often calls him that."

Ruby was listening carefully, urging Imogen on with her expression. She'd never seen her so solemn.

"The family spoke to some people, and everyone put a brave face on it. The boy's family was given something, and it was hushed up, you see. Your father came after and was very kind, but he couldn't do anything to help. He didn't want Dada to give up the peerage, but he was forced to under the circumstances . . ." Imogen sighed. "And everything felt different after that."

When Imogen didn't offer more, Ruby pressed, "Because your father was upset that he'd hurt somebody?"

"Yes, but it was more than that. Granny was as angry as that screaming old lady that came to the house today. She said the papers would find out—that there would be scandal, and disgrace. Grandfather said that in England earls can do what they like. Me and Mummy just tried to stay out of it. There's a danger, still, that people could find out. So don't tell anyone, will you!"

Ruby felt a punch to her stomach. "Of course not, Imogen. I am sorry."

Imogen looked up at Ruby, and said again, "Your father was kind to all of us then."

"Yes, he likes to sort things out."

"Well, I don't think he was in charge, but he had connections to other people, and they made things better, more bearable."

"I think that must have been Mr. Montgomery. That's what he seemed to say the other day," Ruby said quietly.

Imogen carried on, concentrating. "I was only six, but my father hasn't been very kind since then. He goes out a lot more, now. It's affected many things, even my schooling, apparently, though I am perfectly happy at St. Aubyn's." Imogen took a heavy breath. "My mother says that Dada is just far away in his head, but I don't know . . . it isn't just that. He can be different with others. He loves your father. And he likes you."

Ruby stirred uneasily. "No, I don't think—"

"And now my mother is having a baby and it's a boy." Imogen seemed lost in her thoughts. "So he'll be the heir. Granny is quite pleased, and he's not even born yet. I expect Dada will adore him, and Mama doesn't have time for me anymore, either."

"Do you like your grandmother?"

"She doesn't really like girls."

"Oh, I'm sorry," Ruby said, thinking how different her grandmother was from Imogen's.

"It's all been dawning on me here," Imogen carried on. "At school I'm always busy. I never have to think about it. But here, suddenly—"

"You'll be a good sister to the baby, Imogen," Ruby interrupted.

"How do you know?"

Ruby answered instinctively, "Because *you* are kind."

"Oh." Imogen hesitated. "Do you really think so?"

"I think you are one of the kindest and friendliest people I've ever met, and I am sorry that I haven't always been as nice to you. I'm sorry that other people haven't been, either. I'm sorry that this holiday has been . . . difficult."

Imogen was silent for a long time. Then she said, "Thank you."

Ruby said in a rush, "I wish we could be friends. Perhaps you could show me how."

But Imogen didn't respond. She rolled away, her back to Ruby, and changed her voice. "I miss Annie. I hope she is all right. I shouldn't have told you all of that. Mama says we must always be demure and keep things to ourselves. So please forget everything I have said."

There was another peal of laughter from outside. Ruby said desperately, "All right."

She turned her face to her pillow, squeezing away her tears at the dismissal.

THE FOLLOWING MORNING THERE WAS nobody at breakfast. The two girls eyed the empty terrace warily before returning inside to creep through the dark hallway, the even darker dining room, and the passageway, where they could hear the soft banging of Lisette in the kitchen.

The stray black cat appeared in the kitchen doorway and darted past them, fleeing from the noise.

Inside the kitchen, Lisette spoke in furious French. Ruby balked at the barrage of her crossness, not understanding a single word, but taking in the terrible mess on the kitchen counter: stained wineglasses; cracked tumblers soiled with the blunt ends of cigars; too many empty bottles to count; a stack of dirty plates, topped with two half-eaten apricots stabbed through with cigarettes. There was a strange dead smell, too, and Ruby's eyes lingered over an inexplicable bloodstained napkin. Imogen went to the side table, where a fresh stack of pastries peeked out of a paper bag.

She pulled out a *pain au chocolat,* slightly tearing the bag, and turned to Lisette hopefully. *"Excusez-moi, Lisette, je peux?"*

Lisette nodded, her hands buried in the soapy water of the sink. Imogen offered one to Ruby, who had no appetite, but took it anyway.

They dashed back through the dining room and into the hall, Ruby holding her unwanted *pain au chocolat* as it softened in her hot hand.

Outside, Imogen took a bite of her pastry, and said in a muffled voice, "This is wonderful, Ruby. No one is awake. Shall we go in the sea?"

"We're not wearing our swim things."

"Doesn't matter," Imogen said merrily, "let's swim in our knickers. I feel better today."

"Really?" Ruby said doubtfully. "I'm not supposed to go without adult supervision."

"Oh, come on!"

Ruby looked at the refreshed joy in Imogen's face, and remembered their conversation from last night. "All right," she said.

Some hours later, Ruby left a cheery Imogen sunning herself on the lower lawn to go for another *pain au chocolat*—her first had been discarded and was now being pecked at by birds or ants or both—for the sea had reinvigorated her appetite. Ruby had to admit that she felt lighter; the seawater had been soft and welcoming. Both girls had laughingly left their wet underwear hanging by the steps, and put on their dresses to cover up their temporary nakedness. Imogen took herself to the hammocks to wait for Ruby's return, giggling that they could imitate their mothers, and Ruby felt boosted by the suggestion.

Ruby bumped into her father coming out of the front door. She recoiled, first because he smelled so strongly of drink, and then due to his rebuke. "Buzz off, Ruby, for God's sake. What are you doing? We're all hanging like dogs." Toby rested his shaking hand on the door handle. "Your mother's at the doctor, so be good today, please."

"Why is she at the doctor?" Ruby felt a sting of alarm.

"She's not well, all right? Stop asking questions. She's not alone— Polly went with her, wouldn't let her out of her sight." Toby furiously lit a cigarette.

Ruby stood on the threshold, half inside and half out, caught between sun and darkness.

"Ruby!" called Harley, seeing her framed in the doorway. He was seated at the table, being served by a huffy Lisette. Ruby hadn't seen him as she'd raced across the terrace.

"Ruby!" Harley demanded, slamming his fist on the table. "Come and sit on my lap!" Ruby obeyed, if only to appease her father, who led her to the table, scowling at Harley's repeated roaring and squinting around him without his glasses.

"Hair of the dog!" Harley lifted his glass at Toby, who took his seat, unfolding his newspaper in an exhalation of smoke. Ruby hesitated at her chair, not wanting to sit down. Harley's soft shirt was unbuttoned and his hairy paunch was littered with flakes from his croissant.

"Did Rhoda manage her hysteria—anything the doctor can do?" Harley asked Toby, patting his lap and gesturing to Ruby. She didn't move.

Toby grunted behind his paper. "Not sure yet. He'll say to try the dentist, which is what I said . . . Seems the obvious option for a knocked-out tooth."

"Yes, well," Harley smirked, "if she's going to get so drunk she falls over . . . Spitting up blood, what a sight it was!"

"Thing is," Toby muttered dryly, "she couldn't find the bloody tooth."

"Probably swallowed it, dear boy. She'll have to examine her stools in the days to come." Harley chortled. "I imagine good dentists are hard to come by around here; she'll probably return with a brand-new tooth—a different color from the rest."

Ruby listened, horrified. She burst out, "Will my mother be all right?"

"Yes, of course, darling," Toby said plainly. "Hardly life or death—is it?"

Harley turned to her. "Quite right. Lovely dress you're wearing, Rubes. Is it gingham? See, I do notice these things. Come along." Harley patted his lap again. "I'd love Imogen to have a good go on my lap after you . . . but she's got hardly any meat on her arse at all."

Ruby set her reading book on the table, and reluctantly hoisted herself up and onto Harley's knees. She could feel the heat of his breath on the back of her neck as she tried to settle across his bony legs. He utterly repulsed her. She tried to lean forward, or a little to the side. But there was no use trying to get comfortable, so she kept her buttocks tight and stiff, just to have some way of warding him off. She felt so vulnerable with only the protection of her thin dress, and no underwear.

"Honestly, these girls." Harley patted the side of Ruby's thigh. "When I think of my boy Hugo . . . Well, teenagers, don't deserve their sex drive, do they, Tobias?" He laughed jerkily, and Ruby moved about with him.

Ruby's father turned a page of his newspaper and grunted.

"How about a kiss, eh, Ruby?" Harley moved his knees to the side and tried to tilt Ruby toward him. "A birthday kiss—didn't I promise you that? Didn't I promise I'd have you?"

"That's all right, thank you." Ruby glanced at her father, but he was hidden behind his paper. She leaned on her hands and tried to shift her weight away from Harley's lap, and perhaps even slide off him entirely. In the next moment, she managed it. Ruby stepped off, but Harley took her by the waist, circled her with his wide hands, and drew her back to him. He lifted one hand to Ruby's face, and cradled the other around her chin. His breath reeked of wine and something foul.

"Birthday kiss, Ruby Boobs?"

His knees seemed to pin Ruby straight as his hands caressed her cheeks, his fingers touching the tendrils of her hair. Ruby tried to shirk away, but he held her head there, examining her with his eyes. She stood, immobile, terrified, her small figure caught between his knees and his hands. He seemed to be an impending mass of rolling, gray-gristled flesh. With hooded eyes and heavy breath, Harley finally leaned toward Ruby and placed his withered lips on hers, pressing lightly, then harder. When he finally released her face, she pulled away bitterly.

"Baby's first kiss!" Harley's mouth spread into a grin. "There you are—you're a young lady now. You've been kissed."

Ruby turned away, touching a hot hand to her mouth, looking back at Harley and what had just passed between them.

"Harley!" a sharp voice shouted from the main doorway of the house. "What are you doing to Ruby? Let her go."

"You've missed the action, dear Gus. She's quite at liberty to go," Harley retorted coolly. "Nothing stopping her."

Ruby's father lowered his paper, his cross demeanor gone with the appearance of his dear friend. He squinted across the terrace and called, "Angus, good morning, and how are you feeling?"

Through the tears in Ruby's eyes, she could only see the shape of Imogen coming up beside her, her happy face now struck with a strange, sad, dead look.

"Ruby, what was that?"

Ruby still felt the rough grip of Harley on her legs, her thighs, her buttocks— all the more raw for her lack of underwear. She felt keenly her burning face and her stinging lips as she swayed with momentary faintness.

She tried to say, "I don't feel very well," but no words came out.

"And you, Imogen, have a turn on my lap!" Harley roared. "I insist, or I'll curl each of you up into a ball and throw you into the sea, one after the other."

"No," Ruby whispered, looking back at Harley. His face and torso seemed to blur in the sun, like some quivering shadowed image. She added, louder, "Not Imogen."

"Oh, yes, Imogen." Harley's smile spread wide, and Ruby felt a thud in her head.

But his smile faded just as Imogen let out a cry. "Ruby!"

"Imogen?" Ruby replied softly.

"You're having a nosebleed! Ruby!"

"Bloody hell!" Harley cried out, standing, appearing taller and darker than before. "Looks like a bloody hemorrhage!"

Ruby put her fingers to her nose and felt the rush of fluid. It slipped past her mouth, over her chin, down across her chest. She looked back at Imogen, her face full of alarm.

"You're supposed to tilt your head back!" Imogen tapped Ruby's head, but too sharply, and Ruby felt a sudden rush of blood slip back into her throat. She coughed and fell forward, a stream of blood sputtering out of her mouth now. Everything went white. Ruby heard cries of horror before somebody picked her up and held her close, pressing a piece of thick fabric against her nose.

Ruby thought she recognized the musky scent of whoever it was who held her. His arms were strong, quick—not her father's arms, but thicker, safer. Ruby tilted her head against the man's shoulder, her hair falling across her face. She heard his muffled voice vibrate through his chest.

"Toby," Angus said, "I think she's fainted."

She heard a dim response, but nothing as comforting as this embrace. Angus shifted his grip around her, his fingers grazing her face to hold the collar of his shirt more firmly against her nose. He shuffled a little to accomplish this, and she worried he might let her go, but he held her tighter. She took a heavy breath of relief.

"This is all very tiresome. Where's Rhoda?" a shrieking voice seemed to say, but Ruby wasn't sure whose it was—perhaps Georgina's. Angus rocked Ruby gently as her head thudded once more with heat, with pain, with exhaustion. He turned his face to speak to her, his hand touching her hair. "You're all right, beautiful little thing." She closed her eyes, and pressed her face against the cloth of Angus's chest.

22

2010

Mrs. Cosgrove moved jerkily down the staircases. In the hallway she hesitated, and turned to look into the long mirror mounted on the wall. She imagined taking a great hammer to the glass and shattering it, spilling blood over her hands like it had spilled here once before.

But there'd be no such destruction today. She found her reflection, and felt as if her soul passed through the place where the dim hue and dark spots of the mirror had collected. She saw herself clearly, clearer than she ever had as a child, when her height had only reached to a low, cracked corner, reflecting back her distorted and twisted face.

Gone was her calm from before, her memories tearing through her thoughts and beating at her heart with conviction now.

On the mantelpiece below the mirror was a pile of books—a line of vintage Agatha Christies, with their colorful abstract covers. She couldn't believe they had been collected and displayed there, so prominently, like some crucial murder weapon that the police had never discovered.

Mrs. Cosgrove left the house. She crossed the terrace and hastened toward the balustrade, to better see the glittering strip of the sea, the flat bathing slab of rock and its wooden pontoon, undisturbed by human recklessness, but continually burned by the bleach of the sun. She wondered when exactly the château had started rotting. Had it been like this throughout that summer, or had it started earlier, when the Ashbys bought the house after the war, for the bargain price—the "steal"—that they always bragged about? But what would a house like this cost, with everything its walls had absorbed, from the war to that fateful summer? And would she pay it?

Standing now on the terrace, great gasps of memories, voices, visions, noises flooded over her. The adults and their drunken evenings, the card games, the shouts of laughter, the shouts of pain. Harley's dominance over them all—his words and actions like a weighty sword of Damocles held just above his so-called friends, ready to strike at any moment. And then Max Fuller. Their faces seemed to merge together in her mind, and the unspooling tape of her memories stuttered to a halt. The heat was too much for her—she thought she might be sick. She gripped at the balustrade and leaned forward.

Mrs. Cosgrove remembered a better day, the wind whipping through her thick hair, and across her father's face, a face she hadn't seen for so long now. His smile as he held her on the terrace—so serene, so rare, his eyes closed with contentment. She closed her eyes now, too.

But her memory painted his face, his expression, so clearly, like a still from a film. Which could only mean that—surely—she'd been watching from afar, and he hadn't been embracing her. No, it was Ruby he'd held. It was always Ruby. It was never her.

Ruby's young face came to her now, her strawberry-blond hair, her pale skin, always holding herself back, always watching, her face fixed with disapproval.

"Madame Cosgrove, are you all right?"

The estate agent's voice seemed to punch her into place. She was here now, and she needed to get on with it. She held the château brochure in her hands, and she could hold its future in her hands as well—its destruction, its obliteration, or something worse.

"I'm fine." Mrs. Cosgrove stood up straight and took a deep breath.

She removed her sunglasses from her pocket and put them on. "And please do call me Imogen."

The estate agent studied her for a moment, and she smiled in response, grateful for the obscuring effect of her sunglasses. He nodded briefly. "Would you like to return to the château—we have not seen all the bedrooms—or would you prefer to see the grounds?"

Mrs. Cosgrove looked past the far edge of the terrace. She brushed her hand over her hair and pushed off from the balustrade. "I would prefer to see the grounds," she said shakily. "There's no need to return to the house. And then, let's have a talk about the price."

The estate agent's face creased into smiles. "Oh, I would be delighted. The price is indicated in the brochure, madame, but of course we can discuss any offer."

Mrs. Cosgrove nodded tactfully, before asking, "Why does the owner sell?"

"She has no wish to hold the place up . . . *soutenir*, as we say in French. She spends no time here and finds it vastly expensive." The estate agent shifted uneasily and braved another smile. "They say she is an Ashby, but she does not carry the name. And she is not *true* to the name, since she has abandoned the Château des Sètes. Perhaps you know her, in your circle? The surname is—"

"No, no." Imogen raised her hand to interrupt. "I have no use for circles. My circle is growing smaller by the day."

"You are very humorous, madame. I am sure that if the château were to become yours," the man said, trying to inject a note of charm into his voice, "you will bring your husband and friends and have many parties—"

"My husband is dead," Imogen interrupted brutally.

"Oh, I am sorry."

As they wandered around the pool area, Imogen took in how overgrown it had become, the crawling creepers Annie had noticed now wild and throttling the pool house. The pool itself was covered by a thick green tarp, stretched out and held in place by tight steel pegs. The estate agent was watching her carefully throughout, and as they returned to the terrace he declared, "Well, madame, is the Château des Sètes not the most beautiful house in the area?"

"Yes," she agreed blankly, a spot on the flagstones capturing her attention. There was no crack there, no stain of blood. She took in a deep breath, somehow relieved.

The estate agent was beside her, adopting a serious tone of voice. "Before we continue, I must tell you, Madame Cosgrove, that we expect to hear from the other interested party tomorrow. If you wish to proceed, you must do so quickly."

"Who is the other party?"

"He is English, like you. Though, not so glamorous, perhaps."

"I see." Imogen gritted her teeth, trying not to let the flare of her emotions rise up again.

"He is staying in your hotel, I believe," the estate agent added helpfully, "and has a man with him. I understand that he has been making inquiries with the mayor about the history of the house, and the Ashby family. He insisted on consulting the prints of the château, and any documentations we had concerning its history."

Mrs. Cosgrove turned her head toward the estate agent. She looked directly into his face for the first time that afternoon, ready for the answer. "And what is this man's name?"

"Monsieur Hugo Montgomery."

Imogen's eyes flashed as she looked intensely at the estate agent's face. There it was, pronounced out loud and true.

"Perhaps you do know him, after all?" the estate agent added coyly.

Mrs. Cosgrove responded with a twist of her head. "No, I do not. Has he visited the house?"

"Yes"—the man raised his eyebrows—"he found the upstairs very interesting, like you."

Imogen had no more patience. "Indeed, and I shall make sure to trump his offer. I am much obliged to you, Mr. Berne; thank you very much for this tour. I need time to think. I have this"—she clutched at her brochure—"and I shall call you. Please let me know if anything changes. For now, I shall say goodbye."

She put out her hand. He let out a burst of dismayed laughter. "But, madame . . . you do not wish to return to the village by car?"

"No, no," she said, removing her hand, and turning away from him, "I shall take the coastal path." She remembered herself in the next moment. "That is . . . is there . . . a coastal path?"

"Yes, of course." He nodded slowly, gesturing at the far end of the balustrade. "There is an entrance in that corner, but it is concealed. From there you will find a path. It is a charming route."

Barely listening to his instructions, Imogen moved forward with a quick nod and another *"Merci."* She needed time to think. *Montgomery.* The well-known and well-respected name of that monster, Harley. This Hugo was the son he'd mentioned so dismissively, the son who'd forever been his disappointment, who had now grown into a man with a cane and a tortured face that Imogen recognized from society dinners. Had he always looked at her that way—had he always known? Was he a son returning to avenge his father? Was this Englishman a very real enemy, more alive and present than the château behind her, uncontrollable and unknowable, biding his time and gathering ammunition against her?

Mrs. Cosgrove hurried along the coastal path. The sea's waves seemed to lap at the wall with the same urgency as the beat of her heart.

23

1985

Ruby feigned sleep for most of the day. Angus had carried her up to her bedroom, with Imogen following softly behind. Nobody spoke as Angus dropped Ruby gently on the bed. He touched his hand against her forehead to check her temperature, before brushing her hair away from her face. Imogen moved aside for him as he pulled at the shutters and left the room.

Ruby waited for Imogen to go before sitting up to peel off her stained dress, dabbing it against her nose in the semi-darkness. She threw it aside before pushing herself under the covers, trying to catch that musky scent of his, hoping it had rubbed off on her skin, on her hair. She buried her face in the pillow, not caring about the dried blood that flaked around her itchy nose and her mouth.

A half hour later there was a knock at the door, and Ruby opened her eyes.

"Ruby, here's your book," called Ned's voice as she cracked open the door. "Angus insisted."

"Shush. She's asleep. Put it on the side of her bed," Imogen said crossly from behind Ned, "or just leave it outside the door as I suggested?"

"It's got blood on it, Ruby. The book, I mean," Ned continued loudly, moving her arm around the door to drop it. "Just wanted to warn you. Hope you feel better."

Ruby waited for them to go before rushing to the door. There it was, her *Death on the Nile,* splattered with her own blood. She imagined that it looked just like the book's victim and her bullet-wounded head. A wave of dizziness passed over her, and she brought the book back to bed. She put it under the pillow, and closed her eyes.

WHEN RUBY AWOKE, THE AIR felt different. The early evening light wasn't its usual golden, but a muffled gray blue. Even with the shutters closed, she could feel a cold nip come through the gap.

She pushed them open. The pine trees were swaying wearily in the wind. The parasols were folded up, the terrace cleared, the chairs up-turned on the table, and the cushions removed from the loungers. For a moment, Ruby thought that summer was over, that it was the end of the season and everyone had left the house. Her heart leaped with relief, before she realized that no, everybody was still there.

The trees rustled again, and the sky seemed to turn on itself. Rain, Ruby realized, an impending storm. She thought of how she and Imogen had strung their bras and knickers on the balustrade that morning. She wanted to dash down and retrieve them before they were pelted by the rain, or torn away by the wind; she was sure that if she left them outside—even for a moment longer—something dreadful might happen to them.

A sharp voice interrupted her thoughts. "Oh, you're awake. You've been asleep for ages. Are you feeling better?"

Ruby nodded slowly without turning around. "Yes, Imogen, thank you."

Imogen wandered into the room as she said, "Your mother's really gone, you know."

"Gone where?"

"And mine is keeping her company," Imogen added resentfully. She moved over to her bed with her eyebrows raised. "Your mother came back to the house and packed a bag for them both—your father almost didn't let her! They're staying in some hotel in another village." She cleared her throat before asking, "Are your parents getting a divorce?"

Ruby felt a rush of horror. "No," she answered quickly, before adding quietly, "I don't know."

"Jessica Dearden's parents are divorced, and she's all right. Didn't you hear your father shout? He was furious."

"My father never shouts," Ruby said heavily, trying to smother the tremor in her voice.

"Well"—Imogen lay back on her bed wearily—"he shouted this afternoon, almost as loudly as *my* father does."

Ruby's thoughts were jumbled. "What happened? Is my mother really not coming back tonight?"

"I don't know." Imogen looked up at Ruby queerly. "She'd been to the doctor—perhaps she's ill. She said she was very cross about the way people were behaving. She said it didn't feel like her house anymore. Also, I think it's going to rain."

"Did Ned see her?"

Imogen pulled a face, "Why do you ask that? I suppose she must have. You missed out on her story about another woman: Clytemnestra. She was married to Agamemnon, do you remember? The one who sacrificed his daughter for the war. So when he got home, all triumphant, his wife stabbed him in the bath."

Ruby frowned. "Yes, she mentioned that one before."

"Ned even wrote her name out for me in Greek; Annie would have loved it. You should have seen it, all spikes and squiggles."

"She stabbed her husband," Ruby repeated carefully.

"It was vengeance for her murdered daughter. But her other children were furious, and so they killed her. It started a new cycle of revenge, Ned explained . . ." Imogen sighed. "But it got confusing, with all the names."

Ruby tried to imagine Liv stabbing Harley in the bath. Hadn't Liv seemed to encourage Ned to tell this very story, on the beach?

Ruby returned to her bed and lay flat on her back again in an attempt to settle her spinning head. With an empty voice, she spoke to the ceiling. "Our underwear is still outside, from this morning. Will you go and fetch it? I don't think I can go downstairs."

Ruby tried not to think about it, but she could still feel the bony press of Harley's knees on her buttocks, the strength of his hands about her body, the thin push of his lips on hers. Perhaps she should stretch herself across the balcony and wait for the inevitable rain to drench her, to wash away her seething skin—anything to let her feel something other than his touch.

"If my mother isn't here," Ruby said tentatively, "perhaps I can eat up here, and stay away from the others."

Imogen didn't respond, and Ruby wondered if she'd lost her loyalty, if it had passed on to Ned. She wondered again if Ned had heard her father shout, and seen her mother leave. With Rhoda now gone, who knew what Georgina might do?

Ruby had a restless night, helped along by the continued rumble of the storm. She awoke many times, and once she was even convinced that the black cat was darting like a quick shadow at the foot of her bed.

In the morning, the water was still dripping past the shutters. Ruby's stomach was curling with hunger, and she and Imogen made their way downstairs. Ruby felt a peculiar shyness—would anyone ask about her sickness? Would her father blame her? And what were they saying about her mother leaving?

But a sorrier business had Harley shouting in the living room. The girls heard him as they descended the stairs, his dark voice seeming to crack and hum like a continuation of last night's storm.

"I'm not going anywhere—it's my son's blasted fault! Bloody motorbike—I was *hoping* it would make a man of him."

"Give him a call, Harley. He needs to hear from you," Ruby heard her father plead. "They say it was a bad accident. He'll need an operation."

Ruby peered into the room, trying to understand their hurried words.

"There's people at the house, *they* can tend to him! There's Nanny."

Harley screwed up his face. "He's in hospital, anyhow. Best place for him. I've no intention of shortening my holiday here."

"He has no mother, Harley," Toby implored, glancing at Angus for support. "You forget, I think."

"And Liv *wants* to return home to him, old boy," Angus added, he and Toby banding together.

Harley shot his friends a furious look. "Of course she does, and ruin my bloody holiday! Since when are we listening to our wives, boys? Yours have bloody scarpered! Using excuses like doctors and swollen bellies and broken teeth, when really they just can't bear to be around either of you!" Angus turned away abruptly, and Harley declared, "Oho, I've touched a nerve, have I!"

"This is about Hugo, Harley. Be a *father*," Toby attempted.

"Like *you*, you mean; like *Angus*—his wife off gallivanting with his unborn son?"

"Polly's fine, Harley," Angus spluttered. "I'm not worried about her."

"Yes, you only worry about yourselves, don't you? Neither of you would know how to father a boy—and neither of you have been kind to Hugo before. I don't know why you're so interested in his well-being now. I suppose he reminds Angus too much of his late mother Clara, doesn't he?"

"Go home, Harley!" Angus cried out hoarsely.

Harley pushed past them into the hallway, and his voice resounded louder than ever. "You two just want to get rid of me. Well, I'm not going anywhere!"

Angus followed through the living room door. Seeing Ruby and Imogen, he hesitated, his eyes full of concern.

"Morning, girls. You've found us in a sorry state today. Come on— brunch . . . Lisette's prepared a feast."

"What's happened, Dada?" Imogen asked softly.

Angus didn't respond, but urged the girls across the hallway into the dining room, where a glorious brunch had indeed been laid. Lisette seemed to be in as thunderous a mood as Harley. She huffed her way through serving tea and coffee to the strange group in the gathering dimness of the dining room. Ruby kept a cautious eye on Harley, who said little through his tight-lipped fury. He wore a thick cricket jumper and silk knotted cravat, and remained withdrawn until the plate of ham and cheeses slid into his lap when he mishandled it.

"Oh, dash it all! Bloody hell."

The only person at the table who seemed comfortable was Liv, who took a second croissant and asked Ruby kind questions about how she was feeling, and whether she often suffered from nosebleeds.

"No, never."

Harley made a large enough gesture that his fork clattered to his plate. "You needn't make such a fuss of the children, Liv. Pretending to care about Ruby and my Hugo, indeed."

Toby wiped his mouth and threw down his napkin. "Harley, honestly!"

"Why don't you do everybody a favor and leave!" Ned blurted out.

"Just because you've said that, Edwina," Harley stuttered fiercely, "I'm staying, and I'll count on you to entertain me. In fact, I demand it. And you two"—he gestured at Imogen and Ruby crossly—"you used to chatter about when I arrived, prancing around like little butterflies. Now you're as sullen as this weather, and as sour as your mothers. Spoiled rotten, both of you—and Imogen in more ways than one!" His eyes landed on Imogen's soft mouth. "I'll put both of you over my knee and punish you for it, mark my words!"

"You will do no such thing, Harley," Angus said stiffly, his hand tightening into a fist, "and if you continue to speak like that about my daughter, and about Ruby, I—"

"Yes, Angus will take you over *his* knee!" Georgina cackled, her laugh breaking across the dining room. "I'd like to see that . . . The two of you as big as each other . . . You've been aching for a fight ever since you first met, all those decades ago! Quite ridiculous!"

"You can keep quiet, George," Harley hit back. "I see what you've been up to, how you've managed to get rid of the lady of the house!"

Ruby speared some melon with her knife, not knowing what else to do. Her father was stiff with rage.

Lisette leaned over Toby to lift the near-empty basket of bread, but he twisted back to scold her, *"S'il te plaît, Lisette. Arrête!"*

Lisette stood up straight with shock. She turned swiftly back to the dresser as Toby seemed to feel the table's judgment. "What?" he spluttered. "She's been in a terrible mood all day—I can't have a missing wife *and* a miserable housekeeper!"

"Exactly my point!" Harley declared. The old woman moved to the sideboard to chop up more slices of baguette, Ruby following her jerky movements with mournful eyes.

Imogen addressed Harley, her eyes round. "What did you mean about me being spoiled in more ways than one?"

Harley's face shifted; he was delighted at the question. "Oh, let me see, what do I mean?"

Angus spoke up again. "Imogen, don't play up to it, please. And Harley, I've already told you to stop speaking to the girls."

"My dear boy, you don't think you can stop my mouth, do you?"

"Perhaps I can't, but Toby can, in his house," Angus answered, his voice low.

Lisette tried to drop the refreshed breadbasket beside Toby, but he threw his arm up so quickly that she again had to dash out of the way. "*Laisse-moi tranquille!* What's wrong with you today, Lisette?"

Lisette stared at her employer, her mouth agape. Then she seemed to break, and cried out, "*Ce n'est pas moi, c'est ma copine! Je ne croyais pas, mais c'est vrai, vous êtes des hors-la-loi!*" Her face seemed to crumple, and Ruby bolted back in her seat as Lisette continued in a hysterical voice, "The boy, he died! The lady's son, my friend! And *your* friend, he hit him with the car! *Monsieur Ashby, je ne supporte plus!*"

"Whose boy?" Georgina said, almost indifferently. Toby glanced from her to Lisette, pressing at his mustache apprehensively.

"*Son fils! Il est mort, à cause de vous!*"

Harley blurted out, "Oh, here we go again. Is this about Max's bloody crash? What a wretched day—shall we have no peace?"

Lisette gave Toby a terrible look, and darted from the room to the passageway and the kitchen beyond. But her cries of fury seemed to hover around them.

"The bloody insolence of it!" Toby stood up decidedly. "For fuck's sake."

"Tobes, it's all righ—" Angus started, stooping forward to reach his friend.

"It isn't, and I'm getting new pressure from the mayor . . . You've no idea what Fuller's blasted accident has cost me. I've got to go and sort her out."

"Can I—" Liv started, but Harley interrupted joyfully. "Good luck, old boy, but if she's friends with the mother, then"—Harley pulled a jeering face—"soon you'll have to silence the whole village. Don't know how you'd manage that! Oh, how their high opinion of you must be crumbling!"

Toby seemed to suddenly acknowledge the presence of Ruby and Imogen. His face was as agitated as his voice. "Upstairs, girls, now!"

They obeyed wordlessly, and gratefully.

"So that old lady from the other day, the one who stopped you in the village—the one who showed up here, shrieking," Imogen said carefully, "had a son who died. In a car accident."

"Yes," Ruby said dully. The frantic voices from downstairs had stopped. And yet the hallway, the stairs, the corridors seemed to beat with Lisette's accusations—her hot and terrified voice had cast a strange spell over the house. Outside, the rain beat down.

Imogen sat on the edge of her bed, her face taut and deep in thought. "And both our fathers knew about it?"

Ruby hesitated before answering, "I think so."

"But they didn't do anything to help the lady?"

Ruby let the question hang in the air as Imogen went on unhappily, "And the reason they didn't do anything is because the car was being driven by . . . Annie's father?"

Ruby went to tidy her dressing table, but there wasn't much to do there. She answered, "Perhaps it wasn't that; perhaps the lady was confused."

"And so . . . Mr. Fuller . . . killed somebody?" Imogen almost whispered, and Ruby's ears started to ring. She imagined that Imogen was unraveling some weak plot totally unworthy of her beloved Poirot mysteries.

"He killed that lady's son . . . and got away with it! He really is a monster!"

Something stung at Ruby, and she blurted out, "It wasn't Annie's father, it was her mother. Don't you remember, the night of the concert?"

But Imogen seemed not to have heard her. "He'll get away with it . . . just like my father did. And your father helped." Imogen looked up at Ruby, her soft face and round eyes growing more anxious. "That horrible man, Mr. Fuller, he must go to prison!"

Ruby sat on her bed with a new thought. "He must have blamed his wife instead. He was the one with the bloody nose, not her. She only had blood on her fingers . . ." She held her breath. "But I don't think we're supposed to talk about it. And I don't think my father would ever do something so awful."

"This is just like how it was with my father." Imogen put a hand to her mouth. "But worse, because Annie's father wasn't sorry."

"Poor Annie," Ruby said. "Thank goodness she's at home and away from this."

"But your father never checked, did he? That she made it home?"

Ruby hesitated, glancing at the curling wildflowers on her dressing table. "No, he didn't. I'll ask him again . . ."

Imogen's thoughts were hurtling forward. "Does the fact that this accident happened in France mean that people truly won't find out?"

"I'm not sure. Stay here, I'll speak to my father." Ruby hurried down the stairs to find her father, and Angus. She needed answers. For Imogen's sake, for Annie's sake, for the old lady who'd lost her son. Ruby felt fiery and nervous. Why had her father worked so hard to cover for the Fullers? Was it Annie's mother who'd driven the car, or Max? And was Annie all right?

Ruby stopped on the first-floor landing. She'd spotted Ned hovering near the double windows. "What are you doing?" Ruby demanded.

Ned answered with a shrug. "Just—"

"Your room isn't on this floor, in this part of the house." Ruby felt another wave of crossness toward Ned, but as she blinked up at her, the black cat seemed to dart past the window curtains.

Ned moved toward her. "Ruby."

"Go away! You don't belong here."

"Ruby, you're having another nosebleed." Ned stepped forward to touch under Ruby's chin. In the next moment she pulled off her top to expose a skinny bikini beneath. "Here, take my T-shirt."

"No!" Ruby pushed Ned's hand away, and touched her nose. Sure enough, there was that strange sensation again, and that long flush from her nose, over her mouth, down her chin, and onto her dress.

"God"—Ned's eyes widened as she pushed her T-shirt into Ruby's face—"it's really gushing out. Jesus, Ruby."

Ruby dashed around her and down the stairs, feeling the warm flow of blood drench through the T-shirt's fabric. She didn't know where Angus was—the dining room had been cleared and only held her father and Harley. Toby looked defiant as he listened to Harley's rolling drawl.

"I won't leave until I've had a decision from you regarding the château, Tobias. Everybody knows you're sailing too close to the wind, dear boy. Perhaps it's time to call it quits. As I've told you, I'm willing to strike a deal, with Max's financial support. Georgina could contribute too, I'm sure." Ruby moved into the doorway and her father's eyes flashed to acknowledge her.

Harley carried on, "Mind you, Georgina shouldn't need to. That girl of hers is your firstborn, not Ruby, and born of truer love than that shared by you and your wife—soon to be ex-wife, if she's really left you. Yes, Château Number Seven ought to be Ned's by rights—even if it is cursed. I've always told you to do the right thing there. And you can call Angus off your guard—one word from me in the wrong direction and he'll be locked up."

"I refuse to listen to this!" Toby bolted upright, and the table shifted with his movement. "How dare you speak to me like this in my own house, and in front of Ruby!"

Harley turned, and was surprised to see Ruby there. His mouth twisted into a snarl as he said, "Oh, everybody knows—why shouldn't your little flower be told?" He narrowed his eyes at her directly. "Your father is a swine, Ruby. Always has been, always will be!"

Ruby blinked as her father approached her. She felt a strange wave of dizziness, and tried to duck away into the corridor—but her father gripped hold of her shoulder with frightening strength. He muttered through his teeth, "Ruby, we will discuss what you've just heard, you won't have understood—"

"Oh, won't she? Too late now!" Harley laughed uproariously at his friend, just as a rumble of thunder seemed to reverberate through the walls. Ruby pressed the fabric against her face again, seeing in the next moment Ned's face cowering in the shadow of the door, hearing every word. As she caught Ruby's eye, Ned's face stretched into a grin and she nudged at her glasses with her finger, her gaze unblinking. Their father's glasses, their father's gaze. Ruby took a breath into the damp fabric against her face, wanting to scream her humiliation.

She pulled away from her father and stumbled back into the hallway, dizzy again and desperate for a hit of cold clear air. The rain was coming down and bringing the inky blue of a new storm with it. Ruby dashed outside.

She stumbled through the rain, her wild, cruel thoughts pushing her forward. Ned was her father's firstborn child; Ned would have the house, Harley would insist on it. Harley, Georgina, and Ned would move into the house. Mr. Fuller would be able to return. He'd terrorize that old woman, would challenge Ruby's father, torture Annie, and then manhandle Imogen again.

Ruby's eyes creased with distress as she tried to reverse her imaginings: Ned and Georgina out of the house, and Harley with them. Mr. Fuller in prison for his terrible crime. And Annie left behind, like she had been at the airport. In a French village, lost and fading like a blot on the landscape, just like Ruby now.

She ran.

24

As the sky slid into darkness and the village lights flickered on, Ruby sat outside the café, at the edge of the awning, since she had no money for drinks. She was grateful to the rain for washing away her blood-stained nose. She'd discarded Ned's bloodied T-shirt, and sat in the rain even as her hair dampened and rivulets of water slipped into her eyes, even as a few villagers glanced her way.

The waitress made to approach, so Ruby quickly moved to the other side of the square, hovering instead in the doorway of an *agence immo-bilière.* Ruby shivered in her clothes, now plastered against her body. She didn't care. It was good to feel something other than the hammer of her heart, than the heavy agitation bearing down on her shoulders.

She didn't want to go back to the house. There, she felt like she was witnessing the slow commencement of an explosion—like the first-lit fireworks on Bonfire Night that fizzle and spit for a long moment, then leap into the air with a brightly colored scream. Ruby couldn't face her furious father, who couldn't know whether Ruby had under-stood Harley's remarks about Ned, never realizing that she'd known for some time. Harley, too, brash and unpredictable, whirling around and damaging everyone in his wake, just like those wild and sparkling pinwheels. The truth of Ned's parentage was wedged in the past, Ruby thought, like a stone that couldn't be moved—like the château itself. It would never be changed, but it could be blasted open. Ruby simply refused to be there for the explosion.

The church bell chimed the late hour, startling Ruby from her position in the doorway. She hurried across the square, down the street, and to the safety of the church entryway. She found a safe, deep corner, and sat down. Pulling at her damp clothes, she saw the dirty dribble between her feet, and wondered whether she could fall asleep there, pour herself into the puddle and disappear.

Sometime later, a light shone toward her. It swung through the everlasting rain, before the pop of an umbrella, and a woman's voice. "Ruby!"

Ruby didn't recognize the voice at first, but she soon saw Liv, wearing a haggard expression and a shiny raincoat. "There you are, thank goodness."

Ruby suddenly realized she was crying—with relief or sadness, she wasn't sure.

"I think it's time to go home."

Ruby turned away from Liv's earnest face. "I don't want to. I can't." Her voice was loud, bouncing across the stone walls of the alcove, despite the noise of the pelting rain.

"You must. It's very cold and wet; you don't want to become ill."

Ruby stood, wobbling on her weakened legs. "How did you know I would be here?"

"I had a hunch."

Ruby hesitated. She thought of her gift, her bookmark, and wondered how Liv's hunch had been such a true one. She wondered whether a Joan of Arc statue stood in that very church somewhere behind her, silently urging her on.

"Did—did no one else wonder where I was?" Ruby asked emptily.

"Yes, of course, but . . . they were indisposed. Look, I've brought dry things for you. Go to that corner and I'll turn around."

Ruby shouldered Liv away. "I don't care. I don't want to go back there. There's . . . there's nothing for me there."

"There is, Ruby. There's your father and, well," Liv hesitated, "your mother *is* away, of course. But it's your home, your family's summer home, it's where you belong, and where there are people who love you."

Ruby considered Liv's words, but they didn't seem to make sense. She leaped at a sure thing. "I'm worried about Annie getting back to England. I asked my father, but he didn't check."

Liv tilted her head gently. "Do you have any means of contacting her?"

"No," Ruby said miserably.

"Your father—he should have a number for her, after the orchestra trip?"

"Oh." Ruby remembered the pages of forms and documents from the beginning of the summer. "Yes, I think my mother had a list of them. For emergencies."

"Well, then, this is an emergency." Liv undid a bag from her shoulder. "Put these on now and give me your wet clothes."

Ruby was silent as she took the clothing from Liv. She turned around obediently, stepping out of her wet shoes onto the cold stone, dropping her trousers and blouse, and putting on a pair of shorts she didn't recognize and a large black cashmere jumper that felt soft and warm against her skin. "Thank you for coming to find me, Mrs. Montgomery."

"Of course. The car isn't parked far away, just a little walk."

"You are kind—thank you," Ruby said, surprising herself. She suddenly added, "I'm so sorry about what happened to your baby."

Liv turned to gaze at Ruby, before fussing with her umbrella. She cleared her throat and said, "Oh, Ruby. Thank you."

Ruby blushed a little, hearing the agony in Liv's response. She clutched at her wet clothes, wondering whether they'd do better in the bin, but Liv took them in the next moment. She opened the umbrella and clicked on the flashlight. Ruby tucked her hand into Liv's elbow just as the woman gave Ruby an encouraging squeeze. They went into the dark rain together.

BACK AT THE HOUSE, THE living room lamps were on, as were the lights in the hall. Outside, the sea was a soundless black that had bled through the trees, all the way to the sky. It was as if the storm had washed and dyed everything dark. Ruby had no idea how late it was.

Her father stood in the light of the front door, a bleak and ghostly silhouette. "Ruby," he said.

She hurried up the steps with a shiver, cold again now that they'd reached the house, the night air seeping through the threads of the cashmere jumper.

"Ruby," Toby said again, blocking the doorway. "Where did you go all day? We were worried sick. What would your mother say?"

"I'm sorry, Father."

"Ruby." Angus staggered forward and almost tugged her through the door. "You scared us half to death, little thing. You absolutely cannot leave like that again." She jostled about in his rough embrace. He glared down at her, pushing the hair out of her face with his coarse fingers. "Your hair is wet through. Whose clothes are these?"

Ruby's face was hot with the attention. "Oh. My clothes . . ." She turned to acknowledge Liv before glancing at her father guiltily. "I left them in the car."

"Ruby." Toby stepped forward, patting Angus's arm firmly, and Angus let go of Ruby automatically. "Go upstairs and get dry. I'll come and speak to you about what you heard in the dining room today."

Ruby avoided the gaze of the two men and regarded the stairs warily, uncertain that she could muster the energy to step across the hallway, let alone stride up the steps. She certainly didn't have the energy to speak to her father. She said quietly, "Isn't Imogen in my bedroom?" Toby hesitated, so Ruby filled the silence, relieved, "It's all right, Father. I'm very tired. You don't need to speak to me." She knew her father would prefer it that way. He had never understood what ran through her mind, and this would be no different.

"Of course, Ruby. You must be exhausted. I don't even know how Liv found you." He turned to Liv, who was shaking out her jacket and returning it to the cupboard. "I am so grateful. Rhoda will be too, when she finds out about this."

"There's no need to trouble Rhoda, Toby," Liv said tightly. "Now that Ruby is safe and home."

Angus nodded at Liv, and asked, "Shouldn't one of us take Ruby up, make sure she's all right?"

"I could—" Liv started.

"I'll be fine," Ruby found herself saying without turning her head. She touched her forehead, the pieces of hair Angus had pushed just now, soft but stiff from the rain. She felt newly grown-up—neither embarrassed nor shy. She climbed the staircase alone.

Nobody had thought to close Ruby's windows during the second storm, certainly not Imogen, and the water had run in across much of the floor, past her bloodied towel from earlier that day and toward Ruby's bed, so that even the overhanging bedcovers touched the long pool of water. Ruby looked over at Imogen as the cool air sifted through the room. She was asleep, with her mouth slightly open and one arm draped behind her head. Which fairy was she now, Ruby wondered— the Sleeping Fairy . . . the Peaceful Fairy? Yes, it was peaceful there in that room, even as the soft wind ruffled through the trees outside. Ruby left the doors open and climbed into her bed. But the storm in her chest raged on.

25

Ruby awoke to a fresh heat sifting through the window. She had to remind herself where she was as she blinked in the bright light. Imogen wasn't there.

People were talking loudly on the terrace—was it already lunchtime? Ruby's next thought went to the telephone. The school papers with the pupils' numbers—she had to find Annie's, call it, and check. She'd look in the desk in the living room, perhaps, or in her father's study. Or it could be mixed in with the French phone books?

Ruby picked up her blood-spotted *Death on the Nile,* pressing the Joan of Arc bookmark into the middle, and held it like some kind of talisman. She slipped downstairs, keeping close to the wall, taking care that her bare feet made no noise on the tiles. She dashed across the hall, but smacked into Harley coming from the dining room, laden with plates and cutlery. Ruby edged backward, raising her head sharply; Harley was looking down at her with a grimace.

"What d'you think you're doing? Prancing about in your nightdress! Have you even checked yourself in the mirror?" Harley tutted loudly. "And cavorting off last night—why aren't you being punished?"

Ruby's mouth tightened. "I don't know. I've only just woken up."

"Of course, Rhoda isn't here." A strange and mocking smile lifted his face. "No discipline. No proper punishment. You're wild, and going the same way as your mad grandmother."

Ruby felt a sting of rage. "Stop being rude about my grandmother."

"Oho! You've no idea. Her brain rotted along with this house. She hated the sight of all of us by the end." Harley's eyes creased maliciously as he moved to the front door, nudging Ruby with him. "Even her spirit sours the rooms—she can't bear to have us here, I'm sure of it! Yes, you Ashbys are all cursed, like that black cat. If my dogs were here, they'd eat him up. And if you insist on wandering about at this late hour half-dressed, I'll eat you up, too! Now, get out of here before I do exactly that."

Ruby shifted uncomfortably in her loose nightdress. She glanced at the living room door mournfully as Harley nudged at her again between the shoulder blades. She stiffened, but he pushed back, so she moved through the door.

The flagstones of the terrace were baking hot under Ruby's bare feet, steaming after yesterday's rain. She tried to focus on the table, where so much seemed out of place. Lunch had been cobbled together with leftovers; there was no vase of wildflowers on the table, nor any of the usual napkins. Lisette wasn't there—nor her father. But Angus was, beside Georgina, and Imogen next to Ned, who was happily packing ham into a baguette. With Harley urging her on from behind, Ruby couldn't help seeing them all as insolent strangers. Sitting at her father's table, her mother's, hers—not theirs. Harley dropped the plates on the table, and Georgina stood to hand them around.

"Ruby," Georgina said brightly. "Have some lunch."

Ruby didn't take a plate, but asked, "Where's my father?"

"He's seeing to something. Your mother telephoned to say she'll see us in the village for drinks this evening, with Polly," Georgina answered, just as Angus bent toward Ruby and asked, "And how are you today, little thing? Your father insisted on letting you sleep."

Ruby only nodded.

Ned spoke up, clearly feeling that her voice ought to be heard. "Ruby, don't you look a sight, almost bohemian!"

"She's fine," Angus said, standing up heavily and passing Ruby his empty plate. "Here, what d'you fancy eating, Ruby? You must be starving. We're all so pleased you're safe."

Ruby nodded again, concentrating on the heavy dish of roasted vegetables that Imogen held out to her. She spooned out a splodge, but its oil dribbled across the tablecloth onto her plate. Taking her seat, she didn't dare glance around the group. They sat there as if nothing was wrong, with no mention of the drama of the previous days, no mention of Harley's son in hospital, nor his ultimatum over the château, or Max's car accident, or the truth of Ned's birth. Was it all still unspoken—was the explosion that she'd worried about now suspended?

"So Ruby"—Ned's eyes were wide with mischief—"how *was* your escapade? Liv rescued you?"

Ruby looked around for Liv, thoroughly ignoring Ned's gaze. "Yes, she did. Thank you again, Mrs. Montgomery."

"That's a surprise!" Harley said, tearing the skin of the *saucisson*. "Trying too late to be a mother, I see."

"Harley, your unkindness astounds me more and more every day," Liv said simply, putting her hand on the table. Everybody turned to her as she said, "Now, it's your turn to listen to me. When we return to England, I'm going to divorce you."

The table seemed to stiffen as everybody looked at each other. Harley's expression was one of hilarity, of suspended disbelief. But as he checked his wife's face, he grew angry.

"Don't make me laugh. You can't do that, Oh-liv-i-ahh—you'll lose your situation and position in society without me and my connections. Your precious charities, and all that."

Liv leaned forward and nodded like an old bird. "I'll fight you in the courts, Harley, and I will win. Every penny that you throw about has got my name on it. My charities will last longer than your bank balance."

Harley's face twisted. "You fucking bitch."

Ned stood abruptly. "Imogen, Ruby, bring your plates. Let's go to the pool. This isn't suitable for young ears."

———

AT THE POOL, RUBY DIDN'T know what to do; she didn't know what kind of game Ned was playing. She could still feel her shadowy sneer from the day before, now formed into barbed words; but the truth of it seemed to have evaporated with the daylight. Ruby didn't want to return to the terrace, but if she were to escape to the house, she'd have to pass by them. Imogen settled herself across a lounger with her plate, while Ned sat at the edge of the pool and put her legs in the water.

"Shall we have another story? Let me think . . ." Ned smiled into the sun. "Who are the other women mixed up with the Trojan War?"

"I'm fed up of these stories," Ruby blurted out.

"Don't be so bloody rude, Ruby," Ned shot back, and Ruby felt a flash of gladness at her irritation.

"*I* like the stories."

"Yes, I know you do, Imogen. Good." Ned threw a smile her way. "So. Briseis. She was given as a gift to Achilles. She was a spoil of war after the Greeks raided some town. All the main war heroes had a slave girl given to them."

Imogen screwed up her face. "That's horrible. How old were they?"

"Oh, I don't know. Probably my age?"

Imogen raised her eyebrows sympathetically.

"Anyway, Agamemnon's girl was the daughter of a priest, so the priest was furious, and asked Apollo to send a plague of arrows on the Greek camp until Agamemnon returned her."

"Oh." Imogen's face set with concern. "He wanted his daughter back? He must have really cared about her."

"Yeah . . . something Agamemnon knows nothing about, of course." Ned chuckled, and kicked the water with her feet. "Anyway, Agamemnon was without his slave girl. So he took Briseis for himself. Achilles was insulted and demanded her back. 'No,' said Agamemnon, 'she's mine now! I had mine taken and I'm the boss, so I deserve her more than you do!' But Achilles had formed an attachment, and he felt insulted that his 'prize' had been snatched away, that he had been dishonored.

So he refused to go into battle, and then of course the Greeks started losing the war."

"Why?" asked Imogen.

"Because Achilles was the greatest fighter of them all." Ned pulled her feet up to the side of the pool. "I forgot to say that, sorry. So, without him, the Greeks lose."

"Achilles was the best fighter of them all? Isn't he supposed to be your father, Imogen?" A sparkling thought flitted through Ruby's mind.

"Yes, that's exactly right," Ned said triumphantly. "You see, you *are* interested, Ruby."

Ruby narrowed her eyes and turned her face toward the shade, refusing to meet Ned's look.

"So," Ned continued, gripping at her baguette, "Agamemnon returned Briseis, eventually. But it was too late, really. Achilles's pride was hurt. He had a bit of a temper, old Achilles. He continued to refuse to fight, causing the Greeks to lose. His best friend, Patroclus, went instead of him, dressed up like him."

"I thought his best friend was Odysseus."

"No, Achilles and Odysseus just sort of got on, but they weren't best friends. Patroclus and Achilles actually *grew up* together. Anyway, Patroclus went into battle and led Achilles's men, wearing his armor and everything! But the thing was, even though the Greeks did fight better that day, Patroclus was killed, because the prince of Troy, Hector, thought he was Achilles, and took the opportunity to really go for him."

"The best of the Greeks," Ruby said, toying anxiously with her plate as she resisted sitting down.

"Yes." Ned nodded. "So, Patroclus died, which wasn't part of the plan. Achilles was devastated, and the Greeks had to do full funeral rites and games and things for Patroclus. And then Achilles ended up killing Hector, the prince of Troy, afterward, as revenge. But the most important part—"

"Do you mean to say," Imogen interrupted, chewing on her lunch, "that all those men killing each other was because of a slave girl?"

"Yes. And the Trojan War started because of Helen, if you remember."

Ruby said dully, "I think that everything, always, seems to be about a man and a girl."

"A man and a *woman,* or a *boy* and a girl—like in *Romeo and Juliet.* Yes, that's usually where most conflict lies in literature." Ned wiggled her eyebrows. "Sex, you know. Difficult, but exciting."

Imogen stiffened. "You *haven't!*"

"Oh, my darling sweet Imogen." Ned raised her arm to reach toward her. "Although my mother encourages 'sexual autonomy' . . . I'm only seventeen. Though I can't say I've never been tempted."

"I'll never be tempted," Ruby announced from her side of the pool.

"Oh, well, you're only little . . . both of you." Ned smiled. "You'll understand when you're older."

Imogen had a sick look on her face. Ned didn't seem to notice as she carried on. "Briseis is an interesting one, because she was neither grand nor wellborn. She was a slave of war, but still managed to have an impact—"

"Wellborn?" Imogen repeated.

"Yes, like you, daughter of a lord." Ned regarded Imogen. "The Honorable Imogen Bly."

"Yes, but," Ruby interjected. "What does that even matter?"

"Don't be jealous of Imogen, Ruby." Ned pushed at her sunglasses.

Ruby scowled. "I'm not jealous." She looked between Ned and Imogen, her thoughts running wild at all that was being left unsaid. Would everything just continue on as it always had—or would it get even worse? No, Ruby was determined that it wouldn't. She didn't know how much longer she could cope.

"I'm going for a swim," she announced.

"But you haven't got your swim things." Imogen tilted her head curiously.

"I don't care. I'll swim in my nightdress." Ruby raised her head haughtily. "Don't worry about me."

Ned glared at Ruby as she dropped her plate and waded into the water. The fabric of Ruby's nightdress was billowing out at the sides, so she let herself sink, burying her head straight down, like a drowning person would, breathing out the wide bubbles that burst to the surface.

26

Imogen went with Ned to watch one of her horror films. They had become a blur in Ruby's mind; she refused to watch any more messes of birds attacking blond women, or strange alien newtlike animals bursting out of men's stomachs. In her mind they had become part of Ned's cruel and strange calculations.

Her nosebleeds and her thoughts, Ruby realized, were horror enough.

Ruby lay flat on her bed to read, raising the book high above her with both arms. She left the shutters and windows wide open, so that she could feel, hear, and smell the new warmth drying out the damp château and its environs. The rain had so drenched the stone of the balcony and the nearby floor tiles that Ruby had thrown towels down to soak up the wide pools of water. In some ways she was surprised that the thrust of the thunderstorm hadn't broken off the balcony completely, leaving a gaping hole in her bedroom wall, ready for her to tumble out.

In the late afternoon she finished *Death on the Nile*. Ruby pressed the book against her heart. How could such a story be held in such a small volume, in those bound pages? She stared at the cover, at that ornate pistol with the pearl handle, just as it was described in the novel. It looked like the tiny metal pistol in the Cluedo board game downstairs. Ruby frowned to herself; they hadn't played any board games at all this summer.

The black cat sniffed through the open shutters, itching to go outside. Ruby looked at him. "Don't go on the balcony, it's dangerous," she said.

Ruby's mood hardened as she flicked through the book again. She couldn't deny that she was devastated—infuriated even—by the ending. Of course, she loved to be tricked and surprised by the clever plots of Agatha Christie, but this twist had been too much to bear. Her favorite character had been the killer—the woman she'd liked, and even pitied, had been responsible for the murders. What was worse, Ruby entirely understood why she'd done it. Just like she understood Clytemnestra stabbing her husband in the bath. And Carrie, who killed all her classmates after they tricked and tortured her.

Ruby fiddled with her bookmark. Joan of Arc. Had she been badly treated, too? Did she also want revenge? Better to be a Carrie than a classmate, Ruby thought. Yes, better a Clytemnestra than an Iphigenia. Better to perhaps create the explosion oneself, rather than wait for it.

At least, Ruby thought, she could take Joan with her to the next book. Her grandmother had read these Agatha Christies, too—had she liked these characters? Ruby wasn't sure she wanted to think about her grandmother. She didn't like the fact that Harley had known her, and she definitely didn't like what he'd said about her. Particularly because it niggled at a memory she had from when she was very small.

Once, her grandmother joked that she could take Ruby with her on one of her trips abroad. She'd let Ruby beg and plead with her before giving in, saying she'd check whether Ruby would fit in her travel-case. Ruby's heart quivered as her grandmother placed her inside, closed the buckles, and sealed the case, plunging Ruby into tight darkness. The darkness lasted a long time, and it had scared the young Ruby, who had clamored and fought to get out. Her grandmother had only laughed afterward, insisting that it was play, and clutching Ruby close in a clumsy, apologetic embrace.

There was a creak of her shutters. Ruby looked up, startled and suddenly terribly aware of her dark thoughts. What was wrong with her? She put the book under her pillow and left her bedroom.

27

2010

Mrs. Cosgrove hadn't expected to sleep during the day, but the visit to the house and the return walk to the village had exhausted her. No faces had haunted her dreams this time, only dark corridors ending in even darker rooms with long windows and slamming shutters. Her muscles felt tight and confused, her arm was stiff and numb, and her hip ached. There was a burn mark on her hand, from a cigarette.

She sat up with a twinge, drawing her hand closer to her face to better see the pale pink burn, below the curve of her thumb. The ashtray was again piled high, but beside it was only one tall clear glass of sparkling water.

Robert Payne had left a second message, but she hadn't opened it. She had only one goal for what remained of that day.

Imogen hobbled to the bathroom. Her hand was stinging now that she was awake and aware of the burn. She opened the tap and let the water run, leaning into her reflection to better check her face—her pores, the wrinkles around her eyes, the thin lines of her forehead. Her mother would have disapproved, but Imogen knew that she'd earned every single one of those lines. Her pale skin seemed to flash at her as she turned away.

She was the same age now as her mother was then, with one pre-teenage daughter and one baby on the way. Her brother, who was so far below her in age and even further in emotion, had always been a stranger to her. He'd been born too late, and she'd grown too much after that summer—or not enough, perhaps, since a piece of her had always lingered there. The same helpless piece of her soul that had left the house and run along the coastal path with tears streaming down her face.

Just as Ruby had done twenty-five years earlier.

Imogen's fear over Ruby's disappearance into the night had been trumped by her father's frantic fury. She'd never seen him like that, flustered and out of sorts, positively shaking Toby, his best friend, and demanding that they all go out and find her. No, Toby had replied coolly, we'll only waste our time. She doesn't need to be indulged, she needs to learn, he'd insisted. Imogen had listened to the fathers' discussion at the door, and finally mounted the stairs silently, her chest clawing with anxiety as the evening set in. *"She needs to learn."* She'd turned the words over in her head. She still wondered—had there been something they'd all needed to learn?

Imogen covered her mouth as her eyes creased with tears. She felt again that clawing in her chest, and it pulled great sobs from her in the hotel bathroom. There had been nothing for them, as children, to learn. What the adults had needed to learn was compassion, tenderness, and some parental form of giving love. She longed to climb back into that memory, to take her young self aside, and explain. To move between those adults and turn them toward the children, to fill in that neglected space with the warmth and kindness that had been so badly needed. Her sobs shook her whole body, her eyes brimming over so thickly that she couldn't see. One hand touched the cold tiles of the floor, and she realized she must have collapsed. She curled herself into the fetal position, flat on the cold, unfeeling floor.

The behavior that summer had shocked the young Imogen. She'd never been exposed to such emotional and physical violence. She'd never been turned away from her mother's embrace so repeatedly, or seen the truth of her father's manslaughter so clearly, or been so entirely left to her own helpless devices.

And Imogen had watched Ruby meet every horrifying circumstance as if she expected it, as if she was used to it. But Imogen wasn't; she'd never been. It was as if the silent Ruby had accepted Harley's despicable conduct, his aggressive dominance; as if she were blind to Georgina's taking advantage, and the truth about Ned being her sister; as if she had absorbed the story of Imogen's father's disgrace just as easily as she'd accepted Max Fuller's car accident, and the deaths that the men had covered up. Every moment had rocked Imogen to her core, but she'd had no idea how Ruby felt—until that final morning.

As her breathing slowed, Imogen remembered the cold tiles of an upstairs bathroom, how her small knees had strained as she'd bent over to retch into the toilet, how Ruby had held her hair back, and how she'd held Ruby's in turn.

Those tiles were still there, she now knew. They bore their own memories. The furniture, the walls, the very air. When the place became hers, Imogen thought, she'd clear it out, have the furniture burned, tear up those floors. But the house itself seemed to stand strong—as sturdy as the oldest oak tree in England, with its roots buried deep into the ground and its branches reaching high into the heavens. It would take a great deal for Imogen to cut through.

She wondered what Hugo Montgomery knew about that summer, what he was learning as he lay in wait in this very hotel. Imogen wondered whether she'd managed to soften him, to ease the upbringing of the boy born to the monstrous Harley—Harley who had gathered favors and friends like jewels to fill out his glittering crown and sit himself greedily above others. Here was his son with that tortured face, asking questions with a forensic-looking older man beside him, a lawyer perhaps, or a private detective. Here to cause problems for her and for that strange red-haired child that had run out into the night, who had tried to protect Imogen when she needed it. Well, perhaps it was *her* turn now to do the protecting.

Imogen pulled herself to standing, and turned off the tap. She unpinned her thick black hair and let it tumble over her shoulders. She'd do her face, single out a clean outfit, and have a proper walk around the village. She'd visit the shops, walk along the harbor, smile at people, let her skin see the sun, have a cocktail somewhere near the beach. Play the game of life, just like she'd been taught to do, but on her own terms now. Find new places that her child self hadn't known.

Then she'd return to the hotel to confront Hugo Montgomery.

The phone was ringing again in the bedroom. Was it Alexandra, badgering her to return? Or was it the estate agent with news that the château was no longer for sale, that she'd hesitated too long?

Or was it perhaps only a simple call from downstairs, informing her that somebody wanted to see her?

Mrs. Cosgrove stepped forward to answer it.

28

1985

The telephone stood undisturbed on the table in the late afternoon gloom.

Ruby tiptoed into the living room and made for the dresser, sifting through the phone books, trying to find any useful-looking documents with the St. Aubyn's name. She tugged open a drawer, then another, frantically. She lifted the telephone handle to hear the line drone on enticingly.

Then she spotted it: "Pupil Parent Directory." Ruby dropped her book and grasped at the document, almost tearing it in her hands. F for "Fuller"; her eyes followed the line. There were three numbers given—two that were local to their school, since Ruby recognized the area code, and another entirely different. She'd try that one.

A shape moved past the door, then doubled back. Ruby looked up to see Imogen's face peering at her, before looking away, as if they'd caught each other out. Imogen was braver. She stepped forward.

"Sorry to disturb you, Ruby. Ned's sent me away, she's busy in her room, but I wanted to see where you were."

Ruby kept her mouth tightly closed as she lowered the pages, and slid them between two phone books.

Lisette moved through the dark hallway with her bucket of cleaning materials and a stringy mop. She halted when she saw the girls.

"Let's go upstairs?" Imogen said quickly.

"Yes," Ruby said, taking up her book. At least the number was there, she told herself.

In the disturbing hush of the house, they mounted the stairs. Imogen seemed to bubble with nervousness. "I wonder what my mother is doing today."

"If she's with my mother she'll be right as rain," Ruby said automatically. "Your mother is my mother's favorite person."

"What about your father?"

Ruby carried on ahead of Imogen. "I don't know."

"I suppose they've been fighting, haven't they," Imogen said darkly. "And my father certainly isn't my mother's favorite person. It's funny, isn't it . . ."

"Yes, very funny." Ruby let out an unhappy gurgle of a laugh as she scooted around to the second stairwell, Imogen trailing behind her. There was a sudden noise from the floor above, and Ruby hesitated. It sounded like a joyful cry, or some terrible laugh, and it came through the door to the attic rooms.

"No," Imogen continued. "I didn't mean *funny* funny, I meant—"

"Did you hear that?" Ruby stopped, hearing the noise again.

"It's the house." Imogen shrugged. "Come on."

Ruby's bedroom door stood open along the corridor. She hurried toward it, hearing again that strange cry.

Across the landing, Harley had thrown open his bedroom door and was snarling like a beast as he darted forward.

"What do you think you're doing, thundering about? How dare you wake me up from my snooze! After the day I've had!"

The two girls went stiff with shock. In the next moment Harley was in front of them, yanking at their arms.

"Your bastard fathers think they can get one up on me! I'll show them, by God. Yes I will!"

Harley leaned tall over them and tugged them into his bedroom, before whirling around to slam the door closed.

"Discipline! That's what you both need. Now bend over, and I'll give you a proper smack." Ruby looked around her wildly, at the guest room she used to recognize, now covered with Harley's things. A mess of drained whiskey tumblers, a brush tangled with gray hair, a glass bottle of cologne, and some dark stench coming from the bathroom. In the far corner was an open suitcase, full of Liv's neatly packed things.

"Bend over, I say!"

"No," Ruby said, but her voice quaked.

Imogen let out a sob, and Ruby turned to her. She was shaking.

"No?" Harley laughed with a heavy shake. "No? You'll see what I can do, you little bitch. This bloody book you're always carrying around, for starters. You'll see what I'm capable of!"

Harley staggered toward Ruby. He pulled her *Death on the Nile* out of her hand and began tearing out the pages. Ruby watched them fly apart and wither to the ground. In spite of her agonized fury, she cried out, "It doesn't matter! I've finished it anyway. You can't hurt me, or Imogen!"

"Oh yes I can." Harley's blue eyes seemed to flash. "Now bend over."

Ruby remained standing defiantly. But Harley pushed her around roughly, twisting her body back and down. He hit her. She felt her spine crack and her buttocks wince with the sharp pain of his slap. Each stroke hit harder, Harley's flat fleshy hand pounding through the thin fabric of dress. Ruby gritted her teeth and pushed her arms against the bed, her hair falling over her face as her eyes streamed and her mouth spat with anger, hurt, resentment.

After several thrusts Harley relented and Imogen took her turn.

It wasn't until a long, panting moment later that Ruby could stagger to stand. She saw Harley put his fingers across Imogen's mouth to quiet her yelping, pulling her up by her hair with his other hand. Imogen screamed and spat, desperate to get away from him. Ruby glared at Harley, wanting to fling herself at him, put herself between Imogen and his brutal hand. But she was frozen to the spot, her buttocks aflame, her legs bolted to the floor like steel.

"Yes," Harley was saying, "you will submit, pretty thing, pretty

Imogen. You need a good smacking. Damaged goods, that's what you are. Damaged quite nicely, from what I heard."

Ruby tried to reach for Imogen, but Harley pushed her away. She fell, and her knees burned as they scraped the tiled floor. Harley took another heavy breath. After one final swoop of his hand, he staggered back to survey his work. Imogen was sobbing helplessly.

"There we are then." Harley reared his head and drew his hand across his mouth, deeply satisfied. "Now you have been disciplined. You'll both stay here to think about what you've done. I shall return when I'm ready."

RUBY AND IMOGEN STAYED STILL until they heard the door click shut, then a key turn in the lock.

Ruby quickly began collecting the torn pages of *Death on the Nile*. As her hair fell forward in thick strands, she wedged the pages into the book's cover, now ripped at the binding. With every movement of her body she winced, the pain in her buttocks stinging as loudly as the ringing in her ears. Imogen sniffed heavily behind her, and Ruby's eyes filled with tears.

"He's locked us in." Imogen's voice quivered. "He's locked us in."

Ruby shook her head. "I know. Where is Mrs. Montgomery? She might come back."

"It hurts, Ruby! It hurts so much, it burns!" Imogen raised her dress, and Ruby saw red hand marks across her thighs and her buttocks, staining every spare inch of skin. Ruby could feel the marks of her own pain too, but it somehow felt worse to see it on Imogen, painted on her very flesh.

"I'm sorry," Ruby sputtered.

"How do we get out?" Imogen cried. "How?"

Ruby staggered forward and made her way toward the windows, looking through the shutters, seeing the shape of the balcony. The room was the mirror image of her own. Could they jump? No, they'd break their legs. Could they climb? There was nothing to hold on to. They could only leave by the door.

"Is there anyone outside we can call out to?" Imogen asked desperately. Ruby shook her head. Imogen pummeled at the locked door, lifting her voice to call out through her sobbing. Ruby closed her eyes, willing somebody to hear, to help them. Anyone on the same floor, anyone at all.

Ruby was exhausted. She fell forward onto her hurt knees again, letting her face rest on the cool of the floor tiles. Imogen joined her, breathing heavily. Ruby's eyes went dark as she heard soft cries pass between the two of them.

She wasn't sure how long they lay like that, but it was long enough to hear people downstairs, emerging onto the terrace—long enough for the stench of Harley's belongings to crawl into Ruby's nose, and lodge itself into her mind, where her fury dug in.

Imogen's crying gradually grew louder, and with one heart-stopping squeal the lock clicked and the door pushed open. Lisette was peering through the gap.

The French woman's rheumy eyes blinked, trying to understand what she was seeing. *"Mais qu'est-ce qu'il se passe, mesdemoiselles?"*

Ruby staggered to stand. Lisette stepped into the room, and reached a supporting arm out to Imogen, who was nearer. Imogen resisted Lisette with another sob, and instead fell forward through the door, aching for freedom. Ruby quickly followed Imogen with a *"Merci, Lisette,"* but bashed into her a moment later, and stopped short.

Harley stood, waiting. He had returned, with a swirling tumbler of brown fluid in one hand. His eyebrows were raised critically, and his tone was cool but menacing.

"There, there, girlies. Saved by the housekeeper. Well, you've had a taste! Now you know what I'm capable of if you dare cross me again." He swung toward them as Lisette came back through the door. At the sight of Harley, she bowed her head meekly. His voice grew fiercer. "Your fathers like to rile me up. Well, that's what I can do in return. You just watch that you don't tell anyone of this! I'm only footsteps away . . . There's plenty more I can do to you both in the dead of night."

Imogen shrank back, keeping her sobs low, but Ruby stepped forward, trying to shield her. There was a clunk from above, and Harley tipped his head up to finish his speech. "Now. We're going out for drinks, so have a wash, look sharp, and sort yourselves out. We're meeting your blessed mothers! Liv isn't coming—she's no mother." He laughed hoarsely. "And I warn you both . . . watch yourselves, because I really *will* deal with you again tomorrow."

Lisette stepped aside for Harley to pass. She hadn't understood his words, but took in his meaning very well. She didn't leave the girls' side until Harley closed the door of his bedroom, taking the key in with him.

Lisette lifted her cleaning things and hurried toward the stairwell, moving down the stairs without another look. Ruby pulled Imogen into her bedroom, where they stood silently, their faces full of worry. Ruby stared hard at the keyhole in the door, at the gap there, and wondered for the first time where that key might be.

"What did he mean"—Imogen sniffed quietly as she sat on her bed, gripping her knees to her chest—"when he said I've been 'damaged quite nicely'? Do . . . do you think he might come in tonight? I want my mother, Ruby. What should we do?"

Ruby dropped what remained of her book on her bed, and answered in a muddled voice, "I think we should wash, and pull ourselves together. Yes, that's what our mothers would tell us to do."

29

2010

Mrs. Cosgrove lifted the receiver.

"Hello?"

The voice on the other end was strong and irritable. "Darling, it's me, for heaven's sake."

"Mama." Imogen reeled back with surprise.

"Darling, will you get back here? It's becoming intolerable."

"Are you all right, Mama, is something wrong?" She noticed that her hand shook as it held the phone, the same hand marked with the cigarette burn.

"Yes. People are asking questions, Imogen," her mother continued. "You just disappeared into thin air. And that's not the worst of it! Eleanor says there's a gentleman—Rupert someone—telling people that he's whisked you off to his country pile, that you're hiding there, and planning to elope with him?"

"No, Mama." Imogen's chest flickered with panic. "That's not true."

"And that you've been—*fornicating* with this man, all the time that James was ill? It's horrendous."

"No, Mama, please," Imogen urged. "I'm alone here."

"You'd never do that, would you? It's so uncouth. I can't bear to hear it."

Imogen closed her eyes as if she'd been scolded. She couldn't believe that Robert was talking about her like that. Any thought of him made her furious, and miserable at herself for allowing it to get this far.

"Immy? Answer me!" Polly snapped. "You've always had a spotless reputation, that's what I told Eleanor. She agreed with me."

Imogen's voice grew hot. "Well, I suppose it's a complicated thing, to acknowledge what really goes on in a marriage."

"Perhaps with other people, not us," her mother replied. "I was never unfaithful to your father. I adored him, in my own way. We all did."

"Come on, Mama, please."

There was a knock at the door, and the cleaning lady pushed it ajar, but stopped when she saw Imogen. She gave an apologetic look before backing out of the room. But Imogen waved her in, pointing to the ashtray. Polly prattled on, unaware. "This man tried to get an invitation to the house—he tried to force his way in here."

Imogen's eyes flashed at the phone. "He wasn't violent with you, Mama, was he?"

The cleaning lady moved around her to collect the glasses, keeping her eyes cast down. Imogen's brow creased with concern as she concentrated on her mother's answer. "No. Why on earth would he be violent with me?"

"No reason." The ashtray clinked against the water glass and Imogen frowned with annoyance at the cleaning lady, at the mess she herself had made, at this ridiculous situation.

"Well, all the same, Immy, I'd like you to return and fix this, I don't need this going on, especially now that your brother—"

"I can't talk now." The cleaning woman gave Imogen an apologetic look, pointing at the envelope: a message from Robert Payne. Imogen shook her head. "This is upsetting. You are upsetting me, Mother."

"For heaven's sake, where are you, anyway? Alexandra dialed the number for me but she didn't say where. Are you abroad?"

Imogen swung her head around. "Alexandra is with you?"

"Ye-es, she's here," Polly said testily. "But you're talking to *me*."

"Mama, let me ask you," Imogen said evenly as the cleaning lady left the room. "Have you seen Rhoda Ashby recently?"

"No, darling, you know I haven't," Polly barked back. "She's too far away. You know how things are, after Toby. Why do you ask?"

"Does she know about . . . the house?"

"She did send some lovely flowers for you, though, at the funeral. Not that you noticed," Polly rambled on. "Many people are expecting to hear from you—thank-you notes must go out as soon as you're back. Widows are well loved in society, you know, and you can use it to your advantage."

"Mama," Imogen said fiercely, "if you don't want to have an honest conversation, then I can't talk to you."

"Don't fuss," Polly scoffed again, but then said, "what did you mean, 'Does Rhoda know about the house?' What house?"

Imogen couldn't answer; her voice was stuck in her throat as her mother almost shouted through the phone, "*Where* are you, Imogen? Not the château?"

She heard the sudden twang of her mother's American accent, only audible when she was upset, or angry—when her tight schooling came undone. No foreign influence had bled through to Imogen after her young summers in America; and so as a teenager, and then an adult, she'd become entirely cold and English. The bond between Imogen and her mother suffered the same fate: whatever soft connection they'd shared when she was a child had been wrung out and pulled apart during her long years away at boarding school.

"My flight home is the day after tomorrow."

Polly's voice was low and furious. "What do you think you're trying to do?"

Imogen saw a strange whiteness in front of her eyes. "Mama, do you ever think about what happened that summer?"

"Imogen, I insist you come back here immediately."

Imogen's voice stayed calm. "It's all right, Mama. I know you've blocked it out, just like the rest of them."

"Now, you listen to me!"

"I have to go. Goodbye, Mama."

After a short slam of the phone, Imogen lifted her bag off the chair, and left the hotel room.

30

─────

1985

As the girls washed, Ruby heard the shrill of the record player rise up to her bedroom. Not jazz this time, but a long gush of Puccini. Ruby winced, recognizing her grandmother's favorite.

On the drive to the village they passed Lisette walking slowly along the side of the road. She refused to meet anyone's gaze even as both cars slowed to observe her.

"I wonder why Lisette left early," Toby said from the driver's seat.

"Her husband normally picks her up, doesn't he?" Angus said beside him.

"Yes," Toby muttered crossly. "She really shouldn't be walking. But I suppose she's been upset . . . Thank God Rhoda isn't here to see that."

Swiveling in her seat, Ruby kept her eyes on Lisette, even as the old woman receded and her figure became a thin line by the road. With a strange bolt of understanding, she realized she might never see Lisette again. It seemed as if something, finally, had died, right in front of Ruby's eyes.

She felt a sharp pain in her buttocks as she sat back. She moved her hands underneath her, noticing that Imogen had done the same.

Imogen's hair was wet and clean, just like Ruby's, and both were wearing newly ironed dresses—but nothing could wash away the sting of Harley's beatings.

"I don't know what to say, Toby. What a rotten time you're having." Angus eyed his friend carefully and leaned closer. "How was today? Have you managed to deal with the woman in the village, her son?"

"Not entirely. You see, she's not backing down, and many people are behind her. More than I expected!" He let out a quick, desperate sigh. "But there are no witnesses. Hit-and-runs, you know, are just a matter of perspective. She doesn't know which of our party is the culprit, so that's a mercy. There's also . . ."

"What?"

Ruby saw her father's eyes lift to the mirror to check the girls in the back, and she turned away nonchalantly. Toby lowered his voice. "The question of her sanity, as it were. This old lady's medical records are quite . . . colorful, so we'll use that to our advantage. The police chief seems to approve, anyhow."

Imogen gave Ruby a look of dismay.

"What about you, girls," Toby said in a louder voice, "have you had a good day? I'll bet you have. Gallivanting all over, swimming, laughing, not a care in the world. Oh"—he tried to chuckle—"to be young and free again, eh Angus?"

He jerked his elbow at his friend, who replied with a grim nod.

"Is Mama going to be in the village, and Mrs. Ashby?" Imogen asked quietly.

"Yes, darlings, your mothers have agreed to join us, and I'm hoping we'll bring them back with us," Toby said as he guided the steering wheel around the curve of the bay. "What do you think of that?"

"I would like to see Mama," Imogen replied.

In the village an hour later, Ruby sipped her lemonade. The group had pulled their chairs away from the table, reclining in the evening's dense heat. Ruby had managed to sit as far from Harley—mercifully engaged in conversation with Georgina—as she could, and had wedged herself beside Angus, whose staunch shoulders provided a sort of defense. She kept her head bowed and sucked at her drink. Imogen was gazing around the square for any sign of her mother and Rhoda, her stricken face looking as if she might burst into tears at any moment.

Ruby opened her bag and rummaged through it, just to have something to do. Too late, she realized Angus had followed her movement and spotted the ripped cover and torn pages of her *Death on the Nile*. "Ruby?"

She stared into her bag, completely mortified. She pulled the book into her lap.

"Ruby—what happened?" Angus leaned toward her. "What's wrong, little thing?"

Ruby was shaking her head. Angus turned to Imogen, to the misery written all over her face. Feeling the weight of her father's glare, she quickly glanced at Harley.

Angus's face shifted. He looked from the book to Harley, then took the book from Ruby's lap, the torn pages rippling through his fingers as his mouth gaped open.

Harley seemed to sense Angus's mounting anger; he broke off mid-conversation with Georgina. His eyes grew small and round as he spoke up. "Those books, old boy, they're no good . . . they'll give wild little Ruby all the wrong ideas. Even Rhoda disapproves."

"Don't talk like that about Ruby," Angus snapped, and Toby's face turned to him with alarm.

Harley threw up a warning hand. "Don't be daft, Gus, it was only a bloody misunderstanding. I'll replace the book. Anyway"—with a snort of laughter he nodded to Toby—"at school we used to joke that it was Poirot committing the crimes; he's the common denominator, after all—don't you see, Ruby?" He sneered at her as he continued, "Poirot is killing them all off and blaming the Brits, when he's the damned froggy foreigner himself!"

Ruby somehow mustered her courage to say, "He's Belgian."

"Harley, what are you saying?" Toby laughed, thoroughly confused. "Do you even know what you're on about? Are you arguing about bloody Agatha Christie now?"

"He's . . . mad." A mystified Angus shook his head, his punching fury somehow eased. He put the book down, and Ruby quickly shoved it into her bag, concealing this small proof of her shame.

"Not mad, no, only more *informed* than the two of you." Harley sat up importantly. "I'm not leaving France until you've made a decision about that château. You, Tobias, have a responsibility that you must uphold, even here in France. That place needs to survive. These houses were built to demonstrate power, and influence, just like in England. You need to find a way to—"

"Harley." Angus rolled his eyes exaggeratedly. "The château belongs to the Ashbys, and they'll always take care of it."

"I believe"—Harley threw Angus a withering look—"in rules and traditions and playing our part."

"*Our* part," Angus sneered at Harley. "Viscounts and earls, and their descendants. Which you are not."

"Yes, you have inherited titles," Harley snapped. "But your grand old estate is full of Indian silks and Persian rugs and paintings with African slaves in chains, if I remember rightly. Your money is old and rotten, and it will slip away in a generation, just like Toby's has."

"Oh hush, Harley," Georgina shrilled, "the British class system isn't going anywhere. My father always said—"

"Let the men talk, Georgina."

Georgina sat back as if she'd been slapped; she hid her indignant face with a turn of her hat.

"Your money will dry up soon too, Harley"—Angus smiled bitterly—"if your wife is leaving you."

"Well, I have another source." Harley raised his eyebrows. "And you'd better hope I do, for Toby's sake. Otherwise his little daughter won't be going to any more fancy schools."

Ruby looked up, and across at her father.

"Who is your other source? Not Max." Angus's eyes narrowed with dislike.

"I hope never to have to deal with Max again," Toby said stiffly.

"Well, there's no going back after the events of this summer." Harley gave a wry smile. "Let me tell you, dear friend—if the powers that be in England know you've covered up a murder here, on top of the stuff you did for Angus several years ago, there'll be hell to pay. You'll be disbarred. You'll lose everything, on top of your reputation. So we've got ourselves into a bit of a tight corner, haven't we?"

Ruby coughed, suddenly unable to breathe. She tried to push back her chair to stand, but her buttocks were stinging and she felt glued to her seat.

But Angus was standing. "You disgust me, Harley. Are there no depths you'll not sink to?"

"'Depths,' old boy? I assure you, no one is lower than you."

In a flash, Angus smacked the table. Two glasses fell and shattered to the ground. People at the nearby tables shrieked at the noise.

Out of the corner of her eye, Ruby saw the manager holding back his waitresses as they rushed forward with brooms, dustpans, and brushes. The rest of the café watched too, riveted.

Harley leaned back calmly and raised his glass, still composed. He chuckled at the staring villagers, and said slyly, "Your anger is so unbecoming, Angus. I believe I am the only true gentleman here."

Angus inched his thick face toward Harley's. "Whatever you're scheming—leave us out of it, Toby and me. That includes our wives, our daughters, and our houses. I thought I was rid of you after university, after you betrayed me and broke my heart, and I thoroughly regret ever letting you worm your way back into my life. I wish to God you hadn't. You've always had your clutches in Toby, but I see you for what you are. You're a fucking asshole, Harley."

Harley stood abruptly to face his friend. "Say that again in England, Angus, and I'll have your guts for garters."

Angus whirled back in a wide loop and swung his fist into Harley's face. For one slow second the crack seemed to reverberate in every ear. Harley's puckered face hardened with fury, and his whole upper body leaned forward in retaliation. Angus was too quick for him, and grabbed the man's wrists, holding him tightly, their arms locked like great stags' antlers. Their frantic energy had knocked the table and the rest of the party to the side, everyone pushing their chairs away from the heat of the violence. Toby stood, his body taut, waiting for a moment to intervene. Ruby had leaped back from the table automatically, but Imogen had jumped up to stand, a strange, defiant look on her face.

"Please, Dada! Stop! Please!"

The table seemed to shudder between the two men, and then fell still.

Imogen was crying now, but Ruby didn't want Angus to stop. She wanted him to pummel Harley to the ground, and knock his brains out. But instead he let go of Harley, stood up straight, and marched into the café.

"Well," laughed Georgina, "have you finished making spectacles of yourselves? My word, I wonder whether any of us will be able to show our faces here next year, Toby."

Imogen stepped back as a pair of waitresses frantically cleared the mess around the table. One swept under the table with her broom and caught Ruby's watching eye for a moment. It was Ruby who turned away first, not wanting to see such anxious confusion on another young face. Ruby turned instead to Imogen, who was staring at the table in front of her, where the broken glass had let out a rivulet of her blood, now spreading across the wet surface in short whirls.

"What do you *mean* by that, Georgina?" Toby attempted wearily.

"You know exactly what she means, old boy," Harley said, his cheek mottled purple where he'd been struck.

Polly and Rhoda appeared just as the waitresses were departing.

"Sorry we're late. What have we missed?" Polly brimmed with smiles. "We've had a lovely day."

"Goodness me, what have we here?" Rhoda said, appalled. "What a mess!"

"It was worse a moment ago," Georgina said too cheerfully.

Imogen folded herself into her seat and bowed her head away from her mother. Toby turned to them both. "How is your tooth, Rhoda? And the baby, Polly?"

"The what?" Polly asked, confused.

"The baby," Toby asked again as his wife's searching eyes took in the situation at the table.

"Oh. Yes. All is well with the baby, and my tooth," Rhoda answered, gazing at the swirl of water and blood. "But heavens, what is this? The whole village is looking at us. Where's Angus? Where's Liv—and Ned?"

"Ned stayed at home; she's exhausted," Georgina answered.

"Aren't we all?" Rhoda shot back, looking between Harley and Toby, and at the gap where Angus had been sitting. She looked at Imogen, tucked up in her seat, and Ruby standing beside her, her face aflame. "Heavens . . . has there been a *physical* fight?"

Nobody answered.

"Well, I think we've all had quite enough for one summer, don't you, Toby? I think it's high time for people to make their way back to England."

Toby looked at his wife, and Ruby saw something hard and strong pass between them. Toby bowed his head. "You're right, Rhoda," he said carefully. "We'll discuss it tomorrow. Perhaps it is indeed time for everyone to go."

Ruby felt relief glimmer through her chest. Her mother used her voice to penetrate each lowered head around the table. "Yes, it's high time."

Harley sat down noisily with a knowing glance at Georgina.

"We've been on our feet all day, and you've made a mess of these drinks," Rhoda continued forcefully. "So let's get back and have dinner at the château."

"You'll have trouble finding any dinner—Lisette was leaving as we came here," Toby said dully, touching his wife's arm stiffly. But she pulled away from him.

"What—Lisette gone? And no dinner prepared?"

"I don't think so, darling. She had a heavy-looking bag with her. Certainly looked ominous."

Ruby frowned. She hadn't noticed the bag.

"Well"—Rhoda breathed in tightly—"I'll find something in the fridge. We'll take the girls. You lot can find Angus. Ruby, Imogen, come along."

"Why is your hair wet, Imogen?" Polly said with a frown, touching the ends of her daughter's hair. "And you have a terrific mark on your neck. Did you slip at the pool? You mustn't be so careless, darling."

Ruby found her voice to answer for Imogen. "No, it wasn't that."

"Hush, Ruby," Rhoda said. "Don't be insolent."

Harley let out a bitter chuckle as one of the waitresses leaned over him to spray and wipe the table. He appraised the girl and said aloud, "Ah, these French girls, they don't make them like this in England. Soft and sweet here, not like your stiff daughters."

"Goodness me." Polly forced a smile, but Ruby could see the alarm behind her eyes. "Come on, girls."

31

Polly and Rhoda were busy rustling up some dinner when the rest of the party returned, sooner than Ruby had expected. Ned was watching one of her films, *Fatal Attraction,* which Imogen steered toward until her father stopped her.

"Isn't that a bit of an unsuitable film?" Angus said loudly at the door of the living room, his eyes just as quick and cross as before.

"Oh, do you think so?" Ned said, her voice curling as she turned in her armchair.

"Yes, I do. Leave Imogen and Ruby out of it, please."

"I didn't think you cared, Angus."

Angus frowned at Ned, and patted Imogen's shoulder away. Imogen shirked him off and moved automatically through the front door to the terrace, her face impassive, her hand glued to her neck. Ruby followed her.

Polly and Rhoda had made a large omelet with some mushrooms they'd found in the fridge. "I stirred, she chopped, and we still managed to change for dinner," Rhoda said, setting the dish down on the table beside a great bowl of fluttering green salad.

"Looks like we got here in the nick of time, Rho," Polly said.

"Are you back, then, Mother?" Ruby dared to ask.

"Yes, Ruby," Rhoda answered her daughter hurriedly as she tossed the salad, "it was a foolish thought, my leaving. This is my house, and I'll sooner see them out of here than be chased out myself."

Ruby looked at her mother, surprised. Such a speech was something her grandmother would have said, not Rhoda, who'd never warmed to the French house, and who tended to specialize in silent fury behind her appeasing of others.

Ruby's stomach lurched with hunger; the omelet looked delicious. Someone had put on a record to lighten the quaking mood, and Ruby recognized the husky tones of Nina Simone—but now, with the sea so dark, the food so foreign, the table so empty, such a cooing, gentle voice felt ghostly.

Toby and Angus weren't sitting with them; they'd taken themselves into the study, while Harley could be heard bashing around his bedroom. Liv sat slightly apart, soft and docile, her usual impenetrable self. Ruby was utterly drained, glad that her mother had returned, startled by the rage she'd witnessed, and anxious that her parents might not hold firm on having their guests depart.

"Are we leaving any for the boys?" Georgina asked as Rhoda sliced the slim cake of the omelet.

"We've made them a separate one," Rhoda answered coolly. "They'll have it later."

"Boys, indeed!" Polly laughed.

"They *are* boys, Polly," Georgina insisted. "Quite untamed from their school days, their university days—and I must confess, quite untamed by you two."

"What an unkind thing to say, Georgina," Liv said thinly.

"Yes, quite," Polly said, her expression strained.

Imogen and Ruby began eating quietly, heads bent to their plates. Polly soon turned her attention to Imogen, and said in a sour voice, "Your hair has dried very badly, Immy. I can't think why you washed it in the middle of the day."

Imogen dropped her fork as her face collapsed. She let out a sob.

"Imogen!" Polly gasped. "Whatever is the matter? Why on earth are you crying?"

"I—" Imogen sputtered. "I've got a tummy ache. I'm not well, Mama."

"Oh, really? What a bore." Polly tilted her head to survey her daughter. "I'm sure we've got something for it. Eat your dinner and go off to bed, then. I'm sure there's a mint tea in the larder, or something we could rustle up for your tummy."

"I don't want to go to bed! It's not safe!"

"What in the world do you mean?" Polly huffed, her beautiful face muddled. "This is the safest house in the bay."

"She's overtired, Pol. Ruby, you too." Rhoda set her fork down neatly. "Off to bed with you both after dinner. Ruby, did you see the postcard? Ever so much post these last few days. It was addressed to us, but I rather think this particular one is for you."

"Postcard?" Ruby almost whispered.

"Yes, a thank-you for the orchestra trip. We've had quite a few. Charming, some of them, even though the spelling errors were quite alarming." She widened her eyes and tried a fresh smile for the table. "I've left it under the mirror in the hall."

A postcard! Ruby was thrilled at the very idea. Could it be a message from Annie, a cryptic, secret message letting her know she was safe—or that she was not?

Ruby collected the dinner plates, balancing the weight of the dirty crockery with her expectation of what awaited her. She dropped the plates in the sink, then made a beeline for the hall mantelpiece.

It showed a blue picture of Brighton, a very different kind of blue from the sea outside. She turned it over, and her breath held when she saw Bertie's name at the bottom. She didn't know his writing; she didn't know him at all—he was worlds away, now. But his postcard was polite, and kind. She pushed it against her chest, before sliding it into the pocket of her dress.

"What is it? Is it Annie?" Imogen was bringing the dirty glasses through.

"Not Annie, no."

"Who is it from, then?"

"No one. It's nothing. Come, let's go upstairs."

The light suddenly seemed to swim in front of Ruby's eyes. She had great trouble following Imogen, and she wondered if it was another nosebleed coming. Her head felt heavy, and she wanted to lie down and close her eyes. Her stomach seemed to sink with every lurch forward. At least, Ruby thought dimly, this would distract her from the burn in her buttocks, the pain in her chest.

"I don't feel very well," Imogen said glumly.

An hour later the two girls were sharing Ruby's small bathroom, holding each other's hair as they vomited into the toilet bowl. Ruby heard some low groaning from another room, too, perhaps from Harley's, or one of the others on the same floor. When her stomach seemed to give up, she lay back on the cold tiles of the bathroom. She touched the postcard through her dress, and remembered the phone number on that piece of paper that she'd been desperate to call. She couldn't move. This was where she was, and where she would stay.

There was the growl of Harley's snoring across the hall. Or was it her father's below? Or Angus, howling in his soured mood? Everywhere noise, but around her, the rush of silence. Ruby stretched out her foot gingerly to close the bathroom door. She felt the push of Imogen's fingers reaching for hers. Ruby closed her hand around Imogen's and turned her head to the side. Her hot cheek felt the cool of the floor as she closed her eyes.

WHEN RUBY WOKE THE NEXT morning her cheek was on the pillow, though she still wore her dress from last night. She sat up and her stomach turned again with discomfort, but it was a hollow cry rather than that awful fullness of last night.

Imogen turned her head at the movement.

"Ruby?" she voiced weakly. "What time is it?"

It was mid-morning, judging by the light coming through the cracks of the shutters. Somebody had closed the shutters, then, but not known how to put the two girls to bed properly. Ruby managed to stand, holding on to the bed for courage, her strength ebbing with each step.

Imogen followed Ruby, staggering. She stepped on the postcard, and bent to pick it up.

"It's nothing," Ruby said with a cracked voice, "just a thank-you card after the orchestra trip. Are you feeling all right?"

Imogen studied the postcard and muttered, "How strange."

"Please just leave it on my bed."

Ruby avoided looking at herself in the mirror as she considered running a bath, trying not to pull her hair to her nose to smell again that stink of sick. Imogen would need to bathe too, though she seemed more awake and alert than Ruby felt. Perhaps she'd taken less of whatever it was that had poisoned them.

EVERYBODY ELSE SEEMED WORSE. THE stairways and landings were deserted and dark, and when the two girls ventured down to the ground floor they found no Lisette, no breakfast laid, and the hot beat of daylight entirely shut out. Their quick return to Ruby's bedroom was accompanied by many moans through closed doors. The two girls took to their beds again, covering themselves in bedclothes, their wet hair spreading across the pillowcases. The sun was brighter through the shutters now, but Ruby had no wish to open them, hoping that the day would pass by without them.

"My bed smells," Imogen said after a few quiet minutes.

"Mine too," Ruby answered, "but I'd rather not go downstairs again; we can arrange for the sheets to be changed later." She wanted to add, "If Lisette returns," but she didn't want to upset Imogen with her speculation.

"No," Imogen agreed. "I'm terrified every time we go past Harley's room. What if he catches us . . . like yesterday? He said he would."

There was a short silence, during which Ruby dared consider that possibility.

Imogen added with a voice full of emotion, "I never want to eat again. And I never want to come here ever again."

Ruby didn't need to respond.

"Will your parents check on us, Ruby?"

"No," Ruby said. She was telling the truth; she saw no reason why her father would suddenly take an interest in their well-being, especially if he was suffering too.

Ruby's chest lurched as she thought of Angus in the room below, in pain or distress. She said, "What about *your* parents?"

"Oh . . ." There was new worry in Imogen's tone. "Do you think my mother being ill might affect the baby? Should we do something?"

Ruby tried to suppress the bubble of emotion in her voice. "I don't think we can do anything about anything."

Imogen shifted position in her bed and sucked in a breath. Ruby stretched out her legs, and felt a sting across her thighs. Imogen looked at her. "Is your bum still sore?"

"Yes," Ruby muttered.

"I think we have bruises. The mark on my neck—"

"Try not to think about it," Ruby interrupted.

"But I've been wondering." Imogen took a brave breath. "What if we told Ned about Harley? She could help us."

Ruby sat up. "No. Why? How?"

"She's nearby . . . She could help us next time. I know you don't like her, but if we tell her about Harley," Imogen carried on, wincing as she sat up, "she might be able to help us. Maybe she could speak to our parents for us. Force him to go."

"My father said everyone was going. My mother—"

"He wasn't very clear, though, was he?" Imogen's eyes were worried, but bright. "He doesn't seem very . . . in charge."

Ruby lay down again, heavy-hearted at Imogen's words. "I don't want to tell anyone."

"I'm going." Imogen stood, and Ruby sat up to follow. She dreaded the attics, but dreaded being alone in her room even more.

She needn't have worried, since they halted at the other end of the corridor, hearing Ned's voice in discussion with her mother. Georgina's door was open, and a crack of daylight streamed through into the dark corridor. The two girls hovered beside the door, seeing in furtive moments Georgina plumped up on the pillows of her bed, with one of Ned's sarongs wrapped around her head and shoulders like an ugly multicolored hood. There was a pause, and Ruby and Imogen stood like sentries on either side of the door.

"They're trying to poison us," Ned said, out of view.

"I don't think so, darling. Everybody is ill, not simply the two of us," Georgina replied. Ruby gave Imogen a beseeching look, wanting to abort the mission.

"How can you know that?"

"Toby said so this morning; I found him in his study. He and I were really able to talk yesterday, darling. He said that if I invest that money with him, and arrange my business around his debts, he'd leave this house to you eventually."

Imogen's face snapped to Ruby. Ruby blinked, confused, as Ned answered her mother.

"Really? That seems a bit easy."

"'Easy'? That's why we're here. We had to come, once I'd heard this house was in danger of—"

"You've always *joked* that it should be my inheritance, but—"

"This has been a long time coming. I needed to put you in the foreground this summer, to make sure that they took notice, and it worked."

"What about Rhoda?"

"Well, she has to go by her husband's word. She's always known about you, so that's a start." Georgina sighed gently. "He is sweet, Toby, and he's always had a soft spot for me . . . I did rather play with him when we were young."

Ned chuckled. "You still do, when Rhoda's not looking. Especially during those few short holidays we had together. Well, Mother, I am proud of you. A single parent—look what you've achieved for us!"

As the truth of the conversation washed over her, she avoided Imogen's horrified gaze.

"A lot of that was thanks to Harley and his finagling . . . He's been instrumental, really, in holding Toby accountable. Anyhow, it'll all come out now." Georgina was pleased.

"Yes, I suppose it will. Ruby knows, but I didn't push it, like you said."

"Gently, gently, darling. They are my oldest friends—I know these men better than myself. Harley and Angus tried to persuade me to marry Toby, back in the day, before his silly wife came on the scene. But I wouldn't. Nobody talks about such things openly, that's all."

"Ruby won't want me for a sister," Ned abruptly said. At the mention of her name, Ruby met Imogen's stare. The look was affirmation enough for Imogen. "She's still a brat, and I've tried everything you told me to. I'm sure she thinks wonderfully of her father, and we'll always be the villains."

"Ruby's small—she'll bend," Georgina huffed. "You are the first-born, even if illegitimate. Rhoda can be difficult—but Toby and I have an understanding, now, and once we've signed papers, she can't intrude. Nothing outwardly will change, after all. This is England."

Ned chuckled again. "This is France, Mother."

"Yes, quite."

Ruby stared at the opposite wall, the dark outline of the landing, the staircase, and wished she were anywhere but here.

"But do we really want this place, Mother?" Ned asked. "Isn't the château . . . falling down? You haven't got a bean to keep it up, never mind your investments."

Georgina tutted, and answered, "Yes, darling, we do want it. Think about what it means."

Ruby finally pushed herself away from the doorway and hurried back to her bedroom. Imogen followed behind with quick breaths.

"I don't understand, Ruby," Imogen said, leaving the bedroom door open. "Ruby?"

Ruby looked around at her bedroom, her things, all of which might be taken from her at any moment by this strange sister, who had known all along, and whose mother had always had a plan.

"Is she your sister, Ruby?" Imogen said, more loudly, "How can that be? Your father—"

"She isn't."

"But she said—"

"I don't care what she said," Ruby stuttered, trying to steady herself. She closed her bedroom door firmly. "She isn't my sister! And she called me a brat."

Imogen was silent for a moment. "She didn't mean it."

"*Weren't* you listening? Weren't you paying any attention?" Ruby's voice grew hot. "She hates me, Imogen. Don't you think she feels the same about you, too?"

Imogen hesitated, before shaking her head carefully. "No. You haven't been as nice to her as me, I—"

"She only cares about herself, and you know it, Imogen. Ned is horrible!"

"She isn't, she can't . . ." Imogen's face puckered. "She doesn't really think *I'm* a brat, too, does she?"

Ruby answered cruelly. "Probably."

"But then"—Imogen moved into the bedroom, speaking slowly—"Harley said I was damaged goods, and Max said I was disgusting . . . Does she think I'm a brat, because of them?" Her voice suddenly grew shrill. "Ruby?"

"No." Ruby moved toward Imogen and grasped her arms. "That's not what I meant. Of course none of that is true. You are none of those things. It's not true."

"It must be—they're grown-ups!" Imogen's voice was hysterical. "They know how things work. We don't."

Ruby saw the depths of Imogen's agony as if for the first time, and it frightened her. "Shall we get your mother? Let's tell her everything."

"No. Never," Imogen cried, shaking her head. "I might have been able to before, but not now."

"Why can't you?"

Imogen's soft face was devastated. "Are you mad? She'll say it's my fault! Maybe it *is* my fault—I must have done something to provoke Mr. Fuller, or encourage him. Those horrible names . . . they're true. That's why she doesn't even bother with me anymore, and why my father prefers you. So, if *you're* a brat"—she let out a frenzied laugh—"then I must be ten times worse."

"No, no, please. Please, Imogen." Ruby moved toward her, but Imogen stiffened and raised an arm against her.

"No. I need to wash again." Imogen's voice had a hard edge that Ruby hadn't heard before. "I didn't get all the vomit out of my hair. Leave me alone, please."

Ruby watched her go, then glanced at the door. The others would awaken soon. With her finger she traced that empty keyhole again, wondering if there was something she could place there, something to seal the door, some new line of defense.

32

Some hours later, Liv called the girls' names for lunch, and for a fleeting moment, Ruby wondered whether her mother had left again.

The two girls gathered their courage to go downstairs. The air was empty of noise, but Ruby took no comfort from that. They made their way to the terrace, where the warmth of Liv's voice came as a shock.

"Oh Ruby, Imogen," she called from the table. "I think everyone else is still feeling a bit poorly, but I hope you'll eat something."

Both girls nodded. They sat at the far end of the table, near the dishes of cheeses and breads and various cold meats that were prickling in the sun. The scratch of the crickets and the bash of the sea were louder than ever, while the heat held its own heavy beat. Ruby wanted the rain to come back, today and all the way to the end of August. But it never did that in France.

A new bunch of flowers decorated the table, so different from the usual spray of wildflowers and dry greenery. There were pinkish peonies, with small white roses peeking out in between like a smiling surprise. Ruby felt a sting thinking of Annie, who would have appreciated such a display, before telling them some sweet thing about the Rose Fairy. As she ate she realized that it must have been Liv who'd bought the flowers and the fresh food, knowing that Lisette wouldn't return, knowing that the girls' mothers wouldn't have risen.

"Pardon me, ladies." Liv bent near them, her face kind. All the same, Imogen flinched. "Oh, I didn't mean to alarm you. Not long to go till it's over."

"When is it over?" Ruby asked.

"Tomorrow."

The men came onto the terrace in a buzz of boisterous conversation. Ruby didn't know where they came from—the sea, or the pool, or her own imagination? They strode together in a band, clutching at bottles and glasses, with Toby carrying a heavy bucket of ice. Angus separated from the others to approach the table; as they grew closer, Ruby could see that they were weary and sick-looking.

There was a shadow across Angus's face that matched the dark shade of his voice. "Girls. Are you all right? I found you both asleep in the bathroom last night. But I didn't know . . . Well, we were all suffering, weren't we?"

Ruby's eyes widened. It had been him, then, lifting them up soft as leaves and placing them on their beds. Her cheeks felt hot to think of it. Imogen didn't react to her father. She was stiff, afraid of them all now. Ruby opened her mouth to answer but didn't know what to say, as her father and Harley drew nearer.

"Leave us alone, please, gentlemen," Liv said, turning her back on the three men like a stiff barrier. "This is our lunch."

Harley's face rippled with irritation. "Oh yes?"

"Yes. And I've made the arrangements, Harley," Liv spoke back. "We leave tomorrow, when the roads will be clear for our drive home. Your son is waiting. That's my condition."

"Yes," Toby said, as firmly as he could. "Tonight we can have a blowout and some good fun. It's the *Fête* in the village, and it'll be our last evening together. I'm sure you boys can control yourselves for one more day?"

Angus drew an agitated hand through his thick hair, but his face seemed to crease with relief, and he nodded with an "Of course." But Harley was glowering at Toby. "George too?"

"Georgina too." Toby nodded. "My wife insists."

A queer smile lifted Harley's face. "Then we'll have to get as much fun into the next twenty-four hours as we can. Angus and I can go a few more rounds! I'm game if he is."

"Indeed," Toby said uncertainly. "All good fun, dear Agamemnon."

Ruby couldn't stand the desperate look on her father's face.

"Well, let's continue," Harley said, gripping at his bottles and gesturing toward the sea rocks. Toby followed, though not before placing a brief, appeasing hand on Angus's back. Angus gave his friend a grim smile in return. "Odysseus, ever the appeaser."

Toby chuckled sadly. "And you—Achilles? He doesn't even make it to the final battle."

Angus tried a laugh. "I know."

The men moved away. At least her father had set the date, Ruby told herself, which left only one more day to endure Harley, and only one more day near Angus.

Liv stood up straight again. "Well, there we are. It'll be nice for you to have things back to normal, Ruby, won't it?"

"Are you definitely leaving, too?" Ruby asked. "You don't—"

"Yes, I am," Liv answered, "and I shall make sure I take my husband with me."

Imogen seemed to relax as she studied Liv's face. Liv spoke again, "Now, Ruby. Did you find that phone number?"

"Yes, I did." Ruby looked up mid-mouthful. "But I haven't had a chance to call it."

"Shall we try after lunch?"

"Whose number?" Imogen asked quietly.

"Oh." Ruby's voice splintered with surprise. "Yes, please."

"I also wanted to ask"—Liv put an arm on Ruby's chair—"about *this*. Is it yours?"

Ruby's heart stuttered as she saw a page of her Agatha Christie in Liv's hand. She wanted to snatch it from her. "Yes, it is mine. I'm sorry."

"No need to apologize, Ruby. The trouble is, I found it in my bed-room . . . my husband's bedroom," Liv added carefully. "Do you want to tell me what it was doing there?"

Imogen gave Ruby a maddened look, and Ruby lowered her face with shame. She whispered, "No."

"Ruby." Liv bent to the table again. "Has Harley bothered you? Or you, Imogen? You can tell me."

"No," Ruby repeated. She placed her knife and fork together on her plate.

"Then, what was this doing in there?" Liv asked, as Ruby avoided the offending page.

"I don't know."

Liv gave a small sigh, then said, "Are you sure?"

"Yes."

"And do you still have your bookmark?"

This time, Ruby raised her eyes to meet Liv's. "Yes, I do." She managed a small smile. "Could we try to call Annie now, Mrs. Montgomery?"

"Annie?" asked Imogen.

Liv stood back with a nod. "If you wish to, we shall."

A confused Imogen stood too, and they hurried across the terrace, giving the men a wide berth with Liv's protection. The living room smelled of alcohol and the sallow stink of bodies, and Ruby's nose wrinkled as she noticed the piano lid up, the ivory keys splashed with her father's whiskey. She steered toward the telephone and the dresser where she'd hid the parent directory. Raising the handset, she typed in the numbers, hoping they would grant her what she needed. Liv stood behind her, Imogen by the door.

A woman answered. Ruby's eyes flew open at the young, fresh voice.

"Hello?"

"Hello?" Ruby stuttered.

"Who is it?"

"Oh, good afternoon," Ruby said, "I was hoping to speak to Annie Fuller . . . is she there?"

"Yes, she is. But who is this?" came the confident reply.

"Oh, a . . . friend, from school."

"Yes, you sound awfully young. Well, hello, friend of Annie." The voice laughed, "She's just outside. Annie!"

"No please," Ruby said quickly, "don't trouble her, Mrs. Fuller."

"I'm not Mrs. Fuller; that's my sister," the voice answered lightly. "Annie's just here. Are you sure you don't want her?"

"No, no, that's fine," Ruby muttered. "I'm calling from France."

It was the woman's turn to hesitate. "Oh, I see."

"I wanted to see if she was all right, and . . . safe."

The voice was stiffer now. "Yes, they both are. Thank you."

"Thank you, that's good news." Ruby met Imogen's expectant eyes and waited a moment. "Goodbye, then."

"What's your name? No message, then?"

"No message," Ruby answered, her voice beginning to break. "Thank you. Sorry."

She dropped the phone onto the receiver and dashed out of the room. Liv didn't follow her, nor did Imogen. The long twist of the stairs was a darkish blur, and Ruby almost choked on her breath as she ran.

She fell on her bed and cried for the first time that summer. Her whole being seemed to tear itself apart with relief, with sorrow, with anger as she sobbed deeply into the pillow.

33

2010

Mrs. Cosgrove touched the rim of the empty glass with her finger, before ordering a top-up from the bartender. Her harbor walk and her frozen cocktail hadn't been as freeing as she'd hoped, and as she returned to the hotel she'd ducked aside after seeing the pair of Englishmen hovering beyond the main doors. They'd been waiting for a taxi, and while the older, white-haired man had heaved a suitcase into the back, the other man, Hugo, had leaned on his cane to speak to the driver, handed him some thick bills, stood to shake the older man's hand, and bowed him into the car.

A red file had flashed at Imogen as Hugo followed the departing taxi with his eyes. She took the opportunity to dash through the hotel doors.

An hour later, she'd changed into a soft dark dress that settled neatly over her hips, and had sat at the hotel bar. There was no more running from it: she had to confront this inevitable Montgomery.

The château would be their talking point tonight, the battle she would wage around everything else. She touched the burn mark on her hand, then pressed it against the cold glass of her drink.

He passed through the doors half an hour later, her eyes drawn to him automatically as she sipped her glass of wine. He wore the same clothes she'd seen earlier—a navy blue jacket that squared his broad shoulders, a thin linen shirt of the same color, and soft beige chinos.

He nodded at her almost involuntarily, saying, "Good evening."

"Good evening," she answered just as casually, setting down her glass. He stood two seats away from her, and called to the bartender wearily, "*Vous avez de whiskey?*"

"*Oui, monsieur, lequel vous preferez?*" The barman indicated the line of bottles.

"*Ça.*" Hugo gestured at a wide, square bottle with his hand.

"*Bien sûr.*"

He kicked at his cane and settled on a velvet red stool, which was too nimble for his tall, broad figure. Mrs. Cosgrove turned slightly toward him, taking in his worn face, his matted graying curls. She addressed him abruptly. "How do you find the hotel?"

Hugo stiffened and took a long swig of his drink. Imogen watched the ice clink against his glass, but still, he did not look at her. "Yes, it's rather . . ."

"Have you been to the area before?"

He turned to look straight into her face. "Yes, of course I have, Mrs. Cosgrove."

It was Imogen's turn to stiffen, and he was evidently pleased to see it. He carried on richly, "There's no need for these pleasantries, you know. I will have that château."

"And yet you've not yet put in an offer?" She cracked a smile, but her eyes stayed sharp. She hated this game. Hated how she'd angled her body invitingly, hated that she tried to smile, teasing him, to win him over, just like she'd been taught. She hated even more that he seemed immune to it.

"I might not know you, Mrs. Cosgrove, but I knew your husband. I'm sorry for your loss—he was very well respected. I too have suffered a recent loss." Hugo cradled his drink into his chest, and leaned toward the bar. "But what I don't know is why you've come back here so soon after your husband's death."

"I merely took the opportunity," she answered lightly, without looking up, "to view the château, since it has become available. I don't think—"

"Be serious." Hugo returned to his drink. "You're proud of what you've achieved, what you got away with, and now you're here to—"

Mrs. Cosgrove interrupted sharply. "I'm not sure what you're—"

"I can't talk like this." He slammed his drink on the counter, and the bartender looked up. "It's disgusting. You disgust me. You can't admit why you're really here?"

"I . . . needed to see the house," Imogen said desperately.

"Because you were there—that night, that day, weren't you? You know who I am."

Imogen looked at him directly, "Yes, you are Hugo Montgomery."

"Yes." He held her gaze. "I'm Harley's son, although many would say that I don't deserve the name, since I never met his expectations, or fulfilled everybody's hopes. The trouble is, when your father dies, you can't argue with him anymore, can you? The air just sits, empty, on the other side."

Imogen saw him clearly now. Hugo Montgomery, his hands tight around his whiskey, his crooked leg, his energy concentrated into a ball of fury and hatred. In the next moment she saw that red file, by his side. He spoke again. "And you are Imogen. Ruby Ashby was a sweet thing when she was little, but a little too cross to be endearing. I never knew you as a girl. So answer me now, Imogen Bly. Were you there that day?"

Hearing him say their young names aloud felt like a punch in the chest. Imogen glanced at the barman, busy with his work, before answering.

"You know that I was."

Hugo's figure seemed to reverberate with triumph, and he urged her on with his eyes. "I need you to tell me what happened to my father."

"You already know what happened to him. There were two of them—it was an accident." Imogen blinked, fearful for the first time this evening. She'd seen something of the father in the son's eyes just now, and she hadn't liked it. Her voice remained small. "The police, here, dealt with it. They must have reports—they can tell you every-thing you need to know."

"Yes." Hugo tapped his whiskey glass violently with his finger. "They 'dealt' with it— that's exactly right. But the truth of it from the locals, all these years later, is very different." He leaned forward and pulled a withering face. "Haven't you got that version for me, little Imogen Bly?"

Imogen drew her knees in tight under the bar, and said, "Do not speak to me in that manner."

"Do you have any idea the information we've gathered? The cover-up from the mayor's office? Accounts from villagers, everything that people saw that summer. Even the kitchen woman made a statement. Oh yes"—Hugo chuckled hoarsely, tapping the red file—"there's plenty here. Plenty."

Imogen gripped at her wineglass. "Hugo, please—"

"No, no." He raised his glass in mock celebration, and the ice cracked. "I will expose you all. First, I shall buy that place. I have all the money I need. My stepmother—"

"Your stepmother," Imogen cut in desperately. "Liv! Olivia Mont-gomery. I *knew* her."

Hugo pulled an incredulous face. "Hardly, if you didn't even know she had died. Don't pretend you gave a damn about her. She wasn't like you, or any of your styled-out women. She was different." His eyes glazed over as he nodded vigorously at the space in front of him. "How dare you even say her name!"

"I didn't know she had died—I am sorry, Hugo." Imogen's voice rose to meet his. "I wish—"

"What?"

"I wish . . ." Imogen was confused; she turned back to her glass, which was somehow empty. The bartender had moved off, away from their heated conversation. The bar was entirely deserted. Imogen's eyes narrowed, and she felt a sudden wave of terrible, bitter grief. "I wish I'd known her better. That summer, she was the only one not to cause us harm."

"She died just a month ago, and very few people cared to know about it," Hugo said brutally. "I rather think she was the one holding me together. I'm finding that I simply . . . can't get through the day."

"I am so sorry for your loss."

"But before she died"—Hugo rounded on her—"she told me to come here, that it would set my mind at rest. So I'm here to find out the truth, gather the evidence, and get at that bloody house." Hugo drained his whiskey and shouted toward the barman, *"Monsieur, un autre!"*

The man obliged, and Imogen held herself back as Hugo carried on feverishly, "My stepmother told me that that summer was a grubby fight for the château. Georgina Leonard, some character called Max whom I never met, and my father too." His chest heaved as his voice lifted to say, "But my father didn't have the money, and that's why I'm here, because I do. I want what he couldn't have."

"That's rather ugly of you," Imogen muttered.

"Not as ugly as all of them," Hugo shot back. "Or you. You'll never have that house." Hugo laughed, balling his hand into a fist. "I'll destroy you, and your reputation will be in tatters. You, a Bly! Your father, a lord who rejected the peerage! Your brother, the 'Little Lord' swanning around Oxford like a prince. What about *my* Oxford days? Very different from his, I can tell you, without my father."

Imogen was edging off her stool, but her defiance held her upright. "Whatever you have in that file, whatever it says, it will never tell the true story. We were children. Whatever you are referring to, it is not what you think it is." She tried to keep her voice measured. "It was a terrible summer; everybody was at fault."

"Well, it's high time you all faced up to it. Your childish memories can't be trusted . . . This file, these papers, can." Imogen could see keen anguish behind his eyes, and she wanted to reach into it, just like she'd wanted to reach into her own memory and soothe that tortured child she'd once been. "Everything that you remember, Imogen, is wrong . . . Would you like me to show you?"

He fumbled with the file, the same red as their velvet seats. Papers fell out, slipping to the floor. Imogen's gaze caught a large photo among the pages, a black-and-white image of floor tiles and a dark spread of blood.

Hugo staggered forward to collect the papers.

Mrs. Cosgrove left the bar. She needed no help reopening that seeping wound in her chest. Her memory was as solid as a rock—she'd taken it out to inspect and analyze so many times that she knew every moment of that day twenty-five years ago. She would not sit and be told about it, no matter how menacing Hugo Montgomery's threats, no matter how much he reminded her of his father.

34

1985

At siesta time, a sallow-faced Rhoda appeared to tell Ruby that the group would indeed be going to the village that evening for the *Fête*. Ruby nodded, before returning to her bed. She looked over at her flute, long, slim, silver, and laid flat along the ridge of her music stand, neglected as much as the schedule she'd been assigned to, neglected as much as she had been. Tomorrow could not come soon enough. She used to adore the annual celebration, with bumper cars, shooting games, a haunted house, live music, and dancing—but it felt barbed with frightening final opportunities tonight.

As the afternoon slipped into evening, Ruby got her period again. In her small bathroom, she stared at the dark red-brown spots in her knickers. Three weeks since the orchestra trip. The end and the beginning of another cycle. After the shock and disgust of the discovery, Ruby felt relieved, and renewed, as if she could believe in herself as a functioning human being.

She had no sanitary towels left in her bathroom, and realized that Imogen must have used them. She tried her parents' bathroom cabinets, but found nothing. She didn't know where Imogen was, and did not want to venture downstairs. Neither her pride nor her timidity would allow her to consider Ned's room. Ruby finally thought to ask Liv—but no, she was too shy for that.

If it were possible, she would've locked herself in her room until every car pulled away from the driveway, and then let herself out. Ruby stuffed a wad of toilet paper in her knickers, and chose a dark-colored dress to change into, just in case any blood were to show through.

THE FÊTE HAD OVERTAKEN THE village square and clogged up the narrow streets with garish stalls and booths. The usual car park was overtaken by an arcade, a large bumper car platform, and a flat stage lit up with glittering lights and thumping music. After they parked halfway up some unknown street, the two carloads from the château wandered down into the fray, past a group of French teenagers skulking in a dark corner, smoking and laughing. Ruby felt a surge of optimism; it was reassuringly noisy and colorful in the village, the hours were passing, and tomorrow would bring fresh daylight and the promise of freedom.

Toby doled out yellow tokens for the bumper cars, and Ruby and Imogen took them gleefully, and Ned too. Ruby chose a red car, and insisted on going alone. After a few turns, she gave up challenging Imogen and Ned in their shared car, and found that zooming about smashing into strangers was much more fun, even lifting off her seat with her more focused efforts. After her sixth go and final token, Ruby pushed herself out of the car, a little discombobulated by the beat of the music and the strobe of the lights. She felt stiff and bruised, but satisfied. She left Ned and Imogen and wandered into the square alone, into the milling crowd of unfamiliar faces.

But she heard a musical voice.

"Ruby, I've found you, and you're all by yourself," Angus said. She looked up at him; his warm eyes were creased but smiling, and he looked mightier than ever. "Let me buy you a game."

"Oh, no. Really?" Ruby was quietly delighted that he had sought her out, and that no one else was there to torment either of them—but she had no idea what to say or how to behave.

"Yes, little thing, what will you choose?"

"Well, Mr. Bly"—she gestured at the nearest stall—"what about this?"

He bowed his head toward her. "Certainly, Miss Ashby."

Ruby concentrated on the brightly colored balloons bouncing behind a stringed barrier, and the wall of prizes—from packs of cards to enormous teddy bears—before spotting the hard metal rifles that lay ready. She looked up at Angus quickly.

"Oh no, not this one. I didn't mean—"

Angus frowned, then his face cleared with a small chuckle. "No, little thing, don't worry. You can't upset me. You and I know each other better than that, don't we?"

Ruby smiled gratefully, and Angus paid the man. She lifted the rifle and placed it on her shoulder. Angus went to help her, and she shrank for a moment, feeling the rough weight of his touch. In the next moment she let him move the weapon, lift her arm, point out the zoom, show her how to shoot. Five balloons were waving at her behind their barrier. She cricked her finger, took aim, and shot one through.

"Well done, Ruby!" Angus cried out, surprised. "Two more—have a good go."

Ruby smiled, before tightening her mouth to concentrate again. She shot again, and got two balloons.

"Ruby!" Angus touched her shoulder, almost shaking her with jubilation. "Have you been practicing without telling us?"

"No."

Harley suddenly appeared behind them, grinning snidely as he walked by with Georgina. "She's a sorceress, like her grandmother, I've told you. Look at those eyes."

Angus kept his gaze on Ruby, seemingly determined not to turn around. "Don't talk like that about her, Harley."

"No, indeed," Harley snapped, turning away with a sneer. "Watch how you handle that thing around Angus, Ruby!"

Ruby stiffened as she stared at the remaining balloons. At that very moment she could turn to Harley, aim the gun, and shoot him. She had one bullet left, she thought. In the head, or the heart? Were these real bullets—could they penetrate the skin of this horrible man?

"Don't worry, little thing. It's all right." Angus reached under her chin to lift her face and look into her eyes. His fingers brushed a long tendril of her hair as he spoke again. "I'm sorry you've had to see all this, this summer. It's been . . . Look, it'll soon be over. And I promise I'll always help your dad. He and I—we're not the bad guys, little thing. Flawed, yes, but never the villains. Whatever happens, remember that."

"What's going to happen?" Ruby asked as Angus stood up and let go of her.

"Nothing, little thing." His face shifted into a wary smile, the dark beads of his eyes alight. "You can count on us. You know that you can always count on me."

Ruby felt that sting of regret again, the same sting she'd felt when Bertie left three weeks ago. Now he was far away, and soon Angus would be, too. She frowned unhappily as Angus cleared his throat, gesturing toward the wall of prizes.

"Now, one more shot to go, and two balloons. Let's see what you can do!"

THEY ALL GATHERED FOR THE final dinner. Ruby's father had chosen a restaurant just off the edge of the square, far enough away from the noise but near enough to absorb the joy of the *Fête*. Ruby clutched her shooting prize—she'd wanted a BB gun and bullets in a box, but realized she ought to choose one of the stuffed toys, so she picked out a long-armed monkey with round brown eyes. She and Angus arrived at the table at the same time as her mother and Polly, while Harley, Georgina, and Toby were already enjoying an aperitif. Ruby magnetically went to sit beside Angus, as far from Harley as she could manage, but as she slipped past her mother, she heard Polly whisper to Rhoda, "Like a moth to a flame, isn't she? I've seen this with so many women, but none as young as Ruby."

A wave of embarrassment washed over Ruby as she sat down. Pushing herself into her seat, she felt a fresh twinge in her buttocks, still sore from the day before, or perhaps from the bumper cars. She lowered her face and pushed her hair toward her chest.

"Lovely place! Lovely, jolly evening," Harley said happily, his face pink and his eyes watery. "I shall be happy to see out the night, and look forward to returning next year."

Rhoda's head snapped up. Her voice was somehow both pleasant and bitter. "Oh, shall you return next year?"

"I shall," Harley answered firmly, leaning forward to pour himself a fresh glass of wine. His body seemed to sway, and Ruby wondered if he'd been drinking all day. "Although perhaps *you* won't, Rhoda. Toby might not be able to show his face after this summer!"

"I shall return, too, with Ned," Georgina said easily, nodding toward Toby, more relaxed that evening than she'd ever been. "As things stand."

"There's still a lot to discuss . . ." Toby attempted, as he caught the glare of his wife.

"And I, lady of the house, I have no say in my guests?" Rhoda swung an agonized smile around the table.

"Lady of the house?" Harley echoed mirthfully. "Don't make me laugh."

"Not now, Harley, please," Toby said, signaling the waiter. "Come, Rhoda. We don't want to spoil our last evening together. Everyone's on best behavior."

Rhoda's face dropped furiously, and Polly gave her a sympathetic glance.

There was a loud laugh as Ned joined the table with Imogen, leaving only Liv's seat empty. Ned looked at Ruby, and her prize monkey sitting on the table. "All right, Ruby? Did you win something?"

"She did," Angus answered.

"Good girl," Ned said patronizingly. "And how are you managing to walk? I should think you'll have some bruises in the morning."

"Bruises?" Ruby bristled at Ned's comment, glancing at Imogen. Had she told Ned what had happened? Imogen self-consciously touched her neck and caught Ruby's cautious eye with a swift shake of her head.

"Yes, bruises. From the bumper cars," Ned continued. "You were quite a sight to behold! A crashing, bashing champion. Thank God the rubber bumpers protected us."

"Yes," Harley interrupted, listening keenly, "and she's gifted at the rifle too. You've got a damned wild thing on your hands, Tobes."

"A brilliant thing, you mean, Harley," Angus said in his low voice.

"Ruby?" Toby looked down the table in surprise. "What's that? Did you win a prize?"

Everyone at the table seemed to be staring at her, waiting for some kind of answer; even Georgina was peering over with interest. "Yes," Ruby responded pathetically. "But please, don't look at me."

"Don't *look* at you! What are you talking about, ridiculous girl?" Harley blustered as he reached for a new bottle of wine. "That's what you're there for, looking at!"

"Harley," Angus said stiffly.

"Gus, he's drunk," Toby muttered. "Leave him be."

Ruby's face was hot, her eyes a blur. She wished she still had that rifle in her hand. Harley was still talking. "Yes, I've rather gone off your girls, lads. But then I suppose we've always been terrible with children. Angus and that boy on the hunt. Me and my Hugo. Toby and Ned here . . ."

"Oh, will you *stop*, Harley!" Rhoda almost shrieked. "You are so coarse. I wish somebody would hold your tongue. Where is Liv?"

"She didn't feel the need to come," Harley said, shaking his head, pressing on. "And Angus's girl here, little Imogen. All ruined, at such a young age. These children are supposed to be the future." He raised his voice, and his glass. "Well, here's to a better version of the future. I'm glad we've come to some agreement, anyhow."

Toby spoke up with a polite grimace. "There is no agreement. Not with you, Harley."

"Well," Harley shrugged, "an agreement with George might as well be an agreement with all of us!"

"Oh, Harley," Georgina said.

Harley smirked, "Et tu, Georgie?"

"No, darling." Georgina gave him an exhausted smile, glancing at Ned. "But do be quiet, on the financial count, especially. There are some things that ought not to be discussed so openly. You'd know that, as a gentleman."

Ruby saw the glance between the mother and daughter and felt a pang of anguish.

Rhoda rose to her feet haughtily and let out a brittle sigh. "I've had quite enough of this. Polly, let's take the girls home. This is turning out to be a thoroughly indecent evening."

"Now hang on. We haven't even ordered—it's everyone's last night, Rhoda," Toby interjected, annoyed. "Let's not break up the party like this—I'm sure we can all settle down now."

Polly stood awkwardly, dropping her napkin into her chair and giving Rhoda a supportive nod.

"Oh, let them go, Tobias," Harley jeered. "Leave us here to rot in our revelry."

Ruby and Imogen hobbled after their mothers, Ruby gripping at her new toy, her dark thoughts forcing her feet forward.

35

Ruby woke early, before Imogen had stirred. She chose a clean dress and brushed her hair, taking care to settle her fringe over her eyes. Thereafter she sat on her bed, willing Imogen awake, the whole house awake, and up, out, and gone.

A moment later Ruby opened the shutters, just to have something to do.

She left her bedroom and tiptoed through the silence of the house, down the stairs to her parents' bedroom. She hovered at the door, but their arguing voices stopped her from entering.

"If you change your will, and have that wretched girl inherit—" Rhoda broke off.

"I don't see there being any other way, darling," Toby answered strongly, "the financial—"

"We'll find another way," Rhoda interrupted. "We'll appeal to my brother again!"

"No. Rhoda, that is out of the question. And I absolutely refuse to discuss this with you."

"Well, then, let me make myself clear." Ruby heard her mother's voice lift. "If you endow this entire place to Georgina and her insignificant bastard of a child, then you might as well hand it over now, because I shall never set foot in this house again, and neither will Ruby!"

At the mention of her name, Ruby pushed through the door. She stared from one parent to the other and spoke with a weight in her voice that she hadn't expected. "Please, not this house. Not to her. Not after everything, please. I love it here!"

Her father and mother were still in their sleeping things. They stood on opposite sides of their bed, and Rhoda's face was full of fury as she spoke.

"Ruby, don't listen at doors! Honestly, all the terrible habits you've picked up this summer!"

Toby was moving toward his daughter. "Ruby, I am aware that you may've heard some things talked about over the last few days, but please put it out of your mind this morning, and we will discuss everything after *that* bloody lot"—he gestured wildly—"have gone."

Ruby felt desperate. "But Father, please, not this house. What would Grandmother say? Mother is right, there *must* be some other way . . ."

"Leave it, the pair of you!" Toby hissed. "You're as bad as each other! How dare you challenge me like this?"

Something Ned had said came back to her. "Have you been seeing them during the holidays, Father, without us knowing?"

"Ruby! What did I say?" Toby's voice was hoarse as Rhoda looked at him, aghast. "Get back to your room, and I'll talk to you later!"

"I don't want to talk later—or ever!" Ruby let out a gasping sob.

"Keep your voice down, Ruby!" Rhoda scowled, fussing with the bedclothes in an attempt to regain her composure.

"Oh, I hate you both!" Ruby cried out.

In the next moment, her father strode forward and slammed the door firmly in her face.

Ruby's heart was beating in her ears, her blood thumping and reciting to her: *the house the house the house.* She wanted to breathe the place in, to melt into the walls, cut herself and bleed into the floors, become part of the château and never leave it.

She heard a noise from the Blys' room and moved away, her ears identifying the clunk of a suitcase, the squeak of a hanging rail, the creak of the wardrobe doors opening and closing. She imagined Angus and Polly methodically collecting their things, preparing to leave Ruby with her parents, who would do nothing but argue or fall silent, just like they always did when the three of them were alone.

Ruby hurried downstairs, toward the kitchen, but an enormous mess and an overflowing dustbin greeted her. Lisette wasn't there, would never return. Ruby was furious with Lisette, furious with Georgina and Ned, furious with that old woman for being so hurt and doing so little about it. Ruby even found a fury for Polly and Imogen, and their careless compliance. Her fury for Harley she could not confront, and she pushed him to the side in her mind.

Ruby opened the fridge with a clang. In a glass drawer was a clutch of blood oranges. She set them on the counter, and took out a knife, the sharpest one she could find. She dug deep into each orange with the knife and pushed each half against the knot of the squeezer, before pouring the pulpy juice into a glass. Ruby filled one tall glass, then two, then another, sloppily and badly. She did it gleefully, knowing how much the mess and the waste would infuriate her mother.

In the middle of the fourth orange, Ruby nicked her finger on the sharp, long knife. She wondered whether these oranges had been placed in the fridge deliberately, just like the mushrooms left behind by the traitorous Lisette, designed specifically to poison them. If so, Ruby thought, so be it. She would fill a glass for each of them, every guest who'd sat around the table that summer, every person who'd done nothing while a young man died and an old woman screamed. Let them all drink the poisoned juice, and die. That would be a splendid Agatha Christie ending, Ruby thought, and a better finale than any of Ned's horror films could boast.

Her heart still beat through her ears. *The house the house the house.*

Ruby gripped her glass in one hand, the knife in the other, and walked toward the main hallway. She heard a cry, followed by a grunt, then a laugh. It was a helpless, even delighted sound, coming from behind the stairs—no, behind the living room, tucked around the stairs, in the study, perhaps? The noise grew louder as Ruby approached, and she moved slowly, certain that she was right, uncertain of what she'd find.

Ruby pushed open the door of the study; the glass knocked and splashed the orange-red juice against her chest. But she barely noticed. Ruby was distracted by the curly-haired mop of Ned's hair against her father's desk, where she lay flat on her back, her body naked, her eyes closed in some strange ecstasy. Ned was held down by a pair of thick hands gripping at her slim waist. Ruby recognized those hands. They belonged to Angus, whose bulk was revealed at Ned's groin, his thick head buried there, probing and sucking as she leaned back, entirely thrilled.

"Inside me, please," Ned whispered, "now, get inside me."

Angus stood up to his full height and obliged; he thrust himself into Ned as she shifted across the desk with a joyful jerk. They moved together as she entwined her spindly legs around him, lifting herself to throw her arms over Angus's broad shoulders.

Ruby scrutinized Ned's face, trying to understand. It was twisted not with pain—but with satisfaction. Angus too, his forehead tight with focus, broke into a broad smile as they moved together as one.

"Oh, how I'll miss this," Ned said in a fluttering voice.

"It's risky down here," Angus almost whispered. "We should be in your room."

"I couldn't resist coming to find you." She shuddered with his movement. "Anyway, this place will be mine soon, and I shall do what I like."

Ruby dropped her glass. It smashed and splattered the red juice all over her bare feet and across her legs. A heavy agitation shook her out of the room, just as the two broke apart. The glass scraped at Ruby's toes as she turned and ran, dashing along the corridor to the stairs, up and up, two steps at a time, to the safety of her bedroom. There was a hollow shout from Angus below, but it could have just as easily been the thunder of her own dismay after the horror of what she'd seen.

Imogen's soft face lifted as Ruby entered the bedroom. She was standing in front of her bed, the bedclothes tidy beneath a neat pile of things ready to be packed; but she drew her hands to her mouth when she saw Ruby.

"Oh my goodness, what's wrong?" Imogen started. "What's happened to your dress . . . and your legs! Is that . . . blood?"

Ruby's mind was furiously racing, tripping over every detail of what she'd seen in the study. She opened her mouth to speak, but couldn't.

"What is that in your hand?" Imogen cried, covering her mouth again as soon as she'd spoken.

Ruby turned her face to the door just as Angus rushed through it. His face was twisted with worry, his eyebrows drawn into a sharp arrow, his dark eyes searching hers, his hands reaching out for her. Ruby turned away slowly, her mind reeling at seeing those hands now, knowing where they'd been. His mouth tumbled out beseeching words, but she'd seen where that had been, too.

"Ruby, little thing, I'm so sorry you saw that just now . . . It's not how it seems. I understand it's confusing." He moved her arms, nudged her until she was sitting on her bed, before kneeling on the floor to face her properly. He touched her face, passed his hands through her hair. But Ruby only stared, her jaw stiff and her face blank, as if she were merely watching one of those stories unravel from the safety of the living room armchair.

"Dada, what is happening?" Imogen cried from the other end of the room. "What did Ruby see? Why is she covered in blood?"

Angus sat beside Ruby on the bed now, touching her hair, her cheek, imploring her so roughly that she flinched. "Ruby, darling, I'm so sorry. You're so beautiful, and I adore you . . . How I wish you hadn't seen that. Ruby, please, it wasn't what you think. If only you knew how I—"

"Dada, please, no!" Imogen called out. "What are you saying?"

Angus tried to embrace Ruby, using his strength to draw her close. She resisted; he tried again.

Ruby's hand moved more quickly than she expected, and she plunged the knife deep into Angus's stomach. The ease with which it slipped into him, softly and luxuriously, surprised her; it was almost easier than slicing into the oranges downstairs.

Angus hesitated for a moment, before looking down, surprised. He leaned back, and Ruby pulled out the knife. In its place, a thick ribbon of blood slipped out, shimmering and fast. Ruby looked at it curiously.

Imogen screamed, "Ruby!"

Out of panic, Ruby pressed the knife again into Angus's chest. He gave a dreadful sigh, before leaning forward with a stutter. With one hand, he touched at Ruby's face.

"It's not your fault, little thing," Angus gasped, eyeing her tenderly. "It's not your fault. I deserve it, after everything I've done."

His great chest fell to the side, his face still taut with surprise. Two rivulets of blood spilled onto Ruby's bedclothes, and Angus breathed uneasily, wincing with each slight movement. Ruby held on to the knife, her ears full of Imogen's soaring screams, her head thundering with anger, grief, and confusion.

Another voice was behind her now, in front of her, around her: Harley. Imogen screamed all the more at seeing him.

"Ruby, what on earth have you done? Angus. Angus, can you hear me?"

He lunged toward Ruby, and she flinched.

"Get Toby!" Harley cried out. "Somebody get Toby!"

Imogen had pressed herself against the far wall, surveying the scene with her hands clamped over her mouth.

"What have you bloody done, you stupid child!" Harley growled into Ruby's face. "You fucking bitch! Now they'll really lock you up. What have you bloody done? Gus, old chap, look here, stay with us!"

Harley gripped Ruby's arm, shaking it to make her drop the knife, but she only held on tighter, even as it dripped dark red. "Let it go, Ruby," Harley shouted as she swung her furious face to him, "let go of the knife, you fucking monster!"

She stood and pushed against his grasp. But Harley only gripped her tighter. Angus's face was growing pale, and his blood was seeping past the bedclothes now, soaking onto the floor. Ruby didn't want to slip.

"Ruby," Harley shouted. "Let go!"

It happened very quickly. Harley went to grapple with Ruby again, and again she pushed back, even harder. The bulk of his figure curved around her back, his hands trying to pin her arms, just as he had done two days before. Ruby stood bolt upright, pushing against him. She started to trip backward, slipping, falling. Harley moved with her, driven by the thrust of her dogged and furious energy. Ruby felt the glass shards in her feet and strode backward harder, faster. She felt the warm stones of the balcony, and Harley's body behind her as he stumbled in surprise. Ruby abruptly straightened again, and gave one last heave, just as Harley lost his balance. He staggered back against the balcony railing, loosening his grip on her to break his fall.

Ruby turned in time to see the railing crack and give way, and Harley's vast figure tumble with a low bellow of surprise. Imogen's scream filled the air, like a long, wailing siren. But even that could not block out the loud smack of Harley's body as it hit the terrace below.

A short silence seemed to burst through Ruby's ears. She peered over the edge of her balcony. Liv was looking up at her, her face a serene mask of triumph.

Ruby turned back to her bedroom, and to the tortured face of Imogen, whose father was bleeding through the bed.

Her own father, Toby, was standing in the doorway, gazing at his dearest friend, then running to him, his face rent with horror. Imogen's screams now broke into long dashes of sobbing.

Toby saw Ruby framed by the tall gap of the open windows.

"Ruby," her father stuttered, seeing the knife in her hands, "did you do this?"

Imogen sobbed louder, wedged into her spot against the wall.

"Ruby, did you do this?" Toby repeated, urgently this time.

"Yes," Ruby answered.

"What happened here? Where is Harley—didn't he come in here?" Toby approached her, shaking, his eyes flitting from her to the fractured railing of her balcony. "Ruby, let me have that knife. Please, darling girl. Let me have it."

Toby reached toward his daughter. She saw that his arm was soaked with blood, so she motioned him away. It occurred to her that she might be covered with blood too, and she looked down. Orange juice—or blood; she couldn't tell the difference—had transformed the clean white of her dress. She raised her head defiantly.

"No."

He stepped toward her and attempted a jerky embrace. Ruby held still, but his abrupt and unhappy movements forced the rigid blade to nick his thigh. Toby sucked inward at the pain, and let go of his daughter.

"Please Ruby," Imogen suddenly said in a muffled voice, "let go of the knife."

Ruby dropped it, and it fell to the stone floor with a clatter, a long diamond of red and silver, the same red that spread between her, her father, and his best friend. Toby fell to the floor, retrieving the knife with his shaking hands. Behind him, other figures were coming through the bedroom door. Before she could make out their shapes or their expressions, Ruby nodded at Imogen with a weary smile.

AN HOUR LATER, RUBY WAS in her parents' bathroom. She'd been stripped and washed, her hands and face scrubbed hurriedly by her shocked mother, who refused to meet Ruby's eyes with her own. Ruby was alone now, and sat on the floor in her mother's dressing gown, looking at the perfect beauty of her clean toes. She was relieved to see her toes like this. The summer was over, and she didn't need to go in the sea anymore; there would be no need to dig out sand from her toenails, to scrub the bottoms of her feet, nor worry about any rashes.

Everything had come out with the hot water. She felt clean and fresh, like the latest dress in a fashion magazine, ready for autumn. Not the dress slumped in a bloody pile in the corner—they'd have to throw that one away. Yes, Ruby thought as she twiddled her toes, and splayed out her fingers—things were better now. She might even polish her toenails, have her fingernails match, too—pick out one of her mother's colors. Red? No, she was too young for that, better a pink, or a white. There was no danger of them being too pretty now, and she was pleased at the thought.

Outside the bathroom, many people were moving about the house. Ruby heard the police siren, unexpectedly loud after the difficult fizzing silence of her bedroom. Imogen had thrust herself into her mother's chest, where her sobs had lessened, and everybody else seemed to talk quietly and urgently among themselves. They'd wanted to put Ruby in the study, but she'd adamantly refused, and her mother had conceded by offering the bathroom.

Ruby had heard the bustle of the paramedics, too, taking two bodies away from the house, one from upstairs, one from outside. She wondered if they'd bring them to that strange patch of land, bury them among the war dead in those unmarked graves. No, Ruby thought, her father wouldn't allow that, nor would the authorities. She thought she'd even heard the haughty, official voice of the local mayor join the befuddlement of the rest.

Ruby stood to brush her wet hair one more time. She looked at her face in the mirror, and recognized herself for the first time in weeks.

36

2010

Imogen Cosgrove reapplied her mascara and returned downstairs. She had to speak to Hugo Montgomery, to make him understand. More than that, she needed those papers.

She didn't know what he planned to do—blackmail, or worse, exposure—but she couldn't let him go through with it.

But the bar was empty. She stared at her drained wineglass, still there, and his tumbler, dripping with condensation. The barman saw her looking.

"*Il est parti?*" she burst out.

"*Oui, madame.*"

"*Monsieur Montgomery?*" She realized she didn't have her handbag with her. The barman had removed the bill she'd signed, with an already generous tip. No way, then, to eke out some information with a five-euro bribe. She addressed the barman anyway. "*Quelle chambre?*"

The barman studied her face for a moment, and said, ". . . *Vous vous connaissez, madame?*"

"*Évidemment.*" She didn't look at him.

The barman checked Hugo's bill at the register, *"Chambre numero cent-vingt, madame."*

Imogen nodded gratefully as a bitter blush spread across her cheeks.

She was at Hugo's hotel room door before she knew how she got there. She knocked quickly, and waited. She knocked again, just as the door was thrown open. Hugo's face was damp and red, as if he'd washed and pressed a towel against his skin. His shirt buttons were undone and his eyes were soft, confused, sparked with surprise. He was leaning heavily on the door and she looked past him, seeing his cane set carefully against the desk. Imogen seized upon her courage.

"Hugo. You must do what you need to do. But you must also understand that I was a child. So was Ruby."

With a blink, his face grew hard again. He answered, "Children grow up, Mrs. Cosgrove, and must be held accountable for their actions."

"Yes they do." Imogen gave him a sour look. "And when they're old enough, they realize what was done to them."

"Oh please." Hugo stood aside. "What was done to *you,* apart from gorgeous holidays and expensive schools?"

Imogen averted her eyes, too ashamed to meet his. But Hugo's expression caved in as he began to understand. "Oh my God," Hugo spluttered. "Did my father—did my father—hurt you?"

She only managed to choke out, "He wasn't the man you think he is."

Hugo beckoned her into the room, and with a wave of exhaustion, Imogen obeyed.

"No, no." Hugo closed the door behind her. "He was *exactly* the man I thought he was, Imogen. That's the problem. That's the thing that my wonderful stepmother tried to conceal from me: that he was an unheroic, ghastly man whom his friends truly loathed but put up with because of what he represented." He sat on the bed, dropping his head into his hands as his voice rang out with mock hilarity. "'Jolly good man,' old boy, they'd say. People always choose the kindest memories after a death."

Imogen was looking around her desperately. She spotted the red file on the bedside table, and glanced at Hugo as he carried on.

"I was hoping that you could tell me it was otherwise, that summer. But no. He was horrible to me, and horrible to others, all the time. What did he do to you?"

Imogen couldn't answer such a complicated question, and Hugo raised his head sharply.

"You won't tell me. But when I buy that house, I know I'll find something of him there, and something of myself. I'll do it for my step-mother, for me. I'll live there until the end of my days, haunting it like some strange demented version of Heathcliff. As if I don't hate myself enough as it is." He swung his agonized face to Imogen. "They told me he was killed by his friend, but that's not true, is it? You killed him."

"No," Imogen whispered. Hugo stood and approached her.

"Yes, you killed him, before I could confront him. And where's the justice in that? By destroying all of you, I'll find some peace. Don't you see?"

Imogen's heart beat loudly in her chest as she cried out, "I lost my father too, that same day, that same hour. I've never found him since, in any man I've met. Heaven knows I've tried." She took a quick breath. "But, like you, I don't think I even knew my father in the first place."

Hugo froze, staring into her face, taking in her words. Imogen turned away from his deep wrinkles, the twist of his mouth, the glimmer of pain in his eyes. He looked nothing like Harley, she realized; he was nothing like Harley. His height hung over her in the same way— but she was taller now, she was a woman in place of a shivering child. There was no haunting memory of Harley here—just a sad, grieving man. He hovered over her unsteadily, and took a staggered step backward.

"What happened to your leg?" Imogen suddenly asked.

Hugo's face twisted into a hideous smile. "You ask so boldly— hardly very English of you."

Imogen looked away. "No, I apologize."

"I had a motorbike accident, that same summer. The bike was a gift from my father, hoping to make a man of me, but I crashed, rather predictably. I had to wait for him to return before the operation—they needed a parent's permission. But he didn't return when I asked, and we got the bad news several days later. It took too long to operate, and my leg was never the same."

"I am sorry."

"Oh no, don't be sorry." Hugo cleared his throat. "He couldn't torment me into the grave, like he did my mother. Mind you, both of us were guilty of that—her body never recovered after my birth, you see. I suppose I weakened her; she didn't last long." Hugo hesitated. "Didn't your father love her? I heard my father brag about it—how he won her from him, stole her perhaps, wed her, and then discarded her once they were married, since she didn't fit in with the other society ladies. Your father's title too, he envied hugely. Didn't he help him, and help others—perpetually searching for their approval? I never understood their university chatter, and my stepmother abhorred it."

"Hugo, I don't know what to say. I am sorry," Imogen said again, reaching out to brush her fingers across his shoulder.

He reeled back, shocked at the touch, before lurching forward to grip at her arm. He pulled her toward him, folding her into a rough embrace. Imogen stiffened, terrified.

"Tell me, please, tell me what happened," Hugo said into her hair.

"No!" Imogen wrested herself out of the embrace. "I won't be bullied by you. I've been bullied most of my life, by women as well as men. Your father, and mine. I won't be bullied by you, now."

"I don't mean to," Hugo said quietly. He sat down on his bed again, and Imogen looked back at him with a compassion she didn't fully understand.

"My mother"—her voice was subdued, and she turned to the window as she continued—"always said that there are shades of character within all of us. If that's true, then the darkest shades were there that summer. What was it that your stepmother told you to do?"

"She said I needed to come here and face things for myself, and see things as they truly are," Hugo answered dully.

Imogen gazed at the rectangle of light from the window, thinking of Liv and her downcast face. "All right. I will tell you what your file does not."

"You will?"

"Yes." Imogen let out a small breath and closed her eyes. "My father, Angus, was the first to die. Ruby had seen something that upset her. She never told me what, but she said later that he was worse than all of them—and I think he might have been, however little I wished to see it, then . . . or even now.

"It happened very quickly. Ruby rushed into her bedroom. I was there, folding my things, because we were supposed to leave that afternoon. I . . . felt relieved. But I was scared. I was scared every day of that horrible summer. My father rushed in after Ruby; he was furious about something. He must not have seen me. My father—Angus—he tried to comfort Ruby, to *cuddle* her. And it was as if I wasn't even there. His own daughter, can you imagine?"

Imogen's voice lifted slightly. "His comforting was too—forceful. He smothered her—he was very strong. I saw it, and it frightened me. She was holding a knife, one of the sharper ones from the kitchen. I don't know why. I don't think she knew why, either. She just pushed at it gently, to get rid of him, I think. She was scared. It was"—Imogen whirled around to face Hugo—"terrible. Harley—your father—came in. Because I was screaming, I think; I can't be sure. He saw all the blood, and tried to get Ruby to let go of the knife. But she was very angry, you see. She'd been angry for a long time, only I didn't know that's what it was."

She nodded her head as she gathered momentum. "I was only scared, but Ruby was many things. I see that now. She was more furious than anyone I've ever seen, like a cornered, wild animal. Your father grabbed at Ruby, and she pushed back. I don't know how she did it. But she pushed hard . . . and she drove him backwards, trying to get out of his hold. He lost his footing, and fell over the balcony. One moment he was there, then he wasn't. It was"—Imogen stopped abruptly, and looked up to check Hugo's face—"simple, really. I'm sorry."

Hugo stood, motionless, until she added, "I've never spoken that aloud to anyone."

"You haven't?"

"No." Imogen turned to the window again, her voice weaker now, her body gone completely stiff. She felt that at any moment, she might shatter into a thousand pieces. "No one ever asked me. And we were forbidden to talk about it."

"And Olivia, my stepmother?"

"She was outside. She saw your father . . . fall."

"So this 'duel' story that I . . ." Hugo's voice broke. "That I was fed as a teenager, this fight between the two of them—it was all a lie?"

"Well." Imogen hesitated. "Angus and Harley didn't get on; they often argued. There was so much between them—between all of them. A duel must have seemed like a convincing explanation . . . to save Ruby. And me, I suppose."

Hugo moved around quickly to stand in front of Imogen, blocking the window with his strong silhouette. She looked up at him miserably, and their eyes touched. "Don't be angry with Liv. She stood by us. She was the kindest of any of them."

"But perhaps not kind enough."

Hugo stepped closer to her, and Imogen didn't resist this time. He enveloped her in an embrace. After several minutes, he staggered back and touched her face tenderly. Imogen pulled away as Hugo said instinctively, "I'm sorry."

"No, no." Imogen felt a dim surprise as he let go—she hadn't wanted him to, and she felt crumpled up, discarded, lost once again, "I didn't—"

"I shouldn't have been so impulsive."

"No, it's not that." Imogen frowned, puzzled at herself.

"I'll leave you."

"No, don't." She let out an involuntary laugh. "It's your room, Hugo. It's me that should go."

Imogen avoided the heat of his gaze and wandered to the door. She hesitated.

"You needn't go," Hugo said quietly.

"No?" she asked him, and herself.

"No."

Imogen turned and took in the room again—just like her own, but empty of shadows. She regarded Hugo carefully—he might even be handsome, if only something could soften that haggard look of agony. "I'll stay with you for a bit longer," she said.

He stepped toward her urgently and folded her into another embrace. Imogen kissed him lightly, but he returned it with a huge gulping kiss that lasted a long, desperate moment. In the next, Imogen drew back and checked his face again. Perhaps she could soften him, here, tonight, she thought.

It was the first time she had ever given herself so freely and so willingly. She was surprised to find herself laughing at moments, relaxed in Hugo's arms, so easily wet for him, so happy to move back and forth for him, eager to yield to his strength. And he, in turn, found moments of pleasure all over her body, as Imogen felt herself beginning to awaken. Days, weeks later, she would reflect that it was the first time she had ever felt an equal, both heard and listened to, fully able to love and to give. He touched her hands as her body passed through his, and every touch was truly desired.

It was also Imogen Cosgrove's first night of real sleep since she'd arrived in France, unhaunted by men's faces, or a house full of dark rooms, or that flat red file on a bedside table.

37

1985

For the rest of the day and the one following, Toby took charge. He had no choice, and no time to grieve the devastating loss of his two oldest friends—the consequential fallout thrust him forward. The local mayor and the chief of police spent Monday morning at the house, talking in low but steady voices, pacing the living room. Georgina and Ned quietly left the house with their suitcases, but could not leave the village definitively, since they now had no chauffeur for their planned journey home.

Ruby was told to spend the day in her parents' bedroom. That same afternoon, her own bedroom was cleared by official-looking people and their string of formally attired cleaners, after which Ruby was allowed out for a brief swim, with Rhoda watching. They didn't speak to each other, and as she swam length after boring length, Ruby ignored her mother's rigid posture and her fearful, avoiding eyes. Imogen had moved into her mother's room; Ruby hadn't seen either of them, but she'd heard a terrible, hysterical cry come from the Blys' room when she'd passed it on the way to the pool. Ruby didn't mind the strange stiffness of those hours; she felt safer than she had since the beginning of the summer.

She ate an early dinner in the dining room, again, with her mother, who ate nothing. It was a strange, stringy soup, littered with chopped vegetables and pasta. They'd got someone in from the village to help out in the kitchen; the food was better than her mother's but not as good as Lisette's. Her father came in before she started her pudding, a baked banana with brown sugar and cream. She smiled at the bowl before her; baked bananas were something her grandmother used to have the housekeeper cook on the old barbecue when Ruby was small. There'd been no barbecues that summer, and there never would be again at the château, she realized.

Toby eyed Ruby before taking the chair opposite his daughter. Rhoda rose to leave. Ruby scooped up a soft dollop of browned banana and set it in her mouth, savoring every taste. She then laid down her spoon and raised her face to listen.

Ruby's father informed her that the incident on the previous day was being recorded as an "accident" by the French authorities. It had been a duel between two friends, Angus Bly and Harley Montgomery, with fatal consequences. After all, the two men had been seen arguing in the village, and there had been several witness accounts of physical violence between them, including one from a café owner who was willing to contribute an affidavit.

The most significant witness contribution to the case, however, was that of Olivia Montgomery, wife of the second deceased, who would swear that she observed the entire argument and subsequent double-death tragedy. Liv, Toby told Ruby, was quite insistent that this was the true account of the matter, and it had been accepted and recorded by the local authorities.

Ruby listened to the whole speech. It was a simple story, not particularly clever or interesting—one that Poirot would have solved in an instant. When her father ducked out of the dining room, her mother returned, and Ruby asked her if she ought to play her flute, to cheer things up a bit. Rhoda bowed her tense and anxious face, and answered no. Ruby nodded, realizing that her flute was in her bedroom anyway, and might have been one of the things removed by the authorities.

She carried on with her pudding, touching the edge of the bowl carefully with her little spoon, sure to catch the last bits of cream and sugar. Ruby wondered if Liv was still in the house, and hoped to see her before she went home, once they'd arranged the return of her husband's body to England.

Rhoda seemed to greatly miss her friend's company and confidence, and took any opportunity to comfort Polly, even if it meant leaving Ruby alone. It was interesting to Ruby that her mother would choose her friend over her daughter, but she now understood that their bond was sealed long before Ruby was born. Imogen was kept out of their closeness too, Ruby noticed as she passed her and Polly on the stairs coming back from her swim: the mother and daughter were entangled in a tight embrace, but their faces were drawn away from each other, in crystalized horror. Imogen stared at Ruby as she passed her on the landing; she was the only one who had actually met Ruby's eyes since the "accident."

That same evening, Ruby was permitted to return to her bedroom, to collect any items she wanted. Aside from the removal of her thick mattress and the mosquito net she hadn't used for weeks, there were more things out of place than had been taken. She busied herself returning bits to their proper places, collecting her jewelry and folding it away, lifting her torn-up *Death on the Nile* from the dresser and slotting it into her bookcase. She'd leave her teddy bears in the wardrobe—she didn't need them anymore.

Ruby looked around for her grandmother's playing cards—she must find them, wherever they were. Now that Harley was dead, of course, there was no need to put up with any criticisms of her grandmother. Ruby was glad, since the truth was Nancy Ashby had always insisted to her granddaughter that the "gentry" had pushed her to the edge of her wits, and that she'd found herself very late in life. Ruby had imagined her grandmother caught in one of those labyrinths in those old French palaces, a child in an old nightdress, suddenly coming upon her older, truer self. She understood a little better now.

On her dressing table, Ruby caught sight of Annie's wildflowers, now dry and curled with the heat. Ruby collected each one in the palm of her hand, wandered over to the double windows, and with a swoop of her arm cast them out, past the balcony, to the freedom of the air.

Imogen appeared in the bedroom doorway sometime later, apparently sent to check if anything of hers had been left behind, so that she could finish her packing. Ruby sat on the chair by her dressing table and watched Imogen, thinking that perhaps sending her was a ruse, so that the mothers could have their own private moment together. She thought she heard the phone ringing downstairs, but it seemed to ring a great deal nowadays. Ruby waited as Imogen hurriedly checked the wardrobe, her hands shaking as she gave Ruby a wide berth. Her face was full of courage when she finally spoke up.

"I don't want to be in here."

"No," Ruby said, "I understand."

"No, you don't." Imogen dissolved into tears. "You killed my father, Ruby! Why did you do it?"

Ruby looked at Imogen's round mouth, soft and pink, as she tried to stifle her sobs. Ruby felt a leap of sadness for her as she answered, "I didn't mean to. I never meant to hurt *you,* Imogen, I—"

Imogen burst out, "You killed the wrong one! He wasn't even the worst."

"Your father *was* the worst."

"He wasn't! He wasn't!"

"He was, Immy, because he pretended . . ." Ruby began, hushing her voice so that only Imogen would hear. "He pretended to be better, but he lied. He hid that he was the worst. And he couldn't get away with it."

Imogen stormed toward Ruby and slapped her hard across the face. Ruby felt the hot swell of her cheek as Imogen raged at her, "How dare you, how dare you!"

She stood, and Imogen backed away, but Ruby was too quick for her. She grabbed Imogen's wrists and tried to shake her. "Wake up. Wake *up,* Imogen. You know how it was. Listen to what I've said."

Imogen wrenched her arms out of Ruby's grip and turned her back to her. "Our mothers are sending us away; they're taking us out of St. Aubyn's! Both of us! I don't see why I should have to go too, and I'll be starting a year late besides!"

Ruby felt a flare of confusion at Imogen's words. "Another school—where?"

"Their old school, in Scotland! I don't want to go! Everything is changing now. And it's all your fault!"

"I did what I had to do, Imogen, to protect us." Ruby shook her head and tried to think straight. She looked at her bed, at the metal slats where the mattress had been, at the spot where Angus had died. "But if we are moving schools, I'll take care of you there, too."

"No," Imogen shot back, "you won't! You're a monster. I'll make sure everyone knows. I'll tell everyone what you've done."

Ruby stared at the large dark stain on the tiled floor beneath her bed. "They won't believe you."

Imogen's eyes widened with anger. "Then I'll never speak to you again. I'll ignore you! I'll pretend we've never met!"

She shuddered with heavy sobs again, so Ruby inched toward her. "Please, Imogen, I am sorry."

"Get away from me! I don't need you. I've got my mother now. You've got your parents, too. Leave me out of it!"

"I haven't got them, not really," Ruby said darkly.

"I'll never forget this summer." Imogen cried out. "I *am* rotten and used up. I'm worthless."

"You're not used up," Ruby replied.

"Harley said I was!" Imogen choked out in a sob.

Ruby looked at Imogen's thick hair falling around her face. She narrowed her eyes and said, "Harley is dead, Imogen."

Imogen looked across at Ruby fearfully, before burying her face in her hands.

Rhoda was at the door, Polly moving unsteadily behind her. Rhoda knocked and demanded, "Are you girls behaving?"

Imogen went to her mother, pushing herself around her belly. "Yes. Oh, Mummy."

Polly embraced Imogen slowly, her face stiff and her eyes glassy. Rhoda stepped into the room, casting her eyes over the scene, to the bed where Ruby stood, and to the floor, where that stain would always linger as a reminder.

"We're sending you to Caldonbrae Hall, Ruby. We've just had word that they've accepted your application. They've allowed you a special place on account of your aunt being a housemistress." Rhoda added in a rush, "Imogen is on their list too, thanks to the Bly Beresford family title. Her father—well, neither of your fathers—wished it for you, but now"—she gave Polly a nod—"it's the only way. The fact is . . . it's been a difficult time, and they'll know exactly what to do with you."

"Father doesn't wish it?" Ruby asked her mother.

"That doesn't matter, since he'll now do as I tell him," Rhoda said.

"Yes," Polly suddenly added, lifting her face to cast a pale glare at Ruby, "and they'll certainly squash this out of you, Ruby . . . whatever 'this' is."

Ruby met Polly's glare, and Rhoda blanched worriedly. Imogen whimpered into her mother's chest.

IN THE EARLY EVENING, RUBY settled herself in the living room. Her mother had laid an old and battered school prospectus on her lap and Ruby was glancing through the pictures, hardly able to imagine herself in that bizarre landscape, amidst those terrible rocky cliffs and that gray-blue sea.

Toby came in, but hesitated when he saw the shadow of Ruby's head over the top of an armchair.

"Ruby, I need to make a telephone call."

Ruby pushed the prospectus off her lap and stood. "Yes, Father."

"Thank you." Ruby heard the click as her father lifted the handset and added, "I'm going to the village afterwards."

"May I come with you?"

Toby hesitated. "I'm not sure it's a good idea."

"Whyever not?"

Toby spoke carefully. "It's just a drink at the café. I'm saying good-bye to Georgina and Ned; they leave France first thing tomorrow."

Ruby turned her face to the shuttered windows. "I'd like to come, please."

"You'd like to," her father repeated stiffly.

"Yes," Ruby answered, meeting his tone. "I want to make sure they are actually leaving. I insist, Father."

Toby balked at that, rubbing his mustache before abruptly dialing a number and speaking irritably into the phone.

Ten minutes later, Ruby had collected her bag and followed her father outside, glad to leave the house. They passed Liv as they went to the car. She didn't greet either of them, but her eyes darted to Ruby, before looking away. Liv's face was calm, and there'd been a flicker of relief in those small, kind eyes. Ruby thought she'd heard Liv hover in the passageway outside her parents' room that very morning, but she hadn't come in. She hadn't really needed to.

"How long is Mrs. Montgomery staying now, and Imogen and Mrs. Bly?" Ruby asked her father as she settled in the front passenger seat.

"They leave in a few days, after the . . . remains . . . have been flown home," Toby said carefully. "We'll leave sometime after that."

At the café on the square, Ruby chose the seat next to her father. Toby was flustered, nervously peering at the other patrons. Ruby watched him curiously; she'd never seen her father so out of sorts. He stood as he saw Ned and Georgina approach, but he did not smile. Ned's mouth fell open when she caught sight of Ruby.

"Ruby, I can't believe you're allowed out!"

"Ned, be quiet." Georgina's mouth was drawn tight, and Ruby saw dark circles under her eyes.

"Well, she is a murderer, Mother!" Ned exclaimed.

"Hush, Ned."

"What do you mean, 'hush'?" Ned pulled a face, glaring at Ruby again.

"I mean exactly that, Ned," Georgina said sternly. "Do not make this worse. Our two dear friends fought, and hurt each other. They brought it on themselves. That is what happened."

"It is," Ruby said simply, and Ned's eyes widened, incredulous. Ruby studied the girl's baffled face, but only for a moment, to replace in her mind that final image of Ned bent backward in her father's study.

Toby muttered carefully, "It is, and I'll thank you to keep your voice down, Ned."

Ned settled into the chair opposite Ruby. Her face was set, her mouth twisted, as she surveyed Ruby carefully through her glasses.

"What about that old lady," Ruby asked as Georgina and Toby looked at each other, "the one who lost her son?"

"I think after what's happened"—Toby lit a cigarette, keeping his eyes away from his daughter—"she thinks justice has been served. She's rather had enough of us for one lifetime."

"She got two deaths for her one, didn't she," Ned said significantly, "rather like the blood price, or like a Greek tragedy."

Toby looked at Ned through narrowed eyes as he blew the smoke out of his mouth.

"She'll still be sad," Ruby said as the waitress appeared, handing her a *chocolat chaud* and her father a *pastis* before taking the drink order from Ned and Georgina.

"A lot of us will be sad, for a very long time, Ruby." Toby took a small sip of his drink and grimaced.

"Indeed," Georgina said with a bow of her head.

The rest of the café visit passed easily enough. It was a rather boring half hour, Ruby thought, and she wondered whether those secret holidays Ned had mentioned had been as tedious as this. Her father didn't laugh once, and Georgina wore a severe expression throughout, her eyes creased in sadness. Ruby wondered if either of them, any of them, would ever laugh again.

Her father paid the bill, and Georgina and Ned stood to leave. Ned bent to Ruby's ear, angling her body to prevent the other two from hearing.

"Whatever they say, little thing, I—"

"*Don't* call me that," Ruby interrupted, without looking up.

"Well," Ned faltered, "I wanted you to know that whatever happens to you, I'm rather impressed to have you as . . . a half-sister."

"Don't call me *that,* either."

Ruby turned her face away. She supposed that the "accident" could have been attributed to Ned too, after what Ruby had seen that morning—and yet it would have all come to the same consequence. Ned's part in the matter had just pushed Ruby further, forced her hand quicker. In some strange way, Ruby was grateful to Ned—but still, she never wanted to see her again.

"Well, fine," Ned blustered, trying to catch Ruby's attention. "But I hope you realize that you, little lady, are worthy of the Greek heroines. You're like one of them in real life—fighting back, outliving the men. You've shocked and delighted me as much as they have."

"Well." Ruby met Ned's gaze. "I can't say the same for you at all. I'll never forget how you've played games this summer, and done terrible things behind everyone's back. You say you're impressed by me, but I'm disgusted by you."

Ned's eyes narrowed as Ruby shifted her body completely away from her.

On the way home, Toby asked Ruby to sit in the back but she refused, and settled in beside him. She watched the countryside roll past, the dry green and scraggy rocks along the road. Soon enough, the rupture of the land and the back of the château reared up ahead of them. Toby had left the gate open, and as they rolled down the drive Ruby noted the parched land, so dry and unhappy by the end of the summer, even with the storm that had passed.

"Ruby," Toby said, with an attempt at warmth in his voice, "I wanted to talk to you about Ned. Georgina and I have a friendship that goes back more than thirty years. Before I met your mother, I—"

"Yes, Father," Ruby said flatly. "I understand about Ned."

Toby flinched, and pressed on. "I wasn't certain. Well, Ruby, it comes with a complication. There are several financial issues that we . . . that I . . . am struggling with. So as a result, the house might be taken on by Georgina, and passed to Ned in due course. But not in the immediate future." He took a breath and continued, "The details have not been settled yet. So this might be our last summer here, Ruby."

Ruby watched the house bloom in front of her as the car rolled forward.

"And"—Toby flicked the ash of his cigarette out of the car

window—"we shall see what will become of us all. Either way, I do think that it's important to face up to one's actions, and one's responsibilities. It is best to do that, I think."

Toby was nodding to himself, looking to his daughter for affirmation. But Ruby stared straight ahead, taking in the shape of the château shining in the blaze of sunlight, refusing to meet her father's eyes.

38

2010

When she woke, it took Imogen a moment to realize where she was. The window seemed to be on the wrong side of the hotel room. She turned her head to see Hugo Montgomery's broad back stirring slowly as he slept beside her.

Somewhere beyond the cloud of his brown-gray curls was the red file, beating its own destructive heartbeat. She'd meant every moment of last night, and she felt a thrum of contentment as she remembered. But today there were many things to do.

Imogen put on her dress, which was wrinkled from being carelessly tossed aside last night. At the desk she wrote a note, tore out the page, and went to Hugo's bedside table. She lifted the red file away, and put the note in its place. Hugo's sleeping face was touched with serenity. She gave him a sad smile, and left.

In the bath in her own room, Imogen considered the file. The bubbles had climbed over the edge, and Imogen surprised herself by enjoying the heat of the water. She'd propped the file up against the bathroom mirror. It was a deep red—not the soft blush of Ruby's hair, but the dense fuzz of the curtains in her hotel room. It was foreign and incongruous in the bathroom, just like *The Iliad* that still sat on the floor beneath the radiator.

Imogen bit her lip in concentration as she reviewed the pages inside the file. Should she call Ruby, and make some shoddy attempt at reconnecting with her, or should she deal with this herself? The last time she and Ruby had properly spoken was several years ago, when their cohort from Caldonbrae Hall had been called upon to donate toward the new rebuild. Both she and Ruby had declined, and had been chastised for it by the others. Ruby had staunchly defended her decision, and called on Imogen to unite with her, which she had, from a distance. The rebuilding scheme had never fully taken off—at least not openly—and Ruby had told Imogen that she was glad of it.

Imogen had been surprised initially at Ruby's refusal to donate, since the great Ruby Ashby, head girl, had done very well out of the school; had understood the system better than anyone; and had always managed to turn everything to her advantage. But there had always been things in Ruby's head that Imogen didn't fully see or comprehend, and somehow, after these last few days in France, Imogen's stifling horror around her memories of Ruby had shifted into something like respect.

It was certainly true that Ruby had only one friend she cherished, who belonged to no social circle, and whom the other women considered as some sort of elusive rival: Annie Fuller. Imogen had never understood why they clung to each other, but she did wonder if Annie had ever been allowed to see Ruby's true face. She doubted that Ruby's husband ever had—Caldonbrae had taught them how to suppress and control that. But Annie hadn't been taught the same things; she'd attended a progressive sort of school in London, and retained her sunny spirit.

Imogen had always kept her distance from Annie, fearing the potential brutality of her father, Max, especially once she'd heard he'd been ruined financially around the time Annie had graduated. Imogen still occasionally wondered whether Annie's father ever acknowledged that he'd killed someone with his car that night, a young man, somebody's son, and whether that denial had become a curse that pursued the Fuller family to the end. Perhaps a curse had pursued all of them; perhaps it lay in wait still.

Imogen rubbed the soap on her legs and took up her razor. She knew what held her back from contacting Ruby—the blood price had not been paid. Or had it been paid by Imogen, through the life she'd been living? Her fingers quaked at the thought, and her razor slid out of her hand, but did not break her skin.

Later, out of the bath, Imogen took the time to rub moisturizer into her face and all over her body. She put on no other makeup and nodded at herself in the mirror. It was time.

Imogen dressed in her last clean outfit, trousers and a light shirt, and opened the château's colorful brochure. She squinted at the estate agent's number, before dialing it on the hotel phone.

"*Bonjour, c'est Mr. Berne?*" She waited for an affirmation before continuing. "*J'ai des bonnes nouvelles. J'offre le prix, pas besoin de negotiation.*"

She nodded into the phone and, in spite of herself, a smile broke out in response to the estate agent's ecstatic words on the other end.

"*Oui, monsieur, je suis ravie, comme vous. Merci beaucoup. Cet après-midi—vers seize heures?*"

She replaced the receiver, still smiling.

Downstairs she spoke quickly to the receptionist, a young woman who narrowed her eyes at Imogen's tight French.

"*J'ai un message pour le Monsieur Robert Payne, est-ce que vous pouvez m'aider?*"

"*Aider comment, madame?*"

Imogen frowned. "*Il n'arrête pas de me telephoner. Je ne veux pas parler avec lui.*"

The receptionist was confused, so Imogen repeated in English. "Do not connect him, I do not wish to speak to him. Please read him this message."

The young girl smiled in cheerful understanding, taking the piece of paper with a nod. "*Oui. Je comprends.*"

"*Et un taxi, s'il vous plait.*"

"*Oui, madame, vous allez loin?*"

"*Non, pas loin du tout,*" Imogen said. Not far, she thought, but it had taken her a long time to get here.

The receptionist nodded just as cheerfully as before, and placed the piece of paper carefully beside her on the desk with a small pat.

The taxi came, and Imogen ducked inside gratefully. It was cool and dark, a welcome reprieve from the brief heat between the hotel lobby and the car.

When she arrived, Hugo was already there. She could see him standing beyond the small chapel. The sun was high and lit up his tall figure, stooped over the line of his cane.

He waited for her in front of two flat tombstones, separate from the main bulk of the cemetery. Imogen spoke first.

"Hugo, I am buying the house."

He nodded as if he already knew.

"It will lose the Ashby name," she said, taking a breath as Hugo glanced at her. "None of them will come here again. None of those people you so abhor."

"That house means nothing to me now, in all truth. My demons seem to have been put to rest. Thank you, Imogen, for telling me your story." He turned back to the small stone slab. "The mayor informed me that the Ashbys never returned here after that summer, and he had no idea if Georgina or Edwina visited here afterwards either. I couldn't find much about them via my contacts in England; they seem to have dropped out of society. They received no help from Toby, I imagine."

"Toby Ashby never got over what happened that summer," Imogen said. She looked out toward the sea in the distance, a thin line of pale blue. From here, you couldn't see the house, and she was grateful for that. The heat was dry that morning, and the crickets were loud, scratching their prickly song.

"Yes, I knew that." Hugo nodded his head again, vigorously this time. "I went to see him not along after—I don't know what I was hoping for. But he was a shell of a man. He . . ." Hugo's voice cracked. "He might as well have died with them."

She forced herself to look down at the two memorial stones marked *Harley Montgomery* and *Angus Bly*. Imogen stared blankly at her father's name. There were no bodies underneath; they'd been taken to England. But they were remembered here, their names gazing up to the azure blue sky, Toby's last attempt to commemorate his closest friends.

"It was good of you to suggest meeting here," Hugo said, tipping his weight onto his other leg and leaning forward with a dry cough. "You were right, Imogen. You were right."

He reached out to her, extending his arm behind her back to pull her into an embrace. But she held herself stiff and slightly out of his reach.

"I don't think that's a good idea," Imogen said quietly.

"No?" Hugo let his arm slacken.

"Last night was wonderful, Hugo." Imogen turned her face to him and said softly, "And I am grateful to you in more ways that you can know. But I have a lot of learning to do."

"Learning?"

"Yes. Learning, and recompense . . . to others, and to myself."

Hugo's whole body seemed to loosen as he conceded, "Yes. I suppose I do, too."

Imogen nodded.

"What will you do, now?" Hugo asked into the silence.

"There's a lot waiting for me in England, though nothing that I would choose for myself." Again, Imogen was surprised at how freely and truthfully she spoke. "But I need to make amends to James's family, and move forward somehow. Do something about this sorrow I feel, and this . . . anger. I think I've been angry my entire life. It gets in the way of everything else. The thing is, none of the people who brought us up knew how to love."

"My stepmother did. But you're right." Hugo scratched behind his ear and looked out at the view. Behind them, the stone chapel sat high on the beautiful hill overlooking the Mediterranean—the same chapel where they'd held the concert, at the very beginning of this mess, at the very end of their innocence. Hugo carried on, "Children don't stay young forever. People can torture them however they like when they're small, but they'll always grow up and bite back." He kicked at his father's memorial stone. "Your Ruby was one of the rare ones who actually fought when she was still young."

Imogen prickled with discomfort to hear Hugo speak of her—Ruby and that summer belonged to her. Hugo could never understand, even if he wanted to.

"I have something for you, Hugo," Imogen remembered, pulling out her copy of *The Iliad,* alongside those memories of the ancient stories, of how frightened they'd been—of the men, of the nighttime. "We . . . we talked about it a lot that summer. The three men . . . They joked about each being one of these heroes, comrades in arms, torturing each other, after some impossible prize."

"No." Hugo shook his head, looking askance at the book. "You must be mistaken. Yes, Toby and Angus were Classicists. But my father was a historian . . . yet another distinction of his that I've not lived up to."

"Surely you can stop worrying what others think of you, now?"

"Is that a joke?"

Imogen looked at him; she understood what he meant. Their world was ruled by that very thing. She looked down at the book.

"It's not a special copy or anything . . ." Imogen insisted, nudging the book into Hugo's hand. "But I've read it—many times, actually. And I can't find anything of my father in there. I had to find something in myself to forgive him his flaws, instead. But perhaps you might find something in there to comfort you."

Hugo held the book with both hands, gripping the cover anxiously.

"This is kind of you, Imogen."

"Not at all." She smiled regretfully at his well-practiced pleasantries, and at her own.

Hugo spoke firmly now. "You've got my file. What do you plan to do with it?"

"What do you want me to do with it?"

Hugo shrugged. "You should keep it. Destroy it, frame it, use it as wastepaper. Whatever suits you. I don't think it's my story anymore."

Imogen thought of her hotel room, where the file stood propped up in the bathroom. She thought of Ruby's bedroom, where that stain still spread across the floor tiles. She thought of two young and innocent lives that had been lost, and two others taken in return. She thought of that old woman, whose voice seemed to have been screaming in her head for twenty-five years.

She thought of Mrs. Fuller, whose shriek from the police car had been the starting shot of that dreadful summer. She's what would have happened to them, perhaps, if Ruby hadn't done what she did. The woman who, after enjoying a concert a little too much, was driven to the airport as her husband tried to get rid of her. The woman who, after her husband hit another car, went to see if the other person was all right. The woman who took the blame, perhaps even without realizing, plied as she was with drink, drugs, and the judgment of others. The woman whose daughter took refuge in Flower Fairies since she couldn't bear to witness what was truly happening.

Perhaps Mrs. Fuller wasn't very different from Imogen. Imogen simply had more agency, and an inheritance behind her. Imogen would be all right; she'd do it for all of them, just as Ruby had for her.

"Perhaps I won't destroy the château . . . Perhaps I should turn it into some kind of center for the village," Imogen said, her voice catching. "Give it back to the French, as it were. Perhaps a large library, or even a music school."

Hugo nodded, still staring down at *The Iliad*.

Imogen's emotion was too much to bear, and her tears began to flow freely.

It took her a long time to recover, even as she batted away Hugo's comforting arm. The sun sweltered high in the sky while they walked down the path together, out of the graveyard, past the edge of the house and its grounds. They took the coastal path back to the village. Imogen clasped her hands together in distress, before Hugo took them in his.

As the afternoon set in, Mrs. Cosgrove returned to her hotel room, comforted, alone, and ready to face the estate agent for her final appointment at the château.

39

1985

On their final Tuesday Market Day, Ruby sat at the café in the square, stretching her legs out in front of her, sucking on the straw of her lemonade. Her father was absorbed in his newspaper, furrowing his brow at an article on the front page, his glasses perched on the tip of his nose. Her mother was chatting unwaveringly to Polly, who wore a pained look and gave Rhoda only a few muttered responses. Imogen was glancing between the two mothers, trying to listen. Ruby wasn't listening, but she suddenly had a question for the table.

"What will happen to Max Fuller?"

Imogen stared at Ruby as the rest of the table regarded her apprehensively. Her father raised his eyebrows and answered, "We won't be seeing any more of him, Ruby."

"Certainly not," Rhoda reinforced, "and Polly and I will make sure that Fuller man's name is mud in our society."

Polly blinked and frowned, touching her belly.

"Not Annie, though—don't ruin her," Ruby said, before taking another sip of her lemonade. "We must take care of Annie."

"Annie?" Imogen said with surprise.

"Yes, of course Annie."

Ruby turned away from Imogen's questioning eyes to survey the village square. She took in the fountain, the long paved esplanade, the tall trees that shaded the busy bustle of the market. The *tabac,* the *boulangerie.* Places she knew, places she treasured. She wondered if she'd catch sight of Lisette during the time they had left. She wondered whether that poor old woman, Lisette's friend, really was satisfied with the way things had ended, or whether her father had been mistaken.

Lastly, Ruby thought of the house. The creaks in the walls, the bowed floors, the gaps in the doors, the darkness and the light. Her grandmother's favorite. She saw it all now. And it was time to let it go.

Toby stood abruptly, saying, "I need more cigarettes," but Rhoda stopped him.

The mayor was approaching the table, drawing Toby into a wide and confident handshake. He acknowledged Rhoda, and gave a polite nod to Polly and the startled Imogen. Then, his eyes rested on Ruby. She raised a smile for him, and a *"Bonjour, monsieur le maire."* The mayor's face tensed as he bowed his cautious greeting. Ruby reciprocated with a small nod of her head, and a slurp of her drink.

Rhoda observed the short interlude, then murmured to Polly, just loud enough for Ruby to hear, "I'd like to get her up to Scotland as quickly as I can. Caldonbrae has been merciless about their demands, but I really believe they'll be able to sort her out."

Ruby listened, but did not react. Yes, things would look different now. She had a few days left to go through her room, through the house, to pass her treasured things through her hands, her treasured memories through her mind, to stand on the balcony—not too far over—and breathe in the sea air, the trees.

Perhaps she'd ask her mother if they could stop at the *patisserie* and buy a box of cakes for tea. It might cheer Imogen up a bit, and Mrs. Montgomery might appreciate it too. A mille-feuille, a chocolate *opera,* and maybe even a tarte tatin, glossy and perfect in its layered precision. Ruby could already see it in her mind's eye, and she smiled at the thought.

Ruby wasn't sure what lay ahead of her, beyond this afternoon.

There was only one thing she could set upon, a thought that had just now sparked her mind afresh with glee, and hope. She would write to Annie at her aunt's. Annie would stay on at St. Aubyn's, a happy two years stretching ahead of her—perhaps she'd even be first flute now, since Ruby wouldn't be returning. Perhaps Bertie would come for a visit or a concert, and he might even look for Ruby, but find Annie there in her place. Well, if so, he'd be the lucky one. It was too late for Ruby now; she knew that.

Ruby finished her lemonade. She thought she might have one last swim when they returned to the house later: another memory she could collect, cherish, and take with her into the next sunny square or dark pool that life would bring.

ACKNOWLEDGMENTS

To my agent, Nelle Andrew, who first believed in me, and has unceasingly championed my writing ever since—thank you.

To my editor, Sarah Cantin, who seems to understand my writing voice better than I do, and has incredible instincts with every page, thank you for choosing my writing. To the brilliant team at St. Martin's for their incredible work and support, thank you for everything you've done in promoting and celebrating my work.

To my younger self, who took over my brain and wrote this novel for me. I'm sorry about all of it, and I hope this gets us a bit closer to finding peace. I love you, and we're okay.

To France and the village of Cotignac, where I've spent great portions of my life—words can't express what you mean to me. To the village of Cassis, where I've always enjoyed bright seaside days—you're wonderful, thank you for the memories. Those two villages and the glorious people in them were the inspiration for the places in this novel. I hold them close to my heart.

To my sisters, Loulou and Camille, and my oldest friend, Sophie, who might recognize much of this novel—thank you for talking it through whenever we could. I hope the ending speaks to you in the same way it speaks to me.

To my dear friend Christina, who helps me dig deep, and who lets me explore her brain and pick at it for ideas, inspiration, and answers— I'm so lucky to have you. To Anna, who makes me laugh and supports my every step no matter how tentatively I go; to Marta, who never gives up on me, sends inspiration my way every day, and whose recent joys have added to mine—thank you. To Onyinye, who believes in me when I need it, just as I believed in her when she needed it—together we rise.

To my new friends in France, thank you: Honor, for listening and standing alongside me in difficult moments; Brandi, for reading everything and getting it all; and Fabian, for always telling the truth. The three of you have held a space I didn't know existed, and parts of this book were written in that space.

To my family and friends who support my writing and hold me up, who drag me out of my very solitary writing state and help me connect my creative self to my true self—I'll get there one day, and it'll be thanks to you all.